In the old stories, change came in waves, quick as lightning or a gathering storm. And when the skies turned black, the heroes and heroines had to stand on their feet and their wits and find their way back home with what friends they met on their way.

I turned to the back of the book. The last page and the page glued to the binding, the endpaper, were covered in script that told the tale of a girl who for her father's sake became prisoner to a ferocious beast in a magic castle. One of Momma's favorites.

I found a pencil in my trunk and put a single tick mark in the top left corner of the page.

Mark one. Day one.

I was lost out here on the ocean. But somehow, I'd found a map.

Also by Anna Bright
The Boundless

THE BEHOLDER

ANNA BRIGHT

HARPER TEEN
An Imprint of HarperCollinsPublishers

HarperTeen is an imprint of HarperCollins Publishers.

The Beholder
Copyright © 2019 by Anna Shafer
All rights reserved. Printed in the United States of America.
No part of this book may be used or reproduced in any manner whatsoever
without written permission except in the case of brief quotations embodied
in critical articles and reviews. For information address HarperCollins
Children's Books, a division of HarperCollins Publishers, 195 Broadway,
New York, NY 10007.
www.epicreads.com

Library of Congress Control Number: 2018966093
ISBN 978-0-06-284543-6

Typography by Michelle Taormina
20 21 22 23 24 PC/LSCH 10 9 8 7 6 5 4 3 2 1
❖
First paperback edition, 2020

For Wade, who taught me how to breathe.
You are solid ground to me.

THE BEHOLDER

Il estoit une fois un Gentil-homme qui épousa en secondes nopces
une femme,
la plus haütaine et la plus fiere qu'on eut jamais veuë. . . .
Le Mari avoit de son costé une jeune fille,
mais d'une douceur et d'une bonté sans exemple, elle tenoit cela de sa Mere,
qui estoit la meilleure personne du monde.
—Cendrillon; ou, La Petite Pantoufle de Verre

Once upon a time there was a nobleman, who took for a
     second wife
the haughtiest and proudest woman that had ever been seen. . . .
The husband, on his side, had a daughter, of unexampled
     gentleness and goodness.
She inherited these qualities from her mother,
who had been the best creature in the world.
—*Cinderella; or, The Little Glass Slipper*

1

POTOMAC: ARBOR HALL

Once upon a time always began on nights like tonight.

Candles flickered in the trees that grew up through the marble floors of Arbor Hall, setting aglow the faces of the partygoers beneath them and the garlands of shattered glass sparkling in their intermingled branches. My heart beat like a hummingbird trapped between my breastbone and spine.

I ducked behind an old oak climbed over with ivy, hiding for a moment from the music and all the people, careful to avoid the gap carved around its trunk.

Tonight wasn't truly a beginning. I'd loved Peter forever, even if I'd never told him so. Tonight was growth—a page turned. Tonight, I would reap from seeds I'd sown and tended half my life.

Tonight, I'd go to sleep with a ring on my finger and my

future clear before me. Confident in the promise that tomorrow and the next day and the next would be happy days, always the same, always close to the ones I loved. Ready to do my duty by Potomac and take my place as its head someday, with someone strong and trustworthy at my side. Just as soon as Peter said yes.

I tugged an ivy vine loose with shaky fingers, looped it into a wreath, and pinned it over the loose ponytail I'd made of my curls.

Tonight, whispered my heart. *You're getting engaged tonight.*

My breath came fast at the thought, my knees practically knocking together.

Momma had told me the story of my birthday a hundred times. On the night I was born, she paced here in Arbor Hall beneath the trees, pleading with me to leave the safety of her womb and enter the world.

It was a wild, wonderful, magical place, she said. Back aching, ankles swollen, she walked through the forest sheltered beneath the hall's marble dome and whispered stories to where I waited in her belly, as if to prove it to me.

The tale of the Beauty and the Beast, of the girl who rode off into danger to save her father. The story of the girl so kind to a fairy in disguise that her voice rained flowers and pearls all around her.

Through the years, Momma would tell me those stories again and again. Those, and so many more, as we sat in the shade of the trees outside or in the cool of this very hall.

I only wished she were here to see what would happen tonight.

A hundred couples in wreaths like mine and their finest clothes danced under the great Arbor at the center of the room. Hundreds more wove between dogwoods veiled in bridal white and river birches sloughing off their bark like old paper. Here and there I spotted people I knew. The designer who'd made my gown was radiant in her own, its pale pink silk looking soft as a rose petal against her gleaming dark skin as she danced with her husband, a well-to-do farmer. Nearby, a group of boys and girls I knew from school were laughing, faces flushed as they kept up with the music. Dr. Gold and Dr. Pugh, my father's physicians, stood beneath a willow to one side of the room, debating something I couldn't hear.

I took a long breath, squeezed the rosary in my pocket, and stepped out to join them all.

So many people—but of course I bumped into him. Into Peter.

Finding him in a crowd was inevitable, like everything else about us.

Peter flashed a tight grin as he regained his balance, steadying the laurel crown in his tight black curls and straightening his jacket. "Hi, Selah. You look nice."

He didn't look nice. With his skin glowing smooth and soft brown in the candlelight beneath the oak, dressed in tweed and smelling like springtime, he was so handsome I could hardly meet his eyes. My nerves flared, and I fought the urge to hide from him like a child.

We hadn't exactly talked before Daddy extended the proposal, and I'd acted bright and busy and distracted when I'd run into him in the fortnight since.

I could never have told Peter outright how I felt.

Peter Janesley. Six feet tall, black, with curly hair and a strong nose and full lips. Shoulders that tended to round when he was thinking, his father's light brown eyes, his mother's careful hands. Peter, the boy who was brilliant at math and at sports and didn't feel compelled to pretend he was bad at either. Who could've been friends with anyone, but who never made anyone feel invisible. When I was fourteen, I'd learned how to graft roses from his mother just to spend time at his house. The day Sister Elizabeth scolded me till I cried over an algebra test, he'd helped me at their kitchen table until I understood everything I'd gotten wrong.

"Perfect!" he'd said. "I knew you could get this." He'd tapped the problems with his finger, a smile stretching wide beneath his broad cheekbones. I'd tried not to blush.

Peter was smart, and earnest, and kind. After we'd finished studying, he'd cut us both a piece of cake and we'd sat for half an hour on his porch, cross-legged opposite from one another in the rising twilight. Cicadas hummed and buzzed as the light melted off the facade of the Janesleys' home and the abelias and roses brushing the porch rail.

Once, I made him laugh. Peter had rocked back, lovely fingers clasping his knees, mouth open to show the perfect gap in his teeth, and I'd wanted to trap the moment in a jar like a firefly.

After that, we were friends, and I clung to the fact like a trophy. After I made a perfect score on my next algebra test, he hugged me in front of everyone and ruffled my hair. "Knew you could do it," he'd said, pointing at me as he backed away, making for his next class.

My feelings built themselves from a hundred little moments like these, rising like a castle in the distance, every humble stone growing into something I could already imagine. Into something on the horizon I'd eventually reach.

And here he was. My past and my future, standing right in front of me.

"Peter!" I blurted. "Ah—thank you. You look nice, too," I added, remembering his compliment. He huffed a laugh and put his hands in his back pockets. The jacket strained a little over his shoulders. "How are you?"

"Fine. Good." He nodded. "You?"

"All right," I said.

Maybe if I said it enough, I'd believe I wasn't shaking like a leaf.

I wanted to come out with it all—to blurt out exactly what I was thinking and feeling, to explain why he'd heard it all first through our parents and not from me, to see easy confidence in his eyes again. But somehow, I couldn't say any of it.

Later, I thought. Once we were alone, with the public spectacle over, we'd talk. There would be nothing but the truth between us, and the future ahead.

The music quieted, and Arbor Hall's doors swung open. Peter dropped his voice. "I need to go find my parents before it starts." He raised his eyebrows, as if asking for my approval. I sent him away with a nod and a smile.

Soon enough, we'd have all the time in the world.

2

"His Grace, Jeremiah, Seneschal of Potomac," called the herald, "and Alessandra, Esteemed Consort." The crowd murmured, clearing a path to the Arbor for Daddy and my stepmother.

There she was. My *smother*, more like a bag over my head or a girdle around my waist than a guide or a guardian.

Daddy had married her after we had lost Momma seven years before. Looking at her, it was impossible not to see why.

Her hair and eyelashes were thick and dark, her white gown spotless. Her cheekbones and clavicle and wrists stood pronounced beneath her golden skin, despite the heavy curve of her stomach.

Five months pregnant, she glowed. My father looked haggard beside her.

Puffy bags hung beneath Daddy's glazed eyes, and his black suit drowned his thin frame. I bit my lip, trying to remember when he'd lost more weight.

Not for the first time, I wondered what Peter and the court thought when they looked at my father next to Alessandra—at both of us next to her. My *smother*, the perfect, ice-cold center of the room.

It wasn't kind, to speak that way of family. My godmother, one of the nuns at Saint Christopher's, usually scolded me when I did. *Better pray the Hail, Holy Queen, sweet girl, and ask Mary to correct your wayward path.*

But I'd never had to speculate on how Alessandra thought I compared to her. She'd made her opinion of me perfectly clear.

I drew in a breath as Daddy and my stepmother reached the center of the hall and stepped out from beneath the oak, feeling people draw back from me as they noticed my presence. I swallowed, crossing my arms over my chest.

"Countrymen," Alessandra intoned, perfect face earnest. "Women of Potomac. Welcome to Arbor Hall, and happy Arbor Day. We are glad to have you beside us, as we are every spring. Together," she called to the assembly, "we remember our roots."

"Together," rumbled the crowd, "we stretch ever upward." Their response was a wind at my back, whispering through the trees.

Alessandra beamed. "As every year, the seneschal and I honor the old custom. The sun sets tonight on a thousand new saplings in the southeast quarter, beyond the Anacostia River."

I fisted my hands, feeling the calluses on my palms, and tried to imagine my *smother* wielding a shovel in her new gown and jeweled bracelet.

She looked beautiful. But the seneschal's family was supposed to live simply—to take only what they needed, to feed themselves and Arbor Hall from the same common lands that fed the hungry.

I tried not to think of the public fields we wouldn't be able to seed if Alessandra kept up her extravagance.

"Spring is the heart of our hope." Alessandra pressed her hands to her chest. "It was on Arbor Day so many years ago that word of our independence came from England. So today, we rejoice, celebrating the peace we hold dear and our work toward Potomac's prosperity and growth."

I pressed my lips tightly together. The Council was nowhere to be seen, but they were undoubtedly to blame for this speech. Secretary Moreau, most likely, though Secretary Allen had probably helped. Their glib words—*the peace we hold dear*—were like bile in my stomach.

Our little country of Potomac was at peace, more or less, if only because her once-upon-a-time colonizers had retreated back across the Atlantic, abandoning her for a lost cause, forsaking a costly connection that brought them little return.

We hadn't been liberated so much as deserted because we failed to thrive. We weren't at peace so much as isolated. Occupied with survival, like most every other little kingdom and territory and tribe on this continent.

"And so we welcome you to Arbor Hall, to celebrate the future." She put a hand on her belly. "Welcome, all, and happy Arbor Day!"

Applause burst out. "Do you think it'll be a boy or a girl?"

the woman in front of me whispered excitedly to her neighbor, who shook her head, grinning.

I blinked a little. Alessandra hadn't even mentioned my proposal.

A hush fell again as my father stepped forward to speak.

"Happy Arbor Day, everyone." He smiled faintly, one hand twitching at his side. "Thank you all for coming." Swallowing hard, I dropped my gaze.

I didn't want to watch the crowd cock their heads, strain to hear his words. To see them see how thin Daddy had gotten, how his limbs shook like leaves in the wind.

I couldn't watch them watch him. Barely over forty, my father looked like an old man, voice weak as water as he spoke.

I wished Peter could stand beside me right now. I wished I already had my answers, written out like a story in a book, black and white and certain.

But then Daddy called for *Selah, Seneschal-elect of Potomac*, voice creaky as a brittle old oak, and panic filled me. I wasn't ready. I suddenly wished I could slip back through the trees and hide from his answers and the waiting court.

Instead, I uncrossed my arms and walked to the Arbor, feeling exposed in front of the entire court.

They all knew what I was about to ask.

I sifted through their faces as I passed, ignoring everyone as I searched for Peter.

I'd feel stronger once he stood beside me. I knew it.

When I found him at the edge of the crowd, it was all I could do not to reach for his hand as I passed. But Peter wouldn't look at my face.

His long fingers were twined together, his earnest gaze trained on them.

My pulse sped.

"Captain Matthew Janesley, I've extended a marriage proposal to your son on behalf of our daughter, Selah, the Seneschal-elect," Daddy said. "Will Peter accept?"

The moments between the question and its answer hung like smoke in the air, burning my lungs.

I willed Peter to meet my eyes. I knew I'd see his answer there. But no sooner could I catch his gaze than he'd glance away again.

Yes, I prayed, squeezing my fingers so hard I feared they'd snap like twigs. *Say yes.*

Captain Janesley stared at his broad hands, at his feet, anywhere but at my father. Or at me. "No, my Lord Seneschal. Peter respectfully declines your proposal."

3

I couldn't hold my silence.

"What?" The word was a breath, a whimper. But not a single person in the noiseless room missed that small sound of hurt.

I didn't care that all of Arbor Hall could see as I stared. I couldn't look away from Peter. As the room filled with hissing whispers like water boiling over the rim of a pot, I heard nothing but my own keening heart, was aware of nothing but my own humiliation.

I felt well and truly naked, stripped bare before them all.

I'd never cared for anyone but Peter. He'd been my first and only choice.

But Peter hadn't picked me.

He knew me—he was my friend—and he didn't want me. And all of Potomac was here to bear witness to my rejection.

I'd never have to wonder again what Peter thought of me

when I stood beside my family.

I turned toward Daddy, panicked. His eyes darted between Peter and me, confusion and disappointment in the lines of his weary face.

My heart sank into my stomach. He hadn't reckoned on this. He didn't need this kind of worry right now.

How could I have made such a huge mistake?

In the scene I'd envisioned, Peter said yes. Daddy would've been jubilant. He would've given me a kiss, hugged Peter tightly, welcomed him into the family, worn the kind of smile I remembered.

I hadn't prepared for this, either. I hadn't imagined what would happen if Peter said no.

My father studied me, asking me silently what he should do. I gave him the tiniest shake of my head, the feeblest shrug of my shoulders.

"Very well," he managed to say. And Daddy cleared his throat and said nothing else.

The rest of the ball passed in a blur. I sat with my would-have-been in-laws through dinner, hollowed out with embarrassment, flat and thin as a paper doll, like a child disabused of foolish illusions.

I couldn't stand the pity in Peter's eyes.

I'd told myself he and I would talk after the announcement, once we had the truth between us. But I hadn't prepared for the truth to be this.

Our tense meal was a mockery of the festive night I'd

envisioned, the ball a total farce. But Peter was well liked, and his parents were respected. His father was a captain in the military, his mother a talented florist.

So I contained myself.

Besides, everyone was watching to see how I'd react.

We sat side by side through dinner, hardly speaking. I couldn't produce any words; he could only produce two.

I'm sorry, he said, again and again, in whispers and with looks.

I'd been a fool to choose him.

I'd never risked telling Peter how I felt, always afraid of his reply. Proposing via official channels had felt safer, somehow.

Why hadn't I seen that public rejection would only hurt worse?

What, I wondered, *makes one person want another?*

I knew why I wanted Peter. I had speculated for so long on whether he cared for me, carried the hope of him for so long, I hardly knew how to break it apart and examine it.

The only thing left to wonder now was what made a person stare into a proffered heart and say, *No, no, thank you, not for me.*

After dinner, Peter's parents left the hall, making quiet, polite excuses. I met Peter's eyes, searching for an answer, trying to trace the path to destruction my hopes had taken.

A flush crept up Peter's light brown skin, and as he dipped his head slightly, his laurel wreath slipped a little in his tight black curls. He stood wooden and awkward, fingers clasped behind his back, shoulders rounded. A mere two feet away and a world apart from me.

The gap between us taunted me.

I thought I understood him. I thought we were friends, that I could ask him things. But his refusal had stolen my voice. I couldn't ask the only questions left to me.

And the person in front of me was a boy I barely knew.

"I just wish you'd told me when it was just the two of us," I whispered, staring at my shoes.

Peter hitched up a lean shoulder, his light brown eyes baffled. "The thing is, it never was just the two of us, Selah."

The words stung me.

They didn't merely remind me that I'd been avoiding Peter these past few weeks. They meant he'd been totally blindsided by my proposal.

I saw now I'd been hoping he'd answer my question without my having to be brave enough to speak the words. But he'd never even suspected that I would ask. He had never thought of me as I had endlessly imagined him.

And perhaps, more than that, I'd never known him as truly as I'd wished I did. I'd been hoping, not believing. Imagining, not knowing.

I dropped my eyes, avoiding his confused gaze, taking in safer pieces of the boy I adored. Rounded shoulders. The soft shell of his ear beneath his laurel wreath. His hands, clean and slim and white-knuckled with disquiet beneath their dark complexion.

I would never hold them. And they would never hold me.

Peter disappeared through the trees, and I watched him walk away.

15

Then Daddy crouched beside me, eyes gentle in his thin, drawn face, and took my hand.

We couldn't truly get lost among those milling through the damp, green hall, but as the candles burned low in the trees, the party had seemed to move on and forget me. My father gave my hand a squeeze. "I'm sorry, sweet girl."

My parents' love story was one I knew well. My grandparents had been less than amused when the wealthy Savannah princess they'd invited to visit brought a sharp-tongued nun along for company. But that nun had become my godmother, and Althea told me Daddy fell for the girl from Savannah the first time she smiled at him.

Momma had been his solid ground, and he'd been her open sky. I wondered if anyone would ever see me that way.

I'd been blind enough to think Peter had.

"Is something wrong with me?" I finally asked.

"Oh, honey." Daddy stopped me, hands on my shoulders, weary eyes serious. "You are everything you ought to be. Everything, and more. And that's nothing compared to what I know you'll be someday."

He pulled me into a hug, and I wanted to weep against his chest like a child at the sharpness of his ribs. "Daddy, are you feeling all right?" His too-large jacket muffled my words. "You look like Alessandra's got you on a diet."

He chuckled. "Don't you fret about me. I'm just getting old, that's all. Don't need as much to keep me going anymore, since you do all the work around here these days."

I huffed a weak laugh. "You aren't old. And don't be silly. You do a lot."

"Well, I ain't young." He sighed. "You hear all that racket last night?"

I shook my head.

"Maybe I'm imagining it. But I don't think I've slept through the night in weeks. Always seems to be so much noise." Daddy pressed bony fingers to his temples. The band had struck up again, a boisterous song with a heavy drumbeat. "I thought it would help."

I glanced back to my father, unhappiness curdling in my stomach. "You thought what would help?"

But Daddy wasn't listening, and now people were drawing near us—Alessandra, his physicians, members of the court. I felt the private haven we'd shared for a few precious moments collapsing.

Other people needed his time. Mine was up.

But the sound of my name halted my retreat.

"Selah!" My stepmother shook her head, lips pursed. "The evening isn't over."

Daddy cast me a worried glance. "Alessandra, I think the ball can spare her."

"But the Council can't." Her tone was utterly bare of sympathy. My father's chest and shoulders deflated. "The Roots—now."

"W-wait—" I stammered. But Dr. Gold and Dr. Pugh descended as I spoke. No one heard me excuse myself as Dr.

Pugh began rambling about how much better Daddy was looking.

"Clearly, the treatment is working," said Dr. Pugh. Dr. Gold nodded brightly, an attempt at a smile stretched across his kind, young face.

Daddy had told me not to worry. It didn't look as if his doctors were of the same mind.

I wanted to press him, to pinpoint when he'd become this worn, fragile thing, like a page in an old book.

But no one looked at me. I had no one left to question. I could only obey.

The glass decorations in the branches overhead blurred in my vision as I walked away. And as I pushed through a streaming willow's branches and out the side door, I finally began to cry.

Tears streamed down my face as I shuffled down one, two, three flights of comfortless marble stairs, empty but for the echoes of the party. I pressed my back to the cold wall of the bottom landing and fished in the pocket of my gown until the wooden beads of my rosary whispered against my fingers.

One by one, I choked out the string of prayers Momma taught me when I was a little girl. *Our Father who art in Heaven, hallowed be thy name. Hail Mary, full of grace. Glory be to the Father, and to the Son, and to the Holy Spirit.* The beautiful words eased my blistering pain, smoothing me out and untangling my snarled nerves.

But as my tears subsided, I caught the sounds of quiet conversation—of talk not coming from the ball upstairs.

Vague uneasiness rose inside me again, sickly and clinging like fog. The Council meeting in the Roots had already begun.

If Alessandra came down and caught me crying in the dark, she'd lean into my weakness, press on my bruises in front of the others until they thought me as spineless as she did.

Slowly, slowly, I crept down the stairs.

The marble paths between the twisting bases of the trees were overgrown, carpeted with moss and fallen leaves, so my shoes made no noise as I approached the Roots of the great Arbor at the center of the room.

Conversation ground to a halt as I stepped into the light.

Da rief sie einen Jäger und sprach:
"Bring das Kind hinaus in den Wald,
ich will's nicht mehr vor meinen Augen sehen."
　　—Schneewittchen

. . . and she said to a Huntsman,
"Take the child away into the forest.
I will never look upon her again."
　　—*Little Snow-White*

4

Potomac's Council—Secretary Gidcumb, Secretary Moreau, Captain Marshall, Lieutenant Lefevre, Secretary Allen, and Judge Roth—stood clustered together. They stared at me, tumblers of amber Appalachia bourbon in hand.

I'd never attended a Council meeting before, and I hadn't expected to for many years yet, not until Daddy needed me more. Until he was ready to begin training me in politics, I had expected to be left to my work.

Evidently, tonight was to be full of surprises for all of us.

A trio of strange men sat on the far side of the Council table. Their faces were indistinct in the candlelight, their voices pitched low.

I wrung my fingers, fighting the urge to shrink between my shoulders.

It was bad enough I was going to be chastised for Peter

rejecting me. That's what this was about, surely. I'd miscalculated, and it looked bad.

But the Council was elected to help the seneschal steward Potomac's resources, to oversee its courts and its militia and its administration, small though it was. Did all of them—plus a cadre of strangers—really need to be present tonight?

"Good evening, Your Grace," said Captain Marshall, a thick-skulled man with short brown hair. I'd never liked Marshall. Years of military service had apparently taught him only how to mindlessly obey orders.

"Good evening, Captain. Gentlemen." I was relieved my voice didn't shake. "Happy Arbor Day."

Marshall nodded, swirling his liquor, not answering.

I swallowed hard and moved toward the table, set beneath the Arbor's Roots. The great Arbor domed overhead, its Roots curling and twisting like a globe around the table and chairs.

We all straightened at the sound of footsteps on marble— one *clack*ing step moving briskly down the stairs, one plodding tread following after.

Alessandra swanned into the room, followed by my father, and the Council drew near at a wave of her slim hand, muttering and shuffling papers as they settled into the seats unoccupied by the unfamiliar trio. Secretary Gidcumb, one of the Council's more competent members, lit the candelabra at the center of the table before he sat.

"Now," Alessandra began, eyeing us all significantly. "We all know why we're here."

I bit my lip, bracing myself.

My *smother*'s expression of concern was as flawless as the black curls spilling over her shoulders. "Selah, we need to discuss our official response to your rejection."

Sympathy pierced the weary fog in Daddy's gaze. "Alessandra, I think this is something our family should handle in private."

"I beg your pardon, Seneschal, but this isn't a private problem," Secretary Moreau said smoothly. Moreau wasn't the blockheaded yes-man that Marshall was. He was slick, manipulative, with a pointy face and shifty eyes like a weasel's. "The choice of Selah's eventual spouse is a matter of state. The man she marries will guide her and our country. This is not a job for any woman to take alone, let alone Selah."

I stared at the table, drowning in humiliation.

When I was sure no one was looking at me anymore, I let myself peek up at the three strangers for the first time.

The first, seated beside Secretary Gidcumb, was gray-haired but carved like stone, biceps swelling under his shirtsleeves. His olive-skinned face was scruffy and unshaven, his gaze a stern gray. I thought he might be Mediterranean, maybe from Hellás, or Anadolu.

I didn't know what strangers—foreign strangers, no less— would be doing in a Potomac state meeting. But something about this man calmed me.

He didn't look particularly nice. But the austerity in his face amid all the flattery in the room was a relief. I trusted him instantly.

If sides were taken tonight, I wished he'd take mine.

"Your rejection was public," said Judge Roth. "What will this do to your image as our future leader?"

"Nothing!" My voice was a squeak. "It—won't do anything. Potomac knows who I am."

So did Peter, whispered my treacherous heart, *and he said no anyway.*

Captain Marshall steepled his fingers. "You tend to gardens and fields with the women and to the stock with the men. That makes you one of the people. That does not make you their leader."

"What will it say to the people that one of your dearest friends declined to become your consort?" Allen added, looking blond and impressive and dubious.

The second stranger spoke up. "Unless you wanted to lean on the Janesleys—that was the name, yes?—just a bit."

This man looked around thirty. He was pale and pink-cheeked and dark-eyed, and I felt an unholy desire to squeeze his hands and feel if they were softer than mine. He looked distinctly pampered beside his weathered companion. But he seemed to inhabit his expensive clothes uncertainly, to cling possessively to his crystal tumbler, as though he thought someone might take it away from him. *New money,* I thought.

Alessandra gave him the slightest approving nod of her head.

"Now, there's an idea," Judge Roth said, eyeing the stranger appreciatively.

"Excuse me?" I gaped at them all, though I shouldn't have been surprised. Secretary Allen and Judge Roth were brothers-in-law, and they were constantly moving money around, constantly scheming. I knew for a fact Secretary Allen had conned Lieutenant Lefevre into bailing him out of a tight spot last year. I also knew Allen hadn't paid him back.

"We could make it worth their while for Peter to marry you. Was the problem with the family or the boy?" Roth asked, glancing around.

"How much would it take, do you think?" asked Moreau. Lieutenant Lefevre bobbed his head from side to side, as though running numbers in his brain. I thought smoke might start pouring out of his ears.

"No," I said. "No. Absolutely not." The only thing worse than not marrying Peter would be coercing him, and his own sense of honor would surely forbid such a thing. The councilors stared at me, displeasure clear on their faces.

I wanted to melt under the table and crawl to my room. I wanted to cry. I wanted to shake them all by the shoulders, these men who had never felt their agency or reasoning dismissed out of hand.

"You must marry, Your Grace," said Captain Marshall, brows knit. "And soon. You are eighteen, a grown woman, and Potomac is not a large country. We rely on you to set the example for our young people, in matrimony and in bearing children. And you are ill-equipped to become seneschal without a husband to lead and advise you."

They took my shyness, my privacy, for weakness. I gulped down my embarrassment, a bitter pill. "Captain Marshall, I fully intend—"

But once he'd gotten rolling, Marshall was loath to stop. "England abandoned Potomac because their empire grew weak at the fringes." He eyed me sternly, as though I were a soldier who'd shown up for inspection in a wrinkled uniform. "But we survived their abandonment because our ancestors did what they must. And now, so must you."

I knew our history as well as I knew my duty. But duty had felt different when it had looked like Peter.

I sensed clouds gathering overhead, vultures circling close. But I couldn't read what they foretold.

Something was coming. I knew it. I just couldn't make sense of the omens.

Once upon a time, Godmother Althea had told me, the Old World sought out the New, poachers and pilgrims and adventurers and conquerors pursuing glory and gold and space to breathe. And they had found some of what they wanted. But they hadn't stayed forever.

The future does not roll in great waves, she'd said. *It comes in a thousand tiny moments, turns on hinges too small to see, follows a winding path carved by yeses and nos that change the world.*

Europe taxed and took what it wanted, retreating from the New World only after the Old claimed all its attention—when Bharat, far away in Southeast Asia, began to press back against the men who came first for commerce and coercion and then to outright conquer. When distance and cost made us more trouble than we were worth.

A thousand tiny moments. A winding path of yeses and nos.

I wondered how different my life would be if the New

World colonies had pushed back instead of being squeezed thin in Europe's grip. If we had been the ones to revolt instead of Bharat. If, when abandoned by English overlords cheerfully declaring our "independence," someone other than my ancestor had been the one to save our starving, depleted colony and become our first seneschal.

I wondered how different my future might look if Peter had said yes tonight instead of no.

Bharat's revolt had meant the beginning of the end of the British Empire—and, for a time, of all empires. After England's resources were decimated in Bharat's war for independence, Europe's enterprising crowns abandoned their imperial pursuits in the New World and the Old, determined to stay within their borders and stay afloat.

But Britain was not the last empire to seek to cover the earth. If the reports were right, the Imperiya Yotne—the endless swaths of land conquered by the country of Yotunkheym— was a gaping mouth and a bottomless stomach, swallowing more territory in Europe every year.

I shook myself, tried to focus.

I wanted to serve Potomac. I wanted to marry.

But the tides of history weren't mine to command. And neither was my own heart. Or anyone else's.

"Bharat, al-Maghreb, and Masr balance the Imperiya for now. But we cannot perpetually count on great foreign powers to slap the tsarytsya's wrist away, should she reach beyond Europe's shores," Marshall finished. "Who will you choose, Seneschal-elect?"

"There's no one else," I said, staring at the Council table, my voice barely above a whisper. "There was only Peter."

I lifted my gaze and met the eyes of the third stranger.

The last and youngest of the trio sat the tallest of the group. His tanned face was smooth and unwrinkled, set with an upturned nose and bowed lips. No silver threaded his dark hair, but his expression was grave, better suited for a much older man.

His thick-lashed dark eyes were a little dismayed, studying me as I studied him. I glanced away.

"Give her time," my father said quietly. "And, in time, perhaps we can look elsewhere."

Daddy smiled, and I imagined the day he'd met my mother. A stranger who'd become his wife.

Perhaps I could do the same. Given time.

"But, Jeremiah, we need to address this now. After tonight's events, Selah's reputation will only suffer the longer she continues without a fiancé." Alessandra's face lit up, her smile so bright and beautiful and filled with concern it almost stung my eyes to look at. "Besides, our Selah is lovely, cultured, accomplished. She's a very productive seneschal-elect, and she did *so* well in school."

I froze.

I'd often wondered what Peter and the court and everyone thought, when they looked at Daddy and me next to Alessandra. But my stepmother had never left her feelings for me in any doubt.

She disdained me in every way.

Suddenly, I was very, very afraid.

"Really, Selah's predicament is an opportunity in disguise." Alessandra's tone was broad and sincere; but I read an almost manic tension in the furrow of her brow and the press of her palms on her stomach. "In times like these, we need good friends and long arms. Since our search in Potomac has failed, I suggest our seneschal-elect cross the Atlantic in search of her groom."

5

I waited for the punch line to her hideous joke. But Alessandra didn't laugh. Secretary Gidcumb stared at me across the table, his high forehead smooth, his dark brown face carefully expressionless behind his glasses. I could read nothing in the press of his broad lips.

My vision clouded as I slipped into a daze; my thoughts grew fuzzy, as though my brain had fallen asleep the way my arms and legs sometimes did.

Across the Atlantic? The Atlantic Ocean?

Daddy's brows pinched together. "Alessandra, that kind of planning would take ages. We'd have to dig up protocol officers, pick her out a team of advisers, commission a ship—the whole affair could cost us years. And I don't want her going so far."

My heart rate steadied. *O ye, of little faith,* I reprimanded myself.

Alessandra shook her head. "Jeremiah, don't be offended, but I'm afraid I foresaw this, and I'm glad I did, because I've saved us a wait. Boys like Peter . . . Well, he's extremely well-liked; he's handsome; he comes from a good family. You may be seneschal-elect, but Peter has options." My stepmother reviewed me with a quick glance, shrugging as if to say, *You should've known.*

You should've known he wouldn't choose you.

The oldest stranger narrowed his gray eyes.

Daddy shook his head unhappily, but my *smother* waved a hand. "Several courts have very graciously agreed to receive our daughter."

Our daughter. She never called me that.

"In light of her situation, we should be counting our blessings," Alessandra added. Captain Marshall bobbed his head, eyebrows arched in obsequious agreement. "A fine group of young men from respectable houses have agreed to court Selah. After what happened tonight, what are her chances of finding a husband at home, even should she wish to?" She waved an elegant hand, the other still pressed protectively to her stomach.

My father stared at the table, not speaking. The room seemed to hold its breath. Or perhaps it was just me.

I counted the seconds as they passed. Everything in me strained across the table toward my father. I wanted to shake him, to make him meet my eyes. To make him make Alessandra explain herself.

When Daddy lifted his head, looking resigned, I knew I was lost.

"I want to personally approve her team," he said. "I remember what it was like to choose Violet, and you, too, for that matter. Whole committees scrutinized you both, helped me deliberate."

The day my stepmother arrived, golden-skinned and dark-haired, mysterious and beautiful, everyone had been as delighted with her as they had been with our newfound ties to New York, a kingdom home to more shipbuilding magnates than any other on the East Coast. Alessandra was second cousin to the wife of a prince, born of a wealthy family.

I wasn't sure if we had reaped anything from the connection. As a child, I hadn't cared. I'd only felt the formal angles in her embrace and known she wasn't my mother.

My pale skin, green eyes, and freckles told everyone we weren't blood. Her coldness told them we weren't family.

"Of course, darling. You can approve them right now." Alessandra rested one manicured hand on Daddy's arm and swept the other at the three strangers, still noiseless to one side of the table. The soft-looking one tipped his chin agreeably, but the iron-haired man and the tanned, long-lashed one didn't budge.

I stiffened. I hadn't expected the pieces of her plan to be right here in the Roots, ready and waiting across the table from me.

My thoughts slowed, growing sluggish. I felt sick.

"Have you assembled your crew, Captain Lang?" asked Alessandra.

I was startled when the youngest of them spoke, pushing one tanned fist into the opposing palm. Both hands were smudged with ink, or pencil. "Gentlemen of the Council, Seneschal and Esteemed Consort, Seneschal-elect: I'm Captain Andrew Lang. This is our ship's navigator, Homer Maionides." He tipped his head first at the rugged man to his right.

"You may already know Sir Perrault, my appointed protocol officer," Alessandra added. She waved a hand at the man with the face like a portrait. "I've known Sir Perrault since we were young. He grew up at court in New York, as well."

Captain Lang seemed to shift away from Sir Perrault. I felt myself draw back a little, too, my insides twisting.

Perrault and my stepmother were old friends.

And here he was, ready and waiting.

"I don't want to," I burst out. "I don't want to go!"

Alessandra cocked her head. "You dismissed Sir Perrault's suggestion of further talks with the Janesleys. This is your remaining option."

The captain glanced once at me, eyes and lashes the color of midnight beneath dark brows, then looked back to Alessandra. "The *Beholder* is ready to sail tomorrow, per your request."

"Tomorrow?" Daddy frowned.

"It's a long trip, dear," said Alessandra. "Why delay?"

Horror clenched me between its jaws, gnawed my bones with its teeth.

Alessandra had set us all up like game pieces, just waiting for her opening move. The Council. These strangers. And me, rejected and out of options.

She'd planned it all so, so carefully, for who knew how long, and I hadn't seen any of it.

"Where?" I breathed, able to manage just the one word around the fear choking me. Sir Perrault studied me like a museum piece. "Where am I going? Who am I meeting?"

Alessandra smiled at me. Her relief at her victory rendered the expression more like a baring of teeth. "It's a surprise."

I stared at my father, wordlessly begging him to ask Alessandra why she'd maneuvered behind his back. To tell her that my leaving was not up for discussion. That I was his girl and I needed some sleep.

But my father only watched the candles melting at the center of the table, staring into the flames.

I fought tears. My voice cracked when I finally spoke. "Daddy, aren't you going to say anything?"

"Maybe you should take this chance, sweetheart," he said, voice barely above a whisper. "Don't you want to be happy?"

"I'm happy here, at home, with you." I pieced my thoughts together like a broken mirror; my voice was jagged. "Don't you want me here?"

"Maybe I don't know what's good for us anymore," he said slowly, meeting my eyes. "I think you should listen to your momma."

Your momma.

The words sucked the breath from my chest.

Half a mile away, the clock in the tower at the Church of Saint Christopher warned of midnight's fall. I stood and backed away from the table, stumbling over my chair and over the Roots that grasped at the dark.

I would not be unmade in front of these people.

Alessandra's voice stopped me, low and tight as a hand around my throat. "The harbor, tomorrow, dawn."

I glanced from my blank-faced father to the uneasy councilmembers to the young captain, whose unsettled gaze told me he was sorry.

My stepmother was breathing hard, very nearly through her teeth, like winning our fight had sapped her strength. Her arms were wrapped around the child inside her womb. Around the brother or sister whose birth I might not be home to see.

Without replying, I fled.

I tore up the pallid stone stairs and through halls as white as a bloodless face. I'd nearly reached one of Arbor Hall's back doors when I tripped, losing a shoe as I crashed to the floor.

For a moment I didn't move, my shoulders shaking as a sob split my chest. The clock clanged again and again, brazen, unfeeling. When I gathered myself off the snowy white tile, I hissed at the throb in my knees that told me twin purple bruises would bloom there, like lilacs beneath my skin.

Up-down, up-down. I limped toward the door, my remaining shoe slicker than glass against the marble floor. I had to get out.

Up-down. I had to get to the graveyard.

6

Tears and makeup and moonlight blurred my vision as I flung myself in front of the hazel tree and my mother's headstone. *Esteemed Consort Violet Savannah Potomac. Beloved.*

I dragged my fingers over the words and leaned my forehead on the stone, my hand clasping the sapling at its side. I'd planted it from a cutting of Momma's favorite shade tree when Alessandra had it torn up. It had been our place in the summer; she'd sit and read to me from her book of fairy tales for hours, until the sun grew low and the earth cooled and the air grew thick with dusk and magic.

I clung to the tree and the seven-years-cold headstone, and I sobbed.

My world had burned to cinders when my mother died. And now Alessandra had lit another match.

Something rustled close by, and I glanced up, tensing. "Who's there?"

But a familiar face emerged from the shadows. "Selah, it's me."

I gave a ragged sigh, eyelids sinking closed, but Godmother Althea patted me on the back. "Eyes open, sweet girl. We don't have much time."

I rose, stumbling breathlessly after her white habit through the big double doors of the Church of Saint Christopher. "Godmother—" I blurted, confused. What did she know? And how?

After all, I'd been caught completely unawares.

"Shh." She baptized a handkerchief in a nearby font of holy water and wiped my tearstained cheeks. "Come on, now."

My godmother led me from the nave through a small door, down two flights of stairs and into a room smelling faintly of dust and incense. Candles came to life in their sconces as she circled the room. "We need to talk. Still, best to keep in the light." She ushered me to a table in the corner, and I sat heavily. "Now, to begin at the beginning. I heard what happened tonight, and I find Peter's turning you down more than a bit odd."

I gave a sad little laugh. "And why is that? My being rejected by one of the most popular boys in Potomac isn't all that surprising."

"No fishing, and no self-pity." Godmother Althea's mouth curved in a knowing not-quite smile. "I know you worship the ground he walks on, and Peter's a good boy. But, Selah, he's just a boy."

"He's different. Special," I said hotly. "Peter's good and

handsome and wonderful." I grimaced, feeling the words like salt in a cut.

"You're a little biased, baby. He's a cute kid, sure. Comes to confession twice a week and waited on his mother hand and foot when she got sick last winter." She tipped her head at me. "But Peter's not out of your reach."

I swallowed hard; I remembered how he'd taken care of his mother. When I'd spotted Peter here at Saint Christopher's near a bank of candles one day, I'd recognized him instantly, gone to his side.

"What's all that for?" I'd blurted, nodding at the basket at his feet. It was crammed with a pot of soup, sharp-smelling poultices, and sachets of tea. Peter had opened his eyes slowly, wearily, wilting me. "Sorry," I'd cringed. "You're here to pray. Of course. I—I'll talk to you later."

But Peter had smiled. "No, it's all right," he'd said, a little tired, glancing down at the basket. "My mother's sick."

"I'm sorry." I'd bitten my lip, smiling up at him a little rue-fully. "But tea and prayers sound like a fail-safe cure."

"It's been days." Peter had sighed, passing a hand over his dark curls. "Dad and I just stare at each other at dinner. Move around each other all day. Neither of us knows what to talk about without her. I just want her better."

I'd frowned, grasping for the right thing to say—for the per-fect thoughtful remark that would make Peter feel better and stay with him till later. But with no warning, his brown eyes had widened in horror. "Oh, Selah. I'm sorry. I didn't think."

I'd blinked, confused. Then—*oh*.

Sorry about Momma, he'd meant. About Daddy and me and our loss. Sorry for complaining about a few days without his mother when I'd been missing mine for the better part of a decade.

"It's okay," I'd reassured him, and he'd nodded. And the moment had listed precariously toward awkward silence.

He was sensitive, to think about his words, about my feelings. I'd been desperate to salvage the moment.

I'd chewed my lip, impulsively looked around. "Can I tell you a secret?" I'd suddenly asked.

Peter's brow had furrowed, earnest. "Is it a good secret?"

I'd bobbed my head. "Alessandra's having a baby."

"The consort is—really?" He'd paused, long fingers rubbing his jaw. "I'm not supposed to know this, am I?"

"No one is. I just had to tell somebody. That's why I'm here, actually," I'd said, nodding at the candles. "To say a prayer for her, and the baby."

Daddy had told me that morning. I'd been so full of the secret I thought I'd burst. I'd needed to tell someone.

But mostly, in that moment, I'd wanted to tell *him*. To share something just with Peter.

"That's really exciting, Selah." Peter had put a hand on my shoulder, and the warmth in his voice and in his palm had made me dizzy. "You're going to be a great big sister. Careful, though—you'll cast quite a shadow," he'd added warningly, and I'd blushed.

When he'd bent for his basket and made to leave, I'd caught the bright, citrusy scent he always carried, and my nerves had stood on end. "Peter—"

"Yes?" He'd moved back toward me, closer than I thought he'd intended. My mouth had been nearly at his ear.

If I'd moved at all, I would have been touching his shoulder or his cheek—though I would have never. I couldn't even have imagined.

"Don't tell," I'd whispered, the words two little breaths.

Peter's mouth had quirked, flashing the gap between his teeth I loved so much. "I won't. Promise."

He'd left me burning brighter than the candles.

Now I just felt burned.

I gave a wan smile and cleared my throat. "Anyway, now the Council says if I don't— Well, let me start over. Apparently, no one on this continent will do."

Godmother Althea shook her head. "I already know, sweet girl."

I blinked at her. "How do you know? And—and *why*?" I demanded. "I know I'm not what she wants me to be. I know she thinks I'm country trash. But why is she doing this? Why do I have to go so far?"

My godmother bowed her head a long moment before answering. "My best guess is that she hopes you won't come back," she finally said. She paused, her broad face sober. "It's a long trip you're taking."

My breath came out in a huff. "She's expecting something to happen to me?" My voice cracked.

Godmother Althea wet her lips and put a hand on my arm.

My mouth worked, but it was a long moment before I could form words. "And if something happens to me? What then?" I passed a hand through my hair. "And why now?"

Godmother swallowed. "She's having a baby, Selah. Her hopes for the future may have changed lately."

I thought of Alessandra's hands pressed to her stomach, palms protective and eyes threatening, and something in my chest went still.

"Daddy's still young," I finally said, scraping at a cuticle. "She's playing a long game, if you're right."

My voice told us both how much I really believed that.

"She may be." Godmother Althea paused. "On the other hand, sweet girl, you don't need me to tell you what people are saying about your father."

I met her steady gaze, and my heart faltered.

Godmother's theory was so improbable. Even Alessandra didn't hate me quite so much as to actually expel me from my home.

Or did she?

My father was ill. He might even be dying.

I knew it. Everyone did. It was why he'd grown so thin, why Dr. Gold hounded him about his habits. I wondered what treatment they'd begun.

I prayed it worked quickly.

Godmother Althea shook her head. "I knew she was up to something. But we'd hoped it wouldn't come to this."

"We?"

One corner of her mouth lifted. "Do you think Alessandra is the only one watching and listening? The only one with friends and allies?"

Watching? Listening? Allies? I stared at my godmother, wondering what else she hadn't told me.

"Do I have to go? Could you—hide me somewhere?" My fingernails drove themselves into my palms. The question was cowardly, and I knew it.

But there was no judgment in her eyes. "I would, but your disappearing would only make matters worse with the Council. And ten to one, Alessandra would only speed up her plan, whatever it is," she added. "If you go, she won't get suspicious, or feel pressed for time. And I'll have some space to figure out what she's up to."

Neither of us spoke for a moment. In the silence, I added up the cost of a ship and a crew and food for all of us, and tried not to imagine how many more public fields would lie fallow to cover the cost.

"Am I really supposed to marry a boy I don't know?" I asked in a whisper. "Is that what I'm going to have to do?"

Althea sighed. "If I knew who your suitors were, I could help, but that's a secret half the Council doesn't even know." I raised an eyebrow at this, but my godmother just smiled archly.

I didn't know who my allies were. But secret allies were better than enemies on every side.

"Thank you," I said softly.

Althea stood. "Stay safe, sweet girl. Be good. Be wise."

I nodded, and she kissed me on the forehead.

"Rest, if you can. Your bags will be at the harbor in the morning."

Outside Saint Christopher's, I knelt beneath the hazel tree I'd watered with my tears not an hour before. Unpinning the ivy circlet from my hair, I set it in front of my mother's headstone.

I miss you.

I scooped a little dirt from her grave into the damp handkerchief Godmother Althea had given me, tied it off, and put it into my pocket beside my rosary. I left the graveyard with my limbs weary, my head throbbing.

There would be no rest for me tonight.

7

Dawn broke as I reached the harbor, bitingly cold and swathed in a haze that seeped into the fabric of my dress.

Somewhere far away, a rooster crowed. Though I'd left them sleeping a couple hours before, the cows would be stirring in their meadows and in the barns, the sun rising over the fields. Any other day, I would already be on my hands and knees, acquainting myself with my morning chicory coffee, letting damp earth cradle me as I began to work.

But today, a few people on the pier and a rookery of ships waited for me instead. The ships hovered on the foggy surface of the Potomac, their white sails folded like albatross wings.

And as I approached the river, another figure appeared in the mist.

Carved into the prow of one of the ships was a girl. Her long arms were flung wide, fingers splayed, and apples and olive branches rippled like hair around her shoulders. Sinuous carvings like ocean waves hinted at a flowing gown, with high-heeled shoes visible beneath, but she was ready for battle: a sword and a bow and arrow were crossed over her chest. Her face was blank but for enormous stars etched where eyes, ears, and a mouth would be.

Overhead, a tough-looking, tanned girl in black scaled the rigging to fit Potomac's blue-and-gold flag above the crow's nest. Sails unfolded like daylilies around her as two East Asian men, one young, one older, secured the ship's lines. Striding over the deck with Homer Maionides and a stocky, boyish-looking sailor with black hair was Captain Lang.

This must be the *Beholder*.

Lang caught sight of me staring and waved. Homer and the boy turned to follow his gaze.

My cheeks burned. My dress was damp and dirty, my hair disheveled from the night I'd spent walking through the humid air, saying goodbye to all the places I would miss. My remaining shoe I carried in one hand; I raised the other arm, stiff and cold, in reply.

At a tap on my shoulder, I spun, and met Peter's eyes.

My mouth opened and closed. I didn't know what to say to him. I wondered now if I'd ever really known what to say to him.

Hadn't I seen how sparse words always were between Peter and me? Hadn't I known it was a sign of everything else that was lacking?

I dropped my gaze and crossed my arms over my chest. "So everyone knows I'm leaving," I mumbled. "I'm surprised you came."

"My dad told me this morning. I wanted to catch you before you went." Peter lifted a hand to my shoulder, uncertain at first, and then solid pressure. I reluctantly met his light brown eyes. "Selah," he whispered again, "I'm so sorry."

"Don't feel sorry for me." I tried to smile, to get the words out quickly, but my voice cracked at *don't*.

"I know you want to know why, and I wish I could explain it." Peter quietly cleared his throat. "I can only tell you that it wasn't about you. That I had to make a choice for my family."

The hollowness I'd felt the night before swelled inside me again, so bare and cold I thought the wind might echo through me like a reed.

"Can you ever forgive me?" Peter asked. He knitted his long brown fingers together, eyes sincere, lips pressed tight and unhappy.

He'd said this, over and over again, the night before. As if I wanted an apology instead of his affection.

As if he'd done me wrong, rather than return me to reality from the fantasy I'd been privately living.

I tried to see him standing there as Godmother Althea had insisted he was—cute and kind, a perfectly ordinary good heart. Just another boy.

I saw what she'd been trying to show me. But I also still saw him the same way I always had. He was perfect to me. A star of a boy. A king of a boy. The only boy I'd ever cared for.

Maybe a little distance wouldn't be a bad thing.

"Peter, believe me when I tell you: there's nothing to forgive." I forced another smile and peeled my heart from the hands that had held it without knowing for so many years.

We both turned at the rattle of wheels and the *clop-clop-clop* of horse hooves. A carriage stopped at the edge of the pier, and Daddy and Alessandra climbed down.

My *smother* took in my appearance with a roll of her eyes before leading my father aboard.

"I have to go," I finally said. "Take care."

"Take care," Peter said gently. And then he turned to go.

As Peter walked away, I dug my toes into the earth that had raised me, feeling Potomac's soil beneath my feet for the last time for I didn't know how long.

Then I crossed to the pier and trudged up the gangplank after my father and stepmother.

Up on the forecastle, Alessandra exchanged goodbyes with Sir Perrault. I couldn't catch their words, but my stepmother spoke in low, icy tones, and Perrault looked pale—almost seasick, though we'd hardly left solid ground. I almost pitied him.

Almost.

Godmother Althea and my father waited a little space away. On my way to Daddy's side, Alessandra intercepted me. "You couldn't change?"

Heat splotched my chest and cheeks. "I like this dress." I gripped one elbow with my free hand, my shoe dangling from the fingers of the other. "And I was short on time."

"And a shoe." She rolled her eyes again and nodded at Perrault.

He carried a slim folder. "Those are your suitors. Prepare to meet them as you see fit. But fail the Council, and the Council may fail you." She glanced at my father, looking thin and breakable in the early light. "I think you know what's at stake."

I clenched my fingers around my arm, staring first at the folder in Perrault's hands, then at Alessandra's abdomen. At the child she'd made my enemy before I could ever become its friend.

"I'll do what has to be done," I said.

Not that I knew what that was. Not that I knew what it would cost. Not that the words would mean the same thing to Alessandra that they meant to me.

But when I looked at my father, at my godmother, at the little brother or sister I already cared for, at the banks of the land whose absence I already felt in my bones—I knew I'd do what was necessary to come home and protect them.

Alessandra put her hands on her stomach and turned away, eyes victorious. "We'll see," she called over her shoulder.

That was all the goodbye I got.

After she was gone, I wobbled to Daddy's side, and for a moment, there was no sound between us but the gentle lap of waves against the *Beholder*'s hull and the words trapped in his throat.

Abruptly, he pulled me into a tight hug. I stifled a whimper and hung on to him, gripping his reedy frame, wondering if they'd still send me away with this ship full of strangers if I never let go.

"Be careful," he said quietly. "And get home, quick as you can."

A tremor twitched his shoulder, and he released me. I fought tears, furiously memorizing his face—the green eyes and freckled skin like mine, the graying stubble he hadn't shaved this morning.

When he kissed my forehead and followed my stepmother off the *Beholder*, I watched him walk away, head bowed. I swallowed and blinked to keep my tears from falling.

I was on the verge of collapse when my godmother descended upon me, crushing me in an embrace. "Everything is ready," she said breathlessly. "I've done everything I can."

"*Everything's* ready?" The edges of my voice were raw, my fingers tight around the shoe in my hand. Its beading scratched at my fingers. "My bags are ready. Perrault has that stupid folder. But what about me?" Godmother Althea's gaze darted to the file in the protocol officer's grip, but Captain Lang was already approaching, the set of his lips apologetic, as they had been the night before. We had no time.

It wasn't Lang's fault, but my hands fisted themselves, frustrated—at him. At Alessandra. At the slowly rising sun, for not ceasing to move so I could stay where I belonged.

Whatever my godmother said, I wasn't ready.

Althea turned back to me, habited frame tense and vigilant, eyes blazing. "Yes. Yes, you are," she said quickly. "You have a keen mind and a kind heart. You have everything you need."

She believed I would make it through this trip.

I will get through it, I swore silently. *And I will get back to them.*

The captain cleared his throat in our direction, raising his voice over the crowd that had gathered on the pier. Out on the dock, the Council formed a line behind Alessandra and my father, all but Gidcumb looking like they'd enjoyed too much Appalachia bourbon the night before. "Sister— Seneschal-elect—we have to get going."

I put my free hand on Captain Lang's arm. "Please." The word was a breath and a plea. "Just—please. One minute."

The captain watched me for a long beat. His expression was composed, but there was reluctance in his pause, in the push of his fist into the opposite palm. "Of course."

"Godmother." I turned back to her, desperate. "The prayer for travelers—before I go." I'd heard nuns and priests speak it a hundred times over ships leaving port and the rare family that moved away. I never imagined she'd say it for me.

As she whispered the short plea to God into my shoulder and hair, her words hemmed my fraying edges, bracing me where I threatened to come apart. I stood quiet in her arms, thumbing the shoe in my hand.

And then it was time.

Trumpets rang out from the dock. A bottle of wine hung from my stepmother's elegant fingers like a man on a gallows. One end of a rope was tied around its neck; the other, around the prow.

"Potomac," Alessandra called over the crowd. "Our seneschal-elect goes in search of a husband across the sea. Brave Selah," she said, dark eyes staring me down, "do your duty to

Potomac, and don't come back alone."

Come back engaged, she might as well have said, *or don't come back at all.* The Council behind her was a moat, a blockade, an iron gate locking me out of my home until I'd done her bidding.

Alessandra spoke the words like a death sentence or a curse, releasing the bottle of wine as the final piece of her incantation. It swung in a wide arc and smashed a gory stain over the *Beholder*, leaving the girl carved on its prow bleeding.

My father had never looked so defeated.

Einmal im Winter, als es steinhart gefroren hatte
und Berg und Tal vollgeschneit lag,
machte die Frau ein Kleid von Papier, rief das Mädchen und sprach:
"Da, zieh das Kleid an,
geh hinaus in den Wald
und hol mir ein Körbchen voll Erdbeeren. . . ."
Dann gab sie ihm noch ein Stückchen hartes Brot und sprach:
"Davon kannst du den Tag über essen,"
und dachte:
"Draußen wird's erfrieren und verhungern
und mir nimmermehr wieder vor die Augen kommen."
    —Die drei Männlein im Walde

Once, in winter, when everything was frozen as hard as a
        stone,
and hill and vale lay covered with snow,
the woman made a frock of paper, called her step-daughter,
        and said,
"Here, put on this dress
and go out into the wood,
and fetch me a little basketful of strawberries. . . ."
Then she gave her a little piece of hard bread, and said,
"This will last thee the day,"
and thought,
"Thou wilt die of cold and hunger outside,
and wilt never be seen again by me."
    —The Three Little Men in the Wood

8

THE *BEHOLDER*

Godmother Althea blew a kiss as the *Beholder* sailed away through the fog. I watched Daddy—broken expression, bent head—until the mist on the water swept him from my view.

When my home was out of sight, I stood by myself, avoiding the gazes of the sailors hustling around the deck and imagining how ridiculous I must look, filthy and staggering around in a ruined dress, one glittering shoe in hand. A complete disaster, to the eye discerning or oblivious.

Not that it mattered what they thought. These were Alessandra's people, not mine.

Captain Lang didn't turn his head as I wobbled near, arms akimbo so the ship's woozy sway wouldn't send me sprawling. But he rapped his ink-stained knuckles on a barrel beside his place at the helm, and I sat, drawing up my legs beneath me to hide my dirty feet.

He glanced away from the horizon for a long moment, studying my face. "You had no idea before last night, did you?"

"None," I said quietly. "I don't like this—feeling blind. Not knowing the plan."

Lang's dark eyes shifted under his lashes. "What can I tell you?" he asked quietly. "What would help you not feel so lost?"

I was missing so many details. There were so many questions I wished I had the courage to ask.

Where am I going?

What am I going to do?

When can I go home?

But all these questions felt unwieldy. Their answers would be large enough to crush me. I wasn't ready for them.

"Is the *Beholder* your ship?" I asked instead.

Captain Lang's mouth quirked. "No. It's yours."

The curve of his thin lips made something in my chest flutter. I gave my head a slight shake. "Beg pardon?"

"Well, it's Potomac's, anyway."

"Oh."

Alessandra had been so determined to get rid of me she'd bought a ship.

"Have you been a sailor long?" I cocked my head to one side. "You look so young."

"I'm twenty." The captain's jaw tightened, and his eyes grew sharp—not on me, or at me, but clearly I had touched a nerve. "There would've been more competition for this job if it hadn't—" But Lang broke off.

My stomach sank a little. "If it hadn't what?"

Lang shook his head. "I should let Perrault do the explaining. You'd do better to hear the plan from him."

I swallowed hard, at once scanning the deck for the protocol officer and his folder and afraid to spot him.

I needed to find out what was coming. I wanted to hide from it.

"Have you been where we're going?" I asked carefully.

"Europe?" Lang shook his head. "Never been on that side of the Atlantic. But I've done a lot of jobs up and down the Misiziibi." He scrubbed a tanned hand through his hair. "A few years back I sailed the Pacific from the Koniag Archipelago, way up north, clear to the west coast of México. That's where I met Skop—in Koniag. Before this, I was in Zhōng Guó for over a year, running cargo for their national government."

Europe.

I was going to Europe.

"That's so much traveling." My voice sounded young in my own ears. I suddenly felt a little embarrassed by the awe Lang must have heard in my voice. I cleared my throat. "How'd you hear about this . . . job from so far away?"

Job. The word felt odd on my tongue. This was my life that had been turned inside out in the span of one night.

"Ports, pubs, passing ships. News about work travels." Lang flicked another glance at me. "Especially work like this."

"I've never gone anywhere."

"Well, you're going somewhere now."

I watched his face, where a spare grin hovered beneath his

upturned nose, and something flickered in my chest, like kindling catching a spark. "Ready or not," I said, not taking my eyes off him.

Lang didn't look away for a long moment. "Skop!" he called.

I must have leapt six inches off my seat. A boy jogging by changed course and headed toward us, face flushed with exertion. I guessed if he was from Koniag, as Lang had said, he was Yupik, one of the people indigenous to the coast of Alyaska and the islands beyond. Skop wasn't much taller than I; but he had a durable look to him, with strong arms and hands, and fawn-colored skin that grew ruddy over his cheeks and knuckles. Angular, heavy-lidded dark eyes were set in his round face over high cheekbones and a broad nose that looked as though it had been broken at least once, but probably a few times.

Lang nodded between the boy and me. "Seneschal-elect, this is Skop Koniag, our first mate. Skop, this is Selah."

Skop dipped his head, chewing the inside of his cheek and considering me.

"Skop, take the helm. I'm going to show the seneschal-elect to her room," said Lang. He glanced at my ragged dress, my ruined makeup. "I imagine she'd like to rest."

"Sure thing." Skop nodded efficiently, and took the wheel from Lang's hands.

The captain strode off, hands in the pockets of his navy-blue canvas jacket, and I followed him off the forecastle.

It was kind of him to pretend I wasn't drowning.

9

My head spun as I followed the captain across the deck, through one of two doors in the stern, and down a flight of steps. "Captain's quarters," he said, jerking his head at a blue-painted door off the landing. "Or—rather, my quarters." He said the words like they came as a surprise to him, too.

My vision adjusted slowly as we descended. "This is the lower deck," he announced. "Crew's cabins are at the far end. Stores are here and in the hold, below."

I squinted, just able to make out an aisle lined with benches. "There's another level below this one?"

"Yes, and don't go poking around," Lang said sharply. I stared at him, and he hesitated. "The ladder's not quite right, and you're liable to get hurt. Besides, it's dark below."

I crossed my arms, a bit taken aback. "Fine."

Lang fumbled with the knob in the door beside him. "Good. And here's your room."

The door swung open, and I winced at the daylight streaming in through the portholes on the far wall. By the early morning sunlight, I could see the room was plain—a little bunk with a blank white quilt and bedside table, a worn leather chair, an armoire beside all my trunks. Its open cabinet and drawers looked like an empty face.

I thought of my room in Potomac, of my own bed and my bookshelves and the walls I'd scribbled on when I was three, and felt my chest go tight.

"All your things have been brought down. You should be comfortable enough here." Lang stuffed his hands into his pockets again, eyes trained on my luggage. "I'll leave you be." He nodded, sparing me a single, searching glance, and ducked into the hall.

And then I was alone.

I sank onto the floor, fiddling idly with the brass fastenings of my luggage, and began with a sigh to unpack.

I found my trunks full mostly with new clothes—gowns, more casual dresses, shirts, and pants. The process of smoothing and sorting and fitting them into my wardrobe should have been comforting, but I grew more and more apprehensive at their endlessness, at the rising expense I calculated in every layer of finery.

How far was I going? How long would I be gone? And at what cost to Potomac?

I thought of Perrault on deck with Alessandra, my folder in his hands.

I wanted to seek him out, to pore over its pages and make a plan.

I wanted to find the folder and fling it overboard, and let salt and water have their way with paper and ink and Alessandra's plans.

Two-thirds of the way through my first trunk, I heard something shifting between a green lace gown and my favorite old waterproof boots. Curious, I paused.

Beneath the impractical dress was a blond wooden box. As I took it from its resting place, its contents made a rustling sound, like fingertips on pages.

Inside the box was a tiny library of rattling white packets. I lifted them against the light streaming through the portholes, one after another; some held curling shoots; others, black seeds small as pinpricks.

Taped inside the box's lid was a note in Godmother Althea's handwriting.

> I sneaked bags of soil onboard for you.
> Go find them.
>   Stay muddy, sweet girl.

A lump formed in my throat.

"Gardening?" I asked her, giving a laugh that was half a sob. "On a ship?"

But my godmother was miles away. Too far away to hear. Too far away to answer.

A wave of exhaustion and misery collapsed over me at the scent of the box, of Potomac's kitchen garden and *home*.

My heart missed it all already.

My hands kept unpacking.

Godmother Althea's last gift I found cocooned in a soft yellow sweater that had been Daddy's. I lifted it to my face to breathe him in, worrying for him so badly it hurt, then stared at what was left in my lap.

It was a book, a foot tall and a foot wide, as big as the Bible on the altar at Saint Christopher's and bound thickly in green leather. Pages thin as butterflies' wings were covered with spidery handwriting and illuminated with blossom-bright colors and gold leaf. The table of contents listed epics, myths, legends, and fairy tales from countries far and near.

My heart caught in my throat.

This book had been my mother's. I hadn't seen it in seven years. I had thought it had been lost after she died.

I pulled Daddy's sweater on, my fingers tracing the book's supple cover. The scent of the fabric and the leather drew me back to warm days beneath the shade tree with Momma. To starlit nights on my parents' balcony. To Momma reading its stories aloud, and Daddy acting out the parts of witches and kings and brave tailors. Momma would always laugh and warn him not to rile me up so much I couldn't sleep. Afterward, they'd carry me to bed, take off my shoes, and tuck me in, and dreams would claim me.

I loved stories of all sorts, but somehow I always came home to these. Alessandra had never understood my taste—"Aren't those for *children?*" she'd ask—but I didn't care. Though not for lack of searching, I'd never met an elf or a witch or found a magic kingdom in the woods. But though the stories weren't real, they were fundamentally true. I'd learned firsthand.

In the old stories, change came in waves, quick as lightning or a gathering storm. And when the skies turned black, the heroes and heroines had to stand on their feet and their wits and find their way back home with what friends they met on their way.

I turned to the back of the book. The last page and the page glued to the binding, the endpaper, were covered in script that told the tale of a girl who for her father's sake became prisoner to a ferocious beast in a magic castle. One of Momma's favorites.

I found a pencil in my trunk and put a single tick mark in the top left corner of the page, above the illuminated start of the story.

Mark one. Day one.

Once upon a time, there was a man with three daughters. The youngest was called Beauty.

My fingers traced the illustration of a girl reaching out to her father on horseback, their hands not quite touching, his eyes already on the road ahead.

I was lost out here on the ocean. But somehow, I'd found a map.

10

Perrault was waiting for me when I stumbled onto the deck, squinting into the setting sun. Homer stood at the helm, his shadow streaming out before him.

"There you are!" Perrault's dark eyes studied me, evidently approving my change of clothes. I'd fallen asleep after unpacking. When I awoke, I'd washed my face and put on a cozy gray dress and Daddy's sweater, apparently just in time to wobble to the galley after the rest of the crew.

"I was tired," I said, not looking at the protocol officer.

"Hmm. Well, we have a lot to discuss." Perrault opened the galley door and pointed at a table along the wall. "Sit there and wait for me."

Dumbly, I watched his retreating back, then shuffled inside the galley.

A few lamps swung from the low ceiling, illuminating a room divided by a counter. To one side sat the crew, eating and talking over one another; to the other, a stocky brunet boy rushed around cooking, clanging pots on the stove, clattering loaf pans against oven racks.

I wasn't sure how many sailors crewed the *Beholder*. But as the door banged shut behind us, it felt like a hundred eyes darted my way.

The sturdy, square-faced brunet boy stopped hurrying around the kitchen and hauled an enamel pot out to a sideboard as I approached. "Good evening, Seneschal-elect," he said with a nervous dip of his head. "Will Grimm. I'm the steward. I cook and manage our stores." He gestured behind him, at a tanned girl in black leaning against the galley counter and stabbing at her soup bowl as if it annoyed her. "And that's my sister, Cobie. She's the ship's rigger."

"Pleasure to meet you," I said, trying to smile.

Cobie didn't look pleased to meet me. She didn't look anything.

I took a bowl of soup from the counter, conscious of being watched. Anxiety simmered in my stomach as I glanced around, trying to take everyone in at once: a thin, jumpy old man with graying tawny hair sat between Lang and a boy in his early teens with a cap pulled low on his brow. Skop and an East Asian man of about sixty with silver hair and a round face sat across from them; he and Cobie had been working on deck this morning when I'd come to the harbor. Skop and the old man both smiled at me in greeting.

I sat quietly to eat, grateful when Perrault bustled in and attention shifted to him. He placed a folder on the table. "Your appointments," he said crisply. I reached for the first sheet inside, but Perrault rapped my hand with his pencil. "You can peruse the profiles at greater length later. I need to talk you through our journey now, and I don't want to waste time while you dawdle over your suitors' portraits." I blushed. At the sailors' table, Skop rolled his eyes at Perrault.

I crossed my arms, forcing my embarrassment into irritation. "Waste time?" I frowned, leaning forward to whisper at him. "Sir Perrault, I'm not sure if you've noticed, but we're on a ship. On the Atlantic. You have no meetings to attend. No nobles to look after. It's just the—" I glanced around, trying to count.

"Fourteen," supplied Lang's neighbor, the fidgety older gentleman. He nodded at me, slurping his soup, pushing long gray-gold hair out of his face. An origami ship sat beside his plate, half-folded, and his accent was Savannah-soft, like my mother's had been.

"I'm Andersen." He nodded at his silver-haired neighbor, the older East Asian gentleman with the full cheeks and the kind eyes. "That's Yasumaro."

Yasumaro beamed. "Hello, young lady."

"*If* you please, Sailor Andersen," Perrault snapped. "I'm attempting to do my job."

I turned back to Perrault. "The fourteen of us."

"Seneschal-elect, do you want to know where you are going or not?" Perrault cocked his head elegantly.

I crossed my arms, determined not to jump and plead like a puppy.

Perrault opened the folder and produced the first profile.

"Your first suitor is Bertilak, a prince of England and the Duke of Exeter," he intoned.

My jaw dropped. *"Prince?"*

I'd anticipated courting well-to-do sons of great houses. Wealthy boys from prosperous families. Royal hangers-on, even, or minor nobles.

I had not expected to be courting princes.

Perrault eyed me severely, and I stilled. "Prince Bertilak, firstborn son of the king of England, is well-known for his intellect, having studied both at Eton and Oxford. We will meet the prince at Winchester Castle, where the court is currently convened."

I schooled my expression. I didn't know anything about this man—fancy degrees aside. I'd probably have nothing in common with him.

Still. *England.* I was going to England.

I'd read a lot about England.

Something hungry and curious stirred inside me.

Sir Perrault switched pages. "Your next appointment will convey us to Den Norden—specifically, to Norge."

I took a sip of water, shrinking a little inside Daddy's sweater, grateful suddenly for its weight and warmth. Den Norden, a too-small cluster of still-unconquered countries, was the region northwest of the Imperiya Yotne.

"Prins Torden Asgard is nineteen, son of Konge Alfödr of Norge. He is reputedly"—Perrault rolled his eyes—"extremely handsome. Red hair, brown eyes, muscular, and six feet four inches tall."

"Are they selling me a horse or introducing a suitor?" I swallowed a spoonful of soup. "I'm surprised they didn't give his height in hands." Someone in the galley snickered—Cobie, I thought. Skop seemed to be stifling a laugh, as well.

Perrault glared at me. He straightened his papers, breathing hard through his nose. "Your next suitor is Reichsfürst Fritz of the Neukatzenelnbogen. He's twenty-seven."

"Twenty-seven?" I burst out. "Meaning he was nine when I was born?"

"Yes, but—"

"And he was finishing secondary school when I was still playing with dolls?"

"You were still playing with dolls when you were nine?" Perrault asked. I glanced away and found Lang and the rest of the sailors staring at us. The boy in the hat had soup on his shirt.

"J.J.," Andersen sighed, passing the boy a napkin. J.J. dabbed unselfconsciously at the stain, hazel eyes big in his thin little face as he gawked at me.

I flushed and turned back to my bowl. Perrault sighed. "Reichsfürst Fritz is supposedly very clever. He is the oldest son of Hertsoh Maximilian of the Imperiya, Reichsfürst of Terytoriya Shvartsval'd, and has a number of sisters you may find enjoyable companions. . . ."

But whatever Perrault said next, I wasn't listening.

Shvartsval'd. *Terytoriya Shvartsval'd.*

The *terytoriy* were the conquered lands of the Imperiya Yotne. Each country they conquered was resegmented, renamed, its rulers replaced with loyal followers of the tsarytsya.

"The Imperiya?" My voice was a breath, ragged and insubstantial. I pulled my hands inside the sleeves of Daddy's sweater, wishing I could hide the rest of me as easily. Wishing he were here to hide me—though if he were here, he'd be in no condition to take care of me.

Worry for him, and for me, flooded my thoughts.

Alessandra was sending me into the Imperiya.

A shiver ran up my spine. "No," I said, shaking my head. I pushed back from the table, my chair screeching against the floor.

Perrault looked down at the rest of his papers, affronted. "We've still to cover Prínkipas Theodore of Páfos, as well as all of your alternates—"

"No, I can't," I said. My voice was awkward, too loud. "I don't want to go there."

"Your stepmother has kindly negotiated appointments with multiple royal courts on your behalf, and you will honor those appointments as Potomac's representative," Perrault said, affronted.

The Imperiya.

Tears rose behind my eyes. I stood, nearly knocking my chair over.

Most of the sailors were distracted, laughing at a story Skop was telling, but Lang watched me, brow furrowed.

I pushed through the galley door without wishing any of them a good night. It wasn't as though my wishes counted.

11

I wobbled away from the galley, avoiding the eyes of the few sailors still on deck, making my way toward the two doors in the stern. One of them led downstairs, I remembered. To my room, and to quiet. To safety from Perrault's harassment.

I chose the wrong door.

I found myself inside a cabin, sparse but not cheerless, furnished with a rough bedstead, a shelf lined with beat-up atlases and journals, and a scrubby table, with a map pinned to its surface.

Glittering at the edge of the map was my lost shoe.

I drew closer.

The map was broad and suffused with color, penciled with intersecting lines like spiderwebs. Amid borders and topographical designations were markers for the paths the wind blew, the roll of the currents, the depth of the water and obstacles beneath its surface. Here and there someone had scratched handwritten notes.

I traced the route drawn on the thick paper—over the blue Atlantic, to the land marked *Alba, England, Cymru*. The word *Sidhe* rounded the southeastern edge of the deep green island. I wondered what the name meant as my fingers wandered on to Norge's capital of Asgard, and then on to . . .

My hands shook as I skimmed the borders of the gray mass labeled *Imperiya Yotne*.

England had been the last empire to fall in Europe. But it was not the last to rise.

Some time after England's struggle in the south for Bharat's ports and people had ended, war broke out on another front in the north.

As trade ground to a halt and economies collapsed and countries retreated within themselves and stomachs went empty, a headwoman in the little country of Yotunkheym grew hungry.

She made herself tsarytsya, and when she found her own larder empty, she made Europe her table. The tsarytsya—the young headwoman who became the ravenous old crone they called Baba Yaga—devoured her neighbors to the north and the south and the east and the west, hungry as a Wolf.

Or so went the story. I'd found the book—a newer one— in the Roots, at the Council table. Momma had taken it away from me, but not before I'd read the tale whose memory still left me cold.

* * *

A boy and a girl once upon a time wandered into the woods. Brother and sister they were, hungry and orphaned and defenseless. They hoped to find roots or birds' eggs or berries to eat. But though they wandered for days and days, they found nothing.

The house, you see, found them.

The house was in the woods, waiting, when they were hungriest and thirstiest, tiredest and saddest.

The little boy frowned at the house, tall and spindly as if it stood on bird's legs, its face away from them, toward the forest.

"Yzbushka!" he called. "Little house! Turn away from the woods and look upon us."

"And be kind," said his little sister. She was a tiny thing, bones straining against her cheeks, her face dirty. "Please, please be kind, for all that our village has lost."

All their villages, and all others. All the children in all the towns around them had been disappearing, and they knew not where. Perhaps they were somewhere better. Perhaps they were somewhere safer. Perhaps they had plenty of food to eat.

Perhaps not.

The spindle-legged house stalked over to them, shrieking and groaning on rusty old joints, then dropped as if to its knees to let them inside. An old woman welcomed them from its threshold.

"Hello, Grandmother," said the little girl.

(She was not their grandmother; they called her so out of respect.)

"Hello, Grandmother," said the little boy.

(Her name was Baba Yaga.)

"Come you here of your own accord, or are you compelled?" asked Baba Yaga.

"We come here of need," said the little boy. His teeth were chattering.

The old woman welcomed them inside, beckoning to them with her long, bony arms and smiling across her long, bony face beneath her long, bony nose. Her teeth and fingernails were sharp. "Come and warm yourselves, children," cooed Baba Yaga. She ushered them to a rug before the fire and gave them potato pancakes heaped with sour cream, and they ate and ate.

It was only when their bellies were full and their bodies were warm that the little girl looked in the corner.

Beside the long, skinny broom was a tall, skinny chair.

Both were made of little bones the size of fingers.

The girl's heart turned to ice in her chest, even as it began to beat hard and fast as a little drum.

Then Baba Yaga wrinkled her nose and frowned. "I smell the blood of the Bear," she said. (For that is what the Yotne called their northern neighbors: the Great Bear.)

"No, no," lied the little girl, terrified. "We are not Bears. We are Wolves, like you."

(For that is what the Bears call their Yotne neighbors to the south: Wolves.)

Baba Yaga shook her head. "A Wolf knows other Wolves."

Baba Yaga locked the door.

After their defeat by the tsarytsya, fifty long years ago, the land of the Great Bear of the North became known merely as

Ranneniy Shenok, the Wounded Whelp. And little Yotunk-heym rose to take its place.

I traced the gray mass of the Imperiya again, feeling as if my own heart might turn to ice inside me. I crossed my arms, breathing in the smell of my sweater.

Daddy had been younger when he'd worn it, and sturdier. And nearer to me. Most important, nearer.

Worry chased me down, nipping at my ankles.

I wondered how he would feel if they knew I would have to cross the Imperiya's dark borders alone, missing him so power-fully I thought I might vanish from the spot where I stood and reappear at his side.

The cabin door groaned. Lang stood in the entryway, star-ing at my arms wrapped around my middle.

Sometimes, when Godmother Althea looked at me, I got the sense that my skin was see-through, that my thoughts were audible, that none of my secrets were secret at all. I felt the same way as Lang stepped forward, dark eyes piercing my armor.

"You seem to have lost this, Seneschal-elect." One ink-smudged hand took my shoe from the edge of the map, its gold beads and embroidery winking in the lamplight, and offered it to me. I took it from him, then dropped my gaze to the map again.

"They say she lives in a black iron castle." I swallowed tightly. "That her throne is built of the bones of her enemies, that she can smell their flesh a hundred miles away."

"The tsarytsya is deep in Yotunkheym, far, far from Tery-toriya Shvartsval'd." Lang dropped his voice. "We're going to keep you safe. You're going to be fine."

"Lang, you're a well-traveled man. You must have heard the stories." I spoke lightly, but my voice was thin and strained with worry, remembering the epigraph to the tale I'd first read so long ago.

> When Baba Yaga locks the door,
> Children pass thereby no more.

I gave a sad, weak laugh. "Inside the Imperiya, nowhere is safe."

12

The next morning, I entered the galley quietly and sat down near the sailors companionably sipping their coffee, grateful for a few moments' peace.

"Always chicory," sighed Andersen.

"*Pauvre* Andersen. *La vie est dure!*" said the woman beside him, pouting in jest—I'd heard the others call her Jeanne. Her skin was a beautiful light brown, her amber eyes almost catlike, and her accent lilted romantically.

"It's giving me a headache." Yasumaro passed a hand over his forehead.

Basile, a thick-muscled sailor with a deep golden-brown complexion and a bushy mustache, raised his eyebrows. "They got the real thing where you're from?"

Yasumaro shook his head, smile benevolent as the moon. "Nihon, and no. Tea."

"Chicory is a staple in La Nouvelle-Orléans," Jeanne said

with an elegant shrug. Made from the little blue flowers that traipsed wild alongside the road, it was our standard in Potomac as well.

Basile gave a mischievous wink, mustache twitching. "In New York, we just go ahead and start the day with whiskey. One glass and you don't notice the city's smell so much."

My stomach and my grip around my mug tightened as I wondered, for a moment, if I should be nervous about Basile being from New York—if he was connected, somehow, to Perrault and Alessandra.

But judging by the affronted look Perrault gave Basile as he joined me at the table, ceremonious, folder in hand, he and Basile were from very different sides of the city.

"You cut our meeting short last night," Perrault said to me superciliously. Jeanne scooted away from him, amber eyes widening a little, making to return to her work.

"I knew you'd find me again." I turned my mug around and around on the wooden table. "There are only so many of us here."

"That sort of emotional petulance is intolerable in a public figure, Selah." Perrault shuffled the pages in the folder, plucking a sheet from their midst and scanning it with a practiced eye. "As a matter of fact, a lot is going to have to change."

I stared at him. "Like what?"

"You need to begin a personal care regimen. Practice with cosmetics. Skin treatments. Diet management. Exercises— in your room, of course; it would be inappropriate for you to be seen exerting yourself in public. I can't believe what your stepmother's permitted in the past, all this field-hand-sheepherding nonsense." He rattled all this off airily, oblivious to the raised brows and stalled conversation at the other end of the table.

I flushed but kept my voice neutral. "We don't keep sheep."

"Sheep, yaks, pigs, cows—it matters not to me. Stay to the point, please," Perrault said lightly.

My jaw tightened. "So I need to be thinner and prettier by the time we reach England?" I managed to ask levelly. Basile choked on his drink, the mug nearly slipping from his broad, golden-brown hand.

"Exactly!" Perrault nodded, pleased I'd cottoned on so quickly. "Putting your best foot forward, as they say."

I stared at the table and said nothing. Andersen, Yasumaro, and Basile quietly slipped from the room.

Daddy had always told me I was beautiful, with no qualifiers.

I missed unconditional approval. I missed *him*.

"You will remain two weeks with each of your suitors," Perrault said, scanning his notes. "Once you have completed your first four appointments, you may choose one of the four, if you wish. Should you not find any of them suitable, we will proceed to your secondary visits, at which—"

"Wait," I interrupted. "Are you saying I can't choose any of those four suitors until I've met all of them?"

"Why would you make a decision without all the relevant information at your disposal?" Perrault looked puzzled.

"Because I don't want to waste time." I opened my hands,

baffled. "Because if I approve of my first option, and he approves of me, why would I proceed with a two-month charade instead of responding definitively to a proposal?"

I thought of the tick mark I'd put in Momma's book this morning—a second mark, next to the first.

Two little marks. Two little marks, and so many left, and a thousand miles still to go. And Perrault wanted to make the journey longer even than it had to be.

I hissed out a sigh. "That's ignoring the fact, of course, that this *entire thing* is a charade."

"It is *not* a charade," Perrault answered in clipped tones. "And you *will not* abandon your tour prematurely, because to choose one suitor without even considering the rest would be a public slight with massive political implications, particularly with regard to Potomac's relationship with the Imperiya."

The Imperiya. My stomach dropped.

"The other boys wouldn't care!" I shook my head, my hands suddenly trembling. "Or—they'd understand."

"You're right. You wouldn't think they'd care." Perrault sat forward, voice sleek as cut glass. "After all, you're a farm girl. You're a backwater princess from a backwater colony at the edge of the world—"

"I am *not a princess*—"

"And the odds that the tsarytsya is even aware of your existence are slim to none."

"And that doesn't have to change if I never cross her borders!" I was going to be sick.

When Baba Yaga locks the door,

Children pass thereby no more.

"But she will," Perrault carried on, as if I hadn't spoken. "She *will* become aware of you if you dismiss her and the potential match she has approved. And believe me, not-a-princess Selah," he said, smooth and icy. "You don't want the tsarytsya taking any particular interest in who you are or where you go."

"Sir Perrault." My mouth had gone suddenly dry. I swallowed, staring into the darkness of the kitchen. "You know what they say about that place. You know the story."

"The singsong rhymes of the fearful," he said coolly. "The Whelp and its armies were not innocent children on the doorstep of a fearsome old crone."

"The Imperiya is evil!"

"Perhaps." Perrault cocked his head. "There is effect because there is cause. There was war because there was provocation. I see we ought to add a proper history education to your finishing lessons. Or perhaps"—he paused—"simply some appreciation for nuance."

My chicory had gone cold. I rose and set it on the galley counter.

"I don't need you to educate me, Perrault." I didn't look at him as I crossed to the door. "I need you to not throw me to the wolves."

Lang had told me not to go poking around, but I didn't wait for a guide or help. Godmother's note had said there was potting soil somewhere aboard this ship. I was going to find it.

I took the second door into the stern—the correct one,

this time—and passed Lang's blue door, slowing down as I descended the stairs.

It was hard to see on the lower deck. Little rings of daylight came from holes in the hull where oars could extend for rowing, and I could just make out a watercolor wash of light from beneath a cabin door at the front end of the ship.

I peered underneath the nearest of the benches lining the aisle. Nothing.

I shifted experimentally toward the next bench. Nothing but a set of cloths that looked like they'd been wound and unwound a few times, possibly to save a rower from blisters.

Under the next bench I found a crate of apples. The crate under the next was empty.

I found a few other things—an abandoned pair of boots, several other empty crates and bisected barrels, containers of food—but no bags of soil.

Lang had told me the ladder to get below was tricky. But the ship was brand-new. How rickety could it be?

Besides, I wasn't a helpless thing, dependent on other people to fetch and carry for me. I was the girl Momma and Daddy had raised me to be.

You're a farm girl. You're a backwater princess from a backwater colony at the edge of the world.

Perrault had reminded me of that.

I crawled along the floorboards until I found the trapdoor and popped it open.

There was even less light down here. But I put one foot on the first rung, and then another, and then another, until at last, my feet hit the floor. I nearly tripped over a sack of something before my eyes adjusted. My hopes rose, but I squatted and squinted down at the fabric bag and found it was labeled FLOUR in enormous block letters.

I moved to my hands and knees, weaving in the dark between barrels marked SALT PORK and SALT FISH and just SALT. Bags of OATS and SUGAR slumped against walls.

"Where *are* you?" I mumbled.

As if in answer, my head knocked into a barrel. I rubbed my head, mumbling, and squinted at the barrel. Its label wasn't in English; they were some sort of East Asian characters, maybe Nihongo or Zhōngwén. I sat on my heels and sighed, still massaging my scalp.

The barrels with the unfamiliar labels numbered at least ten or fifteen, and there were crates, too, with thick cloths thrown over them; too many for soil. I heaved a sigh and pivoted away on my knees, then gave a surprised cry. "Hey there!" I blurted out, delighted.

SOIL sat in the corner behind the barrels, practically grinning at me.

The pale sun warmed my legs as I spread potting soil into a few bisected barrels and crates. Over and over I dipped my finger into the dirt, dropped a beige seed into each hole, and spilled soil on top. Then I jabbed the packet marked *coriander* at the edge of the row and repeated the process with basil, mint, rosemary, and everything else Godmother Althea had sent me. Now and again, my chest grew tight as I breathed in the scent of earth and the kitchen garden and *home*.

"Seneschal-elect, what on earth are you doing?" Perrault's shadow loomed over the bare soil as he loped closer.

I sat back on my heels and grinned up at Perrault and the sailors behind him, all backlit by the sun.

Lang gave an odd half cough, shaking his head as if to gather himself. "Where did you get all that?" he suddenly demanded.

"From below," I said simply, tweaking the label for the mint.

Lang stiffened. "You weren't supposed to go below. You should've asked someone to get this for you."

"And I specifically informed you"—Perrault fluttered over me, forcing me to stand—"that you were not to be seen in such a state on deck." Horrified, the protocol officer straightened my dress, even as he tried not to touch me. A handsome sailor named Vishnu tried not to laugh, crossing his muscled arms so the monsters and mermaids in his tattoo sleeve eddied and shifted like ocean currents against the deep brown of his skin. His brows arched, stretching their empty piercings.

"Furthermore, we don't have water to spare for these." One of the sailors, an East Asian man with close-cropped hair and angular dark eyes, frowned at me. "I'm glad you've found a way to amuse yourself, but we can't waste valuable resources so you can grow flowers—"

He broke off as a blur of black clothes and shiny chestnut hair streaked down from the ropes overhead and fell into a crouch, hitting the deck six feet away with a *thud*. Perrault clapped a hand to his chest. Lang rolled his eyes.

"Enough," Cobie said, dragging out the word. "Lay off her.

Four against one isn't a fair fight."

"We're not fighting her," Perrault said, officious and offended. "I'm looking after her rep—"

"*You're* picking on her," Cobie said, pointing at Perrault, then at Lang. "*You're* high on control." She nodded at the East Asian sailor. "And, Yu, I'm aware you're the ship's doctor, but you're overly concerned with hydration."

"What about me?" Vishnu said with a laugh.

"You're okay," Cobie conceded. Vishnu grinned at her, and she waved him off. "So—three against one. Still."

I turned back to Yu. "These aren't flowers, they're herbs. And I hadn't planned on wasting fresh water—or manpower, or any other *valuable resources* on them," I added pointedly. "I'll tend them myself and set up barrels to collect rainwater, if we get any."

Yu pursed his lips, not replying.

Cobie turned to me. "Now. You—stay out of the lower hold. Lang's right: you don't belong down there, and the last thing we need is our royal charge arriving in England with a broken neck." I jerked back, trying not to let them see how stung I was as Cobie stalked away. Yu and Perrault followed her, apparently not finished with their argument; Vishnu must have had actual responsibilities to manage.

"Do all Potomac's royals enjoy yard work?" Captain Lang picked at a thread on his navy canvas jacket. Three deep furrows creased his forehead.

I sat back, dusting earth off my palms.

Most everyone in Potomac had their own farms—big

enough to feed themselves and their families, and maybe a little to sell or barter when that was done. A few plied other trades. Those who struggled to survive fed themselves from the produce of the common lands. I was responsible for these, helping plant and weed and till and harvest the public fields myself alongside the laborers we paid from taxes. This had once been Daddy's job; I'd taken it over around a year and a half ago. He'd started getting tired, and I was ready to start doing more.

That life was all I knew. All I wanted. All I wanted to go home to.

I thought back to the first months after Alessandra had arrived, not long after I turned thirteen, when she'd tried to arrange cotillion practices and finishing classes for me.

To hide from her, I took to following Daddy into the fields, and to wandering on my own into the kitchen garden. I'd grown my first eggplant that autumn. The morning I found it, I picked it and marched it straight to the cook, and she promptly chopped it in half and grilled it for me. I ate it standing up and thought it was the best thing I'd ever tasted.

Lang was still watching me, curious. I shrugged, cutting him a grin, sharp and rueful. "I wouldn't know. I'm not a royal."

13

"No, not that one," Perrault pronounced over my shoulder. "You're an absolute savage."

I'd reached for my utensils with the wrong hand again.

"Europeans do not *cut and switch*," Perrault said delicately. "You Potomacs put your knife down as you eat, blade in, as a gesture of peace. As if the very necessity of the thing were not appalling." He swore daintily, a feat I'd never before witnessed but sort of wanted to inspire again. Skop made a face, chewing a hunk of potato off the knife in his fist, entirely unbothered.

"It's really hard to eat with my left hand," I said defensively.

"Thus, our present exercise. This is not for my own entertainment, I assure you." Perrault nodded curtly at my plate. "Try to do it properly."

I sighed and stood.

"Where are you going?" he asked, affronted.

Perrault had been hounding me. Earlier, after I'd returned from gardening, I'd found my folder of suitors—a duplicate to his own—sitting on my bed. When I'd realized what it was, I'd tossed it in my trunk as if it were a live coal, then buried it.

I restrained an eye roll. "Can we pause lessons for a moment? I'm getting more carrots."

"Oh, no," Perrault said, imperious. "You've a reasonable portion of food. Sit."

The silence in the galley was complete, deafening. Basile didn't crack his knuckles; Andersen had abandoned the origami dragon he'd begun with a scrap of paper. Lang's fork dangled unceremoniously from his right hand.

I thought of Daddy, crouching at my side at the ball to comfort me after Peter's rejection. He would never be so insensitive. He would never speak to me this way.

I steeled myself, even as I flushed with embarrassment.

"I'm still hungry." I fixed Perrault with a stare and walked around him and into the galley, where Will was elbow-deep in bread dough. The protocol officer had prepared my plate tonight, and he'd served me a meager helping of food.

I put a small pile of carrots on my plate, my eyes drifting over Will working busily, over the unwashed dishes and carrot tops in the copper sink. Flour smudged the counters, and cold ashes spilled from the oven door onto the protective bricks below.

I took a bite of my carrots, dampened a rag, and began to wipe up the flour.

"Seneschal-elect!" Will blurted out. "What are you doing?"

Perrault's face was dark over the galley counter. "Yes, what *are* you doing?"

"Relax," I said to Will. "There. The counter's clean." I turned to Perrault. "I don't know how you do things in New York. I don't know what makes a lady, in your eyes. Where I come from, a lady knows how to help people." I took another bite of my carrots, never taking my eyes off him. "Don't presume to comment on my food intake again."

Vishnu began to clap, slow and grand and exaggerated, his handsome face solemn. Deadpan, Jeanne grasped his clasped hands and pressed them to the table.

I took the top plate from the stack in the sink and began to wash it.

The galley door slammed behind Perrault.

Will shook his head at me and sighed. "At least put on an apron."

The sailors murmured to one another, staring at the door, eyeing me. Lang came to the galley counter. "You can come out. You've made your point. We pay people to work on this ship."

"You're going to start paying me?" I threw Lang a grin.

A surprised smile broke across his face, and he cocked his head, skeptical.

Lang had seemed old for his age the night I first met him, but his eyes were bright and curious now, the arch of his brows teasing.

He pushed a black-smudged hand through his hair and glanced at the steward, abruptly serious. "She doesn't use the oven or the stove, Will."

Will didn't even pause in his kneading. "No fire. Got it."

"And don't tell your stepmother." Lang tipped his chin down to me, leaning on his elbows on the counter. The end of his upturned nose and the curving bow of his upper lip were right at my eye level. "Our secret."

"Right," I said slowly. "Our secret."

Skop broke the silence, nodding at me conspiratorially as he served himself a third portion of carrots. "Homer, it's your turn," he called, brushing glossy black hair out of his eyes.

Homer cleared his throat, darting a look at me. "You don't want to hear my stories."

"Yes, we do," Skop insisted. "You haven't told one in a long while."

Homer was still eyeing me. I nodded silently, once, twice, from my place over the sink. Lang hopped up on the counter, perching just a little away. He produced a pad and a charcoal pencil from his jacket pocket and began to sketch the lanterns swaying overhead.

"I'm too tired for this," Homer growled, scratching at his gray beard. But he told us a story all the same.

The others had heard bits of Homer's account before—a tale of years spent at war on the southern edge of the Imperiya, near Hellás, and years afterward lost at sea with a captain named Odysseus, fighting to get home to his faithful wife.

"Penelope's suitors seemed to descend as soon as her husband left," Homer said. "They were wolves at her door, snapping for scraps, begging where she had little to spare. Though she had always been a judicious steward, they seemed determined to eat her out of house and home.

"She had to figure out how to put them off." Homer eyed me, gray gaze intent. "First, she told them she had to weave a shroud for her aging father-in-law. Every day, she sat in front of her loom, hands busy at work. And every night, she crept back and undid the day's labor. She fooled them this way for three years."

"Her suitors must have been morons," I mumbled, scrubbing at a plate.

"Most of us are," Skop said agreeably, coming to the counter to pass me his dishes. He grinned at me, and I grinned after his back as he walked away.

"But even when her unwanted guests found her out, Penelope simply devised a test for them," Homer said. "She found another way to put them off, by insisting she would only marry her husband's equal—someone who could use the bow he hunted and fought with."

"Sharp girl." Lang smiled and crossed his arms.

"Most of us are," I said lightly under my breath. I kept my eyes on my work, but I could feel his low laugh stir the air just above my right shoulder.

From behind the galley counter, I envied the sailors sitting comfortably at table together, lounging side by side, trusting one another implicitly as they alternately listened or drifted off to sleep. I imagined taking a seat on the bench beside them.

I imagined having a job onboard the *Beholder*, instead of being a job myself. Imagined being one of their friends, instead of cargo.

If I weren't who I was, maybe Lang would've sat beside me.

Still, I found my own kind of comfort as Homer spoke, the galley growing soft and quiet as he told his tale, the only sounds the kneading of dough and the wash of water over dishes and the folding of paper in Andersen's hands.

ἄνδρα μοι ἔννεπε, μοῦσα, πολύτροπον, ὃς μάλα πολλὰ
πλάγχθη, ἐπεὶ Τροίης ἱερὸν πτολίεθρον ἔπερσεν:
πολλῶν δ᾽ ἀνθρώπων ἴδεν ἄστεα καὶ νόον ἔγνω,
πολλὰ δ᾽ ὅ γ᾽ ἐν πόντῳ πάθεν ἄλγεα ὃν κατὰ θυμόν,
ἀρνύμενος ἥν τε ψυχὴν καὶ νόστον ἑταίρων.
—Ὀδύσσεια

Tell me, O Muse, of the man of many devices,
who wandered full many ways
after he had sacked the sacred citadel of Troy.
Many were the men whose cities he saw
and whose mind he learned, aye,
and many the woes he suffered in his heart upon the sea,
seeking to win his own life and
the return of his comrades.
—*The Odyssey*

14

Wonders and horrors filled my dreams that night. I didn't know if the blood came first, or the water.

Blood oozed around my bare toes, sticky and hot and smelling like metal, twisting my stomach until I gagged. Salt water rushed from beneath a dozen doors around me.

The doors shook with knocking. But behind each of them was one intruder. One uninvited guest.

Alessandra.

I could hear her whispering my name just over the pounding of her fists.

I staggered, and suddenly a rough oak altar appeared. Daddy and I lay side by side on top, dressed as we had been for Arbor Day, our bodies slit open from throat to pelvis.

I screamed and ran, tearing down ghastly white hallways. Branches tore at my clothes, and hanging shrouds grasped after me until I burst onto the deck of the *Beholder*, sobbing and gulping down ocean air. That's where she was waiting for me. Penelope, wife to Odysseus, hero of the story Homer had told us while we were gathered in the galley.

"I abandoned him." I sobbed. Midnight-blue hair hung around her face, and gold bracelets rattled on her wrists as she pulled me to my knees beside her. Overhead, the *Beholder's* three masts were olive trees, twisting and spreading beneath a foggy sky, gray as our navigator's eyes.

Penelope gripped my shoulders. "Do you have a plan?"

"I don't have a choice," I choked out. "They made me go look for a husband."

She shook her head, shining curls like dark water over her shoulders. "Not what I asked. I had to receive my suitors. You had to go where Alessandra sent you. But now. You form. A plan." Each word was a blow, but Penelope was fighting on my behalf.

I shook her off. "Your plan fell apart," I pointed out.

"And when the shroud came together and everything went to pieces, I wove another plan," she said sharply, slicing her hand through the air. "I made it through, one day at a time."

I stilled. "What do I do?"

"Not everyone is fast. Not everyone is clever. I could only stay one step ahead of my enemy before my reinforcements arrived." She tapped her index finger on the deck. "But if you're one step ahead of them, they still haven't caught you."

I woke with a painful jerk, heart hammering so hard against my ribs that it felt like the bed shuddered beneath me. Sweat coated my lower back and underarms. Wood scraped wood as I clutched my rosary from my nightstand, crossed myself, and began to pray.

But my mind wandered.

So many of my dreams were vague and jumbled, but this one had been vivid—hideous.

And yet.

Something stirred in me, the same raw wonder I'd felt when Perrault had told me we were going to England.

I made a plan. I made another plan. One step ahead.

Penelope had chosen to resist. To outwit and outlast where she could not overpower. I could do the same.

I pressed my fist and the beads over my thundering heart, thinking of the folder stuffed in my trunk beneath Godmother Althea's book, beneath the words and the tick marks counting every day I'd been away from my father.

I'd buried it like a dead snake. But perhaps it was time to begin facing my monsters.

Those are your suitors, Alessandra had said. *Prepare to meet them as you see fit.*

I lurched out of bed. The moonlight through the porthole was bright enough to see by as I changed my sweaty shirt for a fresh one, retrieved the folder, and curled with it against my headboard.

The first page bore my father's signature, wobbling and childish—nothing like the busy slash his strong hand had once produced.

I sighed and put aside his letter and my own information;

I already knew how Alessandra and the Council saw me. *Not fat but not thin, brown hair, green eyes. Reads too much. Good with a tiller, useless at parties.*

All my information and nothing about me.

Sighing, I flipped through the rest of the profiles.

Bertilak, prince of England, Duke of Exeter. Firstborn son of the king of England. Brown hair, blue eyes, seventy-three inches tall. Thoughtful, wise. No portrait accompanied the long list of academic achievements.

Prins Torden Asgard. Fifth son of Konge Alfödr of Norge. Age: nineteen. Hair: Red. Eyes: Brown. Seventy-six inches tall, muscular. A portrait of him in color featured a square jaw and a serious gaze.

Reichsfürst Fritz of the Neukatzenelnbogen. Brown hair, brown eyes, medium height. Age: twenty-seven. Oldest son of Hertsoh Maximilian of the Imperiya Yotne, Reichsfürst of Terytoriya Shvartsval'd. Fritz was described only as Perrault had noted—"clever."

My hands shook as I put aside his sketchy charcoal portrait, his smirking grin.

Prínkipas Theodore, only child of Déspoina Áphros and Despótis Hephaistios of Páfos. Age: twenty-four. Hair: black. Eyes: brown. Charming, musical, intelligent. Theodore was painted in vivid color, cheeks flushed against olive skin, smile gleaming as though he were laughing.

A half-dozen other profiles followed theirs. Princes in Corse, dukes in Makedonías, nobles in Anadolu and Alsace and Aragón. I huffed a sigh, shuffling the various papers in my hands. The gesture reminded me of Perrault, and I almost laughed.

But suddenly, instead, I froze.

I pawed through the pages again. "No, no, no." The folder slipped off my lap, and I tipped my head back against the headboard, heart sinking.

I knew what Alessandra had done.

Torden was—I checked again, fingers fumbling—fifth in line for his father's throne. But Bertilak and Fritz and Theodore were firstborn sons, almost certain to inherit whatever territory their parents ruled. The others were the same.

Alessandra and the Council had been clear: I had to marry. They didn't trust me to lead without a husband. But if I were to marry any of these men, with their own countries to govern someday, I'd never go home.

She'd planned it all perfectly.

Penelope had been smart, and tough. And she'd had perfect faith in her husband. Whatever happened, she turned her circumstances into currency and bought herself time until Odysseus came home.

But Daddy isn't Odysseus. Loneliness for him crashed over me like a wave, heavy as water, burning as salt.

No one was coming to my rescue.

My next steps should have been clear. With none of my suitors free to marry and become my consort, I should have been able to simply go home, explain their unavailability, and find someone appropriate in my own time.

But my stepmother had known what she was doing. This wasn't a mistake.

Do they expect me to convince one of these boys to come home anyway? Could I ask that of someone I hardly knew? Would I respect someone who'd agree?

Could I afford not to try?

Torden is fifth in line. You could bet on him.

But who was Torden? Who were *any* of these men? I had their information, I had their portraits—well, most of them—but what was that worth? What if I hated the one prince who was free to return to Potomac? Worse, what if I liked one who wasn't?

Maybe there is no long game to play. If I could stay ahead by even a single step, I might make it home unscathed. If I did my best and still failed, maybe the Council would leave me be.

I flung the folder into my trunk. It landed with a light *thud* on top of Godmother Althea's book. I pulled the covers over my head and turned over, determined to sleep.

But then I stilled.

Strange sounds were coming from my trunk. Like a fire crackling or sled runners scraping cobblestones or—*whispers.* Then, they stopped.

I shook myself. It was only the ship—the sailors making late-night rounds or having late-night conversation. I needed to rest.

I will figure this out, I told myself. *I will get up every day and weave a shroud and then pull it apart at night.*

Whatever happens, I'll stay one step ahead, and I will get home to Daddy and Potomac.

I put another tick mark in Momma's book and finished the Rosary. But I still couldn't sleep.

I scrambled out of bed and made for deck.

15

Huffing a little, I pounded up the stairs and burst out onto deck beneath the stars. Fresh air rushed across my skin as my feet carried me up to the forecastle, where Homer stood at the helm.

"Did you have nightmares?" Homer's voice was gruff as always, but I suddenly noticed a warmth beneath his words. Something loosened in my chest.

I lay down on the deck and let the damp wind stir my hair. "Sometimes I'm not sure which are worse," I said. "Nightmares, or the thoughts that come to visit when I wake up alone in the dark."

Homer frowned. "What's got you bothered, girl? I can toss Perrault overboard, if need be."

But I was too anxious to laugh. "I just—tonight, I—" I broke off. Homer's unvarnished manner of speaking, the very thing that made me trust him, was precisely the reason I couldn't haul my folder up to the forecastle and talk with him about boys. Kind he might be, but it just wouldn't do.

He squinted at me. "Let me guess: you're finding complications at every turn. You're—" He halted, scratching at his beard. "The more you learn, the less you're sure."

I swallowed. "You could say that."

"Hmm." Homer edged the wheel to the right, shaggy gray eyebrows furrowed. He said nothing.

In the dark, beneath the sky, I thought I could almost feel the moon as it pulled at the ocean, pulling my thoughts across the waves to all the people I missed. My eyes sank closed.

"We're lucky to have had so many clear nights," Homer said thoughtfully.

"Not much rain," I agreed. "Not a good thing in Potomac, but nothing needs it out here." I nodded my head backward at my little cluster of planters on the main deck. "Not much, anyway. The moon looks beautiful."

"To be sure," Homer agreed, agreeable. He edged the wheel a little to the right. "But, Seneschal-elect, clear skies and light—and you can see more by some lights than others—are no substitute for a plotted course."

I frowned. "What?"

"A clear night is useless without direction. All the visibility in the world won't tell me where to turn the helm. Information is no substitute for decision."

I lay still, feeling my heart thump through my back against the wood of the deck. "You mean I have to know what I want."

I thought of my godmother's words, of *yeses and nos that change the world.*

"I mean you have the power to choose." Homer's gray eyes drifted up to the heavens, over the stars hung brighter than jewels between gauzy clouds. "Set your course and trim your sails, Seneschal-elect. And whatever your heading, keep your eyes ahead."

When I returned belowdecks, an origami dragon was waiting outside my door, guarding my room. I set it on my bedside table and fell fast asleep beneath his watch.

16

For twenty-six days—twenty-six tick marks—I watched the sun and the moon rise and set over the Atlantic, the days passing with a rhythm steady as a beating heart.

Once, we passed a ship headed from West Africa to Quebec, and a few of its sailors came aboard to swap letters. I sent notes to Daddy and to Godmother full of cheerful descriptions of the ocean and my garden and all the love I could put on paper, hoping the letters would reach them.

Better yet, their captain, Anansi, was an old friend of Homer's and a brilliant storyteller. I washed dishes as quietly as I could, determined not to miss a single word as he sat beneath the swinging lamps in the galley, telling us tale after tale of all the times he, Homer, and their friends had tricked their way out of trouble. Captain Anansi's smile was white and wide against his luminous black skin, his voice melodic; I could barely look away as he talked.

When he'd finished his last story, I cleared my throat. "Do you know how we'll find England, Captain Anansi?"

Elbow-deep in the sink, I nearly missed it.

The sharp glance Anansi cut Homer. The slight shake of Homer's head.

I would've thought nothing of the boisterous laugh Anansi gave in reply, of the wave of his dark-skinned, spidery hand, of his glib response. "It's been quiet out of there for months." He shrugged easily, smiled a bright smile. "Who knows what you'll find?"

But I'd been paying attention.

And even as he left, I wondered what Homer had asked him to keep from me.

I did my best to put the exchange out of my mind. I worked on deck by day, tending my plants or sweating and scrubbing in the galley, ignoring Perrault's horror at my indignity and refusing his summons to further lessons. By night I listened to the crew tell stories, peering over Lang's shoulder as he sketched.

I was always on the outside of their circle, but it was better than drifting across the ocean alone.

Every night, I fell asleep reading by moonlight. Sometimes, before I drifted off, I could have sworn I heard whispers in my godmother's voice, her words a melody even when she wasn't singing.

But on the twenty-seventh day after we left Potomac, there was no moon.

Lang had forbidden me to use the stove or the oven, but I needed my book's company, and it was too dark to see. I lit a candle from the galley's little bundle of matches and was carrying it downstairs to my room when his door flew open onto the landing.

Lang strode down the stairs and took the candle from me without a moment's hesitation. "Absolutely not."

"Homer's allowed to have lamps."

"You aren't Homer."

"But it's dark," I protested.

"You're not afraid of the dark." Lang doused the candle with a puff of his breath, and the stairwell suddenly seemed too small, too full of the two of us, our faces bathed in shadow.

"No." My voice was uneven. "I just can't see to read."

Lang snorted. "Of course."

"Don't be rude," I huffed. I reached for the candle, stretching after it as Lang held it high, and found my face very close to his.

"Hush," he murmured. "The others are sleeping."

"I need to read. I need the light. It's your job to look after me."

"It's my job to make sure you don't send this ship up in flames."

"I wouldn't—"

"You wouldn't mean to do anything," Lang interrupted. He

was so close I could feel his breath on my cheek. "But a single stray spark could burn us alive."

I swallowed and stepped back, suddenly flushed despite the cool night. "Fine."

And without another word, I rushed downstairs, into the embrace of the dark.

In olden times
fairies were sent to oppose the evil-doings of witches,
and to destroy their power.
—*The Fairy of the Dell*

[I]f 3e wyl lysten þis laye bot on littel quile,
I schal telle hit, as-tit, as I in toun herde,
with tonge;
As hit is stad & stoken,
In stori stif & stronge,
With lel letteres loken,
In londe so hat3 ben longe.
—*Sir Gawayn and þe Grene Kny3t*

. . . and if ye will listen but a little I will tell it you
with tongue
As I have heard it told,
In a story brave and strong,
In a loyal book of old,
In the land it has been long.
—*Sir Gawain and the Green Knight*

17

WINCHESTER, ENGLAND: WINCHESTER CASTLE

We beheld land the next day. The sight was like an arrow through my stomach.

I was in my room packing a trunk when he knocked on my open doorframe. Lang.

I sat back on my heels. "What can I do for you, Captain?"

He shrugged and sat down on the chair beside my bed. "I wanted to look through the folder Perrault gave you."

I stopped folding a dress, startled. "My suitors' profiles?"

Lang nodded. "Perrault seems to forget that I'm leading this expedition. He has an odd talent for somehow avoiding my questions by pretending I haven't asked any."

I pressed my lips together, reached into one of my trunks, and passed Lang my folder. He was kind enough to pretend not to notice my hands were shaking.

Lang flipped through the pages as I sorted through boots and gowns and a jewelry box full of things of my mother's. "Twenty-seven is way too old for you," he blurted suddenly, dark head jerking up.

"The Yotne prince?" I asked.

Lang nodded, mouth twisted in distaste. I folded a sweater.

"It doesn't matter," I said quietly. "With any luck, I'll never see him."

"What do you mean?" Lang frowned. "Selah, you have to. It's an official stop on your tour."

"I know. But, Lang, I can't," I said, suddenly fretful. "I'll choose one of the first two, or bypass that stop and go straight to Páfos, or—"

"How do you think this ship will get to Páfos without passing through Imperiya territory, once we're in Europe?" Lang asked. "Do you think there are wheels on the hull you've somehow missed that'll just carry us over land?"

"I don't know," I bit out. "But, Lang, I can't go there. I have to figure out something else."

When Baba Yaga locks the door,

Children pass thereby no more.

I couldn't bring myself to recite the stupid nursery rhyme. It had chased itself, singing through my head, too often lately.

Worse yet, it had begun to feel too little like a nursery rhyme. Too little like a story in a book. Too much like reality, growing closer every moment.

"I know," Lang said quietly. "I know."

I resumed folding my clothes. Silence stretched out between

us, tense and uncomfortable.

Lang cleared his throat and picked up another paper. "Why isn't there a portrait for this one?"

One of my calluses snagged a beaded dress. I winced. "Which one?"

"England. There are portraits for three of them— Oh, no, wait. Here it is."

I glanced over, wondering how I'd overlooked it, and lunged at him when a flash of magenta in the folder caught my eye.

"What are you—" Lang lurched back, eyes wide beneath his lashes. A second before my fingers could close around the thick paper, he realized what it was.

"Don't look," I pleaded. I leaned toward him, braced on one hand, the other stretched out expectantly.

"Why not?" Lang batted my hand away, and I flushed as his ink-stained fingers brushed mine. His brow furrowed, and a grin stole over his face. "What's wrong with it?"

I rose and sat behind him on the bed, cringing at my portrait over his shoulder.

I'd begged to be painted in the library, but Alessandra had dismissed the idea with a roll of her eyes. "We might as well have you in overalls, on your hands and knees weeding the squash."

Perfect! I'd wanted to say. Instead, I'd kept my complaints to myself, sat straight-backed in the fine velvet chair, worn the flashy fuchsia gown she'd picked.

"It just wasn't what I wanted," I said, my face as pink as the ridiculous dress.

Lang slid the portraits and profiles back into the folder. "There's nothing wrong with it. But I think they'll be pleasantly surprised to see you in real life." He looked back at me, eyes dark and smiling.

I huffed a laugh and dropped my gaze. "What, sweaty, covered in dirt and ashes?"

"You know what I mean." Lang's tone was steady. Warm. Dangerous.

"Speaking of Prince Bertilak," he went on, "before you came after me, I was going to ask why there's no portrait of him in here."

"I saw that," I said. "Or rather, I *didn't* see. I don't know. Maybe his looks aren't his best quality."

"Likely."

I hesitated. "What's it going to be like?"

"England?" Lang asked.

"England. The court." I paused. "The prince. Courting him." I held my face in my hands. "I just feel lost right now. In the dark. No course, no clue where to go."

I glanced up when I felt Lang's hand smooth the hair that splayed over my shoulder. "I have good news for you, Seneschal-elect." He smiled. "I know how to read a map."

Lang, Yu, Perrault, Skop, Cobie, and I disembarked in the port town of Southampton, into a wooden rowboat that would take us up the River Itchen. But though there was nothing threatening about the countryside unfurling dewy and deep green around us, nothing forbidding about the willows and farms and small footbridges we passed or about the sky like a pearl overhead, Perrault and I had all the cheer of a pair of pallbearers. Lang and the other sailors seemed cheerful enough as they rowed us up the river, but the protocol officer and I—we were a two-person funeral procession.

He wasn't particularly pleased I'd given up on my finishing lessons. I wasn't particularly pleased to be here.

When we finally reached Winchester, we climbed out and surveyed the village. I wrapped my arms around myself, surprised by the sharp chill in the air so unlike Potomac's humid warmth.

"The Seneschal-elect," Captain Lang muttered to a man on the dock.

"Right this way, Your Grace." One of the men gestured toward a forest-green carriage with gold and black scrollwork on its doors. Skop climbed up after Cobie and our luggage into a nearby wagon, and Captain Lang helped me into the carriage with one charcoal-smudged hand, Yu and Perrault taking seats across from us.

Fish stalls and old buildings swept past our window as we clattered over the cobblestones. Farther into Winchester we passed small homes with thatched roofs, inns with lamplit windows, rows of shops, and then larger houses built of stone. The color of their plaster and the warp of their wood and the tiny, damp sprouts of lichen between their stones told me many of them were older than Potomac itself. Other carts crowded the village streets, but children stopped playing to stare as our carriage rolled past.

Cobblestones quickly became a gravel path rolling past a damp meadow swathed in fog and lavender—soft grays and greens deeper than I'd ever seen before, even during our wettest springs. Then, at the word of the men driving the wagon ahead of us, guards in red jackets and black pants moved in lockstep to admit us through a black iron gate in a low brick wall.

We had reached Winchester Castle.

Milky light sluiced through the stately grove of oaks and poplars just inside the gate, but we came soon to a wide emerald lawn, where blackbirds hopped over close-cropped grass and beds of pink and white roses bloomed tentatively in the mist. Somewhere nearby, water splashed against rock. Elegant topiaries flanked the edges of the path like sentries. I'd never seen such aggressively tended trees at home; I sat up a little straighter beneath their watch. But when the carriage came to an abrupt halt, I flung out an arm to catch myself.

My hand found Lang's as I fumbled backward.

The crunch of footsteps and the slap and thump of luggage being passed from hand to hand replaced the sound of hoofbeats and rolling wheels. Across from me, Perrault gabbled to Yu about dinner or the weather or something. I wasn't listening.

For half a heartbeat I met the captain's stare. Two of my fingers were wound between his, fingertips pressed into the hollow of his hand, the blood beneath my palm thrumming against his knuckles.

His face was almost perfectly composed. But a tiny seam stitched itself between his eyebrows, and a faint pink color rose in his cheeks. Gingerly, as though I were an animal he was afraid to frighten, he unlaced his hand from mine.

Before Yu and Perrault had even noticed us, before anyone could stop me, I shoved open the carriage door and threw myself out. My eyes traced the gray gravel path to the castle steps as I begged my heart to slow to a walking pace.

Winchester Castle loomed elegant and understated a few hundred feet away, dove-colored like the sky overhead, gracious from its low holly hedges to the ivy that climbed between leaded windows over its four stone stories.

I took a deep breath and steadied my shaking frame on the edge of the carriage, feeling it rock as the others climbed down behind me. When I looked down, I saw the wheel had left my green dress streaked with grease. Perrault eyed the mark significantly, his pretty mouth disdainful.

Yu nodded at me. His dark eyes were unbothered, practical, cool and calm as ever. "You'll have time to put yourself together."

I stared at the castle, courteous and dignified in the English morning, and wondered if even with all my thoughts assembled, all my pieces in order, I could put myself together well enough for a place like this.

18

My new room was wallpapered with soothing pastoral scenes, its window draped with chintz hangings that matched the ones around the chestnut four-poster. Smallish framed paintings of green fields and dogs and horses paneled the wall over the wooden mantel, and a fire crackled in the fireplace against the damp gray day, so much cloudier and cooler than late spring in Potomac. But the decor—charming, bucolic, expensive but not opulent—did little for the anxiety grinding at my bones.

Seven o'clock, Perrault had said when he came bearing the news. *A court banquet. Your first official meeting.*

I fretted and dawdled so long that, in the end, I had to hurry, hands fumbling as I put on makeup and the dress Perrault had laid out for me. "This is pretty, very ladylike," he'd said, almost as if to himself, as he'd plucked it from among my things. "Tasteful. The right first impression."

The dress was all right—a demure lavender thing with long sleeves, just another of the too many elegant garments in my trunk. But the fact that he'd chosen it for me, like I was a child, made me want to wear something else.

Hopping into a pair of white silk slippers, I charged into the hallway between our rooms. "Ready?" I was nearly breathless; the contrast I posed to the five of them waiting calmly for me made me go faintly red. Perrault opened his mouth to reply, but with no warning, the door beside Lang's swung wide.

The older of the two men who stepped into the corridor was small and thin, with a gray beard and glasses and papery-white skin so thin that blue veins showed beneath. His younger companion was lanky, a little over six feet tall, his skin tanned, his dark hair rumpled. The boy's blue eyes were narrowed on me, his mouth a thin line.

Captain Lang rubbed the back of his neck. He'd washed the charcoal smudges from his fingers, and he looked strangely formal without them. I drew my shoulders back, straightening politely, feeling almost wistful; we weren't aboard the *Beholder* anymore.

"Seneschal-elect—" Lang nodded at the older man. "This is Myrddin, the king's chief adviser. He'll be escorting us to dinner. Myrddin, this is Selah, Seneschal-elect of Potomac." Perrault drew himself up, looking affronted that Lang and not he himself had introduced us.

The older gentleman gave a slow, deliberate bow. "Your Grace. King Constantine has asked me to express his delight at having you here at court."

"Good evening," I gulped. "And thank you."

"And who is this?" Perrault asked hastily, gesturing to the younger man, as if determined not to be left out of the conversation.

"Ah, yes," said Myrddin. "Seneschal-elect, may I introduce Bear Green, your personal guard for the duration of your stay at Winchester."

The adviser's accent was soft—singsong, even—but I stiffened.

"My guard?"

"Good evening, Seneschal-elect." The young man stepped forward. He uncrossed his arms, but his lofty accent was clipped and cynical; he practically tossed the words at me.

I blinked at him, then turned back to Myrddin. "But—half my crew came ashore. Why do I need a guard?"

"We always assign security to visiting diplomats," the adviser explained evenly. "Merely a precaution, of course, but he will attend you at all times. And Bear's quarters are quite convenient to yours." Myrddin gestured to the door they had just exited, beside the rooms Lang and Yu, Skop and Perrault, and Cobie would occupy for our stay.

"It's a pleasure to meet you." I tried and failed to produce a natural smile. Bear met my attempt with a blank stare.

Captain Lang glanced between us and squared his shoulders. "We should go." He offered me his arm as Myrddin led us from the hall.

I pretended not to notice. I didn't want him to feel my hands shake.

Grand doors opened on a crowded banquet hall hung with red and gold. An unseen voice announced us to the gathered assembly.

Beneath the singeing heat of their staring eyes I shrank between my shoulders, withering like a vine. Cobie jabbed me in the back.

"Would you just stand up straight?" she hissed. "They're not going to cook you."

I straightened, startled by her remark, as a pale, silver-haired man rose at the center of the room. "Welcome, friends! Welcome to you, Seneschal-elect." He drew near us, crown glinting in the lamplight. "It has been long since we have had visitors from your country. I am King Constantine."

I was going to pass out. *Pull it together.* "I'm grateful for your hospitality, Your Majesty."

"And I am pleased to introduce to you my son, Prince Bertilak." One of the men at his table stood and joined him.

My heart caught in my throat.

My mind raced over the details I'd memorized from his profile: brown hair, blue eyes, just over six feet tall, highly educated. As far as I could see, Bertilak met those criteria, but I realized suddenly I'd been picturing Peter with blue eyes, or maybe Lang with lighter hair.

The prince shared his father's coloring. He also shared the

silver in his father's hair. He was forty years old if he was a day.

"Prince Bertilak, it's a pleasure to meet you." I assembled the sentence with difficulty, forced the words out with effort.

The prince gave a low, graceful bow. "Seneschal-elect, the pleasure is all mine."

Every minute of dinner ground past with aching, sandpapery slowness. With Bear at my elbow and Bertilak's sister, Princess Igraine, before me, I floundered along, earning thorny, one-word replies for my attempts at conversation with the guard. Igraine was kind and warm, but I had to bite back a desperate, hysterical laugh when she mentioned she had children my age.

Perrault's best efforts to teach me how to properly hold a fork hadn't prepared me for the evening at hand. I wanted to go back to my room and shriek silently at the perfect little paintings of hounds and horses on the walls.

My muscles turned to butter when dinner finally ended and we retreated to our corridor. Sir Perrault yawned. "Don't disturb me in the morning," he said, glowering at Lang. "I'm exhausted."

But Lang was talking with Yu, their brows serious, their voices low. I caught only one word from him: *she*.

I flushed. *I'm right here*, I wanted to say. *You can talk to me instead of about me, if you want.*

Or were they talking about someone else? Neither of them was even looking at me.

"Lang?" I asked. "A word?" He glanced at me and broke away

from Yu, and Bear draped his long frame against my doorpost, hands buried in the pockets of his faded brown pants, looking almost aggressively pleasant.

"You don't have to wait up," I said quickly.

Bear grimaced, and Lang smiled pleasantly. "I'll look after her."

"Brilliant." The guard pressed his lips together, brows arched, as if in disbelief. "Well, if I'm not needed here—" Bear gave a cynical little bow, and he was gone.

19

I shut the door behind us and leaned against it.

"And you thought twenty-seven was too old," I managed to say.

Lang pushed a hand through his hair, shaking his head.

"Did you know?" I blurted. "Did Perrault tell you? Or Alessandra?"

"Perrault tells me nothing," Lang swore. "And I barely knew your stepmother." He pulled at his tie.

I stopped in front of the vanity in the corner and took the earrings from my ears, planting my palms against the carved edge of the table. "If you barely know Alessandra, then how did a twenty-year-old get hired to captain this ship?" I demanded. "You can't tell me there weren't more experienced—"

"Because I was the only one willing to go into the Imperiya!" Lang hissed. "I was the only one. That's why I was chosen.

Now, can you keep your voice down?"

I stepped out of my shoes, pressing my hands to my temples, and sank onto my bed in silence.

Everything came back to the Imperiya. Its gray mass at the center of the world was a weight, dragging me down, pinning me to this place when my heart longed for home.

"Do you think Alessandra knew?" I finally said.

Lang stood stock-still, hands on his hips. "I don't know." He shook his head. "I guess we know now why there was no portrait."

I chewed the inside of my cheek. "How is he unmarried?"

"Could be a widower."

My pulse rose. I took a fevered breath, staring up at the chintz curtains. "I'm not ready to be someone's second wife."

"Calm down," Lang said, approaching slowly, palms up as though I were a spooked horse. "Look, this is one visit. You've got infinite chances to make this work. There are a lot of profiles in that folder."

"Lang, I don't have infinite *time*," I seethed. "Did you see my father? In that meeting?"

His silence was his assent.

"I have England, and I have Norge, and one of those has to work," I said through gritted teeth. "I can't go into the Imperiya. I can't."

Again, Lang said nothing. His dark brows drew together as he took in the truth.

"And that's not even addressing the fact that that whole

stack is made of firstborn sons," I added, impetuous. I twiddled a loose thread on the drapes. "My stepmother hopes I won't come home, Lang."

"I'll make sure that you do." He knelt in front of me, palms on one knee, dark eyes intent. "Nothing will happen to you."

I wanted—I *wished*—to believe him.

But he didn't know the end of this story, either.

"You can't convince a crown prince to leave his throne any more than you can promise me safe passage through the tsarytsya's territory," I said heavily. "No one can. In Baba Yaga's land, there is no safety."

Lang rose, bracing a hand beside me on the counterpane. "I *can* keep you safe, Selah," he argued. "And as for making someone fall for you—" His smile was grim, lingering just overhead. "Well. You wouldn't want my help with that."

I swallowed hard, glancing down at his hand, its lean fingers and knuckles flexed impatiently.

"Good night, Lang," I said softly. And he left me alone.

I took the fairy-tale book from my trunk and put another lonely tick mark on the back page. I fell asleep reading, alone when my eyes closed and alone when I woke.

But in between sleeping and waking, she found me.

Into the night I was carried, across the grounds and across England and across the Atlantic by the sound of my godmother's voice. I chased her over the waves and through Potomac's fields and into Saint Christopher's crypt.

She was saying my name.

She asked a question, words I couldn't make out; the answer

was muffled. I only heard her reply, her voice that I'd know an ocean away.

England, Althea said. *With nothing but that boy to hold on to.*

And a lifeline, said the other voice. *Thanks to you.*

Thanks to you.

The pause in their conversation was a musical rest, the reflective *selah* for which I was named. Even in sleep, I yearned for its end, to know what she'd say next.

It was only this:

She has everything she needs.

My godmother's voice was a sigh, and I wanted to fall back asleep to it, to dream again of being home and safe.

I was poking at a breakfast tray when Perrault sailed into the room, no knock, no warning.

"Seneschal-elect." He bowed gracefully. Then his face turned hard and efficient. "I've spent the morning in negotiations with Myrddin and Prince Bertilak. We've agreed upon a series of outings for the two of you, in which you will spend time getting to know one another."

I stretched out my hand, and Perrault passed me the list.

Day one of our visit, Sunday, was already over.

Day 1 (Sunday, passed): rest, state dinner

Day 2 (Monday): rest

Day 3 (Tuesday): afternoon tea, Winchester Castle gardens (court ladies and Prince Bertilak attending)

Day 4 (Wednesday): visit Winchester's high street (preselected shops)

Day 5 (Thursday): *family dinner*

Day 6 (Friday): *village school visit (with Prince Bertilak), state dinner*

Day 7 (Saturday): *tournament, ball*

Day 8 (Sunday): *church, rest*

Day 9 (Monday): *fishing on the Itchen (with Prince Bertilak), family dinner*

Day 10 (Tuesday): *walk through castle gardens (with Prince Bertilak)*

Day 11 (Wednesday): *foxhunt (various courtiers and Prince Bertilak attending), family dinner*

Day 12 (Thursday): *private luncheon aboard Prince Bertilak's boat*

Day 13 (Friday): *meeting of the Round Table (various knights and Prince Bertilak attending), state dinner*

Day 14 (Saturday): *tournament, ball*

Affair after affair, outing after outing. The days looked nothing like my life in Potomac, quiet and private and productive.

"I want two events taken off this agenda," I said suddenly. "I can't commit to this many activities."

Perrault stared at me. "It's two engagements or fewer a day for the span of two weeks," he said. "Do you not appreciate how ungracious you will appear, saying you're unable to attend one dinner and one outing a day? What else will you do with your time?"

"I'm not ungrateful," I said sharply. "I'm just—I like more time alone than this."

"You have today to rest," Perrault said. "Have your man take you for a walk. I'll fetch him."

"I don't want you to—"

"Here! Guard!" Perrault opened the door and summoned Bear from where he'd apparently been waiting in the hallway. "The seneschal-elect would like a tour of Winchester Castle," said Perrault, more *at* Bear than to him.

I glanced uncomfortably from the guard in the doorway to the protocol officer, who looked very nearly done with me. "I mean more than today, Perrault. I need some space to breathe. This is who I am. This is how I do things."

Perrault folded his hands. "I'd try to accustom myself to breathing in close quarters. You're not mistress of your days anymore. It'd be a pity to watch you suffocate."

He left me with a smile.

The guard ran his tongue over his teeth and stared at the breakfast tray, his aspect bitter as the dregs of my tea. He turned and stalked back through my door. "Whenever you're ready, Your Grace."

20

He was as unenthusiastic a tour guide as I could have imagined.

I struggled to keep up as Bear strode into Winchester Castle's throne room, empty but for our echoing footsteps and a few maids who scurried out as we entered. Two pillared colonnades swept the sides of the hall. Empty chairs and an empty red-and-gold throne circled an abused wooden table at its far end, its center painted with a lion and rose.

"This throne room is ancient," Bear said blandly, as though he'd given this speech to a dozen dignitaries. "The rest of the castle is much newer." He stopped before a portrait of a red-headed woman in a wide ruff and crown.

A suit of armor stood guard beside the painting, its empty gauntlet closed around a spear. I curtsied gravely to its closed visor and rusted joints.

Bear stared at me, nonplussed. "What are you doing?"

Cheeks hot, I straightened up. "Nothing." I'd forgotten myself for a split second. *Keep your mind on your business.*

Silence crystallized between us.

I stared around, taking in the elaborate tapestries that covered the walls. Gold dragons thrashed on a green field behind the throne; gold crowns were stacked on a blue background on the arras beside it. Bear absently fingered a loose yarn on a tapestry featuring a knight wearing a white tunic crossed with red. A woman in a scarlet gown beckoned to him, leading him off the road he traveled.

The tapestry was old—ancient enough that I wanted to smack Bear's hand away—and beautifully done, rich with color and detail. He stared at it long enough that I wondered if he'd forgotten me.

"What's this?" I finally asked.

"It's an old, old story," he answered flatly. "Or, rather, a piece of one. This is the Lady Duessa attempting to seduce the Redcrosse Knight. She calls herself Fidessa—faith—but represents falsehood. The story's about religion." He eyed me guardedly. "And other things."

I ignored his glance, crossing my arms, pursing my lips as I studied the two figures. "They always do show the evil woman in red, don't they?"

Redcrosse and Duessa were a pair at odds—he gallant and naive and unwitting, she the embodiment of deception. A risk walking. A mistake, ready to be made. The sight of them weighed something down inside me.

I thought of my father, marrying Alessandra sight unseen, left now at her mercy.

I thought of myself, sent away to parts and princes unknown.

"It's very dangerous to trust a stranger." I spoke the words quietly, but my voice broke over them nonetheless.

The following afternoon was crystal clear, the wind just light enough to flirt with the tablecloths covering the tables around the garden. I'd slept poorly the night before, trying to count how many more tick marks stood between me and home.

Bear and Sir Perrault flanked me, Yu, Lang, and Skop having begged off. Cobie had just laughed when Perrault had suggested she join us for the afternoon tea.

"Your Grace." Prince Bertilak crossed the lawn, smiling and offering me his arm. "You look lovely."

I could feel Perrault smirking behind me. He'd been the one to insist on the pale green sheath and fascinator I wore. "Everyone will be wearing this," he'd argued.

"I look like a rooster," I'd said flatly.

He'd pinned the ivory silk flowers into my hair anyway. "So will everyone else."

And so they all did. Dozens of court ladies tottered around amid the fountains and rosebushes in demure day dresses, their high-heeled shoes stabbing delicately at the soft green grass, their hats as ornate as any of the flowers in their beds. All I could think of was how many fields could be planted or cattle fed for the cost of the clothes I was wearing.

Princess Igraine drew near, clasping my hand and pressing her delicate cheek to mine. She smelled like powder and violets. "Please," she said. "Come and meet our friends."

The party was a sea of elegant hands and polite smiles; I drifted through on Bertilak's elbow, Igraine introducing me to ladies, viscountesses, horse breeders, baronesses, socialites, and one extremely old duchess, who sat me down beside her. They left me to her tender mercies as tea was served.

Finger sandwiches, scones, mousses, and petits fours appeared on miniature towers of floral-printed porcelain plates, arriving with steaming pots of tea.

"How are you enjoying your stay, my dear?" she asked.

"Very well, Duchess," I said carefully, considering the pastry tower. Was it too far across the table to reach? Across the party, Perrault eyed me sternly, then shook his head—whether at the sweets or the reach, I couldn't be sure.

The Duchess of Devonshire followed my gaze, then, seeing Perrault, unceremoniously dragged the tea things a foot closer to us.

I raised my eyebrows at her, but the duchess merely plucked a scone from the tower and began to heap it with jam. "I can't abide bossy aides," she said coolly. "Or clotted cream."

I didn't know what clotted cream was. It didn't sound appealing. I took two finger sandwiches and a raspberry shortbread cookie, cutting my eyes at Perrault again. He scowled. I added a strawberry to my plate.

"Now, dear," the duchess began comfortably, biting into her

scone. "How exactly did you become acquainted with Bear?"

I frowned. "Bear? He's my guard."

The duchess shook her head and laughed. "How silly of me. I meant Bertilak, but I was watching that wretched adviser of yours and saw your guard next to him." She dabbed her mouth with an embroidered napkin. "You couldn't have met him at school, you're much too young. Where *did* you study? Sherborne Girls? Cheltenham Ladies'?"

I shook my head, swallowing a bite of my sandwich. "I was taught by the nuns in my parish, back in Potomac."

"Ha!" the duchess exclaimed. "A Catholic. Well, we've moved beyond our fear of that, at least," she said, mostly to herself. "So you knew nothing of Bertilak before your courtship was arranged?" Her eyes were keen on me, her feathered fascinator bobbing as she chewed another scone with the focus of a mathematician.

I shook my head. "My stepmother arranged our meeting."

The idea to pursue strangers away from home wasn't mine, I thought of adding, but decided that wasn't tea-party fare.

"Your stepmother. Interesting." The duchess raised her eyebrows, then reached for a miniature cup of blackberry mousse, spiked with a demitasse spoon. "She and your father won't miss you terribly?"

I didn't know if she meant over the duration of my courtship, or if I married Bertilak. I didn't guess it mattered.

"They're eager for me to settle down," I said politely, sipping my tea. "My stepmother has . . ." I paused, considering. "She has great hopes for me."

"Don't all mothers?" she asked slyly.

I smiled back at her noncommittally. I didn't have the heart to tell the duchess I wouldn't know.

Another afternoon. Another night. I put another tick mark in my godmother's book. A little fence of scratches was beginning to take shape across the back endpaper.

The months stretched out before me, interminable.

21

"This." Perrault thrust a hanger in my direction.

The following afternoon, I was set to formally visit the village of Winchester with His Highness. We were going to patronize three shops on the high street, give me a view of the town, and introduce me to *the common people* all at once, said Perrault. I nearly choked on my tea at the word *common*.

"It feels a little ridiculous to describe other people as *common* when I'm not royalty," I said, setting down my teacup.

"You are not royalty. You are nobility, in the eyes of the court."

"I'm not. I hold a steward's position."

Perrault sighed dramatically. "You will inherit a position of authority from your father, not by your own merit or by election. You are, therefore, nobility, your romantic notions aside."

"Are you saying I lack merit?" I bristled, turning the suit

over in my hands, and passed it back to Perrault. "I don't want to wear this."

He pushed it toward me again, exhaling a sharp breath through his nose. "Everything I have chosen for you I have chosen for a reason. Yesterday, you wore silk. It was important that you look at home among the court ladies. Today, you will wear tweed and sturdy but elegant boots."

I held up the hanger bearing a red-and-white suit skirt and jacket. "I look like a very serious picnic table."

"You *look* like a respectable English lady," Perrault corrected me sternly. "Like a member of the nobility, but sensible enough to be among the people. The red and white is also a nod to England's flag, Saint George's Cross."

"You're saying that wearing a red-and-white tweed suit skirt aligns me with the English common people and a legendary dragon slayer?"

Perrault nodded assiduously.

I pointed at the door. "Out."

And then I put on the suit.

Perrault, Myrddin, and Bear escorted me into a foyer near the mews once I was dressed. When the prince appeared, I curtsied as best I could in my sturdy-but-elegant boots, still stiff in their newness. "Your Highness."

"Your Grace." Bertilak nodded approvingly.

I glanced at Perrault. "Are we waiting for Lang? Should he be joining us?"

"One would think so," Perrault said irritably. "But Captain

Lang informed me that he was occupied with other matters today."

When we boarded a carriage, it was almost a relief to sit next to Bertilak instead of Perrault, who sat opposite me, next to Bear. Apart from the sound of the carriage wheels on cobblestones and the excited cries of the people in the streets, we rode in silence.

Dread sloshed around the pit of my stomach as I remembered a particularly terrible Potomac state dinner. I'd wanted to sit next to Daddy, but Alessandra had tasked me with entertaining a delegation from the Lakelands. The group of eight or nine middle-aged men had plied me with questions about local fishing and then ignored me for two hours.

It appeared my first courtship would be more of the same.

We stopped outside a bakery, and Prince Bertilak helped me from the carriage. The crowds in the streets called to him, and to me. The prince held up a cordial hand; I clasped my hands in front of me, nodding warmly at the people. When Bear opened the door to the shop, the clamor of the crowd gave way to the chatter of a few excited patrons and the smell of butter.

The baker smiled and curtsied. "Your Highness. Your Grace." She smiled at Bertilak, then at me.

"It's lovely to meet you," Prince Bertilak said cheerfully. "Thank you so much for agreeing to have us."

I peered into the pastry case. "Can you tell us a little about what your work involves?" I asked. "I only know a little about cooking, and nothing at all about baking."

"Well," the bakery owner began. "I get up around three o'clock every day. The shop opens at five." My eyes went wide, and I exchanged a glance with Prince Bertilak.

"I can't remember the last time I saw five in the morning," he joked.

"I get up around five most mornings. But three!" I shook my head. "Now—"

"What?" the prince exclaimed. I glanced back at the baker, more interested in hearing about her work than talking about mine, but Perrault widened his eyes, prompting me.

"It's cooler in the fields before the sun comes up," I said with a shrug.

Bertilak cocked his head. "The fields?"

I nodded. "I oversee about three thousand acres—the public fields that feed Arbor Hall and our needy—and a few hundred head of cattle. I help in the kitchen garden. That kind of thing." In my periphery, Perrault pinched the bridge of his nose. Probably trying to plot an outfit that said, *She's not a field hand, truly.*

The shop assistants exchanged glances. "Would you like to see the kitchen?" one of them asked.

Perrault put a hand on my arm, but I shook him off. "Of course!" I beamed. I glanced at Bertilak, and he nodded, bemused.

In the room beyond the bright storefront, two more bakers were hard at work, one rolling out pastry and the other splashing what smelled like beer over chunks of steak in a frying pan. Ignoring Perrault's throat clearing, I peered over their shoulders, crouched to peek into the oven. "Pie?" I asked.

141

"Rhubarb," the baker answered, smiling.

"Have you ever had a pecan pie?" I turned to Bertilak but caught Bear's eye instead. Both shook their heads. "It's pecans, butter, eggs, sugar, corn syrup—"

"Golden syrup," Perrault broke in, glancing back and forth between us anxiously. His smile had taken on a vaguely manic edge.

"Golden syrup *and* sugar?" Bear laughed.

Bertilak joined in.

I nodded. "It was my mother's favorite, before she passed away." Bear's face clouded. I cleared my throat. "It's very popular in Savannah, where she came from."

"It sounds like treacle tart with nuts," the baker mused.

"Maybe?" I didn't know what treacle was, but I was curious about the destiny of the steak and beer sizzling in the pan. "I wish we had time to stay and learn to make something with you."

Perrault's smile was tense. "We're awaited up the street."

"Take something to eat," the baker urged. Perrault shook his head, ever so slightly.

"Money?" I whispered to him. He passed me a few notes, apparently resigned, and I pressed them into the baker's hand.

"Feed someone today who needs it," I said, smiling. Then I nodded at the pastry case, full of pies and tarts. "I'm sure I'll be back."

We carried on, strolling a little farther up the street. When we passed a bookshop, I glanced at Bertilak, then at Bear. "Could we stop here?" I asked. The owner was right inside, considering us curiously.

"No," Bear said quickly. I raised my eyebrows.

Prince Bertilak smiled. "We mustn't inconvenience anyone who hasn't already arranged to have us visit. These things have to be planned."

I nodded, understanding, though still disappointed. We walked on, instead, into a shop up the street where jewelry gleamed in glass cases, intricately shaped and heaped with precious stones. "Do you fashion these yourself?" I asked the owner, awed.

The old woman adjusted her glasses, nodding. "I do. My father taught me." I peered closer at the case. "Would you take a gift, Your Grace?"

This time, I didn't need to look to Perrault. "No," I said firmly. "But I'm very flattered by the offer."

The flower shop we visited next was the most crowded of all. As the florist took us through the gardens behind the store, I admired the trellises climbing with ivy, the rosebushes, the dew-covered clusters of little blue flowers whose blooms bent their heads in the slanting sunlight. I crouched beside them. "What are these called?"

"Bluebells," he said, smiling. "They don't grow where you live?"

I shook my head.

"I'll send seeds with your aide. Please, choose a few for a posy." He gestured widely at the garden.

I beamed at him. "You're too kind." Slowly, mindful of Bertilak's and Bear's and Perrault's eyes on me, I plucked a few of the bluebells and some daisies, admiring the silky blue and white petals side by side. Almost as an afterthought, I wandered to the corner of the garden, where a few yellow blooms grew wild. I picked three of the little flowers and bundled them into the bouquet.

When I turned, Bertilak and Bear were watching me carefully, and Perrault was watching them. They didn't speak as we left the florist's.

When we returned to the carriage, Bertilak climbed up right away, but I paused by the door. "I'd like to go for a walk, if that's all right. To clear my head."

No one clamored over me at home, even when Daddy and I went out together. I needed to move. I needed a moment alone.

"Of course," said the prince. He nodded at Bear. "Accompany her, please. Off the high street."

The guard nodded and turned away. Sighing, I tramped after him across the cobblestones of the high street and over the town common, the placidly grazing animals a stark contrast to the tense silence between us.

"I got the sense I did something wrong back there," I ventured.

Bear kept walking. "Why do you say that?"

"Well," I began. "At the baker's, everything seemed fine. I talked too much and was too friendly, so Perrault was horrified, but that's normal. And then I don't think I was supposed to accept the gift from the jeweler. I'm not a protocol officer, but common sense dictated I refuse that."

"Right."

I nodded, hurrying to keep up with Bear. "Good. But then—at the florist's. Should I not have taken the flowers?"

"They were only flowers, I suppose," he said shortly.

"Yeah, I'd think that, too." I finally caught up to Bear, glancing at him sidelong. "But then why did everyone act so strange?"

Bear stopped short, studying me. "Flowers have meanings, you know."

I thought of Perrault, yammering on about my clothes and their implications. I crossed my arms. "Everything has a meaning here."

"With royals it does," he said bluntly. "And this is an old country, with a long history."

"So?" I demanded.

Bear furrowed his forehead, then looked away. "Bluebells are a sweet flower. They mean humility. And daisies mean innocence, so you can bet everyone watching liked that. Good omens and all."

I nodded at him to continue. "Fine. So what did I do wrong?"

"The cowslips." He narrowed his eyes.

I frowned. "The little yellow ones? I thought they were pretty." I paused. "Was it because they were just a wildflower? I didn't mean to offend the florist."

Bear shook his head. "No. It's just that cowslips—well."

I covered my eyes. "I picked a flower that means death and destruction, didn't I?"

"They have a . . . risky connotation," Bear hedged.

I pulled my hands away from my face, wrinkling my nose. "What does that mean?"

"They are the symbol of choice for a rather—well, a rather reckless group."

My mouth fell open in horror. "Criminals?"

"Not in England's eyes." Bear walked on. "Still, they're enough to make His Highness worry." He glanced back at me carefully. "You really didn't know?"

I know nothing, I wanted to shout at him. *Because I'm told nothing.*

I just shook my head, demure and disappointed. Even Perrault would've had to admire my restraint.

Then, suddenly, I forgot them all.

From the green lawn damp with last night's dew, an arched and towered building strove toward the sun. I stood still beneath its bright stone walls gleaming like the sea, its windows like a rainbow fractured and rearranged.

This was the England I'd dreamed of, the country of the stories I'd loved. Not planned shop visits or wardrobe choices, but grass and stone and beauty enough to leave me breathless.

Bear's shout from a hundred yards away startled me from my reverie. "Oi! What are you doing?" He shook his head, frowning, arms outstretched. "I thought you wanted a walk!"

"It's beautiful!" I shouted back, gesticulating at the huge structure. "Library?"

"Cathedral!" he bellowed back. "Church of England." He put his hands on his hips, head cocked. "Though I don't imagine a Catholic would be struck by lightning just for stepping inside."

Surprised, I stifled a laugh. "Can we go in?"

Bear shook his head and beckoned me on, feigning impatience but grinning slightly.

"Fine." I ran toward him, a little winded. "They brought me here to meet your prince," I said, bracing one hand on my knee and pointing back at the cathedral with the other. "But scenes like *that* are why I came to England."

The guard's mouth twisted into the tiniest of smug smiles. "Library's on the other side of the castle. Not as fine as the ones at Oxford or Cambridge or in London, but I'll take you there in a few days if you'd like."

"You've been to Oxford and Cambridge?" I straightened, suddenly excited.

"Not myself," Bear said quickly. "But—you know. They say." He paused. "King Constantine went to Oxford. Bertilak, as well. Myrddin hails from Cymru, but he was a professor at Cambridge. They don't argue often, those three, but when they do, it's about which university is superior."

"That's funny." I smiled, feeling a little shortchanged that my trip abroad was a husband hunt and not an adventure like college. "We can't go see the library now?"

"Later." Bear smiled, and his elevated accent grew a touch less chilly. "I promise."

Bear didn't slow as he walked on, but his shoulders and his voice loosened as he showed me the rectory and the pub beside the river. "There's the Red Lion, and the miller's, and that way, past the village green, is the smithy." He pointed with one hand and shaded his eyes with the other against the pale afternoon sun. "Shops and houses are there on the high street and Saint

George's, as you've already seen, and the fields are on the edges of town. They finished planting just before you arrived."

A cry drew my eyes back to the village green. Dozens of small children shrieked and tumbled over one another in a game like tag or Marco Polo. "We had May Day there a few weeks ago," said Bear. "The children danced around the maypole for the May Queen, covered boats on the Itchen with flowers. All very charming. And that"—he stepped behind me and swept one lean hand toward the green's grassy expanse—"is where your tournament will be held Saturday."

My tournament. I swallowed but didn't answer.

"Blindman's buff," Bear said.

"What?" I blurted.

He flicked a hand at the whooping children. "The game."

"Ah." I relaxed. I'd startled at the word *buff*. "Looks like more fun than being prodded onto a pedestal for an afternoon."

The heat of Bear's laugh on my neck startled me, sending a shot of warmth through my stomach. "Not looking forward to it?"

He stepped up beside me. I chewed the inside of my cheek. "I'm sure it'll be exciting. But I'd rather not have so many people watching."

Bear's forehead furrowed, blue eyes searching my face. "What are you afraid they'll see?"

I flushed and looked back to the children, unable to hold his stare. "I'm not sure."

22

The prince spent the next day hunting with his men. Later that night, we were summoned to dinner.

The meal wasn't a small gathering, but it wasn't a court banquet, either. The royal family crowded casually around a large table in an elegant private dining room, with green damask wallpaper and gilded molding.

My posy sat at my place at the table.

I'd given it to Perrault when I'd gone for my walk. I'd assumed he would put it in my room. But he looked as surprised to see it as I did.

Lang and Yu paused in the doorway, seeming disappointed at the small size of the gathering. Yu nodded at the flowers, frowning and scrubbing a hand over his close-cropped black hair, and Lang muttered something to him. I ignored them, following the scents of beer and pastry and butter on the air.

I took my seat, several places down from the king and

prince, and trays began to circle the table. I took a chicken-and-mushroom pie from Myrddin's hands on my left and passed the plate to Bear on my right, avoiding Perrault's eyes as I served myself.

The royal family was casual—Prince Bertilak and his brothers hadn't even put on fresh clothes when they came in from the hunt—but I sat tense and silent, wondering what to make of the flowers beside my water glass. When I glanced up, I found Lang staring at the blossoms again, brow furrowed.

Between the flowers and Perrault's eyes taking in every bite I took, I hardly tasted my supper at all. I longed for quiet suppers at home with Daddy, nights with just the two of us when Alessandra was busy entertaining.

It was the children who finally unbound my tight nerves. The smaller ones had spent the afternoon outside, so they carried on for half the evening about the hounds and terriers in the kennels, the horses in the stables, and the cats and cows in the dairy. Tiny five-year-old Alexander told me he was already learning to ride.

"I want to joust!" he bellowed, galloping toward Bear on an imaginary horse. The little boy's face was pink, his dark curls sweaty from the circles he'd been racing around the table. The guard seized him with a bright laugh and, before Alexander could charge into my chair, swung him up on his lap, lean arms holding the squealing child fast.

"One day, little man," chuckled King Constantine.

The boy grinned broadly at me, and warmth filled my chest. "Gemma's only three, so she can't learn yet." Alexander held up a few stubby fingers, shaking his head at a tiny girl with golden hair, then dropped his voice to a whisper. "She got in trouble for sneaking milk to the little kittens in the dairy."

"No," I whispered back, feigning incredulity and giving his tiny shoulders a little shake. Alexander nodded, insistent.

"Not *very* in trouble." Gemma climbed uninvited into my lap. When I twisted to accommodate her, I found myself knee-to-knee with Bear at my side.

He laughed in protest. "Gemma, that's hardly polite."

I shrugged lightly. "Let her. I don't mind." With the child's unself-conscious weight on my lap, warm as an oven in the chilly dining room, I felt natural for the first time all evening. Bear's mouth quirked, eyes softening.

"You oughtn't to feed those cats," he insisted, poking Gemma's button nose.

I passed a hand over the top of her head. "Don't listen to him," I whispered.

Gemma flashed a little row of gleaming teeth. "Shan't!" She curled against me, and Bear and I listened to her talk about kittens until she drifted off.

Alexander joined his cousin in sleep sooner than he would have been proud to admit, given his two years' advantage in age and maturity. "Someone can take them to bed," Bear whispered, leaning over the boy's head. My knees brushed against the rough fabric of his slacks, and I suddenly felt warm from head to toe.

"I don't mind," I said again. Smiling, I adjusted my hold on Gemma's shoulders and knees. Her mouth was ajar and drooling against my green flannel dress. Bear watched me, eyes still and intent.

Perrault's voice cut into my thoughts. "Do you expect many of the gentry to travel in for the tournament, Your Majesty?"

Lang rolled his eyes at the protocol officer's fawning tone. Constantine barely glanced at him. "Yes. With jousting in the morning, a melee later in the day, and a ball that evening, they could hardly stay away."

I swallowed hard and tried not to imagine hundreds of people staring at me, tried not to imagine one pair of blue eyes asking *What are you afraid they'll see?* A nanny suddenly came forward and lifted Gemma from my arms, another taking Alexander from Bear's.

Princess Igraine beamed at me, reassuring. "You'll enjoy it. There's fighting, but there's also wonderful food, and people come from all over to sell pretty things. And the dinner Friday and the ball Saturday will be gorgeous, I promise."

"I'm sure," I said, managing a faint smile.

"It will be," Bertilak said, reaching for another piece of bread, "but I'm afraid preparations are going to keep me busier than I'd anticipated. I may be forced to cancel some of our plans, Seneschal-elect."

I fought to keep the relief I felt off my face. "I'm sorry to hear that, Your Highness."

"But you must keep me apprised of your doings where I am unavailable to join you," Bertilak said, cocking his head. The air around the table grew thick with curiosity, so quiet that I jumped when a burning log snapped on the fire.

"Certainly," I said, startled by his intensity.

"I'm quite serious." Bertilak pushed back his chair and tossed his napkin down on the table. "In fact, I propose this: at the end of every day, I'll present you with whatever I've won or found or fought for, and you shall do the same."

"What if I don't win anything?" I frowned, glancing from Lang to Perrault to Skop, but they looked as confused as I. "Aren't we supposed to be visiting a school tomorrow? Your Highness, I don't understand."

Bertilak shook his head, eyes gleaming beneath the thin circlet on his brow. "You're a sharp girl. You're going to be meeting people, having conversations. That's what you're here to do. I feel confident you'll end the day with something interesting in hand." Bertilak lifted his glass to me. "Do we have a deal?"

I returned the gesture, my half-drunk cup of tea now tepid. "As you say, Highness."

23

I sat alone in the front row of the Winchester village school.
The auditorium was dim, the curtains still drawn on the little
stage.

Mothers and fathers and siblings sat in the remaining rows.
I could feel their eyes on the back of my neck, feel their whispers like a fog swirling behind me.

Sir Perrault and Bear stood against a side wall, half-hidden
in the dark behind a screen. They were my only companions
again today; Lang had been absent when Perrault knocked at
his door to insist he join us.

I glanced over at them, wishing they would come sit with
me.

Well, not Perrault.

Suddenly, a little boy in a sweater and shorts climbed down
from the stage, bowed, and handed me a bouquet. "Your Grace,"
he lisped. I smiled and took the posy from him, lifting it to my

nose. Violets, lavender, mint.

"Thank you," I said sincerely. He retreated, quick as a flash, and the curtain opened. A row of lanterns snaked to life before me, lighting a backdrop of greenery and papier-mâché stones.

A girl in a smock dress stood to one side of the stage, expression serious, curls tight around her face. "Once upon a time," she intoned, "there was a fearless knight named Saint George."

A small boy emerged from stage right, dressed in something shiny and gray, waving a stick. His shield was white, with a red cross quartering it, just like England's flag. "I am Saint George!" he crowed. He lunged and jabbed with the stick, eliciting laughter from the audience, until the girl in the smock dress scowled at him.

"Stop it," she hissed.

He stilled, propping one foot on a paper boulder.

She continued. "Saint George traveled all over England, from Devon to Durham."

The little boy galloped across the stage, shielding his eyes from the imaginary sun. I stifled a laugh.

"But one day," the girl announced, "while riding the cliffs on the Sussex coast, he came across a dragon."

The boy dismounted his imaginary horse as a little girl shambled on from stage left. Blue ridges ran from her head down her back and her fabric-stuffed tail, and green fabric wings extended from her arms. At a nod and a glance from the narrator, the girl gave a roar and stomped nearer to Saint George.

"I eat a maiden every single day!" bellowed the girl-dragon, high-stepping toward center stage. "Will you stop me, Saint George?"

A crowd of children in drab clothes rushed in from the wings, acting—I guessed—as townspeople. "Only our princess is left, Saint George!" one boy cried mechanically, gesturing at a girl in a pink dress and conical hat. "Save her, oh please!"

Reluctantly, the boy–Saint George tossed down his sword. "This shield is magical, full of power." He lifted the buckler, its bright red and white paint gleaming in the dim room. "I will hide us beneath it."

The girl in the conical hat—the princess—shuffled forward, drawing near (but not too near) Saint George. "Me and my village?"

"Yes," said Saint George, spreading his arms wide. "Come and take shelter."

One by one, the villagers circled Saint George and the princess, surrounding them beneath the shield.

The dragon scowled, feigning confusion. "Where are you, you foolish villagers? I will find you!"

"You will not!" shouted Saint George. "I will hide us for as long as I must. Begone, foul worm!"

Saint George may have been invisible to the dragon, but she stuck her tongue out at the boy-knight before she rumbled offstage, growling to herself.

"And so," announced the narrator, "the dragon left the village and its people, and was never seen in those parts again."

The curtain closed, and opened again, to thunderous applause from the audience.

I stood and clapped with parents and friends as the children bowed and then bounded off the stage, running toward the lawn outside, where a reception was waiting for us.

But long after the hall went quiet I stayed where I was, staring at the empty set, confused.

24

Lang came to my room before the dinner that night. "I think half of England's currently quartered in Winchester," he said with a sigh, shutting the door behind him.

"Fantastic," I mumbled.

Lang frowned. "Is something the matter?"

"It's nothing." I sat, squirming as the waistband on my gown pinched my middle—curse all these stupid, expensive clothes—and buried my face in my hands.

Lang dragged a chair in front of my bed and settled into it. "Has something gone wrong with the prince?"

"No, both our conversations have been very pleasant. All two of them," I managed around my palms.

Lang gave a low laugh. He tugged my hands from my face and folded them between his fingers. "If it's not the prince, then what is it?"

I thought of the incident the day before with the flowers. Of the play earlier, and its oddity.

Godmother Althea's book lay on my nightstand. I'd reread the old account after the play, just to be sure I hadn't misremembered it.

In the old story, Saint George had been traveling abroad, in al-Maghreb, when he happened upon a helpless maiden in need of saving. He did defend her, as the children's play had shown; but in the old version, he'd slain the beast after three tries, with a spear and a sword, instead of hiding the villagers.

The changes had been minor enough; perhaps they hadn't wanted the children to pretend to kill one another. But then, why choose that story?

Besides, I'd spent time with Perrault. Enough to know that everything—*everything*—about this trip and my welcome to England was being carefully engineered.

"Something just feels off to me," I finally said. "And not just the prince, and his age."

"You're halfway finished." Lang looked tired, too, I noticed, as though his nerves had been wearing at him as mine had at me. He studied our clasped hands. Carefully, carefully, I withdrew mine.

"A quarter," I said quietly.

"What?"

"A quarter of the way finished," I said, my voice more wishful than I wanted it to be. "Half of England and all of Norge left to go. And then—home."

If the Norden prince proposed.

If Perrault would let me bypass the Imperiya.

If.

Lang's gaze lost its worn-out cast as though a match had been struck behind his eyes. "You are stubborn," he said, baffled and admiring, both at once.

"As a mule," I agreed. "Perrault called me a backwater princess. I guess I've learned how to dig my heels in."

Stubborn, and lonely. For home and for my father.

But I kept my forlorn thoughts to myself. My hands still burned from Lang's grasp. I didn't need him taking them again.

He shook his head, nodding at the door. "Well, knights have traveled from all over to compete and earn your favor, at the dinner tonight and the tournament tomorrow," Lang said, lips quirking wryly. "So go forth, my stubborn lady, and win hearts."

25

The spring night was cool, but the banquet hall was crowded with bodies and hot with lamplight. Lang and Yu scanned the room, muttering to one another.

Perrault eyed the place marker set for me between Bear and Myrddin, huffing. Nonetheless, he was determined not to waste time. As I took my seat, relieved at not being placed near Bertilak, he busied himself pointing out important members of the court to Cobie, Skop, and me. "There's Lord Bedrawt, second cousin to Prince Bertilak, and his son Lord Bedivere," Perrault said, nodding at people I couldn't quite see through the crowd. Then he tipped his chin at a pale man with lank, curling hair and a boy about my age. "And that's His Grace, the Duke of Cornwall, with his nephew, Tristan."

Bear's quiet voice was so close it made me jump. "He goes by Veery."

A servant reached past us to set dishes on the table. I leaned out of her way, and my bare shoulder brushed Bear's sleeve. I tried not to notice how well the deep green jacket fit his lithe frame.

"What?" I asked.

He was so near, I'd felt his breath on my cheek.

The guard took a long drink of wine. "Lord Bedivere. Second cousin, once removed, to the prince. I've been friends with him for years. Goes by Veery."

I nodded, poking at my food, but didn't speak.

"Penny for your thoughts," Bear said, curious.

My palm was sweating around the posy in my hand. "I'm thinking about flowers," I said tightly.

I couldn't read his expression.

Farther down the table, Constantine and Bertilak called out to Yu. "We should get properly acquainted," Constantine urged. "Please, tell us of Zhōng Guó."

They were as intrigued by our ship's doctor as they were bored by our protocol officer. The tables nearby grew quiet to listen as he told his story.

"The floods brought death year after year," Yu said. "My father stole resources from the government to stanch the waters, and he died fleeing capture. I was discovered on the scene."

"How old were you?" I asked.

"Fifteen." Yu's eyes were grave. "I went on my knees to the zǒngtǒng, the president, and begged him for what my father had stolen."

"And?" Myrddin's eyes were narrowed.

"He asked for my plan. I proposed we survey the country,

dig tunnels and canals, and build dams and lakes. So he gave me what I needed, and we got to work."

"You *led* this project?" I was in awe. I'd had no idea.

"Why on earth did you become a sailor after that?" Bear asked.

Skop grinned into his bowl.

"Oh—sorry," Bear said.

Skop shook his head, unfazed.

"I spent ten years on the move," Yu said. I'd never seen his broad face so alight with intensity. "I studied my people, natural medicine, every centimeter of Zhōng Guó. Working in a government office wouldn't have been a reward. It would have been a life sentence."

"Teaching, then," pressed Bear. "You could have gotten a position at any university in the world after that."

Yu barked a laugh. "That would have been even worse! Days spent in meetings? Currying favor for a living? I may be older than you, boy, but I'm not dead yet."

"But Zhōng Guó." Bear asked, "How could you just leave your home and your people?"

Yu took a long moment to chew his bite of pudding, eyes dark and thoughtful. "Zhōng Guó is yet and always the center of my world," he said at last. "Everything I do is for my country. For my people and my family."

Myrddin tipped his head to one side. "Fascinating." And despite his melodious accent, the word and his gaze were sharp.

I glanced around and suddenly realized half the room was following our exchange. "Seneschal-elect Selah of Potomac, of course," King Constantine said offhandedly to some newcomers nearby. "Visiting the prince."

My heartbeat stumbled in the succeeding silence.

"Relax. They're simply curious," Bear whispered. He cleared his throat quietly. "And you look very nice."

You do, too, I almost said without thinking. But I bit my tongue.

"Your Grace," Prince Bertilak called, "we dined tonight on venison my men and I brought home from the hunt. And Dà Yu brought a most intriguing account to dinner." Bertilak cocked his head. "I trust you haven't forgotten our bargain?"

"Of course not, Highness." I rose and passed him the posy in my hand. "From the children at the village school this morning. They performed Saint George and the Dragon and were very sorry to miss you."

Myrddin turned to me, eyes sharp and inquisitive. "What did you think of their adaptation, Your Grace?"

I swallowed.

I knew the story of Saint George and the Dragon. But the children had shown me quite a different myth.

"I rather think," Sir Perrault said languidly, "that the dragon should have been a wolf."

"It should not," said Bertilak sharply.

The room went still.

Everything about my welcome to England was being engineered. I'd been shown that play for a reason. The razor edge in his tone left me in no doubt.

I was being warned. Or, perhaps, if they expected me to

become their princess, being prepared.

If Saint George's shield was England's flag, then King Constantine's England did not go abroad searching for enemies—be they dragons or wolves—to slay.

Indeed, England didn't slay its enemies at all. It hid, waited them out, protected those nearest them. It had repented of its sins, learned from its wrongs. From the wreckage left and the damage done before its brutal empire bled to death.

Constantine's Saint George stayed home and guarded his own.

I merely wished I'd been allowed the same courtesy.

Because there were worse than dragons abroad. And worse than dragons watching Daddy in Potomac.

"I thought they did well," I finally said, smiling as best I could. "The dragon, in particular—she turned in a ferocious performance."

The crowd laughed, and Constantine's and Bertilak's faces relaxed into smiles. And the room forgot me.

I turned to Bear and whispered, low enough that Myrddin wouldn't hear. "The flowers—these flowers. What did they mean?"

The guard squinted down the table, eyeing the posy. "Lavender, violets, mint. Devotion, modesty, virtue."

No sign of the recklessness the prince had found so offensive before. I breathed a sigh of relief.

Beneath the rising din of conversation and laughter, I leaned close to Bear again and whispered in his ear. He wet his lips, inclining his head to hear me. "That day we stood on the green, you asked what I was afraid they would see if they looked at me. That—that was it."

His eyes sobered. "What do you mean? You gave a fine performance."

The tournament hadn't yet begun. But the games had.

And I'd already been shoved onto a pedestal.

"Yes," I said quietly. "But a performance, nevertheless."

The first day of our bargain. The sixth day of our stay. Another tick mark. So many left to go.

I fell asleep with my book open to the story of Saint George and the dragon—the old account.

I'd read it again and again, searching for anything I might have missed. Another warning. Another sign.

When I slept, I dreamed; but in my dream, the princess was out to save Saint George. He pleaded for her mercy, and she rescued him.

"Return home with me," Saint George said when the princess had saved him.

"I can't," said the princess. "I have to carry on."

"Come home, sweet girl," said Saint George; but his voice, suddenly, was not his own. "I miss you."

26

I woke to darkness and a sound in the hall.

Winchester beyond my window was still swathed in deep gray fog as I blinked away my dream, pushed Althea's book out of the way, and opened my door.

Bear moved impatiently in the corridor. "Good morning, Seneschal-elect."

"What are you doing here?" I whispered, squinting against the lamplight. "It's not even seven o'clock."

"And it already looks like a carnival outside." He leaned in, as if to put a hand on my shoulder, then thought better of it; but his face was almost pleading. "Trust me, Selah. You don't want to miss it all because you were asleep."

I met his eyes, bright blue and giddy as a child's.

I didn't know what to make of this. Of him, like this.

How could I say no?

"Give me a few minutes."

Bear's smile was a lit candlewick: tentative, and then glowing. "I'll wait."

Tired though I was, Winchester was alive, dawning pink and orange and luminous. The cool air and the brisk *clop-clop-clop* of hooves against cobblestones swept away my sleepy haze and set my pulse surging. And down the high street, teeming with vendors and tournament-goers leading horses and drawing carts and bustling in and out of stores and homes and inns, Bear kept near me, hand just above my back.

He didn't touch me. But I felt him, close, close at my side.

The village green was a crowded party beneath the glowing morning sky. All around us went up calls from men and women hawking wares and taking bets on who would win the joust that morning and the melee later that afternoon. Bunting strung across stalls snapped in a breeze scented with flowers and tea and roast meat and pastries. As we talked, I did my best to take it all in: the busy stalls and the empty dais beneath King Constantine's green-and-gold coat of arms and the horses, everywhere horses, stamping and snorting and gleaming in the early light. "So," I prompted. "Are you going to compete?"

Bear toed a rock with his shoe, pouting. "I'm not allowed."

"Why not?"

"Because." Bear tipped his head at me. "I'm supposed to be looking after *you*." His mouth was still sullen, but his eyes were teasing.

I opened my mouth and then shut it, suddenly self-conscious.

"I'm so sorry. I don't mean to be a—"

"It's not your fault." Bear shook his head. "Besides, I expect I'll enjoy the day regardless."

I couldn't admit how his smile threw me off-balance. But this time, I didn't look away.

When it was time for the joust, we took our seats on the dais, next to the prince and the king. At a word from His Majesty, it began.

I'd never been afraid of animals in general, or of horses specifically, but the joust was unlike anything I'd ever witnessed. It was noisy and terse and brutal—all the danger of fighting, without any of its necessity. I shrank farther and farther into my seat beside Prince Bertilak, growing tenser with each crash of spear against shield and armored man against earth. It was unsettling, and worse still, it was *boring*.

I stared around the dais, dying for distraction, but the royal family was engrossed, and Bear along with them. Though his chair had initially been a little behind mine, he'd edged forward to get a better view until he was beside me, practically leaning over the rail. Only the *Beholder* crew seemed not to be paying attention—Skop, because he was laughing and beset by the royal children, and Perrault, because he couldn't relax beside Cobie, expression black as her clothing. "Where are Lang and Yu?" I suddenly asked.

Cobie's eyes flicked to the back of Bear's head. "Surprised you noticed."

Skop elbowed her. "I'm sure they'll be here soon."

"I hope they're off meeting the Duke of Cornwall, as I suggested." Perrault scanned the audience, eyes greedy. "A very valuable contact. You can never make too many connections at events like this, you know."

I wanted to hit my head against the railing until I couldn't make out his words anymore.

If the joust was dull, the melee was even worse. It was endless, one long, droning battle beneath the brazen afternoon sun. Dazed by the clash of blunted practice weapons and the cries of the two armies draped in green and gold jerseys, I distracted myself by admiring horses and coats of arms. Bear explained the significance of the colors and symbols splashed across the warriors' shields, never growing annoyed as I peppered him with questions. But when the leader of the forces dressed in gold disarmed the last remaining green knight, he flopped back in his chair, crossing his arms and grunting in disgust.

As the armies regrouped out on the field, preparing to present themselves to Constantine, a lean-muscled boy in a green jersey waved at Bear. He tugged his helmet from his head and shook out his dark, sweaty hair, and even at a distance, I could see the disappointed twist of his scarred upper lip; he'd taken their loss hard. Suddenly, he stopped short.

The boy cut his dark eyes in my direction, and Bear gave a tiny nod. But then Bertilak appeared without warning.

The prince smiled politely. "You and I shall present the winner's reward together, to the leader of the victorious gold army."

"To the victor, Sir Mark, Duke of Cornwall!" cried

Constantine. I started at the name of the *valuable contact* Sir Perrault had mentioned, whom he'd pointed out the night before, along with his nephew, Tristan. He rose from his low bow, revealing longish teeth in a wide leer.

I swallowed hard. "Congratulations, Your Grace."

"Until this evening, Seneschal-elect," Cornwall replied smoothly, not needing to raise his voice much over the crowd. Though they had cheered wildly for the joust's winner, their enthusiasm over the champion of the melee was barely polite.

Bear's friend was lost in his army's ranks by the time I returned to the dais. I leaned near the guard as I settled into my seat. "I have to see the duke tonight?"

"It's tradition for you to dance with today's victors." I hardly heard his answer beneath the delighted screams of the royal children, finally free to play.

Great.

Alexander and Gemma fled the dais, tearing over the green with the other children, shrieking and giggling. I pressed fingers to my temples, trying to massage away the long hours of posturing. "Could we convince Bertilak to replace next weekend's melee with a few rounds of blindman's buff?" I tried to sound light, but my voice came out strained.

Bear leaned against the dais rail. "His Highness mightn't agree, but for your pretty face, the armies would play whatever game you asked."

I gave a breathy laugh, grinning a little sadly. "Is that really all you think of me? That I have a pretty face?"

I expected him to insist he'd complimented my looks, protest I shouldn't be so sensitive. But above his smirking mouth, Bear's blue eyes were bright and serious. "Oh, Selah." He shook his head. "Your beautiful face is the very, very least of you."

27

That evening, for once, I was the first to be ready.

I'd hoped to take a nap after the tournament. But though my body was tired, the day turned itself over so feverishly in my mind that I gave up on sleep.

When I finished getting dressed, I propped myself against the corridor wall, across from the door to Bear's room. I told myself I would be patient, but the curious feeling that had refused to let me sleep shifted restlessly in my chest.

I had no business wondering what was happening behind Bear's door. I was here to court the prince he was bound to serve.

I remembered what Perrault had said, about slights to rulers and their international implications. Remembered Bertilak, awaiting me at the ball. Remembered the folder full of suitors, the Imperiya *fürst* who I would have to court, should I fail here or in Norge.

I walked across the hall and knocked.

The door burst open. His hair was wet and uncombed, and he was tugging a dinner jacket on over his shirt, a tie half-knotted around his neck. Bear stilled with his hand on the doorknob and met my eyes. Arrested.

I was struck suddenly with the feeling of desperately needing to ask him a question and at the same time not being sure exactly what it was I needed to ask—the feeling that the question didn't matter, so long as the answer came from him.

His Adam's apple bobbed, and he pushed his hair out of his face, fumbling lucklessly to fasten his right collar button. "Am I late?"

My mouth felt dry. I shook my head. "You've got a minute."

Against my will, my gaze strayed across his mostly bare room as Bear leaned into a mirror by the door. Water droplets spattered his shoulders as he combed his wet hair. But I couldn't help noticing the books piled on the end table and scattered across the floor, the sheets crumpled on the bed.

Was he tossing and turning, too?

He was still fiddling with that button.

"Come here," I said, and he obeyed, pausing just a foot from the doorframe.

I had no business in his room.

I crossed the threshold to meet him.

With unsteady fingers I unbuttoned the collar of his shirt and flipped it up, staring resolutely at the plum-colored silk tie as I looped it into a knot and slid it up to his neck.

Neither of us spoke.

The pulse flickering in his throat distracted me momentarily, and I accidentally tightened the tie too far. Bear choked a little, hand flying to his collarbone.

"Sorry!" I whispered, laughing and meeting his eyes. They were lit candles over his smile.

I flipped his collar back down, buttoned its corners easily, smoothed its crease. I was acutely aware of his hands hovering between us, of the warm skin and damp hair my fingertips grazed at the back of his neck.

"There." I straightened his lapel, releasing the jacket only reluctantly.

Bear examined the knot. "That's different."

"It's called a Bowery knot." I wrung my fingers. "It's the one my father wears."

Bear nodded, watching me carefully.

"Is something wrong?" I blurted out. I appraised my dress, dark green lace that curved off my shoulders and over my hips. "Do I have a thread—"

He cut in. "No, you look—"

But I never learned what he was going to say. Perrault glided into the corridor. "Your Grace."

I took a large step backward into the hallway and Bear did the same, closing his door behind him with a *click*.

"Hello, Sir Perrault." I studied my gown, my hands, the carpet—anything but the protocol officer's narrowed eyes.

A crowd had already gathered in the tapestried banquet hall when Skop, Bear, Captain Lang, Perrault, Yu, and I reached its doors, our numbers one short because Cobie had flatly refused to come. *You'll do enough sucking up for the both of us*, she'd said. Then she'd slammed the door in Perrault's face.

We found the ballroom a blaze of color, a rainbow of gowns and gems and tailored jackets. I was grateful for the doors flung open to the courtyard and the cool night air, dazzled as I was by the glitter and noise and Bear close—so close—on my left as we took our seats.

"Bear." Skop turned to him, intent and oblivious, as our plates came. "I've been wondering all day: Does Lord Geraint typically joust with a lance that long? He was struggling with it."

I groaned inwardly, wishing Godmother Althea's book weren't the size of a paving stone and impossible to tote around. Here, there weren't even coats of arms to distract me.

Time to start studying tapestries and gowns.

I glanced around the room, taking in the party again. Lang should have joined us—an empty chair waited beside Perrault a few seats down—but the captain stood to one side of the open doorway, scanning the room as if searching for someone in particular. I could probably have abandoned the party entirely and he wouldn't have noticed.

Bear nudged me, suit jacket rustling against my bare shoulder. "The melee and the joust are no blindman's buff, but would you find them less tedious if you understood them?"

His nose and cheeks were so near to mine. My pulse skipped. "Maybe."

Bear smirked. "I'll take that as a personal challenge."

My stomach went warm, then froze when I saw Perrault. Across the room, his eyes on me were narrow slits in his pink cheeks.

I wanted to stare him down. To hold his gaze until he lowered his eyes.

But I was a coward. So I looked away and turned back to my friends.

Bear took his self-imposed directive seriously. Rather than simply talk about past tournament results, flicking through names and places I wouldn't have recognized, he told stories, elaborating for my benefit on the personal tales of winners and losers and his own triumphs and training history. We didn't notice when our empty dinner plates were cleared away and the outer courtyard filled with dancers.

"Scarecrows?" Skop laughed, wiping tears from his eyes. "You fought scarecrows?"

"We beat them senseless." Bear laughed into his hand, shoulders shaking. "Had to be entirely rebuilt. Veery's father was ready to tan our hides."

"And with good reason," I choked. "You young vandals!"

"We were seven. We called it training for the melee!" Bear protested. His blue eyes laughed inches away from where I leaned on my elbows, my forearm brushing the sleeve of his dinner jacket, my insides soaked with a drunken, delirious warmth.

A servant reached around me, setting a pie on the table. I gasped as I reached for a slice.

"Something wrong?" Skop frowned, poking at it. "Looks fine to me." He licked his finger, dark eyes lighting up. "Tastes better than fine."

"Nothing." I smiled at Bear, nodding at the pie. "It's pecan."

"Technically, I believe it's walnut." Bear arched his eyebrows, smug. "Still. Seems as though you've made an impression on someone."

I swallowed, not able to break from his gaze. "Seems so," I agreed.

But at a voice behind us, we both sat up straight. "Seneschal-elect . . . ?"

I turned to face Prince Bertilak, hoping I didn't look as guilty as I felt. He waved a courteous hand at the dance outside. "Of course," I stammered.

My unsettled insides felt wrong among the straight spines and graceful arms of the dancers as we joined the minuet. But Bertilak fit perfectly among them, voice as crisp and civil as it was every night at dinner. "Did you have anything to contribute tonight, Your Grace?"

I mustered a smile. "I had a very good chicken pie today for lunch. But then," I added, "so did you. So it would seem we had identical days."

Eyes like candles in a darkened hallway.

A tie around a neck, fingers grazing a pulse.

I was lying through my teeth.

Bertilak laughed politely, a superficial sound that came from his mouth and nowhere deeper. When the dance ended, he gave a chivalrous bow and moved on.

Perfectly cordial. Perfectly disinterested.

Bertilak was handsome, and kind. And we might as well have existed on separate planets.

Alessandra would have been furious. The Council, too. But I gave a sigh of relief as I watched his retreating back.

Courtiers flitted around me like butterflies when he left. My throat grew hoarse, my cheeks tremulous from smiling at the noblewomen eager to know if I'd stay to spend the autumn at Windsor and Christmas at Sandringham, at the noblemen hoping to dance.

I fumbled through a jig early in the evening with Lord Geraint, the friendly young victor of the joust, but the crowd had thinned substantially before the melee's winner finally approached, bowing low and baring his long teeth in a smile. "Seneschal-elect."

His Grace the Duke of Cornwall made no advances on me—I was Prince Bertilak's potential bride; it would've been political suicide—but as the duke described in vain, exacting detail his houses and his horses and the times he'd hosted the royal family, I felt like a fish on a hook, wriggling desperately, wanting nothing more than to be free of his loathsome proximity. I kept my elbows at right angles as we waltzed, to maintain maximum distance between us, searching desperately for my friends behind the duke's back and catching seconds-long glimpses of them inside the banquet hall.

One-two-three, one-two-three—Yu and Captain Lang swirling glasses of wine by themselves, eyes on the crowd, mouths terse and disappointed.

One-two-three, one-two-three—Skop and Perrault nowhere to be seen.

One-two-three, one-two-three—Bear in a corner with three boys—Cornwall's nephew, Tristan; the muscular one from the melee with the scarred lip; and another, freckled and awkward-limbed, with a mouth shaped for whining.

Over Cornwall's shoulder, I saw the boy with the scarred lip pour drinks from an amber bottle. Bear and Tristan and their other two friends clinked their tumblers together, looking wry and secretive. When Bear caught me watching, I quickly looked away.

"You've heard, no doubt, of my own marriage plans," said the duke, moving finally from the subject of his wealth.

"What?" I asked, startled out of my reverie. "No, I haven't."

"Oh, of course you have. Tristan goes to fetch her within the twelvemonth; no one's been able to talk of anything else tonight. And with the bride-price I paid for that girl?" He shook his head, drawing breath in through a snarl. "She'd better be worth it."

Unease crawled up the walls of my stomach.

As the musicians played the last strains of our tune, I curtsied, poised to escape when I rose. But when I stood, two boys towered over us like pillars.

"Bear." The word was a sigh of relief in my mouth.

But there was no warmth in the guard's face. "Your Grace," he greeted the duke, blue eyes hard.

I expected the duke to respond in kind, but Cornwall stiffened for a moment before his facade dropped again, smooth as oil. "Bear. Lord Bedivere." He coughed. "I was just claiming my dance as the melee's victor. Informing Her Grace of my recent engagement."

"That, and nothing else, I'm sure." The boy with the scarred lip—Veery—rolled his neck and stretched one sinewy arm. "Heard you had to send all the way to Éire for a wife. No one within smelling distance would have you?"

Cornwall tipped his head to one side. "Don't look for trouble, Veery."

Bear put a hand on my shoulder and glanced down at me, fierce expression softening. But his voice was razor-edged. "He's a moth to flame, Cornwall. I'd think carefully before I kindled any fires." Then he lifted his glass to the duke. "May Tristan bring you back exactly the bride and all the happiness you deserve."

I tensed, waiting for the duke to lash out. But he left me with a stiff bow, lip curled, not bothering to avoid jostling the few dancers left in the courtyard.

Veery clinked his glass to Bear's. "I'll drink to that," he muttered.

Bear bent his head, forehead creased in worry as he eyed me. "Are you all right?"

"Am I all right?" I glanced after the duke's retreating form. "What if he—"

"Don't worry, Seneschal-elect." The muscular boy grinned, scarred lips curving in a real smile that improved his whole appearance. "Bear's been around too long. He's untouchable."

"Shut up." The guard rolled his eyes. "Selah, I wasn't able

to introduce you to Veery at the tournament this afternoon. Seneschal-elect, Lord Bedivere. Veery, this is Selah." Bear jostled him, familiar and easy, sloshing his drink a little.

"Oh, well done," Veery scoffed, but he was smiling.

"Oh! Veery. The friend with the—the scarecrows. From when you were little." I glanced between the two boys, abruptly charmed, though it seemed unlikely that such a rangy, thorny creature had ever been a child.

"You total prat." Veery clapped a hand on Bear's shoulder and gave a single, sharply delighted laugh. "Quick bit of advice, mate: don't tell pretty girls that story."

I blushed and looked away, scanning the room. "Weren't there four of you?"

"Yes," said Veery. "Kay and Tristan decided to skip our encounter with his most charming uncle." He nodded after the Duke of Cornwall's back.

"They don't get along?" If Tristan and Bear were friends, surely Tristan was nothing like his uncle.

"Cornwall doesn't get along with anybody," Bear said, scowling. "He only approached you to make trouble in the first place."

Veery nodded. "That's the duke, all right. And speaking of making trouble . . ." He cut his eyes at Tristan and Kay, who'd been joined by a few other boys and a very pretty dark-haired girl. "My services are required elsewhere."

Bear smirked. "I'd expect nothing less."

"See you later, mate. Seneschal-elect—" Veery grinned and pressed a hand to his heart, making me an irreverent little bow. Then he tossed back the rest of his drink, clapped

Bear on the shoulder, and was gone.

"Nice to meet you," I called sheepishly after his back.

Bear gave a quiet laugh at my side. His warm breath smelled faintly of liquor, but the drink hadn't dulled his words. "Do you promise you're all right?"

I bit my lip, shifting my weight from one sore foot to the other. "I just hope the duke doesn't win next week."

"He won't. I'm certain," Bear said, voice intent. "Selah, would you be embarrassed to dance with me?"

I glanced up at him, surprised. "With my fearless defender? Of course not," I said. "Unfortunately, my shoes are killing me."

"Take them off." A grin pried at Bear's mouth. "We're the last ones here."

It was true. The throng that had easily numbered six or seven hundred when we arrived had dwindled with the passing hours. A few exhausted princes and princesses were draped over chairs inside the banquet hall. Nannies chased the royal children or let them be; little Gemma was fast asleep, curled under a table with her thumb in her mouth. Bear and I were alone in the courtyard with soft music and the scent of climbing roses.

He eyed me, expectant.

The musicians' sibilant tune posed no distraction to the weight of Bear's right palm on my waist, the shift of muscle and bone in the warm hand that held mine. He'd loosened the tie that I'd knotted around his neck.

"Thank you for taking me outside this morning." My voice was uneven, treacherous. "I had a wonderful time."

"The prince was pleased," he whispered. Guilt stabbed my stomach and heat bloomed beneath my skin as Bear's cheek grazed my temple. His nose and mouth were a mere heartbeat above mine. "Half the village and the court are in love with you."

My nerves sparked and flared. I gave an edgy laugh. "Why do you say that?"

"I've been paying attention," Bear whispered, thumb tracing a small circle of fire through the fabric over my waist. "You should do the same."

The last notes of the song still hung on the air as he bowed over my hand and kissed it. Though light as butterflies' wings, my skin burned beneath his lips; I half expected their touch to leave a mark.

I was still rooted to the ground when words cold as an icy wind blew my reverie away.

"Seneschal-elect." Sir Perrault loomed at the edge of the empty courtyard like a ghost, black eyes flashing. "Take a walk with me."

28

The protocol officer strode inside, and I lurched alongside him like a marionette. Lang's brow puckered in question as we scuttled through the beautiful hall, but he looked away when our eyes met. He shifted uncomfortably, turning his attention back to Yu.

When we finally reached our quarters, Perrault faced me, eyes hard, voice stripped of all its charm and silk. "It's apparent that your relationship with your guard has progressed beyond the merely professional."

I wasn't cold, but fear spread like frost through my veins, wrapping icy fingers around my throat.

What is he going to tell Alessandra and the Council?

Everything. He's going to tell them everything, and everything is ruined.

And it's going to kill Daddy.

"That's not true," I answered, too late.

"No?"

"No," I said, but the word was brittle in my mouth. "I'm focused on the appointment at hand. The Council's goals are my goals."

He paused, gaze growing distant. I clenched my fists, felt my nails bite my palms. "Seneschal-elect, do you know where I came from?"

I've known Sir Perrault for a very long time.

"You're from New York." An accusation, not an answer.

I'd been stupid to forget how deep Alessandra's claws could sink, to think Perrault was too busy fawning over the king to notice me.

He knew what my stepmother did to people who failed her. I was a walking reminder.

Perrault began to pace.

"Potomac's seneschal is a gentle man, and life at Arbor Hall is accordingly kind. But let me tell you about the court where I grew up.

"Power in New York is a fluid thing, and the court is a structure in motion. Families rise and fall without warning. Artists, scholars, and innumerable other varieties of sycophant spend their existence clawing their way to its apex, regardless of what—or who—stands in their way."

My stomach muscles clenched. "What are you saying?"

Perrault stepped toward me. "I'm saying, Selah, that I am skilled both at lying and at identifying liars when they cross my path." Another step in my direction, and I was flattened against the wall while his eyes dissected me like scalpels. "So *don't lie to me.*"

The protocol officer no longer looked like a portrait. He looked like a fox deciding how to tear a chicken to pieces.

My heart was going to punch its way out of my chest.

I took a shuddering breath. "Fine." I glared up at Perrault. "Fine. So our relationship is—warm. So what? Nothing's going to *happen.*"

The words resisted being spoken aloud, clinging to my mouth as if leaving my lips lent them truth.

But it was true. It had to be. Cornwall flirting would have been socially risky, a surefire way to fall out of favor. A mere guard doing so would be outright treason.

"Do you not remember what I told you weeks ago?" Perrault demanded. "I told you that to choose before completing your appointments was to slight the families who have extended your invitations. Above all, your goal is not to give offense to your host. Word travels, even of a backwater princess at the court of a minor king, even if only in whispers." He leaned closer. "And of this you can be certain: the tsarytsya has excellent hearing."

My pulse accelerated, feverish in my wrists and my neck and in the soft hollows beneath my ankles, telling me to *run.* But I couldn't move.

Cobie's door creaked open, and Perrault jerked back, startled.

She was clad in ripped pajamas, but she hadn't been sleeping.

Cobie's sharp eyes didn't miss my pale face, the protocol officer's guilty expression. "What's going on, Perrault?"

"Nothing, Grimm." He shook out his right hand as though working out a cramp, then dropped his voice. "You have one suitor on this visit. I strongly advise against grooming a second." Perrault stalked into his room.

Cobie watched his closed door, toying with a rip in her shirt. "I know he's overseeing this thing," she said, "but he's not one of ours, and that means I don't trust him. Find me or one of us if he tries to get you alone again."

I nodded, hoping she didn't notice the shake in my hands.

They were shaking still as I fell asleep clutching my godmother's book, reading the story of clever thief Molly Whuppie and the giant who tried three times to catch and kill her. He chased me into my dreams, and I ran, sprinting away from him, stumbling over unfamiliar ground as my Godmother Althea whispered for me to hurry, hurry home.

29

I followed my lengthening shadow to the edge of the woods where the hunt waited, heavy steps echoing in my hollow chest.

"Your Grace?" Bear asked tonelessly. He passed me my horse's reins and tightened her girth without meeting my eyes or saying anything else.

When Sir Perrault had glided into my room unannounced that morning, he'd stared at me eating breakfast sprawled before the fire as if I were something a cat had killed and left on the floor. "This is to remind you that Prince Bertilak has requested you join him hunting this evening."

As if I could've forgotten.

Bear's silence was only recompense for what I'd done. We'd hardly spoken since the ball four days earlier.

Four miserable days of avoiding him. Of words bitten back and swallowed. Four tick marks in my book at night as I clawed my way free of this place.

I'd overtly avoided him at church Sunday morning, and hidden in my room that afternoon and evening. He'd knocked, and I'd pretended not to hear. And when the prince had taken me fishing on Monday and on a walk through the castle gardens on Tuesday, I'd avoided Bear's eyes, and he'd maintained an appropriate distance. Now, it seemed, he'd taken to using my title again.

I'd gone cold on him, and I hadn't told him why, and he'd finally returned the favor.

"Seneschal-elect!" Prince Bertilak called merrily. "So glad you could join us!" He nodded at my horse. "Cotton Nero is pleased, as well."

"Of course, Your Highness." My attempt at enthusiasm sounded feeble to my own ears. "Now, remind me what we're hunting?"

The Duke of Cornwall led a fast-looking black horse toward us, eyes glittering. "Foxes, Your Grace."

"Hunting foxes!" scoffed someone else. "Aren't we all?" A few of the men laughed, easy and confident, teeth flashing. My shoulders tensed.

"Ignore them." Bear's voice was low. "Just keep close to Prince Bertilak and me, and you'll be fine." I nodded, avoiding his eyes as he helped me into Cotton's saddle, then settled himself onto his own mount, Ursa Major.

I tried not to let my heart rise at the protectiveness in his tone.

The Duke of Cornwall gave me another long-toothed leer before lifting a hunting horn to his lips. At its boisterous call, we rode forward beneath the thick canopy of green, the field cheerful and noisy, the hounds and terriers trundling along with their noses to the ground and tails bobbing.

Suddenly, a hound at the front of the pack tipped his dirt-brown muzzle toward the sky and bayed, tail twitching like tall grass in a stiff wind. I jerked at his cry, plaintive and desperate, and Bertilak and Bear exchanged a sharp, oddly familiar glance.

"He speaks!" someone shouted, and the hounds took off. The horses broke into a gallop after them, hooves hammering the earth like thunder rumbling up from underground, sleek torsos straining forward. My heart climbed into my throat as Cotton picked up speed.

Mud flew and thorns caught at my clothes as we clambered through thickets and tore over soggy paths after the dogs. I gripped the reins, white-knuckled, and leaned into Cotton's sprint; but the horse and I were strangers. I didn't know her well enough to keep up. One by one, the riders passed me by.

My heart sank as they vanished through the trees, leaving me alone in the gathering dusk.

"Your Grace?"

I twisted at his voice. Bear sat easily on his horse's back, hands braced on his thighs, as fluid and relaxed as if he'd been poured into Ursa Major's saddle.

"You're still here." I furrowed my brow, surprised.

"I'm supposed to stay with you. This was bound to happen." Bear tipped his head at the path the company had smashed through the trees.

I blushed. "Ah. Glad my incompetence was so obvious. Good to have company out here."

"That's a bit harsh." Bear raised an eyebrow, urging Ursa a little nearer to Cotton and me. "Look, my first time on the hunt, I was quite small, and I fell behind, too. I rode around for an hour before I just went home," he said. "Later I pretended I'd been with them the whole time, but I don't think anyone believed me."

I laughed out loud despite myself. "Really?"

Bear's eyes lit, and a grin caught the corner of his mouth. "There she is," he said quietly.

My heart stilled at the look on his face.

We rode on, following the path the hunt had broken. "When my father taught me to ride, he had me in the saddle every day for a month," Bear said. "My legs were jelly every time I came off the horse."

"Your father?"

Bear had never mentioned his family before.

He nodded, still staring through the woods. "It looks like they went this way."

"Is your father a member of the guard, too?" I pressed.

"No. My father and I haven't much in common. He's not pleased I've taken this post."

He was silent for such a long moment I glanced over at him, brows arching.

"He's not?" I prompted.

Bear pursed his lips, shooting me a sidelong glance. "He worries it's not safe."

"What does your mother think?"

"Mum's approving." His face warmed, and Bear gave me another piercing look, forehead puckered beneath the hair that had spilled over his brow during the chase. "What about your family?"

"I have a father and a stepmother, and they have a baby on the way," I began. But I trailed off as a dangerous temptation suddenly filled me—the longing to brush the hair out of his eyes and tell him the truth.

I pulled Cotton up short, glancing around and listening. Only the rich, green silence of twilight, only our breathing and the spatter of a brook far off.

"My father and I are close, but my stepmother and I . . . are not," I said slowly. "That's why she sent me here."

Bear squinted at me. "What do you mean?" I looked away, not answering, and he ducked, forcing me to meet his gaze. "Selah?"

I blew out a long breath. Cotton's ears quirked backward. "I didn't even know I was leaving until the night before it happened. When my proposal at home was declined, my stepmother and the Council announced I was going away," I finished. "My father's not well, and I'm worried for him. And Perrault's not aboard the *Beholder* because he's much use at sea."

Bear's eyes narrowed. "Your protocol officer has quite the pair of eyes on him."

"Yes." I gave a bleak smile, darkly amused to be confiding in one spy about another. "He suggested you and I were spending too much time together. He's very concerned that Prince

Bertilak extends a proposal."

Bear cocked his head. "Aren't you?"

"Of course," I lied abruptly.

A smile as wry as mine spread across the guard's face. "He's afraid I'll jeopardize your chances."

"I told him we merely—" But I broke off at the steepening arch of Bear's eyebrows, the curve of his grin. Mortified, I hurried Cotton Nero forward, but Ursa kept up with us easily.

"Myrddin and the king trust me implicitly," Bear insisted. "You can, too."

I was growing more awkward by the second. "I know."

Realization dawned on his face, nearly displacing his delight. "And that's why you've been so cool since Saturday."

"I haven't been—" But the knowing tilt of his head stopped me short once again. I bit my lip and shook my head. "What was I supposed to do?"

Bear's eyes tightened, and he opened his mouth to reply, but the distant bark of hounds snagged our attention.

"That's the field," I cut him off, relieved and disappointed, and rode ahead to join them.

The hunters greeted us with a chorus of apologies. A terrier darted between Cotton's ankles; the dogs were jubilant, scampering around the covert as their handlers and the hunters milled around on horseback or on foot. Only the little red foxes lay motionless on the ground.

"Oh, I'm sure the—Bear had you well in hand," the Duke of Cornwall called, long teeth flashing. Most of the men frowned, foreheads wrinkled in disapproval, but one or two snickered roughly. I cringed, not sure where to look.

"Mark." Prince Bertilak's voice was hard as a stone.

"Your—Highness, I—" Cornwall stammered.

"Enough." The prince held up a hand, and the field held its breath. And the duke held his silence.

I ate dinner with the royal family again that night, feeling Perrault glance furiously between Bertilak and me. The prince had taken a seat half a table away.

Perrault's face relaxed when Bertilak called out to remind me of our lunch plans the following afternoon. "I haven't taken you boating yet, have I?" he called cheerfully. As if he could've forgotten.

Maybe he had. Maybe I occupied that little space in his brain.

Heaven knew he occupied a small enough fraction of mine.

My smile was polite. "Not yet."

But the next morning broke gray and chilly, dark clouds hanging overhead. The prince sent a messenger, suggesting we take lunch indoors.

But after the messenger left, and before I could compose a reply, Bear came to my door.

30

You are making a mistake, my rational mind whispered.

Smothery gray clouds blanketed the sky behind Winchester Castle, their edges twisting in the buffeting wind—not benevolent wisps, but claws, malevolent and grasping. Bear stood on my right, nearer than decorum permitted.

I'd thought at first that he must be the prince's messenger, come to carry back my reply. I'd nearly slammed the door in his face, surprised to find him stretched against its frame—exhausted but perfect, eyes ringed like mine with sleeplessness. "I want to show you something," Bear had said, nudging the door open again, running a hand through his shaggy hair.

What could I have said but yes?

I'd sat on my bed, chewing my pencil, and scribbled a note to Bertilak, saying I didn't feel well and asking if we could postpone our lunch.

Daddy and Godmother were counting on me to come

home as quick as I could. My stepmother and the Council had ordered me to return with a fiancé, and the little thatch of tick marks in the back of my book told me that I had only two days left in England. That fewer and fewer days stood between me and the threat of the Imperiya.

Every step I took toward Bear was a step off the path toward duty. Toward my rightful role. Toward Daddy and Godmother and home.

I'd sealed the note and sent it before I could change my mind.

"We're only going about a half a mile as the crow flies." Bear pushed open the back gate, and it gave with a long creak. The woods behind the castle were dark beneath the somber sky. "But the hills are rough, so it's a bit further than that, really."

I eyed the gathering clouds uncertainly as I picked my way down the ridge, over fallen logs and scrub. The exposed skin on my arms and collarbone prickled under a cold wind. "Is it about to rain?"

Bear smirked. "This is England. It's always about to rain."

"It's been mostly clear since we arrived— Oof." My feet slipped over a stone slick with the morning dew. Bear reached out, bracing me.

"Well, then." He grinned, charming but still dangerous, palms dawdling over my arms even once my feet were steady. "I guess you brought the sunshine."

We came at last to a tall stone building nestled between damp green hills, its gray slate roof covered in moss, its leaded windows glowing with warm light. Vast oaks and thick tangles of willows and wildflowers crowded around its sides, trembling in the wind.

"Where are we?"

Bear took me by the elbow. The hair on my arms rose at his touch, at his private smile.

You are making a mistake.

"Come inside and see."

An old grandfather clock marked the time with pensive *ticks* in the dark-paneled foyer, dimly lit and otherwise empty. The sound followed us through a narrow corridor and into an adjoining room. When my eyes adjusted to the weak lamplight and the gray glow of the sky outside, I gasped aloud.

Bear had finally brought me to the library.

Thousands of leather- and canvas-bound books lined hundreds of chestnut shelves, like carved jewelry boxes stuffed with treasure. Rugs covered the walnut floor beneath my feet. The only sounds were the faint wooden *tick-tick-tick* of the grandfather clock and the whispery rattle of branches on the windows and the hum of my nerves.

I ran my hands over the nearest spines—*Parmenides, Plato, Pythagoras*—and silently multiplied the shelves, the corridors, the spiral staircase just visible through a half-open door.

For a moment, I felt the thousand books stacked quietly around us and imagined Bear had heaped them up just for me, like children in a fort of blankets and cushions. "Are we the only ones here?"

"No." Bear shambled forward to peer at another

shelf—*Aquinas, Athenagoras of Athens, Augustine*. His slouched spine and hands in his pockets said *nonchalant*, but the smug set of his mouth said *very pleased with myself*. "Some of the staff are in the third-floor office."

I paled, thinking of the lie I'd told Bertilak.

"Don't worry," Bear said quietly, smiling. "They won't even know we're here. They tend to keep quite busy."

"So I can just . . . ?" I glanced around, disbelieving.

He nodded, grinning complacently, totally self-satisfied. "Go explore."

I tried to make orderly stacks as I pulled down volumes and thumbed through their pages, telling myself that I would catalog the titles and plead that they be lent to Potomac someday. But I was too excited to be organized. More than once I found myself sprawled between bookcases, two chapters into a story I'd only meant to look at.

The old grandfather clock had just clanged a warning—*two o'clock*—when Bear discovered me holding court on the second floor between shelves of fairy tales and folklore. Rain clinked against the windowpanes as he surveyed the towers and cities I'd built of heavy volumes, gold and silver foil gleaming like pieces of jewelry against their deep red and green bindings. "Are you hungry?"

I bit my lip and let the book fall closed around my index finger. "I'm not ready to leave."

"I thought not. Come on." Bear held out a hand, eyes flickering.

I let him help me up. He didn't let go as he led me to the

spiral staircase, as we climbed up, up, up the stone steps. Somewhere on the walk, his fingers laced through mine. I swore to myself that the shaking in my limbs was from the cold air whistling through the old tower wall.

At the top of the stairs, Bear retrieved a key from a chain around his neck and unlocked the door to a small circular room.

Flames inside a crumbling brick fireplace and lamps misted with ash threw light on mismatched chairs and couches. A rickety old desk was stacked with books and papers, and a half-dozen teetering shelves were so crammed with volumes they looked in danger of collapsing. From its patched wooden ceiling to the hodgepodge of worn rugs spread across the floor, the room had a makeshift sort of coziness, its comfort cobbled together from things cast aside or forgotten.

His insistent hands drew me over the threshold, floorboards creaking beneath my feet. I watched Bear, careful, careful, questioning.

"It's mine," he said quietly. "Myrddin thought I'd like a place here, and the library staff don't mind me using the attic."

Myrddin thought.

But why? Why did Myrddin think? Why should the king's adviser care what would make a no-one boy—a castle guard of no name—happy?

Unless he wasn't no one. A spy, certainly. Maybe a nephew or a cousin or a grandson to someone important.

And if that were so, what kind of betrayal to the king's adviser was it that he was here, now, with me?

Unable to hold Bear's gaze, I swallowed and broke away to pace the room's perimeter. I'd studied political philosophy, but even I flinched at the stern, dry-looking tomes on law and justice heaped upon the desk.

"As I said, Constantine and Bertilak studied at Oxford," Bear said quietly. I whipped around, staring at him. "The prince has got as many degrees as he's got limbs. Law and philosophy and such. Makes education rather a *thing* at court." He smiled.

The space between us was silent, but only in the way of a concert hall before the music began.

On a displaced sofa cushion before the fireplace, another book lay abandoned. Not a textbook—a slim thing, with a dark green binding. "*Beowulf?*" I asked.

"I just finished it a few days ago."

I settled onto the cushion, turning the volume over in my hands. "Old English poetry and legal textbooks. I don't know what to make of your taste."

"Skepticism from the girl with what can only be an encyclopedia on her bedside table?" Bear laughed.

I flushed at the teasing shape of his mouth.

"They're about the same things, really. The rule of law can't survive where bravery dies."

He took a basket of food off the old redbrick mantel, tugged another cushion off the couch, and settled in beside me—close, too close.

You are making a mistake.

I knew it was wrong. Infidelity was always wrong. I owed more to Bertilak. To my father, weak and worrisome. To

Potomac, which deserved to have someone honest and steady at its steward's side. And Perrault had warned me: the tsarytsya was always listening.

But my insides ached at the warm firelight thrown over the curve of Bear's eyebrows and his long nose and soft lips.

I had nothing. Months of time had been stolen from me outright, given away to strangers and to courts about whom I knew nothing. But in this moment, I had this: Bear, next to me, and a room full of quiet and firelight.

He is so very handsome, and we are so very, very unwise.

"Will you read to me?" My voice cracked.

I chose a sandwich from the basket and burrowed deeper into the cushion, exhilaration burning bright in my chest as our shoulders and knees brushed.

"Yes," Bear said. "I'll start at the beginning."

Sometimes I watched his fingers move over the old pages; sometimes I shut my eyes and listened to his liquid voice rise and fall as rain drummed on the roof outside. Bear didn't stop reading until the grandfather clock reminded us twice more on the hour that the outside world was waiting.

"Here." He passed me the book. "You should have this."

"Are you sure?" I asked, but already I was thumbing its pages.

"I've already finished it." He traced a finger over the back of my hand.

My breath caught, and I grew very still.

"Read it." Bear's eyes were soft. "It'll make you brave."

We collected ourselves in silence and returned to the great

front doors, waiting fruitlessly for a break in the rain. "Thank you for bringing me here today." I hesitated. "My mother would have liked this place. She would have liked you."

"Really?" Bear pulled off his jacket and wrapped it around me. He settled it onto my shoulders, tugging it by its front snugly around my waist. I breathed in the smell of its leather, soft and warm and aged with work.

Bear's hands pulled me closer as if of their own accord.

I nodded, swallowing. "Momma and I used to hole up in our library for hours. 'It's not what you look like, it's how you see,' she used to always say, and she believed someone who didn't read only ever saw through their own eyes."

But my eyes hardly saw the torrent of rain outside the dim foyer, hardly felt the shrieking wind dashing it into our faces as Bear fixed me for the thousandth time with his heady blue gaze.

"I love your eyes." He ran a thumb along my hairline, his gentle, precise accent undoing my will. "Myrddin insists our fates are written in omens and dreams, but yours is written in your eyes. Green as England. I knew you'd understand." He cradled my jaw with one hand. My pulse tore off in a sprint beneath his palm.

I'd never felt this before. Peter—perfect Peter, with his earnest words and careful fingers and the gap between his teeth that showed when he smiled—had only liked me as a friend. He'd never put his hands on me.

"Bear—"

"Blindman's buff," he broke in, tone strangled. "Did you

know that sometimes the children play so the blind man has to guess who he's captured by the touch of the person's face?" I shook my head; his fingers grew more tangled in the hair at the nape of my neck.

My heart was a burning star, singeing my lungs, setting fire to my nerves.

Was it my fault, really, that my chest couldn't hold it?

I dragged tremulous fingers over Bear's cheekbone and down the corner of his mouth. His breath caught. "I could guess yours," I said, voice uneven. "Could you guess mine?"

Somewhere far off, lightning flashed and split the pewter sky.

He laid his hand over mine, leaning his flushed cheek against my palm. "I could," he whispered, "if only I could catch you."

My heart stilled. I withdrew my hand, taking one, two, three steps back into the downpour.

Rain traced my scorched skin, coursed through my hair and down the back of my neck.

You are making a mistake.

We were doomed, but I was smiling.

"Try," I said, and we were off and running.

31

We chased each other, slipping over stones and moss and catching each other around the waist time and again. I won, and he won, and we both lost, and by the time we got back to the castle, Bear and I were drenched and out of breath and laughing like fools. My neck and wrists and fingers burned everywhere he touched them.

Once inside my room, he tugged his jacket off me and stoked the fire, sending sparks up the chimney. I dragged a chair closer to its flames, teeth chattering as he draped me with dry towels.

Bear knelt and grasped my shaking hands, caked with mud and wet leaves, warming them with his own.

"I would have crossed from Potomac to England," I whispered, "just for today."

Guilt pooled in my stomach, sharp and icy. I had not crossed for this. For *him*. I pushed the truth away.

I knew I was cold. But with his eyes on me, suddenly, I couldn't feel it.

My fingers curled slowly around his.

A thousand tiny moments.

Yeses and nos that change the world.

There would be a price for this betrayal later. I hoped I could afford it.

And then Bear was kissing me.

I'd never been kissed before, except for by family or friends; pecks on the nose when I was little, parting kisses scrunched against cheeks. Peter had never come nearer my lips than a friendly hug permitted, but even with him, I'd never imagined anything like this—brilliant, glowing, breathless.

Kneeling by my chair, Bear's other hand grasped my shoulder. Unbidden, my free hand found his burning cheek, fingertips winding their way into the dark hair clinging damply to his temple. He pulled back only a heartbeat later, questions in his eyes.

He was still crouched beside me, our interlocked fingers resting on my knee, when Perrault and Captain Lang walked through the open door.

"There you are!" Lang said, looking relieved. But they both stopped short when they saw Bear. He patted my hand awkwardly and dropped it, rising to his feet.

Perrault blinked, then his eyes narrowed. "I thought you weren't feeling well."

I swallowed. "I thought a walk would help."

"It was brilliant, until the rain drove us home." Bear dug

back into the linen closet and dumped six more towels on my lap.

Sure, I thought wryly. *That'll convince them.* Lang's stare was as heavy as my rain-soaked clothes.

"You're shivering," Lang said tightly. "Perrault, have someone bring hot water."

Perrault drew himself up. "I'm not an errand boy—"

"But you *are* only fourth in command on this expedition," Lang said tautly. "And I'm the captain. The seneschal-elect needs to get warm. Please, have someone send a bath."

Perrault turned on his heel and stalked toward the door. "I'll call for tea," Bear said quickly, following him.

Later, he mouthed to me. My heart skidded, disastrous, over the reluctance in his eyes.

And then I was alone with Lang.

"You told the prince you weren't feeling well enough to join him for lunch." His voice was quiet, hard as a stone.

I twisted the hem of my shirt over the basin by my bed, watching water run in rivulets down the painted ceramic. "I thought I'd go for—a walk," I said haltingly. "Bear suggested the library. I—"

"Selah." Lang cut me off. His eyes were agitated. "You're playing a dangerous game."

I tried to laugh. "What are you talking about?"

"Vanishing for hours? With a member of the household?" He tripped over the words, voice growing heated.

My face reddened. "What does his status matter?" I demanded.

"He's not the prince." Lang flung his arms out. "Don't you care— Selah, what are you even here for?" He was breathing hard, as if he'd been running. As if my foolish truancy left him breathless.

Lang, who even when we were all together, was always somewhere else.

I narrowed my eyes at him and dropped my voice. "What are *you* here for, Lang?"

He froze, one smudged hand midway through his tousled dark hair. "What are you talking about?"

"I hear the things you say," I said sharply. "You're everywhere but by my side. Perrault follows me around like a nanny, but despite the fact that you keep insisting that you're in charge, you're never around, even when I might need you. You're looking for something. For—someone."

"Selah, trust me." He eyed me keenly, his very words careful enough to walk a tightrope. "That has nothing to do with you."

"Trust *you?*" I asked. "How can I trust you, when you ignore me for days at a time, then come in here making accusations?"

Never mind that they're true.

"I don't understand." Lang shook his head, eyes confused. "You were so concerned about making this work, and now you're—with *him?* Of all people?"

My voice was nearly inaudible when I finally spoke. "What would you do, if you were in my shoes?"

"I'd do what I came here to do," Lang said, low and intent. "Court the prince or not, but stick to the mission either way."

"Fine." I leveled my gaze at him. "Then I'd say the same

to you. Do your job, Lang. If you're concerned about me, be around to see what's happening."

Lang shook his head, and left me alone, silence deafening in his wake, cold anxiety creeping over my bones.

The kiss.

It clouded my brain through the next day and during the final state dinner before the tournament. I hardly heard the prince when he called to me from his father's side during the banquet. "Do you have anything to share with us tonight, Seneschal-elect?"

I'd spent the day with Bertilak, meeting his knights. They'd sat circled at the table in his throne room, discussing the next day's tournament. Bear had stood sentry behind me, hand on the back of my chair, stealing my concentration.

The books. The fire. The rain.

The kiss.

Bertilak sat at the far end of the table, half my entire hope of avoiding the Imperiya.

He smiled pleasantly. He meant absolutely nothing to me.

I would never be his wife. That future would never arrive. But this—this present, with Bear at my elbow, close enough to hear his breathing—was at hand.

I had it in my grasp. I would not release it until it was ripped from me.

So with Bear's palm on my knee and Lang's eyes accusing me silently, I smiled at the prince and lied to the whole room.

"A book from your library. I'm looking forward to reading it."

"And that's all?" Bertilak's brow furrowed, even as he smiled pleasantly. Bear squeezed my knee, shaking beneath the table.

"Yes." I swallowed, hoping the truth would live quietly in my stomach and not make me sick with guilt and fear. "That's all I've got to share."

32

One more day.

The thought persisted in my head as I dressed for the final tournament Saturday morning. One more day in Winchester, and then I'd leave. I would leave Bear.

One tick mark in the book the night before. One single mark left to me.

I'd known all along what I'd have to do, but knowing didn't soften the edges of the hard facts. My pitiful crush had never had a chance.

One more day with Bear began with one more knock, one more meeting in the doorway. My guilty insides were gray, but he was beaming, buoyant, downright sunny. "Why so glum, Seneschal-elect?"

I folded my arms and looked away, throat tight. "How can you be so cheerful?"

Bear ignored my question, eyes glowing as he traced my

cheekbones with his thumbs, cupped my face in his hands. "You must think me the worst kind of traitor. Prince Bertilak—"

"I don't want to think about any of them." I swallowed hard and shook my head. "Just us."

Bear's laugh stirred my hair and eyelashes. "Don't worry, Selah," he whispered, leaning his forehead against mine. "Today is going to be a perfect day."

How badly I wanted to believe him.

Though it had been nothing two nights before but a bitter sky over drenched grass, the village green was a riot of color and cheer. The breeze was clean and fresh and dry; vendors tempted the crowds with flowers, treats, and toys beneath tents and a blue sky shot with pink. I was the only rain cloud in sight.

We walked on and found the lists already crowded with horses and riders. Though I knew it was probably my imagination, I felt their eyes on Bear and me as we passed.

I tried to ignore their stares, but my guilty conscience pricked my skin, sang in my ears.

They know what you've done. Both of you.

I feared them. I feared the prince. I feared everyone at home finding out I could have done my duty, but I hadn't.

"Did you know Igraine rode in the joust when she was a girl?" Bear whispered as we climbed the dais steps. A crown of roses waited on my chair beside a note signed in Gemma's scrawl. I couldn't help but smile as Bear slipped the crown over my ponytail. "Lord knows how she convinced her father."

"Did Constantine disapprove?" I asked. "That surprises me."

Bear frowned and opened his mouth as if to answer, but seemed to think better of his reply.

I imagined Igraine among the men and women now making ready to ride, tightening girths, adjusting armor, talking quietly to their horses. As I watched, one of the women saddling up to ride slipped a ribbon from her hair and tied it to a noble-man's lance. Another lady tugged a handkerchief from inside her sleeve and pressed it into the hand of a tall man on horse-back. He tucked the handkerchief next to his chest, beneath his armor, and bent to kiss her.

"Ladies' favors," Bear said softly in my ear. "Little remem-brances. That ribbon's going to come off the lance before the Earl of Norfolk rides, but the idea is nice." I bit my lip, smiling when he pronounced *idea* as though it ended in an *r*. I'd found his accent so cold when we'd first met. Now, I found it unbear-ably attractive.

"And why don't the ladies get favors themselves?" I asked, smiling.

"Because they don't want the distraction."

I shivered at his breath on my cheek; his lips had been nearly close enough to brush my ear.

The chair beside me moved, and Bertilak took his seat. I straightened, away from Bear.

One more day.

I'd been bored out of my skull the Saturday before, but today, the sun tore through the sky, cruel and unfeeling as a cannonball. The joust was over in a few merciless heartbeats, lances crashing against shields again and again with the speed of a furious cymbal player. My heart ached as precious minutes stole away from me, crumbling like firewood turned to ash.

"I'm going to slip away for a moment," Bear suddenly whispered.

"Where are you going?"

He waved a hand. "I'll come back straightaway." Then he hesitated, tracing one of the blooms in my wreath. "May I?"

I nodded, and with one finger on my chin, he turned my head and tugged one half-blown white rose from the crown beneath my ponytail, grazing the skin of my neck. Captain Lang and Yu were talking privately, eyes on the crowd, and Perrault was trying to ingratiate himself with every titled person on the dais, and Cobie was busy being stony, as usual; but I sensed them all watching. Watching me.

The melee soon began, and Bear didn't come back. Skop and Igraine tried to engage me amid the sounds of the battle, but I was distracted from the warriors in green and gold, glancing over at every sound on the dais steps, expecting to see him. Lang's shoulders grew tenser with my every stealthy look.

Unlike his sister, Bertilak on my left didn't speak to me. He hadn't addressed me at all since dinner the night before.

A creak on the stairs made me jump—but it was only Alexander chasing Gemma over the dais. I slouched, disappointed.

Bear still hadn't reappeared, and if the joust had been short, the melee's pace was downright frantic. Time was slipping away from me, like water through my cupped hands.

But the pace of the event wasn't in my imagination. The crowd sensed it, too, and they roared their approval.

The excitement centered around a tall, rangy warrior in green with an impossibly fast sword arm. The design of his shield—three stacked golden crowns on a blue field—was familiar, but I couldn't place it, and his helmet's visor hid his face.

I wasn't sure who had commanded the green army the week before, but he was clearly leading them today. Seven knights in green surrounded him, identities likewise hidden beneath their helmets. They worked rapidly through the field, voices feral and fierce with strain, weapons flashing as their owners charged and retreated. Like a flower opening and closing they advanced and withdrew, returning always to circle their leader. And though he fought whatever enemy came his way, his gaze returned again and again to the leader of the gold army.

Cornwall. He was fighting well enough, I guessed. My stomach turned at the sight of him.

When the green knight was the last mounted fighter remaining, he jumped down and sent his horse away with a slap on the rump, earning him another almighty cheer from the crowd. The din only rose as a trio of warriors in gold attacked, and he flung away his shield to grasp the dagger at his belt, subduing his enemies even more skillfully on foot than he had on horseback.

The field was looking distinctly green.

"What's happening?" I hollered in Skop's ear.

I don't know how she heard me over the mob and the

mystery warrior's horn, calling to his scattered knights, but Princess Igraine answered, eyes still on the fight unfolding before us. "His men listen for his every word. They're one unit, with one opponent."

"What? Who?" I shouted.

"Haven't you noticed?" Igraine gestured wildly at a knight in a gold jersey.

"Yeah," Skop bellowed. "They've been fighting their way to the leader of the gold army all this time. Drilling him. The guy with the long hair who won last week."

"Right." Igraine nodded appreciatively. "It's as though they don't care what happens, as long as Cornwall is forced off the field. He's determined Mark will not be the champion. And yet," she added with a grin, "they're fighting so hard, the green armies are sure to claim the victory. My, but he's quick—been practicing, I see—"

The princess was still speaking, but I suddenly couldn't hear, couldn't reply, couldn't breathe. Her answer had knocked the wind out of me.

I just hope the duke doesn't win next week.

He won't. I'm certain.

Cornwall had loomed over me at the previous ball, like a shadow I couldn't seem to escape. The very idea of another dance with him—the prize for his victory—had made me ill.

But Bear had promised me that wouldn't happen.

Somehow, I clung to calm, restrained the smile that wanted to break over my face like the sun from behind clouds. I kept my composure even when Veery tore his helmet from his head, even when Sir Mark, Duke of Cornwall, lifted his visor to scream at Tristan for catching a blow meant for Kay.

I propped my head in my hand and hid my grin behind my curled fingers, because I knew where Bear had gone. Because, on the inside, I was like everyone else, throwing flowers and cheering for the mystery green knight.

For Bear, who led an entire army to victory to rescue me from a dance with Cornwall.

By the time Bear's blunted dagger ripped Cornwall's gold jersey, leaving an angry welt on his neck, the entire crowd on the village green was on its feet.

Everyone but Bertilak.

The prince observed in a chilly calm as the boys tugged off their helmets, sat ramrod straight as they ran gauntleted hands through sweaty hair—Veery, and Tristan, and gangling, awkward Kay, as I'd suspected, but also Lord Geraint, the young jousting champion from the previous week, and the boys and the pretty dark-haired girl from the weekend before. They shambled toward the dais, whooping and laughing and slapping one another on the back, fierce and triumphant.

Bertilak rose stiffly, mouth one thin line, and escorted me onto the green.

"You chose to participate," the prince said to Bear.

"I did," he panted.

"I should have thought you'd be more careful," Bertilak said tightly. "Accidents happen in the melee, you know."

Fear jolted through me. Were his words concern, or a threat?

Bear lifted his visor. "And yet," he said breezily, "all was well today."

"Indeed," said Bertilak. "Today."

The prince's expression didn't change when Bear at last yanked off his helmet and shook out a head of shaggy dark hair. But the village green erupted in deafening approval, clapping and screaming, heedless of their aching hands and throats.

"Congratulations, Bear Green, victor of the melee," Bertilak called over the clamor. A man hurried forward to pass me the victor's trophy and I handed it to my guard, biting my lip against the joy and admiration rioting in my chest.

The roar of the crowd was earsplitting, but I was fixed on Bear as he pushed sweaty hair out of his eyes and dropped to one knee in the grass, friends kneeling likewise behind him.

You are making a mistake.

But he was utterly magnetic.

From beneath his armor, near his heart, Bear produced the white rose he had taken from my wreath. He held it up to me, panting, a grin stretched across his face.

My heart was a lit candle, a forest fire, a burning star.

Doomed, but smiling.

I took the flower from his fingers, and the crowds continued to cheer.

33

I got ready slowly, wondering if tonight Bear would be the one to knock on my door. If he would be the one to seek me out for a moment of quiet before the ball.

Our time was up.

I couldn't stay with him. I couldn't take a guard back to Potomac as my chosen fiancé and skip my other appointments. And I couldn't very well take him with me to Norge, a rival to my last chance not to enter the Imperiya.

I didn't know what I would say to him. But I wanted to kiss him again, to feel his hands on mine one more time. I wanted him to say he had a plan.

But his knock never came.

I found Lang in the hallway, waiting in a charcoal suit. He studied the tiara on my head, dark eyes curious. "Is that new?"

The box had been waiting on my bed when I returned from the tournament. I'd blinked, nearly dropping the tiny crown when I'd unearthed it, glittering with emeralds and pearls, from a rich swath of purple velvet. A note written on expensive stationery had been attached, stamped with the royal crest.

> *Dear Seneschal-elect,*
> *For tonight only, or for always,*
> *if you like.*
> *To match your eyes.*
> *HRH Prince B.*

My stomach had dropped through the floor.

Lang swallowed, jaw working. "It suits you."

"Prince Bertilak lent it to me."

Or for always, if you like.

But I didn't.

I didn't want his proposal. I didn't want to be a princess. I was never born to wear a crown.

I missed Potomac—its fields and its heavy heat and Daddy, always Daddy—in my very bones.

The tiara wasn't large, barely more than a crescent of jewels, but it felt weighty on my head. I smoothed my gown, silvery gray to match my borrowed finery. "Do you think I'm wearing it right?" I reached up, reangling it slightly over my hair.

"You're wearing it correctly. This is marvelous." Perrault stepped smoothly into the corridor. "A proposal tonight, no doubt about it. An ace up our sleeve already, and we've barely begun," he added to Yu and Skop and Cobie. The latter snorted as she stomped into the hall in her usual work boots, yanking on the hem of an out-of-style black dress.

Bear's door stayed closed.

"Cobie, you look wonderful," I offered.

"Thanks." She grasped her skirts in her tanned fists, limbs stiff as a board. "Let's get going."

"Wait. What about Bear?" I blurted out. Yu and Cobie exchanged frowns as Captain Lang searched my face, forehead creased.

"Bear has been removed," said Perrault. "We depart tomorrow. There was no need for him to stay."

I stared at the protocol officer, but his mouth was smug, bleakly victorious.

I'd promised him nothing would happen, and he'd made sure of it. Perrault had won.

Loss wrenched through me as I nodded at him, trying to compose my features into an expression that said, *Yes, of course, that makes sense.* But my heart was a splinter in my chest.

I'd known our time was short. That it was something I only possessed in present moments, not something I could hold for the future.

But I hadn't been ready for the present to be taken from me. And the future had arrived a few hours early, and my time with Bear was over.

It hurt.

Captain Lang did not look at me when he offered me his arm, Adam's apple bobbing in the rigid lines of his neck.

And as on the night we'd arrived, I pretended not to notice, and clasped my shaking hands behind my back.

Every ball and banquet I'd attended in England had been an onslaught, from our first night in Winchester to the last tournament ball. Again and again I'd been overwhelmed, astonished by meeting Bertilak, dazzled with glitter and noise, overpowered by Bear's touch.

Tonight, though, I was numb. England had finally done me in.

I didn't care what happened tonight.

I hardly touched my dinner and didn't want to dance, but I opened the ball with Prince Bertilak anyway, only just remembering to thank him for the tiara, even as it pressed down on my skull. Constantine approached next. When he left me to rejoin his son and Myrddin at the head table, the Earl of Norfolk drew near, reminding me he'd won the joust. I recalled with a pang the ribbon tied to his lance and the rose I'd given Bear, now pressed between the pages of my copy of *Beowulf*.

More than anything, I wished the melee's victor were present to claim me.

As I danced with Norfolk, I watched Myrddin, Bertilak, and Constantine at their table. Were they planning Bear's punishment at that very moment? Had they found us out? Or was the whole of our friendship—of *whatever* we meant to one another—beneath their notice entirely?

Yu and Captain Lang stood in another corner, talking to a woman, their conference quiet but urgent. Though on first glance she seemed to be dressed like the other ladies at the ball, as I studied her more carefully I saw that her elegant blue cloak was drawn tight around a worn dress damp with rain. Pins poked haphazardly from the knot styled high on her head, as though she'd thrown herself together in a hurry.

She glanced around and pressed a folded letter into Lang's hands, marked with a green seal. With a jolt, I noticed the yellow cowslip bloom poking from beneath her cloak.

My eyes met Lang's across the crowded hall.

Criminals?

Not in England's eyes.

A rather reckless group.

Lang's face was pale. I shook my head and turned away.

I wanted to shake him. I wanted to go to my room, to cry and lock my door, to fling the tiara against a wall and watch it shatter into a thousand pieces of emerald and pearl. But I couldn't break down, couldn't embarrass someone else or punish them for my foolishness.

So I shook hands over and over as this earl or that baron introduced himself. I greeted Veery's father, Lord Bedrawt, around the lump in my throat. As Myrddin and Sir Ector discussed his son Kay's performance in the melee, I resisted thoughts of Bear kneeling in front of me, hoping they missed the forlorn note in my voice as I agreed the boys and their friends had fought exceptionally well.

Finally, the clock began to chime midnight, and the crowds drifted off the dance floor. One by one, my crew came to surround me where I stood in the center of the room. Lang, his spare lips tense. Yu, keen eyes scanning the crowd. Cobie, sharp as a knife in her black dress. Skop, broad shoulders near to me, cracking his knuckles. And Perrault. Always Perrault, close by.

Once the crowd stilled, King Constantine spoke.

"Ladies. Gentlemen. A good evening to you," he said. "To our guests, it has been our very great pleasure to host you these two weeks—especially you, Selah, Seneschal-elect.

"This evening, however, I must make you an apology." Constantine glanced at Myrddin, kindly expression faltering.

My pulse leapt. Maybe the prince wouldn't propose, after all. But Skop's angular eyes were uneasy beneath their sparse lashes.

"I hope," said the king, licking his papery lips, "that you will forgive the deception and accept that it was committed in the interest of ensuring honor and trust."

Sir Perrault frowned, eyes blank, but gears were working behind Yu's and Cobie's stares. Lang shook his head, eyes disbelieving.

I didn't know what they made of the king's meandering, but his demeanor was too cheery for me to mistake his intent.

My head throbbed beneath the tiara's weight.

He's going to propose. Think. Think.

Constantine's wrinkled face lit up again. "To be perfectly honest, though, dear, I'm rather pleased you're not the whey-faced baby angel they made you out to be."

Myrddin gave a chiding laugh. "Your Majesty, *please.*"

My stomach turned to stone.

They knew.

They knew.

"Well, I am," insisted Constantine. He shook a finger at me, the gesture as playful as his cloudy blue eyes. "You're a lovely girl, but you weren't too virtuous to decide what you wanted and to take it. And yet, there's not an ounce of real deceit in you." He gave a laugh. "You, my dear, are a perfectly awful liar."

The crowd's eyes were a thousand lit matches pressed to my skin.

I looked to Perrault, but he was silent, dumbstruck. Lang was the first to find a reply, lips curling into something that bore no resemblance to a smile. "Do you have a question to ask the seneschal-elect, or not?"

Constantine glanced to Bertilak. "Do you?" he asked.

Princess Igraine crossed to his side. "I'm afraid not," she said with a laugh, putting a hand on his shoulder in a particularly unsisterly fashion.

Prince Bertilak smiled at me, apologetic. "I'm afraid I'm already spoken for."

It was like being tossed over a cliff. I scrabbled and groped, desperate for a handhold, but found only empty air beneath my flailing feet.

"Then why did you bring me here?" I demanded.

Perrault stepped a little in front of me, expression calm but chilly. His face was pale. "The seneschal-elect was here to court your prince. This is a breach of trust. This is not what was negotiated."

"No, it isn't. Or, not exactly," said a voice behind me. "But I did warn Selah to pay attention."

My breath expired. I didn't turn. I didn't need to.

34

Bear crossed the room amid pleased murmurs, parting the crowd. Far from his typical worn leather jacket, tonight he wore a green tunic and sash, a golden crown on his head. *We match*, I thought faintly.

Silence reigned. My arms and legs began to shake.

"Him?" Lang demanded. His eyes tracked Bear as he joined the prince and king.

"As it happens, I've been married to Igraine for some time now," said Prince Bertilak, taking the hand of the kind princess I'd been told was his sister. "So I'm not searching for a wife, myself."

"And you?" My words to Bear were paper-thin.

Bertilak answered instead. "The seneschal-elect was here as potential bride to my only son, Prince Arthur of England, on whose behalf I would like to propose their marriage."

I stood rooted to the ballroom floor, able only to gawp at

the contented family before me. Basking in her husband's magnanimous glow, Igraine smoothed the hair back from Bear's forehead. Bear—Arthur—her son—ducked his head, grinning.

I had fallen for Bear. And it had been him all along. This changed everything, solved everything.

Didn't it?

I'd hoped for this—for *him*—though I couldn't stay, had never planned to stay. I'd never mentioned that point, the last piece of the truth, to Bear.

And if this solved everything, why was my stomach twisting itself into a knot?

I swallowed, finally meeting his eyes. Bear eyed me, expectant, smiling hesitantly. "You used a false name?" I asked, frowning.

"Bear's a nickname. Not even a very creative one, I've just always been tall." He gave a nervous laugh. "Surely you didn't think I'd been baptized Bear Green, even when I was merely a guard."

Bear's exultant smile faltered as I stepped around Perrault, moved leadenly toward him. "You might've been. I didn't think about it," I said. My mouth didn't want to work properly. "I didn't think you'd make up something like that."

I stared at him, stricken.

"Well, you weren't completely forthcoming yourself, Your Grace," Prince Bertilak cut in, twinkling. "We had a bargain."

"Wh— Huh?" I'd half forgotten Bertilak's presence.

Bertilak raised his eyebrows at me, feigning hurt. "Our deal.

Our exchange at dinner. I brought my quarry to our table every evening, but you failed to do so yourself. Completely ruined our game, lying about your romantic dash through the rain."

Constantine chuckled.

"What are you *talking* about?" I demanded. My breathing was ragged.

Bertilak faltered at the crack in my voice. "I'm sorry. Do forgive me," he said, all traces of mirth gone from his voice. "That was unbecoming. But I— Selah, dear, I was only joking."

"Joking?" I breathed. "You find this funny?"

"No, I'm merely—" Bertilak broke off, dismayed. He glanced to Constantine and Myrddin as if for help.

Myrddin stepped to His Highness's side. "It had to be this way, Seneschal-elect," he said simply. "We rather thought you'd be pleased to learn the truth."

Understanding was a series of *clicks* and *snaps* in my brain, the sound of the truth fitting itself into place, unfolding itself into its natural shape.

Why Bertilak had left me alone, day after day. Why Bear hadn't feared the wrath of his prince or Perrault. Why a guard would study statesmanship or sit at dinner with the king and his children. The old duchess at tea had nearly told me herself—had asked me when I'd met Bear, instead of Bertilak, and then corrected herself as if she'd merely misspoken.

They'd watched me for two weeks, watched me try to please and impress them when they knew they'd set me up. I felt as though they'd sliced open my abdomen to pick through my innards and augur all the secrets I'd thought were mine and Bear's alone.

I'd been blind to it all.

I was going to throw up.

Briefly, fighting nausea, I imagined accepting Bear's proposal, imagined us blissfully in love. The picture tugged at my heart and my will, but how would the court see us?

I saw in the way Constantine nodded reassuringly at his grandson how Bear would be perceived—a romantic, helplessly in love with me. Whatever his sins, they would be forgiven. But I would be remembered quite differently.

I would be painted England's flightiest princess—the girl with no self-control, who gave her heart and lips to one man while being courted by another. Even the truth—their purposes—the fact that I was *right*—would not justify me.

Most of all: If I stayed, if I married him, would I ever really trust him when we'd begun with a lie?

Perhaps another girl would have found the whole affair romantic. But standing before the court, raw and exposed and sadly mistaken, I felt as if I were back in Potomac all over again, searing from the acid sting of Peter's public rejection.

I just wish you'd told me when it was just the two of us.

It never was just the two of us.

Except I knew Bear—I really knew him, and he knew me, and we cared for one another. And still, somehow, I'd found myself naked in front of a crowd.

I shrank back and bumped into Yu, who caught my elbow.

His lips were pressed tightly together, his expression sharp and cold. "Steady," he whispered. Skop, on my right, squeezed my hand.

I cleared my throat, blinking hard. "This is extraordinary."

Bear shook his head, trying to soothe me. "Selah, you don't understand."

"No. I do." I took a shuddering breath. "Was any of it real? Was that even your study?" I asked. My thoughts were shattered.

"Ah. I told you the study was a good idea." Myrddin looked approving. "The melee, too. You worry over him so—but I knew she'd appreciate it," the adviser added, nodding at Bear.

I pressed a hand to my forehead, feeling faint. "So many lies."

"It was one lie." Bear drew near, voice low and reassuring. We were at the center of a crowd, but he put his hands on my face, forcing me to meet his eyes, blue and bright and utterly sincere.

"One enormous lie," I said. "One you told again and again."

"Yes, but just the one," he insisted. "All the rest was true. I wanted to tell you so much, but—but Selah, we got to know one another without any formality, with nothing to come between us. If you knew then what you know now, how difficult it can be to get to know someone on an official basis, would you choose any differently?" He glanced at his father, who nodded encouragingly.

I took one, two steps away from him. The distance grew

between us as it had the day he'd chased me home from the library in the rain.

Except this time, I didn't know if I wanted him to catch me.

I gripped Skop's fingers again, faint with horror and humiliation. Lang simply stared at them all, his dark gaze raw and astonished. "What an elaborate invention."

The weight of the chaos was going to flatten me.

"I think we all ought to calm down," Myrddin suddenly said. His keen eyes were abruptly concerned.

"Calm down?" I bleated.

"Yes." The adviser shook his head, forehead creased. "Discretion was necessary, but all has worked out for the best. No lasting harm has been inflicted." He gestured at Bear, then at me.

No mortal wounds, perhaps, but the scars these boys had left me would remain.

I studied the king and the prince and the royal family, feeling my pulse high and wild at my throat and wrists and the arches of my feet, telling me to *run, run, run.*

And I'd thought Sir Perrault was the only fox I should fear.

My trembling left hand clasped Cobie's palm, Skop's in my right. "Prince Bertilak, thank you for what hospitality you extended. But we're leaving."

Not a sound could be heard in the hall. The royal family stared, speechless.

Shaking from head to foot, I turned to my crew. "The *Beholder.* Let's go."

We pushed out of the ballroom, leaving pandemonium in our wake.

Back in our quarters, Cobie packed my things with joyless efficiency. "Selah, is this your blanket? Or did you find it here?"

"It's not mine," I managed.

She flung open the wardrobe. "Are these all your clothes? Are there more anywhere else?" I shook my head mutely.

I couldn't help her. I couldn't move. I stared blankly into the fire, at the chair still beside it, until she slammed the last trunk closed. "Done. Let's get you out of here."

"Lang and Perrault are handling the formalities," Yu announced grimly as we stalked into the night. He and Skop piled bags onto the waiting cart, boots crunching on the gravel path.

"After what Bertilak's done, this should be simple," Cobie muttered. Lithe as a cat, she leapt onto the tail of the wagon and began arranging our luggage.

Suddenly, we all paused, glancing back at the castle's gray facade. Skop flexed his fingers, then fisted them. "Oh, no way."

But there was no mistaking the sound of the approaching crowd.

Bear skidded onto the gravel path, panting, the end of his sash and the hem of his tunic billowing behind him. "Selah!" Servants and nobles poured outside behind him, Kay and Veery and Tristan at the head of the throng. They surrounded him, wide- and worry-eyed.

"Keep moving," I said darkly, fumbling with the handle on one of Perrault's suitcases. It tumbled from my grasp, its corner tearing a hole in my skirt.

"Selah, please let me—"

Skop put a protective arm around me, and Cobie pulled the knife from her boot, fingers flexing around its handle. "You're going to want to back away from her."

Veery surged forward. "Steady on!"

"Cobie, no," I blurted.

She shoved the knife back into place but continued to glare at Bear. He waved off his friends, and they backed into the crowd, expressions ranging from fury to fear.

I shook my head at him. "Don't make this worse than it already is."

"I can't let you leave without explaining," Bear said, desperate.

"Explain?" I demanded. "You had two weeks to explain the truth to me! You missed your chance to come clean."

"You *must* see, we had to be sure—"

"What? To be sure your whole family had the chance to thoroughly humiliate me with their lies and that stupid game?" My shout was jagged in the damp night air. I dragged the back of my wrist across my tears, clenching my rosary in my other hand. "No. In violation of all convention and my trust, you tricked me." My voice cracked, thin and weary. "I broke the rules for you. I never break the rules, and now I remember why. I won't be so naive again."

233

I turned away from him, making to climb onto the cart.

"Selah, we were worried about your stepmother!" Bear blurted.

I froze. Turned back to him. Drew near.

Bear's chest rose and fell in agitated breaths.

"What did you say?" I whispered.

"Your stepmother," he said again. "Her letter came mere months before your arrival. It was—urgent, pressing. Aggressive." Bear shook his head, eyes luminous, dying to make me understand.

"You lied to me because of a pushy letter?"

"It was more than that," he said. "We take years to consider and plan these unions. She was eager to send you within the twelvemonth. The dowry she offered to send you with was unheard of." He cocked his head, forehead wrinkled with worry. "Besides that, she insinuated that an alliance with you, her stepdaughter, was an alliance with New York." Bear scraped a hand through his hair. "We need willing trade partners. It was all too tempting."

I swallowed. "And you thought—"

"We thought she might be staging something. In league, perhaps, with the tsarytsya. Using you to establish a beachhead from the west. So we took precautions. Father didn't even want me as close to you as I was—he wanted me sent away." Bear wet his lips. "Surely you understand."

My heart throbbed painfully.

The problem was, I did understand.

The Saint George of Constantine's England did not seek dragons on foreign shores. His Saint George didn't slay dragons at all.

It hid from danger. It waited. It had repented of meddling and theft. It defended its own, kept to itself, kept its borders.

I had only ever wanted to do the same.

I had never wanted to be standing here, in a foreign court, navigating such harsh waters as these.

"My father began that game with you when he thought you might be a spy. He was opening negotiations with you. None of us knew you were ignorant of your stepmother's actions."

Sir Perrault and Captain Lang strode toward us, the latter's posture and drawn brows forbidding.

"It's done," said Lang.

Cobie loaded the last trunk onto the wagon and jumped down onto the gravel path.

"It is not done," Perrault said. "The seneschal-elect is not to give her final answer until she has completed her tour."

My throat was tight as I took the tiara from my hair and pressed it into Bear's hands. I watched hurt fill his eyes as he palmed it, gemstones glittering between his fingers.

"Perhaps someday I will return to claim this," I said brokenly. "If I do not, you will be advised."

And if I do not, I thought, *you will know precisely why.*

Bear nodded once, then twice.

I looked to Lang. Gone from his eyes were the frustrated remains of our argument; his jaw was resolute, protective. I could practically see the chip balanced on his shoulder.

He shrugged out of his dark blue jacket and draped it across my shoulders, the canvas heavy and comforting over my thin dress.

And I walked away from Bear. And I walked away from England.

The prince didn't speak as we climbed into the cart. And I didn't look back as we drove off, even as the crowd's murmurs rose into a dull roar. But as we rowed back to the *Beholder*, I cried the entire way.

35

If the *Beholder*'s crew was surprised at our early return, they were even more shocked at the state of us. Cheerful shouts went up as our rowboat drew near, but when Andersen glimpsed my face, they were abruptly cut short. Lang only left my side long enough to summon Will and Vishnu to carry my things downstairs.

More tears and smeared makeup. Another ruined gown. Six weeks had passed, but I was the same girl who'd left Potomac.

Their eyes were more sympathetic than my pride could stand.

As I rushed belowdecks to my room, I would have given anything for my godmother's company, or Daddy's. But the people I loved and trusted had never felt farther away.

Lang went away just long enough to bring me a mug of tea from the galley. He sat by my bedside until I cried myself to sleep.

He was beside my bed again when I woke, my copy of *Beowulf* in one hand, Godmother Althea's book in the other.

"Is this yours?" He held out the smaller volume. "I tripped over it in the hallway."

I tossed it into my trunk. "Bear's."

"I'm sorry."

"Did—did I deserve it?" My voice quavered. "After what I did?"

Lang frowned. "What you did . . . ?"

I rubbed at my eyes, puffy and soft from crying. "The—you know. The lying."

The kiss.

Lang shook his head. "Selah, they set you up to fall for him. The entire court spent two weeks pretending. Like I said, it was an incredibly elaborate lie." He paused, scrubbing a hand through his hair. "You may have broken the rules, but they fixed the whole game. What a stupid gamble."

I didn't respond. I remembered Bear touching my face, sitting in his study in front of the fire, coming to my door at dawn.

I'd known my courtship was a farce. I just hadn't realized I was the one being played.

And now, I had one fewer buffer between me and the Imperiya.

Lang's brow furrowed. His eyes were soft. "You're going to be all right," he said.

He offered me my godmother's book. I cleared my throat and accepted it, dropping it on my bed and flipping quickly past the English fairy tales.

Something crackled, and I froze. I stared up at Lang, wide-eyed. "What was that?"

And then I heard her. My godmother.

"*Selah.*" The voice was muffled, but it was unmistakably hers. "Selah, if you can hear me, I'm here."

"What is that?" I scrambled backward, sitting upright in bed.

"Selah, it's been over six weeks, so you must be through your first visit by now. I don't know if you can hear me." I clapped a hand to my mouth. Lang seized the book and flipped swiftly through its pages, jewel-bright illuminations blurring past.

The back endpaper was covered with the story of the Beauty and the Beast. A calligraphed poem filled its center.

> Welcome, Beauty, banish fear,
> You are queen and mistress here;
> Speak your wishes, speak your will,
> Swift obedience meets them still.

I froze as Lang took a knife and deftly pried the endpaper from beneath the thick green cover. "What are you—"

But there, buried inside the binding, was a small black box.

My godmother was still speaking from its mouth.

"I've mostly tried to talk to you at night, when I thought you'd be alone. But I hope you can hear this, sweet girl, and I hope you're on your way again. I hope your first visit is over, wherever it was. And I want you to know that everything is all right here. Your father is fine. Alessandra hasn't made any moves. Everything is fine."

I turned the box over in my hands, clumsy and desperate. "Godmother?" I blurted. "Godmother Althea?" Tears pricked at my eyes. My heart was a stampede. But she didn't answer.

"She won't be able to hear you." Lang's dark gaze was careful beneath his lashes.

I wiped my cheeks. "How do you know?"

"It's too small to be a transmitter. Without a tower to send out a signal, it's a receiver only." He paused. "It's called a radio."

A *radio*. I swallowed. "How do you know?"

Lang studied me. "The same way I knew that cover was thick enough to smuggle you something." He eyed a dial on the radio, then pointed to the bottom corner of the endpaper. "Do you see this number, three-point-four-four?"

I frowned, then flipped a page back. "It's the wrong page number. And anyway, an endpaper wouldn't be numbered."

Lang nodded. "Because this isn't a page number. It's the frequency your godmother's using."

What is Lang, I wondered, *besides a sailor?*

He studied me. "You haven't been communicating with her. You had no idea this was here."

I shook my head.

Everything is all right here. Your father is fine. . . . Everything is fine.

"I've been so worried," I whispered.

"I know. This is good." Lang smiled and passed a hand over my hair. I stilled at the feel of his palm against my neck. His lean fingers ran down a stray lock and tucked it behind my ear.

"Will you help me find a—" I broke off. "What did you call it?"

"A transmitter?" Lang asked. I nodded. He frowned, thinking. "I've seen only two in my life—both in Zhōng Guó."

"They're rare?"

He nodded. "This radio is powered by a battery; I'm not even sure where your godmother would have found one. The transmitters are much larger, and require much more power. The kind of power we hardly even have on our side of the Atlantic. I'd guess it's rare in Europe."

Maybe whoever helped her smuggle the radio to me had helped her first lay hands on it.

I wouldn't know. Nobody told me anything.

I chewed my lip, running my fingers over the leather I knew so well and the black box so unfamiliar to me. "I want to talk to her," I whispered. "I have to."

"I'll help you," Lang said. "I promise."

Even with the weight of the radio in my hand, I felt lighter. Bear had ripped me apart, but Godmother Althea—just her voice, spirited to me by magic and machine—had pieced me back together.

I sat forward on the bed, cross-legged. "Thank you for last night," I said. "You and Cobie and Skop and Yu—you stood with me."

"That's our place," Lang said, voice quiet and tight. His knee bumped mine; he didn't move it. "That's where we belong. Between you and everyone else."

I glanced up. Beneath his arching eyebrows and heavy

lashes, I read not quite an apology but a ceasefire. And when I said thank you again, Lang understood, too: I'd accept his truce and let him keep his secrets.

After all, I had mine.

After that, Godmother Althea spoke to me every night. Lang showed me how to adjust the radio's volume and frequency, how to angle its antenna to hear her more clearly, how to replace it within the book's thick binding to hide it when I was done.

Night after night. Story after story. Five marks on the back endpaper, each little scratch a step closer to Norge.

Their prince was my last best chance. The only one not bound permanently to his home by the responsibilities of a firstborn son.

If I could persuade him to propose, I could be mere weeks away from home. From Daddy.

If I couldn't, the Imperiya *fürst* was waiting.

I tried to forget about all of them. The ones ahead, and the one behind.

Ne pisses pas dans un violon, Jeanne had told me in indignation when the crew heard what had happened at court.

Don't . . . urinate in a violin? I'd asked, confused.

Her amber eyes had flashed as she'd shaken her head. *Do not waste your efforts on good-for-nothing boys. Do not cast your pearls before swine.*

I'd tried to laugh. I wanted not to believe Bear's eyes and hands and heart had left their marks on me for good.

I tried not to fear I would never make it home at all.

When I wasn't falling asleep reading fairy tales, waiting for the sound of my godmother's voice, I was working in the galley, gardening on deck. Will had cared for my plants as best he could, but they'd withered a little while I was away. I dug into them now, softening up the earth around their tender shoots, watering them carefully. Within a day or two, life came back into their leaves, green and full as they ever were. I plucked sprigs of rosemary and put them under my pillow, hoping their scent would ease my sleep.

And the crew filled my head with words, drawing me into their circles and their stories. We sat side by side on deck late into the night all that week, Skop and Yu at my sides, Lang at the helm, or sketching, if Homer or one of the others was steering. Perrault stayed in his quarters, but even Cobie kept company with us, in her own way. She sat in the crow's nest overhead, her black clothes flapping in the wind like a pirate's flag beneath Potomac's blue-and-gold standard.

We were a mere day from Norge the night I turned to Yu, my voice quiet beneath the sailors' voices and the waves washing over the hull.

Lang had told me their place was between me and everyone else.

I wondered if that applied to Alessandra and the ones who'd forced me away from home. If the crew would stand by my father, as well as by me.

I believed they would.

"Yu," I whispered, "you're a doctor. Can I ask you a question?"

He nodded, looking concerned. "Of course. Are you all right?"

"I'm fine," I said quickly. "But—if someone lost a lot of weight in a short time—someone who wasn't trying to, they just didn't have any appetite—what would you suspect was wrong?"

Yu frowned. "Well, weight loss can be symptomatic of many conditions, but without more information, it would be difficult to say."

I thought of my father, of how weak he'd looked before I left. "Sleeplessness. Tremors. Says he has pins and needles in his hands. I think his vision's getting worse, too." I shook my head. "He's just not himself lately."

"Who are we talking about?" Yu's broad forehead creased.

I studied my hands, picking at a cuticle. "My father."

How I wanted to get home to him.

For a brief moment, I wondered if accepting Bear would have saved us. If returning home right away with a fiancé at my side and the English crown behind me would have put an end to all our problems.

The question had risen in my mind again and again, threatening to follow me around like a shadow through my days aboard ship, to stand at the foot of my bed at night. I cast it away once more and turned back to Yu.

Yu was from Zhōng Guó. I'd heard medicine there was more advanced than it was at home. Surely Yu could help me. Surely he would have the answers I needed.

He rubbed his forehead. "Let me think on that," he said

slowly. "I want to consult a few texts before I wor—" Yu broke off. "Before I weigh in."

Before I worry you, he was going to say.

I walked the deck that night before I went to bed, savoring the feel of the wood against the soles of my feet, walking heel-toe, quiet beneath the dark sky full of stars. As I crossed the forecastle, the breeze ruffling my hair, I caught sight of the fig-urehead at the prow.

The ocean had washed away the hideous wine stain Alessandra had smashed across her chest. Her bloodied body had healed, scrubbed clean by salt water and time.

When I crawled into bed, I studied the tick marks I'd made at the back of my book.

Time was passing, and time would heal my hurt.

But time was running out for me.

And time was running out for Daddy.

Hwæt! We Gardena in geardagum,
þeodcyninga, þrym gefrunon,
hu ða æþelingas ellen fremedon.
—Bēopulf

Lo! the Spear-Danes' glory through splendid achievements
The folk-kings' former fame we have heard of,
How princes displayed then their prowess-in-battle.
—*Beowulf*

36

LYSEFJORD, NORGE: ASGARD FORTRESS

Five days after departing Winchester, we sailed into the Lysefjord.

I sat cross-legged against the foremast of the creaking ship, arms wrapped around my knees, wonderstruck beneath the cliffs towering to our left and right. Though the day was cloudy, the hulking walls of stone on either side of the fjord gleamed with an otherworldly light, ethereal and substantial all at once. Veins of greenery running down the pale rock were the only hint that summer was coming.

This would be a forbidding place in winter, but even in early June, the fjord was ancient and weather-worn, sparse and lonely in a way that Winchester and Potomac were not.

Homer summoned me from the helm, pointing with a chapped hand at the cliffs. "The northern edge of Mount

Kjerag, Your Grace, and the home of Asgard Fortress."

I squinted at the summit. "I don't see a fortress. All I see is a grove of—" But my own gasp cut me off.

From the cliff top grew what must have been a hundred trees grown into one, mountainous in size, its branches spreading wide enough to obscure the stronghold behind it. What I had taken for an irregularity in the rock face were its knotted trunk and curling maze of roots grasping at the fjord. The oaks and maples that twisted through Arbor Hall were saplings, by comparison.

The tree felt like an omen, though whether good or evil I couldn't say.

A faint gleam in Homer's gray eyes was his only acknowledgment of the wonder in mine. "The great ash tree, Yggdrasil. Those are its roots in the Bilröst—that's what they call this fjord."

I swallowed. "What do you know about this place?"

"I've never been here," Vishnu offered wryly, rubbing at the back of his neck, "but I'll tell you this: from what I hear, if they throw you a tournament, the king won't be watching from a throne."

Below the cliffs and the great ash tree, Lysefjord's harbor was a menagerie of ships. Bright rowboats bobbed like golden finches and bluebirds alongside huge vessels whose swooping prows and sterns were carved like horses and sea snakes. As Homer called out orders and the crew brought the *Beholder* to port among them, Andersen pressed my hand between his. "Good luck, girl. I hope you find what you're looking for."

I smiled at his kindness, at his soft Savannah accent that so reminded me of my mother and Godmother Althea. "You, too." I paused, laughing. "I mean, thank you."

Andersen gave me a funny look, pushing his graying blond hair out of his eyes, and nodded. "I knew what you meant."

The crew carried our bags down the gangplank and onto a wagon. I waved feverishly back at Vishnu and Homer and Basile and Yu and the others as huge golden horses drew our cart away, up a road carved into the cliffside that led us past wide fields of grain and a village of long, low homes. Tall, broad-shouldered people wiped their hands on rough-knit sweaters and paused in their work as we rattled by.

Sitting between Captain Lang and me, J.J. shrank from their stares, biting his nails and jiggling his leg.

I thought of asking Lang why he was bringing J.J. ashore instead of Yu. J.J. was barely in his teens, and while he made himself useful aboard ship and made good company in general, I wasn't sure what he'd do for two weeks at court. But even after several days at sea, my peace with Lang felt tentative— delicate, even. I hesitated to question him, even in this.

In the meantime, Skop rambled, warm and reassuring, on my left, and Perrault and Cobie bickered quietly in the other cart. But when the fortress came into view over a gargantuan stone wall crowned with iron spikes, none of us could find words.

Asgard Fortress was a soaring thing built of earth and sky. Massive gray stones were fitted tightly between wall-size windows. Strong iron beams marked its corners and the seams between glass and rock.

But what took my breath away was the tree. Arbor Hall was a cloistered forest, but Yggdrasil's trunk was part of the fortress itself, its branches and leaves spreading higher than the highest chimney rising from its slate roof. Fitted snugly between the summit of Mount Kjerag and the great tree, Asgard was a stern, proud thing, both airy and solid on the precipice overlooking the fjord. Guards waved us through the forbidding gates, and I climbed down after my friends, openmouthed and still as they began to unload our carts.

"Now? Right now?" came Perrault's voice, irritated. The guard at his side nodded, authoritative.

"What's going on?" Lang asked, approaching the guard.

Cobie hopped down from her wagon to join him, nimble as a cat.

Lang turned to me. "We've been summoned to meet Konge Alfödr in Valaskjálf, the great hall, immediately." He shook his head. "I'm sorry."

Perrault pursed his lips, pretty face tense, as if our being beckoned so abruptly had thrown him off-balance.

I had no time to prepare—and no time to fret over it. "It's fine." I nodded tightly at the guard and the fortress's broad front doors. "Lead on."

Loud laughter and boisterous conversation rang down the

fortress's corridors as we followed our guide toward Valaskjálf, dodging and darting out of the paths of large, broad-shouldered strangers. I slid my trembling fingers over the rosary in my pocket and thought of the suitors' files I'd studied so many times.

Prins Torden of Asgard was the only one not set to inherit his throne, the loophole in Alessandra's plan.

He was my only chance if I hoped to meet my stepmother and the Council's demands and return home with a fiancé.

He was my only chance if I hoped to avoid the Imperiya.

I was jostled out of concentration as a half-dozen or so unruly boys and a girl pushed past us. To a one, they were good-looking and tall—I hardly reached the shoulder of the boy with glasses who apologized as he knocked into Perrault—and most of them were broad and blond. But one boy was fine-boned and narrow-shouldered with a shock of dark hair, and another was redheaded with the coppery scruff of a beard on his chin. I squeezed out of the way as they hurried on, feeling my pink cardigan snag on the corridor's stone wall. But somehow I caught his eye.

I stopped short, and so did he—the redheaded boy, his jaw tense, raw shock burning in his gaze. The remnants of a greenish-yellow bruise brooded over his left cheekbone.

I knew him on sight.

Halfway down the hall, the pack of boys and the girl halted at a word from the black-haired boy. He held up a hand to them, studying me through narrowed eyes.

"Torden," called the blond boy with the glasses. "Pappa will be angry if we're late."

I forgot to breathe as the redheaded boy's brown eyes slid from my face to my sweater to my nervously clasped hands. I watched the space where he'd stood long after he'd cleared his throat and marched off with his friends.

Torden.

37

We caught the rumble of male voices before we even reached the great hall's entrance.

Valaskjálf was enormous, imposing as the fortress itself, as unlike Arbor Hall's quiet, green warmth as possible.

Three walls were of stone; one was formed entirely by Yggdrasil's hundred trunks. Huge, roaring fires threw light on men sitting shoulder to shoulder at long wooden tables, on high, vaulted ceilings, on tapestries and weapons and armor and—

I gripped Skop's arm. "Why are there dead animals on the walls?" Deer and moose heads and preserved fish leered from on high, bodies still, eyes glassy.

"Calm down," he hissed. "They're trophies."

An outstretched spear stopped our progress into the hall. "This is Selah, Seneschal-elect of Potomac," said Lang, eyes flinty as he faced its owner. The guard shook his head, calling to another soldier. I only understood one word—*Engelsk*. English.

"No stranger enters Valaskjálf who carries war-graith," said a second guard, extending a basket. His accent was melodic, with flattened *a*s and guttural *l*s and a pleasant lilt unsuited to his scowl.

Cobie and Lang exchanged a glance. But Skop was already tugging a knife from his boot, and another from a belt beneath his shirt, so the others did the same, though Cobie looked sullen. J.J. pulled a dagger from each pocket, grinning at my wide eyes. Sir Perrault only scoffed as the first guard looked him over.

"And her weapons?" asked the second guard, nodding at me. "What sort of princess travels unarmed?"

"I'm not a—"

"Does she look like she's armed?" Lang broke in, brows arched.

The guard surveyed me briefly and, evidently deciding I posed no threat, strode up the center aisle toward the front of the room, calling out first in Norsk, and then in English. "The Seneschal-elect of Potomac seeks an audience with you, my liege, and your royal sons."

Across the room, all eyes turned toward the head table, awaiting the response of the man at its center.

This was the king of Asgard, famed Shield of the North.

His hard-muscled forearms lay on armrests carved with the head and a tail of a snake, and a cast-iron horse strode across his chair's high top rail. Konge Alfödr looked to be in his midforties and wore a patch over his left eye, but his visible right eye was knife-sharp blue, and powerful muscles moved under his homespun shirt; age had not softened him.

I thought of Daddy, thin and brittle-boned, and suddenly felt sad.

I wished he would even have the chance for the years to render him soft and comfortable. I wished even more that he possessed a tenth of the strength this man wore like armor.

I wished most of all that I were in his hall, instead of Alfödr's.

Broad-shouldered and stone-faced, with a thick head of graying blond hair and a full beard, he was immediately identifiable. I knew the king of Norge at once, as surely as I'd known the redheaded boy now sitting a few places to his left was his fifth son, Torden Asgard.

The king rose and beckoned us, and silence fell as we trooped up the middle of the room. "Strangers," he said in a gravelly voice, accent lilting like the guard's. "Long have we awaited your arrival. Well met, and welcome to Asgard Fortress."

He gestured to the woman beside him, perhaps ten years younger than he. "This is Dronning Rihttá, my wife." His queen, the *dronning*, was dark-haired, with a round face, fawn-colored skin like Skop's, and a beautiful figure. Her narrow, angular eyes were a deep, smoky shade, and strikingly sad.

"Hail, Seneschal-elect," she said, "and welcome to Asgard."

I curtsied low. "Thank you for your hospitality, Your Majesties."

The queen cast a canny look to Alfödr's left and right. "And this," she added, "is our family." I sucked in a long breath, clasping my hands behind my back.

The king nodded. "First: I present Kronprins Týr, and Vidarr and Váli." Three blond, burly men rose from their seats, two of them twins. Their features were weak, their eyes watery blue and disinterested.

At a wave from the king, another pair stood—two of the boys we'd passed in the hallway. They had their older brothers' coloring but lacked their enormous physiques, though they were still sturdier than the boys at home. "My sons Bragi and Hermódr," said Alfödr. Bragi had curly blond hair and a face almost too symmetrical to be real. Hermódr—the one who'd jostled Perrault and beckoned Torden in the corridor—pushed up his glasses and smiled reassuringly at me, apparently not missing my locked knees and trembling limbs.

"It's a pleasure." I cringed at the creak in my voice, and a few of the men who'd been close enough to hear gave low laughs.

"Baron Aleksei, not of the house of Asgard, but of Yotunkheym." The *konge* nodded, and another boy stood, pale and as dark-haired as the others were light—the sharp-boned, sharp-eyed one who'd studied me so carefully in the corridor.

One of the Yotne, at Asgard?

The boy's mouth curved slowly at my evident surprise.

"Prinssi Fredrik, and his sister Prinsessa Anya, of Varsinais-Suomi." Alfödr nodded again, and the last blond boy and the only girl at the head table stood together.

The boy was almost as cute as Bragi—another charmer, for sure—and the girl was slender but broad-shouldered, with blond hair braided into a halo around her head. A necklace sparkled against her pale skin, woven strands of cloth of gold dotted with amber stones that reflected the firelight. "Anya will be your companion while you remain here," added Konge Alfödr, and she gave me a smile.

But I could only stare. The eastern Norden countries—including Anya and Fredrik's kingdom of Varsinais-Suomi—had fallen to the Imperiya Yotne a decade earlier. Even its name was no more. As a *terytoriya*, Yotunkheym called it Finlyandiya.

So the tsarytsya did. With teeth like knives and spears and armies, she chewed up an independent nation and spat out something entirely different.

And here was one of the Imperiya's sons, sitting at table with them. Disquiet was a deep, cold pool in my stomach.

What was he doing here?

Konge Alfödr cleared his throat. "Last, may I present to you my son Prins Torden." As the red-haired boy rose, only the fireplaces continued to whisper.

The Asgard boys were an attractive group. They had clean jawlines and straight noses (except where they'd apparently been broken, and they couldn't fault nature for that). Muscles that bespoke years of healthy eating and hard work filled out their button-up shirts and the rough pants tucked into their boots. But Torden stood out among them. He defied comparison.

Torden Asgard was handsome in a way entirely indelicate and unpolished—rough and ready and serious, deep-chested and thick-limbed and fair-skinned. Dark brown eyes burned above his snub nose, and a scruffy, red-gold beard lined his jaw. Sleeves rolled to his elbows revealed arms and hands as freckled as his face, and a tattoo inside his left wrist.

He was so good-looking it made me nervous. Just the sight of him made me hesitate to try to win his affections.

But I had to try. He was my best—my only—choice.

I fought the urge to fiddle with the hem of my cardigan as he sat back down with his brothers, gaze still fixed on me, guardedness mingled with something else I couldn't quite read.

Trying to drum up some bravery, I glanced from Captain Lang to J.J. to Cobie. She nodded, eyes bracing.

"My father, the seneschal, sends his greetings and his gratitude for your welcome," I called. "Allow me to introduce the crew of my ship, the *Beholder*." The sailors dipped their heads or bowed as I gave their names. When I introduced Skop, he straightened, blushing and shaking himself out of a daze. I followed his gaze and found he'd been staring at Anya.

"Well met, and welcome," said Konge Alfödr again. "Please, join us."

Sir Perrault must have seen the sheer cowardice in my eyes as I started toward an open bench nearby. "No." He took my wrist. "The head table. Sit with the *prins*."

I yanked my arm from his grasp and glared at him. Lang stepped between us, a dangerous look on his face.

"Do not repeat the errors you committed in England," Perrault said. His voice was quiet—but his tone was almost pleading. I exhaled a long breath, gritting my teeth in frustration.

We were interrupted by Anya rushing forward, beaming at us. "Come and sit down!" Skop returned her lilting invitation with a blank stare and slack jaw, so I took his elbow.

Then I nodded at Perrault, begrudging, and followed Anya toward the boys seated on Alfödr's right.

Lang watched me walk up the aisle and took the rest of the crew to the *konge*'s left, near the older of Konge Alfödr's sons. As Cobie, Perrault, and J.J. followed him, I noticed the queen watching J.J., her expression unguardedly sad—almost hungry.

A stuffed, silently *yawp*ing moose head on the wall caught my eye as we wove up the aisle. "Unbelievable." I shuddered, nudging Skop.

But Skop didn't answer. His eyes didn't leave Anya as she led us to the front of the hall, pausing here and there to smile and fill mugs from foaming pitchers scattered across the long tables. Glasses rose to her as she passed.

I nudged him again gently with my shoulder. "You're going to burn holes through her, Skop." He blushed bright red.

"She's perfect," he said, disbelieving.

"You met her three minutes ago," I pointed out, not very helpfully.

"So? You only have two weeks at each court. Your time crunch elevates our whole situation."

I had two weeks to succeed with Torden, if I hoped to avoid the Imperiya and get home to Daddy quickly. My pulse rose suddenly. "It's protocol," I snapped, "it's not *my*—"

"Shush," he cut me off. Anya stopped short, and I walked right into her. Right in front of Torden and his brothers.

38

I gawked at the five Asgard boys. "Evening," Skop supplied, finding me temporarily mute.

Anya directed me to a chair across from Torden, and I pulled it out, wincing as its legs screeched.

"The queen seems glad to finally meet you," offered one of them.

Dronning Rihttá was still stealing glances at J.J. at the far end of the table. If this counted as upbeat, her melancholy must be miserable.

"I'm glad—um . . ." I trailed off.

"Hermódr." He winked behind his glasses.

"Right. Hermódr," I repeated, serving myself from the platters of roast goose and cabbage at the center of the table. "This would be much harder if your mother didn't like me."

Aleksei scoffed. My throat tightened as I studied him— pale and dark-haired, an Imperiya Wolf sitting at a table with them as though there were nothing strange about it at all. But he sat just as easy as the rest of them. "Rihttá is actually their stepmother," he answered me. "Shame. Inheriting her face would have been lucky. You all got stuck with your father's looks, Torden excepted."

Anya's brother, Fredrik, rolled his eyes. "Yes, poor, ill-favored Bragi suffers especially." One of the boys—Bragi, the perfect one—barked a laugh. At my side, Anya's fingers tightened around her knife and fork, and her mouth thinned.

"Dronning Rihttá is from Sápmi," she said quietly in my ear, referring to the land of roving hunters north of Alfödr's kingdom. "The *kongen* had never been married before he married her about fifteen years ago."

"I—oh. Of course." I glanced over again at the queen. She was obviously too young to be their mother. Alfödr's oldest sons looked at least twenty-five.

"None of us here are hers by birth, but Hermódr might as well be." Torden scratched his beard and nodded at his brother. I blinked, caught off guard by his deep voice. This close, I could see his eyelashes were the color of rose gold.

I didn't know what he meant by *none of us here*—were they hiding more brothers somewhere? "There are a lot of you," I mumbled, poking at my plate.

"Well, you're not going to confuse any of us with Týr and the twins." Hermódr pushed up his glasses and nodded down the table, where Alfödr's oldest sons tore into their dinner, shouting over one another. I cringed. Týr had food around his mouth—goose fat and foam from his beer. Cobie, no manners

264

mistress herself, sat among them in grim silence.

"Poor Selah." Aleksei leapt up to stand behind me. "Never fear. We are easy to remember, once you get to know us."

I only had time to register Torden's horrified expression before Aleksei seized my shoulders and twisted me toward Anya. "Our *prinsessa* is beloved, but no one is prettier than Bragi." He flicked a hand past her at Alfödr's fine-featured son. Bragi smiled tightly.

"And yet"—Aleksei gave my shoulders another tug, forcing me to face Anya's brother—"no one does better with the ladies than Fredrik."

Fredrik opened his mouth to protest, but Aleksei only raised his voice in my ear. "Hermódr is studious, impressively responsible, the only real grown-up among us."

"Hmmph." Hermódr rubbed his eyes beneath his glasses as though he had a headache. "Perhaps if I'm in a room alone with you."

My head was spinning. "What about you, Aleksei?"

"Me?" Aleksei jerked my shoulders backward with no warning, looming over me, eyes dark in his pale face. "Oh, I'm trouble, and that's all you need to know about me."

Perrault had warned me what a slight to the Imperiya would mean: danger, a massive misstep with political ramifications for Potomac. Did that apply here, to Aleksei, as oddly as he was behaving?

But when I glanced at Anya and the other boys, I found them rolling their eyes and shaking their heads, as if they found the whole display a little childish and nothing more.

I gave a trembling laugh, all nerves. "I consider myself fore-warned."

Aleksei winked. "Doesn't matter. The only person you have to impress on this visit"—he set me gently upright—"is Torden."

I faced the redheaded boy across from me, cheeks burning. "Any advice?"

"He's got a nasty temper." Aleksei leaned down to stage-whisper in my ear. "And he gets physical quickly." He glanced at the others for their reaction.

Fredrik laughed generously as I gaped. At Skop's sharp glance, Anya swatted at Aleksei. "Stop it. You know what she thinks you mean."

Torden cracked an embarrassed smile and scratched at the scruff on his chin. "I never pick the fights."

Oh. I'd misinterpreted Aleksei's comment—he'd intended me to. Relief flooded me. But Torden's siblings had dissolved again into scoffing and eye-rolling.

"What?" Torden demanded. "I do not look for trouble. I don't begin fights."

"You finish them," Bragi teased.

"Someone has to. You never complain when I am taking your punches," Torden said calmly. "Come on, don't make me look bad in front of Selah." He glanced at me, a smile catching the corner of his mouth, and something jolted in my stomach.

I thought of Bear—how, time and again, I'd felt my heart in my throat at the look in his eyes. *Too soon,* chorused my thoughts. I bit my lip.

Fredrik elbowed him. "She ought to know what to expect."

I changed the subject again. "What *should* I expect?" I asked. "From this visit, I mean."

Hermódr shrugged. "Most of our days proceed according to routine. We train together. Eat here together. Visit the village to help out as we can."

"And you'll be here for Midsummer's Eve!" Aleksei exclaimed. Hermódr swallowed hard and glanced away, silent. The others suddenly seemed very interested in their plates.

"Midsummer's Eve may be different this year," Torden muttered, sawing at his food.

But Aleksei ignored the warning in his tone. "We have to!" he protested. "It's bad luck not to have the bonfires."

"Did the bonfires bring Baldr or Hodr any luck last year?" Torden asked, suddenly fierce. "Or the rest of us?"

"Boys," Anya said softly, laying a hand on each of their arms. Torden's tensed, veins rising; Aleksei's looked fragile beside it, his bones delicate as a bird's. Neither boy said anything.

Suddenly, Fredrik threw down his fork and knife, stretching and yawning. "I need to get some sleep."

"You mean you need to go meet Kjerstin or Ida or Janne or whoever it is this week," Aleksei snickered.

Fredrik glared at Aleksei. "It's Lisbet, and this time is different." At this, even Torden gave a good-natured snort.

Hermódr leaned forward to tousle Fredrik's hair. "Where have we heard that before?"

Fredrik slapped Hermódr's hand away. Before I knew what was happening, Anya's brother had seized Hermódr by the collar and they were wrestling over the stone floor. Men nearby cheered as Bragi and Torden jumped in—Bragi to defend Fredrik, Torden taking Hermódr's side. I jumped back, and so did Aleksei, casting a quick glance at Alfödr, but Skop and Anya hovered close, amused.

"But Hermódr's glasses . . . ?" I asked sheepishly.

Skop gave me a wry look that said, *Don't be a stick in the mud.*

"Will be fine," Anya hurried to reassure me. "They are only playing. Brothers," she sighed, flashing Skop a winning smile. His ears turned pink.

I shrugged, envying her the easy companionship of the boys whooping and tumbling over the floor. Her friends—her brothers. "I wouldn't know."

The Asgard boys jostled Fredrik good-naturedly—Bragi calling after him with advice, Aleksei with inappropriate suggestions—as they headed off to bed and he left to find Lisbet, wherever she was.

Anya installed the *Beholder* crew where there was space for us to stay—Captain Lang, J.J., and Perrault in a room near Valaskjálf, Cobie with a stranger. I pitied her, but she didn't seem to mind. Skop was given a room just large enough for one, and from the coats and boots heaped along the far wall, I suspected it had been a closet before our arrival. His single bag waited on the iron bed that filled the rest of the space.

"Please call on me if you need anything, First Mate Koniag," Anya said with a smile. "We are not far."

He pushed his dark hair off his forehead, grinning

unselfconsciously. "Please, Prinsessa. Call me Skop."

"If you like." His smile broadened as Anya batted her lashes and pushed through the very next door.

Yes! Skop mouthed, punching the air.

I stifled a laugh. *Sucker,* I mouthed back. I ignored his gentle but profane silent response and followed Anya into her room.

Anya flopped on her bed, blond wood like the rest of her furniture. I held up my rosary and pointed to one of the bedposts. "Do you mind if I . . . ?"

She shook her head, unconcerned. "Not at all. We'll have this room to ourselves."

It had never occurred to me that we wouldn't, though Anya's quarters were much larger than Skop's. Her room was built of stone, like his, but its far wall was a single pane of glass, reflecting the crackling fire and the tapers in the angular iron chandelier. I pressed my face close to its chilly surface and found we were nestled in Yggdrasil's branches, overlooking the Lysefjord.

"The boys aren't so lucky," she added. "The *drengs,* the young warriors, sleep four to a room in the *brakker.*"

"Isn't that a little crowded?" I'd never even shared a room with *one* person, let alone three.

Anya laughed. "Welcome to Asgard. Everything here—the big windows, big rooms, big tables—is designed for people who don't care about comfort and who can't stand to be indoors. Or alone."

As I sank down on a fur rug in front of my trunk, staring out Anya's window at the ash tree, a memory flooded my mind—a game of hide-and-seek I'd lost to Momma when I was little. I'd startled a bunch of butterflies from the trunk of an American ash in Arbor Hall, and she'd come running at my shouts. Momma found me shrieking with laughter, twirling in a cloud of raven-dark mourning cloaks and brown-winged hickory hairstreaks.

I wanted to hide somewhere quiet with my book and my godmother's voice. I wanted to climb out Anya's window, out of this fortress of stone and too many soldiers, and hide in Yggdrasil's branches until I could breathe again.

Careful not to jostle the radio in the binding, I opened my book and made one more tick mark on the back endpaper.

Thirteen days left. Thirteen days, and then I would be faced with the Imperiya: with crossing its borders, or with convincing Lang and Perrault to spare me and let me go home to my father, with Torden or without him.

"You get used to it." Anya's gentle voice broke into my thoughts.

I considered how charming she'd been at dinner, how awkward I'd been, by comparison. "You certainly have."

She gave a low laugh. "I didn't have much choice. Our people—the ones who survived—fled to Asgard after the Imperiya took my father's throne."

"I'm sorry," I said softly.

Anya's bed creaked as she peered over my shoulder and crawled onto the floor. I shifted, shielding my book; but then I saw her eyeing the contents of my trunk with interest. "We should hang up some of your things."

"Oh. Thank you." I set my book aside and passed her the green lace gown I'd worn in Winchester. Anya placed it in her wardrobe, fingers reverent. "And Aleksei?" I asked, tentative. "When did he arrive?"

"Yotne-born, but he's lived at Asgard since he was seven. His father was the tsarytsya's ambassador to Norge until he died."

"And he stayed here after?" I asked.

Anya frowned, dropping her gaze. "In the Imperiya, few parents raise their children at all; the tsarytsya claims and fosters most of them, some in her very house. Alfödr didn't want to send Aleksei back to her, so he adopted him—Fredrik and me, too."

"That was kind of him."

Anya nodded. "Aleksei had lived in Asgard for several years by then. Who knows what he had learned about Norge in that time?" She shrugged. "Alfödr was kind to adopt him, but it was a strategic decision, as well."

I nodded, fiddling with a pair of pajamas. Thoughts of the tsarytsya made my stomach tight with anxiety; but Torden and the others had seemed at dinner to look on Aleksei more as an endearing annoyance than anyone dangerous, or even upsetting.

How must it be to have your enemy's son for a brother?

But if Aleksei hadn't lived in the Imperiya since he was a boy, surely that made him more a son of Asgard than a son of Yotunkheym.

I glanced back at Anya, passing her another dress. She hung it. "So you just live here like brothers and sisters?"

Anya bobbed her head side to side, as if she were thinking. Her eyes and her smile were so bright, I almost didn't notice the way she tugged at her gold necklace as she cleared her throat. "Something like that."

She was asleep when the transmission came.

Anya's breathing had long gone steady beside me when I heard my godmother's voice, muffled through the leather covers of the book and the trunk around it.

Hey there, sweet girl. I hope you can hear me; I just got back from services.

I crept silently out of the bed and sat on the floor to listen as Godmother Althea made quiet, one-sided conversation, as though I were a sick or elderly relative, too tired or confused to respond. My failure to reply didn't matter; she was simply keeping company with someone she thought might be lonely.

So on and on she rambled, about how the lector had lost his place during a reading, about the flowers they'd arranged on the altar that week.

It was almost as good as being at home.

They, ah, brought a wheelchair along for your daddy this past Sunday, Godmother added. *Just in case. They do that a lot now.* My throat tightened.

Did Torden and his brothers know how lucky they were, to know only their father's strength and power? To know he would always be there, would never fail to protect them?

But he's carrying on, sweet girl, she added. *I hope you are, too.*

I am, I thought at her, wishing she could hear me. *And I will.*

39

I awoke to find Anya traipsing around the room like a fairy princess, practically singing with the dawn.

"Good morning," she lilted.

I blinked at her. In the golden light sloping in through Yggdrasil's leaves, she reminded me of nothing so much as a ballerina on the stage.

Anya gave a cheerful laugh at my nonresponse and forced me into an outfit nearly identical to hers—a dress, undershirt, and some wool tights—and dragged me to Valaskjálf. Heads turned from their breakfasts to follow her willowy frame and halo braid as she flitted between the tables.

"Just a minute," I told her, glancing at the other end of the high table.

Perrault sat near one of the twins, eating fruit with a fork and a knife. Properly, of course. I made my way toward him.

"Good morning, Sir Perrault." I planted my hands across

from him on the table, still standing. His eyes slowly wandered up to meet mine.

"Good morning, Seneschal-elect. In what way can I be of service?"

I cleared my throat. "I was wondering if you'd determined my schedule for this stay." I glanced nervously back at the boys seated around Anya.

Watching them, big and boisterous and entirely too many, I suddenly longed for the safety of an agenda. Of order. Organization. A plan.

Perrault's brows arched sardonically. "Oh, I won't be coordinating engagements for your time in Asgard."

"Why not?" I drew back, feeling like someone had dumped cold water down my back. I needed a plan to survive the next thirteen days—and the days thereafter.

Perrault cocked his head. "First of all, that is not the way of this place. Second of all—it's not as if you put much store by the schedule I appointed for you in England."

I gaped at him. "You're going to jeopardize my trip to punish me?"

"I'm not punishing you." Perrault was serene, unflappable. "I'm simply not going to squander my expertise."

"Winchester was different," I protested. "My pretend suitor was forty years old!"

"*Norge* is different," Perrault said neatly. "Make your own way, Seneschal-elect. I won't make it for you this time." He ran his eyes over the hall distastefully. "I'll be fully occupied with enduring this stay. Make no mistake, I'll be watching, but you're on your own."

I gaped at him, dumbstruck.

Without a fiancé, I could be forced to travel to the Imperiya. I'd be that many more weeks away from seeing Daddy, from protecting him from whatever Alessandra was planning.

If Torden didn't propose to me, I'd be left at the mercy of boys I could not afford to love. To boys who could never come home with me to Potomac.

My stomach plummeted.

Perrault dismissed me with a smile and a nod at the Asgard boys. I turned and made my way to the other end of the table, his mockery still ringing in my ears.

Skop fit in well among Anya's freshly scrubbed, sturdily built brothers, already well into huge plates of porridge and eggs and brown cheese when I reached them. I flopped down beside Skop, and he pushed me a cup of coffee—or something like it—and exchanged a knowing smile with Anya over my rounded shoulders.

"Thanks," I mumbled, dumping cream in the mug. There was no sugar anywhere on the table. I rubbed at my eyes, weary and unsettled from my conversation with Perrault.

Aleksei smirked. "Only children drink milk in their coffee."

I took a long slurp and half glared, half squinted at him. "You let children drink coffee?"

"Leave her alone. She can have whatever she wants." Anya

slid me a plate of food and turned to Hermódr. "How were your times this morning?"

"Fine." Fredrik rolled a shoulder forward. "Today's route felt longer."

Torden laughed. "You always say that. It's never longer."

"Well, it *felt* that way," Fredrik grumbled.

"Enough groaning, squeaky door." Anya smiled and ruffled her brother's hair. "It is always twelve kilometers. No more, no less."

I choked on my coffee. "Every day?"

Bragi speared a piece of scrambled egg and nodded. "Týr leads the *drengs*; Pappa leads the *thegns*—the older warriors. Twelve for us, eight for them, every morning at sunrise."

I stifled a whimper.

"You might wake up faster if you opened your eyes all the way," said Torden, leaning across the table. My heart stuttered at the teasing shape of his grin, and I felt a sudden stab of guilt. *Predictable.*

"Yes, but then she'd have to see your whole face," said Aleksei.

Fredrik jostled him. "Nicer view than yours."

"Boys," chided Anya. "Leave her alone."

They didn't. I poured another cup of coffee.

"Now." Torden passed me a practice sword. "How should you hold this?"

It was a mercy the Norden summer was cool. Already I was sweating beneath the mail shirt Anya had draped over my shoulders, though whether from anxiety or exertion I wasn't sure.

I'd gawked when the five Asgard *prinsene* and Anya first led us into Konge Alfödr's armory, a long, low stone building designed to evade notice. Past a maze of weapons and equipment smelling strongly of oil and polish were rows of lockers; a bow and a half-dozen daggers and swords hung in Torden's, with a shield, two helmets, and other armor heaped on the floor. An enormous hammer was propped in the back corner, its impossibly short handle engraved in elaborate knots.

They carried their gear to a quiet, grassy hill outside the fortress walls. "I'll work with Skop," Anya announced, testing the edge of a broadsword. Skop grinned to himself as he stretched his muscles, rolling out his neck.

"And her?" Aleksei nodded at me.

Torden's searching gaze was like a sunburn. "I will work with you. If you like."

Make your own way, Seneschal-elect.

Perrault had been deriding me. But this had to work.

Torden was my last—my only—chance.

If I was going to do this, I was going to have to do it my way.

I swallowed hard. "If you need to get in some real practice, I can just watch. But I'll do whatever you're doing, if you're willing to teach me."

The *prins* passed me a practice sword in answer, nodding firmly. Hermódr and Bragi exchanged a meaningful glance and got to work.

Skop learned quickly under Anya's guidance. She was a

natural, quick and graceful, the gold and amber around her slim neck flashing in the sunlight with every movement, and she sent Bragi and Skop tumbling into the dirt more times than I could count. Over and over, Anya offered them a hand up, and they accepted her each time, their faces never growing less admiring.

But I grew more and more anxious working nearby with Torden. He began by teaching me to parry a thrust, but I kept fumbling it: I failed to shift my weight correctly, my wrists were too slow to reangle the blade, I held the sword too far out and opened my side to attack. Worse yet, I couldn't read him at all, his quiet study of me so unlike Bear's open watchfulness.

"Again," he said simply, over and over. Over and over I got it wrong, but his serene scrutiny never faltered.

I needed his approval. But his patience in the face of my inability—his total, steady calm, such a contrast to my rapidly fraying nerves—was unsettling.

Wasn't he irritated, to find me so slow to learn? Wasn't my incompetence getting under his skin?

Either way, his expression betrayed nothing. It unnerved me.

After about an hour and a half, the muscles in my arms and back were aching, and I eased down onto a patch of grass to rest. Most of the others dropped down beside me, but Torden wasn't finished. Careful and deliberate, he kept working, practicing a single maneuver with the blade until I thought his arm might fall off.

"Slow and steady, old man," Aleksei taunted.

"You are going to hurry yourself into an early grave," Torden returned.

Aleksei's face tightened. "Care to help me get there?" He opened his arms, and the boys began circling one another.

Torden was taller than his dark-haired brother by half a head, his arms the size of the other boy's legs—but Aleksei struck first. Anya scooted close to Skop and me as they went around, their armor and the faint sheen of sweat on their foreheads gleaming in the sunlight.

"Won't Torden flatten him?" I asked her. "He's so much bigger than Aleksei."

"It's not so simple." Anya flashed us a grin. "Torden is not just strong—he is focused, and fearless. He works very hard, and he always makes the bold choice."

"But?" I prodded.

"But this isn't a wrestling match, and Aleksei is fast and tricky—creative," she said. "He isn't afraid to dance around or retreat when it will catch Torden off guard. He isn't afraid of looking silly or cowardly, if he wins."

Hermódr, sprawled nearby, nodded in agreement. "Still, you would beat him more often if you trained more, Aleksei."

"He's right, brother," Torden called. "*Skjerp deg*. Some discipline would do you good."

"Is Aleksei lazy?" I whispered to Anya.

"Famously," she hissed back. "He has not made it to a single morning run in two weeks!"

I groaned again, remembering the boys had put in a full day's work before I'd shown up to breakfast.

Torden glanced over at my voice, and Aleksei surged forward, spotting the gap in his focus. "Too much practice makes *you* predictable," he snapped.

The tip of his sword was aimed at Torden's stomach.

Torden snapped back to attention and just barely blocked the attack, metal screeching against metal. I wrapped my arms around my legs, cringing as his arms strained, forcing Aleksei's blade away. Then, in a blinding flash, Torden threw his brother off and brought the point of his own weapon to Aleksei's chest. They were finished.

Elation flashed beneath Torden's nonchalance as I whooped with the others, congratulating them both while they stripped off their armor. But resentment flickered across Aleksei's face as he sat down in silence.

"Should we go for a ride?" Bragi asked eagerly.

Please, someone else say no.

I tried not to sigh audibly with relief when Anya held up a hand. "Relax. Let's eat something."

"Is it lunchtime already?" Skop asked.

"No." Hermódr helped himself to a large serving of bread and brown cheese. "But have some *brunost*, anyway. Aren't you hungry?" Skop grunted in concession, and Anya passed around more food and a leather canteen.

We lay in the grass for a while, the boys joking and horsing around as though their full morning hadn't wearied them at all. Anya braided tiny flowering weeds into a crown for herself, then wove one for me. I beamed at her as she tossed it over my hair, but she and Skop were lost in conversation.

"This is pretty," he said quietly, running a finger along her glittering necklace.

Anya darted a look at Bragi and bit her lip but didn't pull back. "Old boyfriend," she murmured. I turned away quickly, cheeks burning, glad the other boys weren't paying attention. Fredrik had made a joke I hadn't heard to Bragi and Hermódr, and the three were a rolling jumble of elbows and knees and fists.

Unsure whether to be concerned or amused, I glanced at Torden and found him leaning back on his elbows, studying me. His hair was tousled and he'd rolled up his shirtsleeves, and though my limbs felt heavy enough to sink into the ground, he didn't look tired. "You're not going to jump in?" I asked lightly.

He shook his head. "Not interested today."

"Ah."

A pause wider than the sky overhead stretched between us.

"I take it you are not a great lover of sports," he finally said, tone as casual as mine. Or was it? Either way, I couldn't pretend just to please him.

I picked at my borrowed wool tights. "I like to think I just haven't found my game yet."

Torden took the bait. "What have you tried?"

"Whatever Sister Agatha made us play in school." I chewed the inside of my cheek. "Football. Rugby. Basketball. I wasn't any good at any of them. I once hit myself in the face with a tennis racket."

Torden's lips twitched, and he scooted closer. "What about track and field? Badminton? Cricket?"

"Scratched every day for two weeks in the long jump. Would not touch a badminton racket after I hit myself in the face in tennis. And in cricket, I'd just jump to the end of the line over and over when my team was batting."

He gave a broad laugh. "Really?"

I buried my face in my hands, peeking out through my fingers. "You're probably really good at all of those." Torden didn't answer, but the set of his mouth said, *Of course.*

I felt full to the brim with embarrassment—awkward and silly in front of this flawless specimen of a boy. But a note of happiness sang through the blush I felt like a burn on my skin.

"I'm not even much of a runner," I confessed, smiling despite myself. "I like to ride, though. On a beautiful day I can walk for miles. Or garden for hours."

Torden's gaze grew serious. "Are you telling me you are a competitive gardener? Is this a sport in Potomac? How are the matches structured? Because—"

"All right, enough," I said, unable to hold in a nervous giggle. "So, no, I don't like sports. What's to like?"

"Well, training and competition channel our energy," he began.

I cut my eyes at his brothers—Fredrik had Hermódr in a headlock. "I see."

Torden gave another quiet laugh. "Well, it helps, anyway." Then he paused, considering. "We live for Norge. The kingdom needs us at our strongest. Besides, is there anything like it?"

"Like—sweat dripping in your eyes? Like screaming lungs

and a side stitch and people watching me fail?" I shook my head. "If I could avoid being in the public eye forever—avoid all that pressure—I would do it."

Torden hesitated, scratching at his beard, squinting at me. "Who cares about the people watching?"

Spoken truly like a boy who's never been teased in his life.

Or, my brain rejoined, *like one who's been teased all his life and knows how to give it right back.*

"No one knows how many years he has, Seneschal-elect. Life is short and death is certain." Torden shot me a glance, tugging absently at the top button of his shirt. I gulped and dropped my eyes. "So every moment I am aboveground and not below it, I want to feel the difference. We'll all be in our graves soon enough."

I smiled at my shoes. "Your profile failed to mention what a philosopher you were."

He opened his mouth, but Hermódr cut off his reply; the boys had quit scrapping. "Time for a horseback ride?"

Torden got to his feet. "Let's see if you like to ride as much as you think you do." He offered me a hand up, smile unreadable.

Bear had been sullen, cynical, romantic, and charming by turns—emotional, and disposed to talk about it. I'd understood him.

I had no idea what to make of the boy in front of me, or what to do with him, except to play his game and see if I liked it.

And what does it mean if you do? It's too soon for any of this to be real.

But I pushed back.

No. What I had with Bear wasn't real.

But this could be.

I needed it to be.

Everything calling me home—my father, my fear of Alessandra's plans—needed this to work.

I swallowed hard and swatted Torden's arm away, dragging myself upright. Though my legs were weary, I jogged past him after Hermódr. "Let's see if you can keep up with me."

Torden cocked his head, amused. "My horse is very fast."

"I meant keep up with me in general," I called over my shoulder, grinning. His smile broadened, and he broke into a run.

40

Konge Alfödr's stables were a thing of wonder, home to row after row of enormous beasts bred to be ridden by warriors. As we trotted into the paddock on the backs of black-coated Friesians and dun-colored Fjord horses, the wind flapped the hem of my dress and pulled loose strands from Anya's halo braid. Skop couldn't look away from her face.

"Easy," I muttered.

Skop shook his head. "She's glorious. A sweet force of nature."

I blinked at him. "Well, I'm glad your crush has turned you into such a poet."

Skop arched his eyebrows at me. "Well, let's hope yours turns you into an athlete," he teased quietly. I gaped at him, indignant, but he shook his head. "Oh, Selah, I'm not in any deeper than you are."

I flushed. "You—!" I lunged, meaning only to smack Skop

on the arm, but the horse sensed my sudden movement. And before I knew it, we were off and running.

I'd always spent a lot of time alone, or with people who let me be. But Anya and the Asgard boys were happier and more whole together than apart. Where I craved stillness in written words or in the dirt or in church, they longed to be side by side, racing and chasing and crowding each other, only able to breathe if their lungs were burning. Over every hill was a sight they couldn't wait one more moment to see, and Konge Alfödr had raised impeccable riders.

I couldn't help but wonder, as we rode, how it would have been to grow up raised by a pack of wild animal boys instead of nuns and libraries. Would I be less fragile and anxious if I'd spent my earliest days being teased by brothers, more confident if I'd been conscripted into wrestling matches, taught to fight and race?

I watched Torden lean into his gallop, so handsome it hurt to look at him.

With a breath in, and a breath out, I resolved at least to find out if I could still be that person. Hardly knowing what I was doing, I gave myself up to the North.

My gibe at the *prins* notwithstanding, I had to fight to keep up with them. But as the clear air and their happy shouts flooded my system, I found I didn't mind the physical struggle.

I imitated my new friends, howling at one another over the wind like so many feral animals, ignoring the growing ache in my limbs and the wind that stung my face. I'd never been less self-conscious in my life, and it was intoxicating. We were a racing pride of lions, a stampede of horses, a herd of beasts running wild, invulnerable and free and thrilled with the mad beating of our own hearts.

We tore across the cliffs over the Lysefjord until the light began to grow golden, and Aleksei suddenly stopped and dismounted. He barely paused to tie up his horse before sprinting between two rocky hills to the edge of a blue lake. The others took off after him.

"What—" I started. My heart seized as the Asgard boys began peeling off their clothes, stopping at the sturdy shorts they wore under their pants. I froze, more immobilized by the act of undressing than their state of undress, but I couldn't look away. Aleksei's thin form was vivid with tattoos: a snake, its jade color dull, wrapped itself around his upper arm, and a gray wolf stalked the sharp ridge of his spine toward his neck. Its lean charcoal body was warped and bizarrely elongated, as if its wearer had grown.

I stiffened at the sight of the wolf. But I shook myself and looked away.

Torden, Hermódr, and Bragi wore ink, as well—a mark like a slanting letter *F* over each of their hearts. I gasped as they streaked toward the water and jumped, and then again as they burst above the surface, pushing water off their faces and shaking droplets from their blond and black and red hair.

"Anya, that water's got to be freezing," I panted, palms braced on my knees. A stiff wind tore across the cliff top; a sultry Potomac summer day this was not.

Anya tugged off her dress, leaving only her wool tights

and shirt. "Then you'd better hope that ride was enough of a warm-up." She winked and hurtled toward the lake, flinging herself in after her brothers.

I seized Skop with shaking hands. "They're insane."

"I know," he laughed raggedly, yanking off his sweater and pants. "Isn't it great?" As he jumped, I backed away from the bank, stomach seething.

Torden swam over, grinning and blinking water from his eyes, waving me in. "Come on!" Goose bumps formed over his thick-muscled chest and arms.

I shook my head fast, worrying the cuff of my shirtdress. "I can't swim."

Hermódr gaped. Bragi and Aleksei groaned, beckoning me anyway.

"Don't think about it. Don't be afraid. Just do it. I'll catch you." Torden held both his arms out.

I shook my head again, taking another cautious step back. "I'll just wait here."

"No!" Anya called, looking disappointed.

Torden swam a little closer to the water's edge. "Come on, Selah." His smile was sincere, lit with no trace of mockery. "I promise, I'll catch you and I won't let go. Jump. Trust me."

Could I?

Was it foolish to trust so soon, having learned just how easily trust could be broken?

Or would it be worse, letting Bear break my heart *and* my faith in people?

Panting, shaking, grateful above all that Anya had forced

me to wear her stupid wool tights, I turned around. I couldn't fiddle with the buttons of my dress as they watched. At least one catcall—Fredrik, I thought—joined the cheers echoing off the rocks, but the offending noise was silenced by what was unmistakably a slap.

I stood shivering in my tights and undershirt for a moment when I was done, wringing my fingers. Then I turned, sprinted toward the lake, and jumped, hitting the icy water like a sack of flour and sinking like a stone.

Before the pain in my skin and lungs had stilled, strong hands seized my upper arms and dragged me to the surface. The others whooped as I came up coughing.

"You did it!" said Torden. "That was not so bad, was it?"

"No," I gasped, trying not to cough in his face.

"Still—" Torden shifted his hands from my forearms to my elbows, drawing me closer. "Maybe we will work next on diving instead of swordplay." Though his expression was serious, his lips twitched.

Torden began to laugh, and then so did I—nervously, foolishly, each of us watching the other. I hoped it hid the shaking in my limbs. My heart thumped as his grip traveled to my waist.

Barely a week ago, I'd been wrapped up in someone else's arms.

Too soon, too soon, too soon.

"So, are you just going to hold me here and not swim around?" I tried to sound nonchalant.

"I told you I would." Torden pushed his hair off his forehead.

He had. He'd caught me, just as he'd said he would.

It was so small a thing. We were children playing in a pond, wasting time on a summer day.

But the strength of Torden's arms around me made me feel, for the first time, that my plan—hoping he might save me and my father—might not be a leap destined to end in bruised skin and broken bones.

Suddenly, a stream of water hit me in the face—Anya had swum up to spit water at me through her teeth. I squealed and shrank against Torden's shoulder, laughing and splashing at her.

"Come on." Fredrik beckoned to Anya, and she swam back to her brother.

Torden maneuvered me behind himself. "Climb on."

"What?"

"You have to push Anya into the lake," he said, lifting me up easily when I didn't do it myself.

"Okay, but why?" I tried not to wobble, thankful that a thick layer of wool lay between my unshaved knees and his palms.

"Don't you want to play?" Anya, already steady on her brother's shoulders, looked disappointed.

Torden looked straight up at me. The corner of his mouth curved, and my insides spun dizzily.

Too soon.

But—*Jump*, he'd said. *Don't be afraid.*

I lunged at Anya, seizing her shoulders. She squealed and grabbed one of my arms. Hermódr, Skop, and Bragi gave supportive hoots and cheers, but our fight was over as soon as it had begun. Anya shoved me and I fell backward with a *smack!*, swallowing a gallon of lake water before Torden dragged me to the surface. I climbed back on his shoulders, spluttering but determined.

Anya won easily, over and over again. The last time she upended me, I righted myself and dog-paddled feverishly toward her, barely afloat, not saying a word. She stared at me blankly until I dove forward and ducked her underwater, crowing, "I won this one! I win!" Anya shrieked delightedly, swiping at me wildly.

Torden finally intervened and the two of us tried to duck him without success. He flipped Anya and me over his shoulders, arms around the backs of our knees and both of our heads just above water. We screeched and hooted and flailed, and when he released us, Anya somehow managed to flip over his back into the lake, but I wound up in his arms, close against his chest.

I pushed my hair behind my ears with one hand and clung to his neck with the other, shaking from nerves and the cold as we bobbed silently together in the water.

Neither of us moved until another catcall from Fredrik split the air.

"Time to dry off," said Torden, voice so low it rumbled in his chest. He hauled us both out of the lake easily, as though I weighed nothing at all.

The others climbed out after us, blue-lipped and shivering likewise. But as Fredrik heaved himself onto the bank, Torden gave him a playful shove and he flopped backward, hitting the water with a huge splash.

Fredrik clambered back toward the bank and dragged himself onto dry land. "What was that for?"

Torden eyed him and gave a long wolf whistle, as sharp and silly as Fredrik had before I'd jumped in. We all collapsed into laughter.

We retreated to the fortress freezing but exhilarated, and Anya and I both took scalding baths before I collapsed into her bed.

When I woke, Anya was aglow with excitement, her hair a mess and eyes so bright I wondered if she'd napped at all. "Time to get ready?" I asked hazily, wiping my eyes.

Anya nodded eagerly. "Time to get ready."

We pawed through each other's things while we got dressed, like little girls playing dress-up. Anya talked me into red lipstick and a bright ruby pendant of my mother's with my yellow gown—but only on the condition that she wear her own golden tiara and the green dress I'd worn in England. She'd refused at first, her tone all well-bred protest, but her hands traced the patterns in the lace even as she shook her head.

I thought of the tie I'd knotted around Bear's neck the night I'd worn that dress, of the way he'd watched me and held me when we danced.

It felt foolish to give away something so expensive. But it wasn't as if I was ever going to wear it again.

When Anya was dressed, she didn't fasten the amber and gold necklace around her neck. Smug on Skop's behalf that she'd set aside the relic of a former flame, I dragged her to my jewelry box, and she chose a delicate chain with a little golden charm shaped like a kitten from its depths.

"I used to have cats in Varsinais-Suomi," Anya said sadly. "Alfödr says pets are a waste of resources."

He would. I fastened the chain around her neck, smiling. "It's all yours."

When Skop came to our door to escort us to the Valask-jálf, I checked myself one last time in her mirror, almost shy at the sight of my own reflection. I turned to Anya, twisting my fingers together, clinging to the remains of the dizzying confidence I'd felt earlier that day. "What do you think?"

Skop smiled as Anya seized my hand and tugged me toward the corridor.

"Don't change a thing," she insisted, then winked. "Come on. Torden's waiting."

41

My eyes found him the moment we walked into Valaskjálf.

The Asgard boys were dressed like the rest of the *drengs*, their white military dress trousers and gold epaulets and brass buttons gleaming in the firelight. Alfödr's sons were an imposing crowd, handsome, laughing and shouting over one another—but I could only watch Torden.

He quit roughhousing with Hermódr, a smile hooking the corner of his lips as he took me in. My heart went abruptly still, my skin warming beneath his stare.

Hi, he mouthed.

I gave a tiny wave, though by now we were halfway across the hall. *Hi.*

Fredrik rolled his eyes and elbowed him in the ribs. Torden grunted, grabbing at his side. I stifled a laugh.

Valaskjálf's long tables had been pushed nearer its perimeter to free up space for dancing. Colorful dresses and military jackets in Norsk blue and Varsinais-Suomi red filled its benches and aisles—though no one wore their clothes quite as well as Torden. When he caught me staring at him again, I flicked my gaze to the tapestries on the walls, woven not with images but foreign words.

Torden drew a chair out for me beside him. "Our library," he said in my ear.

I gave a shivery laugh. "What?"

"We have few paper books here. The København royal library down in Jylland is much larger." Hermódr settled down across from me, sounding wistful.

"But our most important tales we keep where everyone can read them," said Bragi. "Well, everyone who can read, anyway."

Skop frowned. "What do you mean?"

"The hangings are worked with the names of the dead and their deeds, so our past is always before us," Torden said. "And we wear the words that matter most. Here, and here." He tapped his heart and pulled down his glove, so close to my side I caught the smell of his soap as he moved. I glanced at the symbol like an angular letter *R* tattooed over his pulse, thinking of the ink on his chest beneath his shirt.

My shoulders tensed at the memory of how close I'd been to that tattoo this afternoon.

Too soon.

Anya's expression gentled, seeing I was stalled. "Do you keep many books in Potomac?" she asked helpfully.

But my mind didn't go back to Arbor Hall. Suddenly, in my head, I was in Winchester's library, with more volumes than I could read in a lifetime and a boy reading *Beowulf* aloud to me before a fire in a tiny, shabby attic room.

I nodded tightly. I was warm in the memory, but its recollection burned.

"Ah, but how do your storytellers compare to ours?" Bragi flashed a brilliant smile.

"Storytellers?" I sat up straight.

"Yes," said Bragi. "Reading is solitary. But a storyteller, everyone can enjoy together."

"Bragi's not a bad storyteller," said Anya.

"Not as good as you." Bragi fixed her with an admiring stare. Anya cleared her throat and looked away.

Skop rubbed the back of his broad neck, eyes darting between them. "What kind of stories?"

"Our *skálds* tell the kind that are . . . mostly true," Torden said. "Wars, great hunts, survival. Some love stories, too." He smiled at me, dropping his voice as Alfödr rose from his seat. "I suppose we will see what Ragnvald has for us tonight." But Torden's smile froze when Aleksei entered the hall.

He wore military dress like his brothers, but his uniform was Imperiya gray.

I nearly dropped my fork, staring as if a ghost stood in the foyer outside the hall. Alfödr was at his side quicker than seemed possible.

They were too far away to overhear, but there was no mistaking the fire in the king's gaze, his fury as he hauled Aleksei back through Valaskjálf's great doors. The king pointed down the hall, shook a finger in his son's face, then strode back inside.

At my side, Torden rubbed his temples and exchanged a glance with Hermódr. Both boys were silent.

His choice of clothing was probably a joke.

But part of me—a tiny part, speaking only in whispers—wondered if the uniform was some sort of message to me.

I'd failed to read the omens back in Potomac. Here, again, I had no idea what this one could mean.

Jaw tight, Aleksei brushed himself off and cast a backward glance at his father before heading down the corridor. But the king was already greeting his guests.

Alfödr spoke to the crowd in Norsk before turning to the *Beholder* crew. "Seneschal-elect and her guardians, you honor Asgard with your presence. Please accept these treasures. Use them well."

His voice was strong, powerful; his people watched him admiringly. I thought with a sudden pang of how the crowd had watched my father on Arbor Day, barely able to hear him, their eyes concerned and confused.

I wished I were home with him right now. I wished I could help him.

My very bones felt pulled toward Potomac.

Six men carried bags and cases to the head table, passing brilliant copper rings, swords, and knives from hand to hand, both new gifts and their own weapons that had been confiscated the day before. As my gift, a bronze suit of armor, was unveiled in the corner, I wondered when I'd ever wear such a thing.

I swallowed, shaking off my sadness. "Skop, can I see?" I

whispered across Torden.

"Sure." Skop nodded absently and passed me his ring. When I finally handed it back, he didn't notice my frown; he was watching Anya as she rose from the table with her stepmother.

The ring was finely engraved with Skop's name and the outline of the island of Koniag. But such delicate work took time—clearly, more than had passed since our arrival.

How did Alfödr know of Skop's homeland? His name?

A low cheer from the crowd distracted me from my thoughts. Dronning Rihttá had filled a drinking horn from a large cauldron warming over the fire and offered it to Konge Alfödr. As Anya passed the horn she carried to Fredrik, five other noblewomen rose to repeat the ritual at other tables, answered by every face in Valaskjálf with admiration. I glanced in question at Torden.

"Only a few women are allowed to serve the first mead. It's tradition," he whispered in my ear, eyes tracking Rihttá as she approached, statuesque in black. "Their hospitality forges and preserves peace."

Silently, the queen passed her etched silver drinking horn to Torden.

"Baldr," he said, voice lower than far-off thunder.

I didn't understand the word she mouthed as he replaced the vessel in her hands, but her dark eyes said, *Thank you.* Torden nodded, gaze full of something like sympathy with a bracing edge.

When the drinking horn came next to me, I raised it to

Torden, a nervous thrill chasing the alcohol through my blood.

After everyone had drunk, clamor rose again around the hall. Utensils scraped bowls and plates as everyone helped themselves to lamb and cabbage stew, pork and herring, cooked onions and carrots. Loud talk and jokes went up on all sides as Alfödr's *thegns* and *drengs* and *heerthmen*—his householders—bragged loudly about their past and future exploits.

"In three months, I'm going to be able to finish the morning run in half an hour," said Fredrik.

"That is impossible," said Hermódr, ever practical.

"You will see how impossible it is when I do it," Fredrik fired back. I wasn't certain exactly how long a kilometer was—I'd only ever measured distance in miles—but twelve seemed like a lot in thirty minutes. Torden returned my blank stare with the tiniest shake of his head: Fredrik was bluffing.

"What's your best time?" I asked Torden offhandedly.

He shot me a sideways smile. "I always finish last."

I squinted; this didn't agree with his reputation. "Well, you'd still have me beat," I finally said. "I could probably handle twelve kilometers, if I were allowed to crawl the last eleven."

Torden shook his head, apparently considering my comment seriously. "You could do more than that, with training. You have very long legs."

Bragi and Aleksei glanced at one another wordlessly, stifling laughs. Only when Fredrik snorted over his stew did Torden seem to realize what he'd said. Torden rolled his eyes at them, elbowing Bragi as his brother clapped him on one broad shoulder in a silent, sarcastic compliment.

My heart swelled, watching them, trading glances and the barest gestures for whole meanings as if they all spoke a secret language.

For the first time, I wondered how on earth I could ask Torden to leave them behind. The mere thought made me press my lips together, afraid the question would blurt itself out of its own volition.

When Torden's brain finally caught up with his mouth, he didn't bother trying to backpedal.

"Well, you do." He shrugged and scratched at his beard, brown eyes impenitent, his crooked smile rebellious, as though challenging me to ask why he'd been looking at all.

Hermódr reentered our conversation two steps behind, as if from a dream. "Torden isn't a slow runner," he said matter-of-factly. "He keeps pace with Týr at the front. But he is the only *dreng* who runs to the rear of the pack when he is done and finishes again with the runners who have fallen behind."

Fredrik made a disgusted noise under his breath, half-hearted envy on his face; Aleksei cocked an eyebrow at him, silently agreeing.

"You liar." I nudged Torden gently in the ribs. "You said twelve kilometers every morning."

"It doesn't matter," he murmured, avoiding my eyes as he sawed at his food. I could've counted the freckles on his cheeks at this distance, could see each of his red-gold lashes.

I bit my lip. *It does*, I wanted to reply. *It does to me.*

Finally, the meal came to an end, and a hush fell over Vala-skjálf. As knives and forks and cups and voices fell silent, Bragi and a white-bearded man rose to stand between two of the roaring fireplaces along the far wall.

The old man began in Norsk, his accent cradling the unfamiliar words at the back of his throat before he spoke them. Bragi watched him recite, as still as the hall around us, before interpreting. "Of Kvasir we have heard, the man a gift, and gifted of old with wisdom."

The *skáld* spoke again in Norsk, and again, Bragi translated, blue eyes focused. "Of mead we also know, and of its gift to us, poetry."

It should have been a stilted performance, in high-sounding English and Norsk words that meant nothing to me. But I was helpless against the spell the two of them wove and cast like a net over the room—powerless against Ragnvald's husky accents and the subtle movements of his hands, against Bragi's clear voice and careful rhythm.

"I should have been studying," I whispered to Torden, only inches away. "It would be nice to be able to understand the story in your language."

He fiddled with a ragged cuticle, white gloves abandoned on his lap. "If we get married, I'll help you." Torden shifted, and his shoulder bumped mine.

I stuffed my elbows inside the arms of my chair, nerves abruptly on edge, and nodded over at Bragi. "Do you ever . . . ?"

He shook his head. "No, never. I'm a poor speaker."

"I don't believe that for a minute," I said quietly.

He glanced at me, eyes startled again beneath their guarded cast. Torden wasn't an attention seeker—that, I believed—but there had been no mistaking the respectful looks that had followed him all day, that were trained on him even now.

"People would listen. *I* would, anyway," I added quietly.

Torden shifted again and took my hand under the table.

From that point, I heard nothing. The hall could've caught fire around me and I wouldn't have noticed, so keen was the thrill of panic in my blood. Torden's large, callused hand made my own look almost delicate. It also made my palms sweat.

I *wanted* to be near him. But barely a week ago I'd been wanting someone else, kissing someone else. What sort of fickle heart could feel so much for two people, a week apart?

Did it matter, with what lay in wait for me ahead and at home? Could I afford to move slowly, the risks being what they were?

If I hoped to get back to Daddy and avoid the Imperiya, I had to get engaged.

If I hoped to fall in love—truly in love, recovered from my hurt—I ought to take my time.

I couldn't breathe. I wriggled my slick hand from Torden's grasp to reach for my cup.

The move would have been more convincing if I hadn't used my right hand to stretch for an object well to my left. Skop winced.

As the story ended, the musicians' instruments were nearly drowned out by the shriek of boots and bench legs on the floor. Torden and I remained seated after our table had emptied.

"I'm sorry," I blurted out.

Torden's eyes sought mine. "Do not apologize," he said

steadily. "I would not compel you, not even to something so minor."

I bit my lip at the earnestness in his voice. "You surprised me, that's all. And . . ." I trailed off.

The books. The fire. The rain. The kiss.

The thought of my naïveté paraded in front of England curdled in my stomach.

Bear had lied to me, and for good reason. He'd been wry and sulky and difficult, and that had made him all the more charming.

His kiss had been perfect.

Even now, I had to force myself to close the book on those memories, warm to the touch, searingly painful, too tangled to sort out.

Torden wasn't forbidden fruit, appealing because I couldn't have him. Torden could save Daddy and me. He was necessary to a degree that tore me in two.

I needed him, and I needed to want him, and I needed him to want me. I felt the pressure like a bruise on my heart.

Perhaps Bear had made things easier for both of us by disguising himself all that time.

Perhaps, when I thought of all the things I would do because I had to do them, I understood Bear better than I'd thought I did.

"What is it?" Torden asked.

I slumped a little in my chair and stared hard at the table, running my fingernail over a rough spot in the wood. "How much did you hear about my last visit?"

He hesitated. "Not much."

"And?"

"The rumor is that it ended poorly," he said.

"The rumor?"

Torden nodded at two men I didn't recognize standing near the edge of the dance floor. One was wispy and white-haired, the other younger, his features unremarkable but for bright, intelligent eyes. Both wore black cloaks that flapped and waved like massive ravens' wings with their every gesture. "Huginn and Muninn—Muninn is the older one, and Huginn is the younger—are my father's advisers. They know everything that happens in Asgard, and probably everywhere else." Torden paused. "They told him the prince proposed and you declined because of a misunderstanding."

"That's a fairly misleading version of the story," I said flatly.

"What happened?"

"They tricked me."

Torden's brow furrowed, and I slid deeper into my chair, shaking my head.

"It's a mess to explain. My suitor's father pretended to be my suitor; my suitor pretended to be my guard."

He drew back slightly. "Why?"

I leaned forward, watching the dancers, unable to meet his eyes. "They distrusted Potomac," I said. "I don't think it was personal."

Neither of us spoke for a long moment.

"Selah, I am not perfect," Torden finally said, his tone frank.

"My brothers could—they *will*—offer you a long list of my failings."

I swallowed. "Like what?"

Torden raised his eyebrows. "Will you tell me yours if I tell you mine?" he asked baldly. I considered this a moment and nodded.

He blew out a breath. "I am rash," he said. "Impatient. Not as wise as my father or as thoughtful as Hermódr, and Aleksei is much cleverer. And I am too ready to fight when I should try to talk."

I didn't agree out loud, but he'd spoken truly. I could see those things in him.

And yet, I thought, *you confess quickly, too.*

His fingers flexed, a few inches from mine on the table. "Your turn."

"I question myself ceaselessly," I half whispered. "I have no confidence—I'm afraid to fight. Afraid even to be laughed at."

I thought of myself fleeing the ball in Potomac, fleeing the ball in Winchester. Running away from watching eyes and whispering mouths.

Torden scratched at the wood grain on the table, then turned his gaze on me, searching my face. "That's the worst of you," he said in a low voice. "Now tell me the best. Don't be shy. Don't be modest."

I swallowed hard and reached for his hand.

This list took longer to assemble, my brain buzzing at our touch. "The best things about me are gifts from the people I love," I finally said. "Kindness. Loyalty. Faith." I paused. "More than anything, faith that a larger story is being told all around us, even when it's beyond our view." I swallowed and glanced at Torden. "Your turn."

His voice was quiet but sure. "I'm not afraid." One thumb rubbed my knuckles. "I keep my promises. And despite what he did, you can trust that I will never lie to you. Whatever I tell you, you can believe it is the truth."

I squeezed his fingers and faced him, blood pounding in my ears.

Just do it, he'd said. *I'll catch you.*

Across the room, Perrault was eyeing us. He nodded, pleased.

I didn't want his approval; it washed over me like icy water. But somehow, it drove me nearer to Torden.

"Will you dance with me?" I asked.

Torden didn't answer, but he didn't let go of my hand as he led me from the table.

42

The Asgard boys had ribbed Fredrik in English the night before, but the way they hassled Torden while we danced made me grateful I didn't speak Norsk. He ignored them for an hour until something else made him falter—the twins, Vidarr and Váli, at the head table with his father and stepmother. They were too far away to hear, but their hands were unmistakably tense and argumentative, their mouths surly.

"It— Selah, I am sorry," he said, looking perturbed. "Excuse me."

"Of course."

Lang gave an anemic smile as I approached his perch on a table near the edge of the room. "Your Grace." He raised his mug to me in an ironic salute, wiping foam from his upper lip with an ink-stained finger.

"Captain." I sat on the bench next to his feet, studying the room. Cobie stood alone in a corner, arms crossed over her worn black dress as though daring someone to approach her. Perrault seemed to be busily ingratiating himself with a group of *thegns*, though I wondered whether his flattery would find purchase in a place like this. J.J., I hoped, was in bed. "Enjoying yourself?"

"Sure." Lang shrugged. "And you? Things look like they're . . . moving along."

I glanced at Torden. He stood at his stepmother's side, listening to her intently. My heart warmed a little. "He's kind. He's handsome. He's genuine."

"I'm sure he is."

I frowned at Lang, and he laughed wryly. "He's so honest and brave, he's like a prince in a fairy tale."

My eyebrows shot up. "Excuse me?"

Lang gave a sardonic half grin. "He's a paper doll." He eyed me, curious. "I'd just think after what you've been through, you'd have a bit more appreciation for . . . chemistry."

The kiss.

Bear and me, in front of the fire.

Lang's words sent a flash of heat and shame through my blood.

I sat up straight. "After what I've *been through?*" Across the room, one of the twins had stalked away from the head table. Torden stood, resolute in his blue military jacket, between his stepmother and whichever twin remained. "Lang, what I've been is lied to. And what I appreciate now," I said, jerking my head at Torden, "is solidity. Sincerity. And those things can coexist with attraction."

He shrugged. "I'm sure you're right. I just don't see it, that's all."

"Well, you don't have to worry about that," I said awkwardly. "You run the ship and keep us safe, and I'll worry about figuring out how I feel."

"Ooh, are we talking about our feelings?" With no warning, Aleksei slid down the bench and careened into my side. He draped an overly familiar arm around my shoulder, and I shrank away, laughing uncomfortably. I had no idea when he'd returned, dressed now in a black suit.

"Good evening, Baron Aleksei." Lang's barely disguised grimace belied his greeting.

"Delighted to formally meet you." Aleksei gave the captain a broad, ghastly smile. "Mind if I steal her?"

Lang looked away. "I'm not Selah's keeper. She's made that abundantly clear." He gave a tight nod and leapt from the tabletop, striding off toward Cobie. I frowned after his back, feeling a little deflated, though I didn't know why.

"So. I see you've tamed the stallion." Aleksei nodded at Torden, grinning wolfishly.

I cringed. "I wouldn't phrase it that way."

My stomach twisted at his insinuation. Did Aleksei just want to get a rise out of me? Or was his behavior about something larger—meant to unsettle me, throw me off course?

"Goodness, you women." Aleksei smiled, but it was a hard expression, cadaverous. It tightened the lines of his face, emphasizing the curve of the skull beneath his pallid cheeks. "Anya lets Alfödr's *drengs* chase her hem and tortures Bragi endlessly, and you shy away from the word *tame*. A heartless beauty and a shrinking violet."

I squirmed and looked away.

Aleksei sighed, abruptly serious. "You ought to know what things are really like in Asgard, Selah. Don't let squeamishness get in the way."

When I turned back to Aleksei, his expression was still sour, but he suddenly looked tired, and very young. I studied him, torn between suspicion and sympathy. "I think I like it here," I said tentatively.

"Of course you do," Aleksei said, smiling bitterly. "Because you haven't made a mistake yet and been forced to taste the consequences."

Alfödr had thrown Aleksei out of dinner in front of everyone for what could've been an honest mistake, or—more likely—a joke in poor taste. I'd been publicly humiliated often enough lately to imagine quite clearly what it must have felt like.

I chose to let sympathy win.

"You sound like you're having a bad night." I smiled and put a hand on his shoulder. "Maybe things will look brighter in the morning."

"Maybe the sun will rise in the west." Aleksei rolled his eyes as I left him.

Wincing, I hurried to the fireplace where Torden stood talking with Fredrik. They stopped speaking as I approached, but their faces were pained.

Fredrik furrowed his brow at me. "You look like someone

just told you a dirty joke and then explained the ending when you didn't get it."

Torden grimaced and nodded back at their brother, who was busy now with a trio of pretty girls. "She looks like she's been talking to Aleksei."

"Or that." Fredrik bobbed his head.

I rubbed my eyes, abruptly weary. "His, uh, party tactics are something."

"Aleksei loves to stir the pot." Torden sighed, rubbing his neck. "Let me walk you back to your room."

He wrapped a heavy arm around me as we walked out Vala-skjálf's doors. "You look beautiful tonight."

I smiled, grateful for his warmth; my shoulders were bare, and the corridor was chilly. "Thank you. You look nice, too." I paused, studying his downturned mouth, his tired eyes. "Is something on your mind?"

"What do you mean?" he asked, suddenly guarded.

I hesitated. "You look . . . troubled. You said I could trust you. I don't want to pry, but you can trust me, too."

Torden paused, considering, cautious longing in his face. "If I tell you, will you tell your companions?"

"No," I said quietly. "Your secrets are yours. But if they're heavy, I'll help you carry them awhile." I put an arm around his waist, my blood surging. This close, I could hear his heartbeat through his jacket.

Torden's answering smile was a sunrise.

He shook his head, beard scuffing my temple, apparently

uncertain where to begin. "I love my brothers and my sister, but sometimes I do not understand them. I would trust Anya with my life, but she . . . complicates things," he said vaguely.

Aleksei had said as much. I nodded.

"And I would die for Aleksei, but trouble follows him."

"Trouble like—his showing up in an Imperiya uniform to dinner?" I suggested gently.

"Among . . . other things. This year has been too much." Torden passed a hand over this forehead. "I don't know what he could have been thinking. Another bid for attention, I imagine." He frowned. "He's determined to shock, if that's what it takes to get Pappa to notice him."

I squeezed Torden's side. Aleksei's behavior—his prurient comments, his determination to instigate conflict—suddenly made more sense.

What had made him this way?

"But things are hardest between my oldest brothers and Dronning Rihttá," Torden said. "She is the only mother I have ever known. But Týr's mother and Váli and Vidarr's mother are still living, and my brothers are old enough to remember Pappa choosing Rihttá over them.

"When her sons, Baldr and Hodr, were small, my brothers tried to understand. But now they are gone, and Týr and the twins resent her marriage to my father. And Rihttá's pain makes her fragile."

Her sons. Torden had mentioned them at dinner the night before. *Did the bonfires bring Baldr or Hodr any luck last year?*

"Your toast earlier, to your stepmother," I said. "What did that mean?"

"*Minni*," he said softly. "When we drink, I always drink to Baldr's memory. He was just twelve. My mother suffers."

My heart ached as I suddenly realized why the queen watched J.J. so wistfully. "That's terrible."

"My father is at his wits' end. Sometimes I think I'm holding this house together with my bare hands." Torden shook his head.

I couldn't imagine Alfödr frustrated. He seemed so controlled—so powerful. As unlike my last memories of Daddy as possible. But Torden's sigh rustled past my ears and settled in my hair, his breath heavy with doubt.

I'd wanted to comfort him. Had I merely opened old wounds instead?

When we rounded the final corner to Anya's room, a sudden chill bit my skin as he took his arm from my shoulders.

Anya was leaning against her doorframe, face tipped up toward Skop, who stood much closer than seemed friendly. They flew apart at our approach.

I stopped short, feeling like an intruder. Torden's jaw worked. He faced me, then leaned toward my ear. "Remember—you promised." And he strode off into the dark.

I got ready for bed and lay thinking silently until Anya bid Skop good night and burrowed beneath her covers. The moon colored her pale blond hair almost white across her dark red blanket knitted with stars.

My godmother's book was only a few feet away, fresh with another tick mark; but I didn't reach for it. I didn't want to read; I wanted her company and her comfort.

Worry pooled in my chest so deep I thought it would overflow, run down my ribs and over my collarbone. Worry about Aleksei and the Imperiya. About Daddy, about myself. About Torden. His reaction to Skop and Anya in the hallway had surprised me.

Skop. Now I was worried for him, too.

Anya lets Alfödr's drengs chase her hem and tortures Bragi endlessly.

"Don't break his heart, Anya," I said softly.

She took in a sharp breath. "I could say the same to you."

"You could, but I have no idea what I'm doing," I said hollowly.

Boys like Peter. Boys like Torden.

Alessandra had sized me up so unsentimentally at the council meeting that night. If she weren't practically his sister, Anya—gracious *prinsessa*, mead-bearer, tall and lithe—was the kind of girl I would expect to see with a boy like Torden.

"Skop's my friend," I finally said. "And you're really beautiful. So just—be careful, okay?"

I felt, rather than heard, her assent as her nod rustled against her pillow and the blanket. "*God natt*, Selah."

"Good night."

43

Wondering and worry stole my sleep, but I was at least better off than Fredrik. As the Asgard boys set us up for archery practice on the edge of the woods, checking the targets fixed at the tree line and stringing their bows, Fredrik lay flat on the grass and closed his bloodshot eyes.

He'd rubbed his temples all through breakfast, gagging as his brothers passed around smoked salmon. He'd looked near tears at J.J.'s too-loud *good morning* when I'd flagged him and Cobie down in Valaskjálf and asked them to join us. J.J. had said yes, but Cobie declined, rolling her eyes in Perrault's general direction.

While Anya and Skop helped J.J., Torden held out a single arrow and the bow he'd strung for me. It looked absurdly small in his hands. "How should you hold this?" he asked, testing me, just as he had the day before.

I glanced over at Hermódr, the most deliberate of his

brothers, and tried to notch the arrow as he had, feeling the string wobble beneath my fingers as I drew it back toward my cheek. I looked to Torden for his review.

He grinned. "Not bad. Ah, let's widen your stance." I flushed as Torden braced my hips and hooked his boot around my ankle to drag my right foot a few inches. "And ... straighten the wrist, rotate the front elbow ..." He adjusted my arms and hands with gentle fingers, rose-gold eyelashes glinting inches away in the morning sun.

A tremulous laugh escaped my lips. "You aren't going to break me."

"I might," he said quietly.

I gulped and cast a nervous glance at his brothers.

Torden put a hand on my shoulder. "They're not paying attention. And if they were, they would be rooting for you."

He cared so much for them. Fleetingly, I wondered again how I'd ever ask him to leave them all behind.

I pushed the thought aside and released my arrow with a shaky breath. It hit the ground ten feet short of the target.

"Here, try again." Torden passed me another arrow. When it flew three feet wide of the wooden circle, he handed me another one, and then another. The third passed within a foot of the target, but the fourth and ninth and twelfth bounced off its painted edge. The thirteenth arrow stuck.

Torden grinned, stretching so his sleeves strained over his shoulders. "Good! Again." He held out a fourteenth arrow.

It hit an inch inside my previous mark. "Again."

The muscles behind my shoulders and above my elbows

were quivering before Torden strode over to examine my target, now studded with eight arrows. "Selah, I think you've found your game," he called, sounding pleased. I shrugged modestly, but I was thrilled.

Marvelous, I imagined Perrault cheering. *A proposal, no doubt about it.*

I needed Torden to propose. I was making my own way, as Perrault had said to do. Riding. Fighting. Verbally sparring with sarcastic boys.

I hoped I recognized myself when I was finished making it.

I wanted to want him more than I needed him. And I wanted him to propose to *me*—the real me.

Anya rumpled J.J.'s toboggan affectionately. "It's because she has patience, a trait bred entirely out of the Asgard line," she called to us. J.J. beamed, basking in her attention, nodding as Skop called out pointers—quietly, so as not to wake Fredrik, who lay fast asleep with his face on his arms. He'd slipped away once or twice earlier, I suspected to throw up his breakfast. I had no idea how he'd survived their morning run.

As Hermódr and Bragi kept shooting, I eased myself onto the ground, and Torden took a seat beside me. I knocked him with a weary shoulder. "Done already?"

Torden shrugged. "I practice archery because I should. But it's not my favorite weapon."

"You like the sword better?"

He shook his head. "The hammer."

I nodded, remembering the one I'd seen in his locker. "Can you—don't be offended—can you actually fight with that thing? It looked heavy, but its handle was so short."

"Only wide enough for one hand." Torden flexed his fingers thoughtfully. "We buy most of our weapons from the *dvergar*. They are master craftsmen, and do not usually make such mistakes. But I like it that way."

Aleksei winked at me. "Since only he can manage it, none of us ever borrows it."

"Which I cannot say for most of my possessions. I still want to know what you did with my helmet." Torden glared at his brother. Aleksei tore up a fistful of grass and blew it into my hair in reply. I flapped at him, annoyed.

"I don't think I could fight with a sword or a hammer. I'd rather fight enemies at a distance." I paused, suddenly a little ashamed. "Being so sensitive is a luxury, I know."

I could afford to be delicate about fighting. War would almost certainly never come to my doorstep in Potomac as it had to theirs.

Threats to our safety were subtler.

Torden passed a warm hand over my arm. The gesture seemed instinctive, a reflex. "A luxury for which I am grateful, on your behalf. I—do not be offended—would have you far, far from your enemies." His eyes drifted, thoughtful. "I will fight, if I have to. But if I have to break another's body, I deserve at least to feel his suffering in my own arm. I think the powerful would love less the fruits of violence if they had to deal it out by hand."

I stared at him mutely.

Was this really the boy whose siblings teased and scoffed

when he protested he didn't pick fights? Would I ever learn what seeds he sowed that bloomed in bruises on his cheeks? His reputation was so at odds with what I saw that I doubted whether that other boy even existed.

"Lunchtime!" Anya called, rescuing us, as she always did. But I hardly had the energy to eat the food she passed around. Our conversation grew quiet as, one by one, we joined Fredrik in sleep.

I felt every second of the past two days when I woke up in the grass. I lay still, muscles miserably stiff. *If I don't move, maybe no one else will wake up.*

But then I heard them.

"Do you think she likes it here?" Torden asked. I froze.

"How should I know?" asked Aleksei. "Do you like *her*?"

I strained my ears over the wind and the rustling trees, but Torden gave no answer. My heart stilled, disappointed.

I shouldn't have been eavesdropping; Daddy always advised against it. Nothing good ever came of snooping, he insisted; people didn't always mean what they said in front of others, and besides, others' opinions of me were neither my business nor my problem.

But perhaps if I'd snooped a little more in England, I wouldn't have been caught so off guard.

"Okay, okay," Aleksei said. "Something easier. Do you think she's attractive?"

"Of course," said Torden. "Don't you?"

Breathe normally.

"We aren't talking about me. On a scale of one to ten, how attractive?" Aleksei prodded. "Do you think she's as good-looking as Ida or Janne?"

Torden's voice came out in a growl. "What is wrong with you?"

"I'm sorry." Aleksei's tone was placating. "I am trying to help you sort this out."

"Ida is gorgeous, but she is such a gossip. It's boring." Torden sighed. "And I don't care if Janne is pretty. She flirted with me for weeks before I realized she was just trying to get closer to Fredrik."

"So?" Aleksei asked.

"Selah is very pretty," said Torden. "Her eyes. Her freckles. Very . . . sweet."

"Too sweet," Aleksei said acidly.

Torden didn't acknowledge this. "I don't know what to do around her. I'm afraid I'm going to ruin her with my clumsy hands."

There was a long moment of silence between them.

I wanted to reach out to Torden and tell him his hands were just fine. That I didn't believe he'd hurt me, on purpose or through carelessness.

"I didn't even notice she had freckles," Aleksei said absently.

"I can't *stop* noticing," said Torden, and something flickered inside me. "On her nose."

"Too wide, in my opinion. And so is her waist."

I flinched.

"I like her waist just fine." The tiny spark in my chest flared.

Torden sounded lazy, sleepy.

"Ah. Speaking of," Aleksei asked, "has anything . . . happened?"

"No!"

"You haven't even kissed her?" Aleksei demanded.

"When?" Torden answered, now sounding annoyed. "In front of everyone at the ball? In the lake, with everyone around?"

"You're the one who keeps telling her not to worry about who's watching," said Aleksei. "You walked her back last night. Could have done it then."

"Anya and Skop beat me there."

Aleksei's tone shifted. "Really?"

"Just talking," said Torden quickly. "Anya knows better. Knows what is expected of her." He sighed again. "She'll be married off and gone sooner than we would like, I am afraid."

My heart sank at his words. Poor Skop.

Aleksei snickered. "Anyway, you'd better get moving before she falls for Fredrik and he swipes her, too."

"He wouldn't." But Torden sounded suspicious.

"Well, he might if you don't do something," retorted Aleksei. "Or she might, if she thinks you are not interested." I thought of Fredrik turning green over breakfast and almost laughed aloud.

"I don't want her to run!" Torden groaned. "What do I do?"

"You need to make sure your father lets us celebrate Midsummer's Eve," Aleksei insisted.

Torden paused. "After last year? Are you sure that is a good idea? Pappa has hardly—"

"Come on," Aleksei wheedled. "You'll get cozy at a bon-fire, we'll split up into the woods, you can sneak some of the imported Bordeaux out of the cellar—"

My eyes went wide.

"All right, all right," Torden said unevenly. "Aleksei, I'm getting to know her, not trying to trap her." He sounded as nervous as I felt, and somehow, that calmed me.

"So? You arrange your circumstances." I couldn't see Alek-sei's face, but I was sure he was rolling his eyes. "Set the right scene, set the right things in motion, and everything will work out the way you want."

Torden sighed. "You really don't think it's a bad idea? Things are just beginning to calm down."

"No. Trust me, brother," Aleksei said smugly. "I'm looking out for you."

44

Arranged or spontaneous, the next few days were bliss.

I felt at home walking the barley fields with the boys, comfortable by Torden's side as he talked to the farmers and carefully checked the crop. And when he yanked off his shirt to straighten out a warped beam in a plow, I studied the grain below and the thatched houses all around with just as much care, my face heating as I caught glimpses of Torden's fair, muscular back and straining arms.

Some days we rode or sailed. Cobie was never free, but Anya taught J.J. to walk and trot, and the Asgard boys taught me to fish for salmon and herring off Fredrik's boat, *Skidbladnir*. I even found myself agreeing to come with Torden to watch the sun rise over the Bilröst. "It will be early, by necessity," he said, baiting my hook and avoiding my eyes. "But it will be worth it."

"I can make an exception," I laughed, heart stuttering

clumsily, feeling suddenly that I'd make any number of exceptions for his sake.

As he took my hand, I tried to ignore the need pressing against my skin, the worry about my father and the Imperiya whispering reminders of the consequences should I fail to secure his proposal.

And the more I let Torden's words and his smile drown out that voice, the more I believed I could truly fall for him.

I knew I was changing as I spent time with Torden. But somehow, it didn't feel like change under pressure. Or if it did, it was pressure like sunlight and rain and soil.

It felt like growth. It felt good.

Hours and days raced by like clouds over the Lysefjord as we hiked, ate, picked strawberries in the woods like children playing a massive game of hide-and-seek. The others didn't care what we did as long as we were together, and much as it shocked me, I didn't get tired of their company.

What surprised me more, though, was that none of the boys seemed to notice how close Skop and Anya were becoming within the larger sphere of our group. I said nothing, since they were only talking. Until, one day, they weren't.

We tramped through the woods in twos and threes. Sweat beaded on my forehead and under my clothes, though the air was cool.

"Cloudberries are my favorite," Torden said, "but they grow later in the summer."

"What do they taste like?"

"Sour. But they are delicious with cream."

"Yes, heaven forbid you sweeten anything," I grumbled. I switched my bucket to my left hand. Its handle left a sulky red crease in my right palm.

Torden nudged me. "If you want honey, all you need is to ask."

"It's never on the table. I don't want to be a bother."

"That is why our teeth are so strong. The *drengs* aren't allowed sweets." He grinned at me meaningfully. "Well, most sweets."

I laughed. "Torden, that was a terrible pun."

He stepped in front of me, eyes warm, only inches away. "Then why can't you stop smiling?"

Just then, I caught movement in my periphery. I flushed and turned, expecting to see Anya or one of the other boys running over to say they'd found more fruit.

I did *not* expect to see Skop's mouth fixed on Anya's, her hands trapped in his shiny black hair.

But my mortified giggle broke off when Torden's face went abruptly dark. "Anya!"

They pulled apart at once. Skop reddened and grinned good-naturedly. But Anya's fair face went ashen, blue veins standing out in her forehead.

Anya knows what is expected of her, Torden had said.

I thought of Bear pretending to be my guard as we fell for one another, of Captain Lang's advice and Sir Perrault's threats.

How well I knew the distance between knowing and doing what was expected of me.

"Skop, we need to speak." Torden's voice was grave. He emptied all the berries I'd picked into one of his buckets, lifting it with ease, and brushed my hair off my shoulder. "I will find you later," he said to me somberly, and together he and Skop made for the fortress, leaving Anya and me faltering beneath a dense silence.

"Please, do not say anything to the others," she said heavily.

"I wouldn't." I shook my head. "But—why?" I'd overheard Aleksei and Torden's conversation, but I didn't understand it at all.

She fingered the end of her braid, blue eyes faraway. "Because if Asgard's sons are its walls, its daughters are its bridges. This choice was never mine to make."

I'd cared for Peter. If he'd loved me the same way, there would never have been any question of sending me away—of forcing me to choose someone else.

Would there?

Doubt ran a cold finger down my arm, and goose bumps rose over my skin.

Maybe it was paranoid. Maybe it was wishful thinking. But for the first time I wondered if Peter had turned me down of his own volition, or if someone else had been involved and made the decision for him. For me.

Fear of Alessandra and all she had done to banish me sang again through my blood, a strident, eerie song. Fear for Daddy. Fear for Potomac.

Maybe Anya and I were in more similar situations than I'd thought.

Anya didn't go back to the fortress with me. I sat on her bed in her empty room, peeled the endpaper from the back binding, and switched on the radio.

I needed my godmother's familiar voice in this strange place, her comfort, her guidance.

Daddy needed me. And I needed to know what to do next.

But there was only silence from the other end, only an empty hiss like a foreign language I couldn't understand.

Dinner was awful.

Anya said she was sick and didn't feel like coming down, so I pretended to believe her and got ready alone. Skop didn't wait to walk me down; he, Lang, and Cobie were deep in conversation when I reached Valaskjálf.

"Do you know when he'll be back?" Cobie asked as I passed them.

Lang shook his head. "Soon, I hope."

I didn't know what they were talking about. They didn't acknowledge me as I walked past, and I tried not to show that it stung.

I thought of Lang's absence in England, of his search for the woman he'd finally found at the ball, and wondered what he was up to now.

None of Torden's brothers mentioned their sister's absence over dinner. Fredrik and Bragi hardly spoke at all, and Hermódr was distracted, sitting nearer their father than usual.

I leaned near to Torden. "Can we talk? What is going on?"

"Hermódr and Pappa are discussing a trade agreement with Sápmi," he said, a little enviously. "Most of us are better soldiers than politicians, but not Hermódr."

"And Fredrik and Bragi?" I asked. "What's wrong with them?"

"Fredrik is angry at me for warning Skop off. And Bragi—well. This is hard for him." Torden rubbed the bridge of his nose. "I'm more concerned about how Skop is handling things."

I swallowed. Down beside Cobie, Skop was deeper into his cups than I'd ever seen him, the pitcher of mead at his side vanishing with startling rapidity. His voice rose and fell, sloshy with alcohol.

He wasn't the only person in the hall who seemed to be getting carried away—he wasn't even the only one at Alföðr's table. Perrault was pink in the face, giggling to himself, and even Bragi looked a little glassy-eyed; mead flowed in Valaskjálf, stronger than what the rest of us were used to. I wasn't worried until I heard Skop say something about Anya.

I thought of Skop taking my hand in Winchester as I crumbled in front of Bear and the court. Now it was time for me to look after him.

I caught Cobie's eye and nodded in our first mate's direction. As we helped him from the table, I smiled wanly at Torden. "Family first."

He nodded, a little rueful.

"Torden's in love with you," Skop mumbled as he staggered

from the hall. "Lucky you. Lucky yours is free," he slurred. "Why is yours *free* when mine isn't?"

"Skop," I said gently, "between you and me, only one of us is actually free. And it's not me."

"Selah." Skop sighed, eyes mournful. "I'm so sorry."

And then he threw up on my shoes.

45

Back in his room, I murmured vague encouragement as Skop evacuated his stomach into a bucket, rambling between heaves.

"Is Lang mad? Is it why"—he hiccupped—"is it why because we're under orders?"

I glanced at Cobie, but she just shrugged.

"I *love* her. He's the worst. 'Stick to the mission, Skop.' He's one to talk," he slurred. Skop poked at me, pushing his index finger right into my forehead.

I stared at Cobie, wide-eyed. *Mission?* "What is he—?" I began.

"Okay. Okay, that's enough," Cobie announced, swatting Skop's hand away. We both jumped as the tiny room's door swung open. Then Cobie and I sighed in relief.

Skop lifted tired eyes to the doorway. "Hi, Lang."

"Anything?" Cobie asked.

Lang pressed his lips together, darting a glance at me, and shook his head. "I went to Valaskjálf, and they told me you had already left." He eyed the bucket and my discarded shoes, grimacing. "I can take over from here. You and Selah wait outside while I get him changed."

Out in the corridor, Cobie wilted against the wall, half-heartedly beating her head against the stones.

"Tired?" I asked pointedly.

She closed her eyes with a groan. "I just knew Anya was going to do this to him."

It was Aleksei's gossip all over again. "Don't say that. You don't know her."

"And you've known her for a week," Cobie said sharply. Then she opened her eyes and sighed. "I'm sorry. That was harsh."

"You're always kind of harsh."

She cracked her knuckles. "Yeah, but I'm not usually unfair."

"You should give Anya a chance," I said quietly. "She's not toying with him."

"You give out a lot of chances." She paused. "As long as we're, you know, analyzing each other."

I shrugged, grinning thinly. "I gamble on forgiving people as often as I can."

You didn't let Bear explain himself, said a critical voice inside. For the first time, I thought of the sadness in his face as I'd left him behind, and felt a little guilty.

"I'm counting on that," came a low voice from the end of the hall.

My head shot up. "Torden."

"I came to see if you were all right," he said simply. "May I speak with you?"

I nodded but didn't move until Cobie gently shoved me in his direction. "Do I smell like barf?" I hissed in her ear.

Cobie gave a tiny shake of her head as Torden led me around a corner, listening for a long moment before he spoke. "I do not want us to be overheard."

"Just—explain." I flopped against a wooden door post. "Anya was miserable today. When I asked her why you hauled Skop off, she just said something about Asgard and bridges and walls."

"Anya cannot be with him." Torden ran a hand through his hair, avoiding my eyes. "Pappa will not allow it."

"Why not?" I demanded. "Skop's steady and smart and good."

"The *konge* says a time will come when—" Torden paused, his jaw tight. "When we will need Anya to marry and forge peace outside our borders as she has within our halls."

The words were noble. But all they meant was that Anya was a resource, not a person.

I wondered if the Council thought of me any differently. Or if it was any better to be sent away simply because my stepmother loathed me. At least Anya's marriage might serve Asgard, help keep her family safe.

But she deserved to choose for herself. *I* deserved to choose for myself.

I frowned. "Is she engaged?"

Torden shook his head. "But she will be, and likely soon."

"To whom?"

"That has not been decided."

I raised my eyebrows. "So this engagement is still just an event—it isn't even a *person* yet. Torden, they care about each other."

"I didn't say I thought it was fair," he said quietly. "Pappa knows nothing, and no one will be concerned about Skop and Anya talking at dinner and dancing at balls if they stay close to the rest of us. But . . ." He trailed off. "You have to understand, we are not supposed to be too private. Pappa says we belong to each other. To Asgard and to Norge."

"So it's better if their flirting means nothing?" I asked. "He'd rather she just use people so he can use her when he needs to?"

Torden looked away. "My father means well."

"Were Bragi and Anya really in love?" I suddenly asked.

Torden's mouth fell open.

"Aleksei told me, but I'd already—"

"Don't *talk* about that." There was no anger in his tone, only desperation. "That is a secret."

"Is it because they were as good as brother and sister?" I asked, curious.

Torden shook his head, weary. "No. No one worries about that; they are not related by blood, and our communities are small. Besides, families take on wards all the time, and these things are bound to happen when people grow up so close. Just—please." He took my hand. "I don't want anyone else punished. Bragi never saw her as a sister, but that is what Anya is to me, just as Skop is your brother."

I massaged my forehead, thinking of Anya and Skop kissing in the woods, so lost together they'd forgotten they weren't alone.

What would it be like to kiss Torden that way?

My stomach swooped.

Bear's kiss had been a single stolen moment with a forbidden boy, like something out of a daydream. As fleeting and dubious in its reality as my imagined relationship with Peter, perfect Peter with kindness in his heart and laurel in his hair.

I had never seen how distant Peter had been from me before. I saw it now when I felt how little space remained between Torden and me.

When I looked up at Torden, I saw a boy I was learning at close range, in a deeply specific way. The burdens he carried. His love for his brothers.

It was difficult. And I knew it was real.

"What if we're caught down here? In—private?" I stumbled over his word. "What then?"

Torden came a step nearer. I pressed myself harder against the wall behind me, the cold stone raising goose bumps over my skin. He put a hand on my bare upper arm. "Anya and Skop are not supposed to be together," he said, voice husky. "But we . . ." He trailed off again, thumb skimming back and forth over my shoulder.

I pushed my lungs open, pulled in air and courage. "We what?"

"I am terrible at this." Torden shook his head. "But I would face worse than an older brother for a chance with you." He slipped his hand down my arm to twine his callused fingers through my own. That chaste gesture alone made me dizzy, but I reached for his other hand.

"I don't have any brothers," I said faintly. Torden smiled, eyes burning.

But as he bent, pressing his rough cheek to mine, a door somewhere nearby snapped closed, and Lang's voice split the silence.

Hidden though we were around the corner, we jumped apart, the spell broken, our breathing ragged. "I should probably get back." I fiddled with my shirt cuff, unable to look at him. "Skop's fine, but he's going to have a headache tomorrow."

But Torden shook his head. "I have to make this up to you. Did you mean what you said, about going down to the fjord one morning?"

I stilled. "For the sunrise?"

"I can be outside your door first thing tomorrow." Torden's eyes were guarded but so serious, so earnest.

"Can you miss your run?"

"I'll run double the day after tomorrow. Besides," he said, "I never break a promise."

I bit my lip at the light burning in his eyes.

I didn't want to just watch the sun rise with this boy. I didn't want to wait alone for dawn through the long hours of the night. I wanted to leave together, right then, to spend the night talking under the stars wheeling over the Lysefjord, coaxing truths out of him until the sun rose and kindled the black sky.

But Torden wouldn't abandon a friend, and I wouldn't, either. "I can't wait."

When I stood up on tiptoe to kiss him on the cheek, it felt like standing on solid ground.

Lang bid Torden a distracted good night when we met him around the corner, and the *prins* left me with a small smile.

I turned to the captain, hoping my flush wasn't visible in the dark. "Skop?" I asked. "Cobie?"

"Cobie went to check in on Perrault," Lang said. "And Skop's fine, but I'm going to stay with him, just in case."

"Wait here." I slipped into Anya's darkened room and returned with a pile of fur rugs, pushing them into his arms. "Take these. His room's cold."

"Thanks." Lang rubbed one red-rimmed eye. A long eyelash fell onto the soft, shadowed hollow above his cheekbone.

"I'd do anything for Skop." I shrugged and gently plucked the fallen lash from his tired skin, blowing it lightly off my fingers and wishing for a clear dawn.

Lang opened his thin lips as if to reply, but for a long moment only our breath disturbed the hallway's silence. "And for him, too?" The corners of his mouth and his eyes were drawn down, intent and bewildered.

I didn't have to ask who he meant.

I swallowed and stepped backward into the dark of Anya's room. "Good night, Lang."

"Good night, Selah," he finally said.

I closed the door behind me.

46

My nerves roared to life with Torden's arrival in the small hours of the morning. I dressed, trembling, in Anya's still-dark room, wringing my hands as though my fretfulness could be shaken off like water.

But he wrapped me in his arms when I stepped into the hallway, the scruff on his chin catching at my hair. Close against his chest, the soap-and-water scent of his skin and his steady, certain breathing softened the jagged edges of my anxiety. "*God morgen*," he whispered.

Out by the stables, Torden set me on his palomino, Gullfaxi, before swinging into the saddle himself. With no reins to cling to, I clasped my hands tentatively around his waist. "Do you mind if I—?"

I felt the moment his heart began to thunder beneath my hands. "Of course not. Hold on to me."

We rode to a skinny stretch of flat rock between the

Lysefjord and the base of Mount Kjerag. I was speechless, awe-struck; bound to the mountainside, the trunk of the great tree was half the length of a football field, its twisted roots each thick as the body of one of Alfödr's horses. "Is all of this . . . ?"

"Yes." Torden dismounted, then helped me down, his hands lingering a moment when he'd caught me around my waist. "Yggdrasil." He led me along the narrow bank, the only sounds the water and the birds and, far off, the deep rumble of Alfödr's *drengs* and *thegns* preparing for their morning run.

We are not supposed to be too private, he'd said. But here we were on the edge of the water, alone, far from his brothers and sister and my friends. My hands shook as we clambered across the roots that snaked into the fjord and settled into a wide fork.

Torden Asgard, fifth of Alfödr's sons, the boy with his arm around my shoulders. Could I have known, reading his profile aboard the *Beholder,* how his very nearness would sear my skin, wreck my pulse, blur my focus?

"Torden, why am I here with you, and not one of your brothers?"

I'd blurted out the question without thinking.

"Would you rather be here with someone else?" he asked. He shifted away, his stare so raw and frayed at the edges that I wondered if he was remembering Aleksei's warning not to let Fredrik too near me.

"No. It's just—" I shook my head, mouth going dry as I clawed for words. Torden stretched out his legs, studied his pale, muscled hands, suddenly seeming far away.

Can I trust Torden with the truth?

He'd trusted me with his.

"I haven't told you much about my home," I began. "Yours is so different, I was afraid you wouldn't understand."

Torden's eyes were wary. "What do you mean?"

"My father's unwell, and my stepmother wishes I weren't part of her family. All my suitors were first sons—boys in line for their own thrones." I cleared my throat. "You were the only exception to that rule."

Understanding dawned on his face. "And all my brothers are unmarried, so . . ."

"So I'm wondering," I said softly, "how I was lucky enough to be invited to visit you, of all the Asgard boys, instead of Týr."

Torden swallowed hard. The pink light blooming faintly on the horizon colored his face rosy and hopeful. "You once told me that you would listen if I told stories," he said, arm circling my shoulders again. "Does that promise still stand?"

"Of course."

"All of it?" he pressed. "You have to hear the ending, if I begin."

"I will." I squeezed his hand. "I promise."

Torden leaned back into the fork and looked off over the Bilröst. "There once was a boy who feared for the fate of a girl who did not even know his name." He paused. "The boy hadn't intended to involve himself at all. In fact, his father intended her for his eldest son."

I glanced up at him, and his beard grazed my forehead. "Then how did it happen?"

"How do these things ever happen?" Torden shrugged.

Banners of orange unfurled over the horizon, the promise of warmth and daylight. "He was enchanted."

My soft, red heart began to riot beneath my skin.

"I'd been brawling with Vidarr again, more of his—never mind." Torden flexed his fingers, their nails bitten short. "But I had come bruised to Pappa's study so many times it hardly mattered. He didn't even pause his meeting with Týr when I came in."

I tried to imagine Daddy summoning me to issue a scolding and couldn't. Certainly, I'd disappointed him through the years. But he'd always come to *me* afterward—to talk, to discipline me if the situation required. And then, always, to forgive.

How my heart ached for him.

"My oldest brother has been focused solely on learning warfare for as long as I can remember," said Torden. "When Týr has a spare thought, it is for food. Or drink. But he is twenty-six. My father has been insisting he choose a wife for years, but he could never be bothered. Until one day, when a portrait arrived from across the ocean."

I gave a shiver, either from his words or the chill of the rock underneath us. Torden snuggled me against his side. "I stood in my father's study, waiting for my turn—for my reprimand—as he pressed Týr. The girl was beautiful, Pappa said. Old enough to be married, young enough to have many children. It would be simple.

"I'm not a curious man by nature," he mused. "But when neither of them was paying attention, I looked at the file on his desk. And there you were."

Torden shook his head. "You had on that pink dress, pretty enough to sway my brother. I could hardly read your information, because I was trying to be—subtle. But what I could read concerned me."

I bit the inside of my cheek. "What?"

"Huginn and Muninn had done extra research," he said quietly. "Your official biography was marked with their notes—'quiet,' 'withdrawn,' 'bookish.' Their interpretation of what their contacts reported."

Shots of white and gold rang through the sky. I grew very still at his side.

Torden's voice was a low rumble when he spoke again. "I told myself it was nothing more than chivalry. You would lose the chance to be queen, but I could not watch a gentle, unsuspecting girl be crushed under the weight of Týr's thoughtlessness."

I remembered his older brother that first night at dinner, shouting and shoveling food into his mouth. I could never have reciprocated his feelings—if he'd managed to produce any.

"Pappa had almost convinced Týr—after all, he might never find a wife so easily again. He was nearly ready to move forward."

Move forward. As though I were a village to attack and the oldest Asgard brother were organizing troops. "So what happened?"

Torden wet his lips. "I asked Pappa to let it be me, instead."

A pause. My voice wobbled treasonously. "What?"

"I asked Týr to defer to me," Torden said. "Potomac was furious, because plans had already begun, but in the end, they conceded."

In the end, I thought, *it had mattered most to Alessandra that I go.*

"The visit might end in nothing, but I hoped at least to spare you two hideous weeks with Týr. He is not very inclined to marry, so he agreed. Pappa just looked at my black eye and said that maybe a woman would do me some good." Torden cracked a grin.

My humorless laugh echoed off the rocks as I shifted away from him. "I guess it's lucky for Týr and me that you felt sorry for me."

"Stop," Torden said evenly. "Wait for the end. You promised." His arms didn't restrain me, but his tone held me fast.

"Fine." I avoided his eyes, choking on confusion and embarrassment. "Finish."

"I called it chivalry in the beginning because I didn't know any better," he said. "I didn't know how it would be."

"How *what* would be?"

"How everything would change when you arrived," he said heatedly. Torden scrubbed a hand through his hair, gleaming red gold in the sunrise. "Your portrait was a weak still life. But when I saw you face-to-face . . ." He shook his head. "It was all over for me."

The sun stole over the horizon, stretching across the water, and Torden dragged in a breath as though he were coming up for air. "I never needed anyone before. Not me, on my own," he said quietly. "I had my brothers, my kingdom. But you told me that first day you would listen to me. You let me lean on you, and not because you had to."

My blood stuttered, but I held my silence, fearful to speak and break the spell.

"You've been hurt," he said. "And we seem nothing alike."

"We *are* nothing alike."

"That isn't true."

I breathed a mirthless laugh. "Have you *looked* at us side by side?"

My pulse was the brittle *tick* of an old clock. But there they were—the words I'd dreaded saying, the truth I couldn't avoid when I remembered my stepmother's criticism.

Boys like Peter. Boys like Torden.

I realized I'd been waiting for this moment, this inevitable point when he would look at me—soft, scared, unremarkable— and see that he could do better.

Torden was a tempest on the edge of the dawn, a self-contained thunderstorm as he gripped me gently by the elbows and forced my eyes to his. "The things we like are different. The things we love are the same."

A strangled noise escaped me. "What does that mean?"

"Courage is the heart of me," he said. "The thing I pray to be. And I see it in you. It's in your eyes every time you tell me something you are afraid to say or try something you are afraid to do." He took a breath. "You are so brave, Selah, and so beautiful, and I want you beside me always. I will keep you safe, and you will be my home."

Torden shifted around me, curving my body against his, and I found myself sheltered beneath his arm. "I have seen how we look side by side," he whispered into my ear, "and it has changed how I imagine my life. With you, I see a wider world."

I forgot how to breathe as he ran a thumb over my cheek-bone. "Would it work?" My voice was desperate. "Could it possibly?"

"Who can say? But I am not afraid to try." Torden pressed my palm to the hammering in his chest, voice growing fierce. "My heart is not a liar."

"Mine's beating just as hard," I whispered, laughing weakly. Torden smiled and leaned his forehead against mine.

"It will not be easy, but we could build something good together. Something that would endure."

Something that could save Potomac. And Daddy.

My heart rose.

The sun made its way over the horizon, its advent coloring the Bilröst and the cliffs and Torden's face warm with light.

Through this whole affair, I'd been yanked like a marionette from one place to the next. I'd left Potomac on my stepmother's orders. Bear had deceived me. Even as I believed I was mak-ing my own decisions in England—following my heart, taking risks when I dared—I was merely reacting to circumstances tailored to control me.

Torden, my only suitor not set to inherit a throne, had felt like a foregone conclusion before I met him.

I'd thought I had no choice. But Torden had chosen me.

He had given me the truth. He was offering me himself. And that meant everything. It *changed* everything.

Something molten and glowing crystallized inside me, in my chest or my guts, and I wasn't scared, for once, to do what I wanted to do. I took Torden's face in my hands, brushing his hair from his forehead. His wonderstruck eyes held mine only a moment before I stretched forward and kissed him on the mouth.

Dawn over the Bilröst was rosy and mild, but our kiss was thunder and lightning, burning my body. And in that instant, I didn't feel even the faintest trace of fear. I could have fought Alessandra, scaled Yggdrasil clear to the foot of Asgard, tied myself to the prow of the *Beholder* with my arms outstretched and dared the wine-dark sea to defy me.

Torden lifted me easily onto his lap, gathering me in. I was awkward at first, out of sync, but his lips were so steady, his hands so certain as he slid his fingers into my hair, that I fell into his rhythm.

When we drew apart, flushed and smiling uncertainly, I shook my head. "That was . . ."

"Beautiful." Torden glanced down at me, panting. "You're beautiful."

Shaking, I kissed him once more, softly this time, and leaned my head against his chest. "I'm glad you chose me," I said. "I'm so glad it was you."

"I may have chosen you, but I hardly had any choice in the

matter," Torden said into my hair. "It was clear as day to me from the beginning that you were the one."

My heart ached with the rightness of his arms around me, of his voice in my ear and his hands in my hands.

He was my rescue. And together, we'd save my father.

As the sun climbed over the water, I knew with as much conviction as I'd ever felt that I belonged with Torden, and he belonged with me.

47

Our kisses and our confessions opened a floodgate.

I told Torden about my momma, about my godmother and Daddy and Potomac. He told me about growing up at Asgard, about visiting his uncle Heimdalr, who guarded the mouth of the Bilröst, about life before and then after Anya and Fredrik and Aleksei came along. He even told me about the scuffles he still insisted weren't his fault. "They insulted our mother!" he'd protest, or swear he was only backing up his brothers.

I held up my palms. "I've never had the urge to hit anyone."

Bragi laughed at this. "Marry him and you'll come to know the feeling."

We only held hands in front of his brothers—and that alone was enough to invite their mockery. But when the others weren't looking, he'd catch me around the waist and kiss me until I was dizzy, upright only because of the constant echo of his heartbeat in my chest and his arms around me.

When the *konge* announced that Midsummer's Eve would be celebrated on Friday, two days thence, Hermódr, Bragi, and Aleksei became more cheerful and boisterous than ever. We passed two more perfect days together, tromping through the woods and the barley fields, riding and practicing swordplay and archery until my arms ached. The afternoon of the bonfire we sailed across the fjord just to play in a waterfall. Torden never let go of me as we shouted and splashed beneath the rainbows that rose through the mist, Fredrik and Anya and Skop the only missing pieces to our happiness.

We finally rode back to the fortress when the sun got low, the wind so strong at our backs that it whipped my hair out of its pins. I was next to last to return, faster only than Aleksei, who wasn't trying, but my legs didn't wobble when I jumped off Skeithbrimir's back to let Hermódr and Bragi and Aleksei lead our mounts into the stables.

Torden sidled near, eyes narrowed in the fading daylight. "Are you excited for tonight?"

"Mm-hmm." I nodded, pinching my lips around my hairpins while I looped my hair into a tidy knot.

He wound his arms around my waist, grinning mischievously. "You open yourself to attack when you raise both arms at once." His voice was low, his nose and lips nuzzling my ear. "Your sides are defenseless."

Euphoria clouded my brain. I tripped over my own feet, incoherent, and gave a shivering laugh. *All of me is defenseless.*

"You aren't a threat to me," I murmured. I let my hair fall, resting my hands on his chest.

"No. Never to you." When he pulled me onto my tiptoes, my hairpins fell from my lips, lost forever as he lowered his mouth to mine and I melted like snow in the late-afternoon sun.

A wolf whistle startled us apart. "We were gone for less than a minute!" Hermódr protested, tumbling out of the stables ahead of an elated Bragi and a gaping Aleksei.

"What was your hurry?" Torden called back, grinning. My cheeks grew hot; I couldn't quite meet anyone's eyes but his.

I adore you, I wanted to tell him. *I'd kiss you in front of them or anyone else and not care at all.*

I'd told Torden all about my godmother. Suddenly, more than anything, I wished I could tell Godmother Althea all about him.

I cleared my throat. "I should go check on Anya." I gave him a featherweight kiss and backed away, resuming my efforts with my hair. "See you tonight."

Torden scrubbed at his beard and shook his head, casting about for words, as hazy from our proximity as I was. "See you tonight!" he finally yelled back.

As I turned toward the fortress, the boys burst out behind me, jubilant beneath their mockery. Just once I looked behind me on the scene I'd left: Aleksei was smirking, but Hermódr and Bragi slapped Torden on the back and jabbed earnest fingers at his chest, arms slung around his shoulders. Torden was triumphant, face brighter than the sky overhead.

I bit my lip, thrilled. Stupid. Happier than anyone had a right to be.

* * *

Anya wasn't in her room when I got back.

Nerves surging, I unearthed Godmother Althea's book from my trunk and turned to lock the door. Except it didn't *have* a lock.

"This *place*," I groaned. I flung the book on Anya's bed.

My godmother's voice filled the empty room.

Our Father who art in Heaven, hallowed be thy name.

I froze, choking back a laugh or a tiny sob. How many times had we said prayers together? I scrabbled for my rosary, fumbling past the book's pages as if my godmother herself were trapped in its binding.

Hail Mary, full of grace.

Free of its hiding place, I let the radio carry her voice to me from an ocean away, carry the prayers that were my roots and bones, wishing she could hear my voice join with hers. One by one, the beads slid across my fingers.

With the book flopped open before me, the little rows of hash marks on the endpaper caught my eye. I'd forgotten to keep count the last couple of days. Guilt soured in my stomach as my godmother continued to pray.

Glory be to the Father, and to the Son, and to the Holy Spirit.

Yggdrasil began to rustle in a stiff breeze outside Anya's window, and I hurried to turn up the radio over its noise. But instead of growing louder, suddenly, my godmother's voice disappeared.

"No," I blurted, almost a whimper. I lunged for the radio and found I'd adjusted the frequency, not the volume. "No, no, no." I fiddled with the knob, trying to find Althea again, but only a hissing sound came from its mouth.

I gave the dial one more frustrated twist, and the scratching stopped. But my godmother wasn't speaking.

"Gretel," said a man's voice. "Gretel, this is Hansel. Can you hear me?" His accent was square-sounding, somehow, sheared of its end *rs*, as if he were English, but he pronounced his *ths* like *zs*.

There was silence.

"Gretel?"

"Hansel," said a woman. "We're here. We've considered your invitation, and we accept."

"Burg Cats?" asked the man—Hansel, I supposed. "Or Burg Rhein—"

"Hansel, *stoy! Ty s uma soshol?* Are you crazy?" Gretel demanded. Her voice was sweet and high-pitched, all soft consonants and swelling vowels, but her words were sharp. "Anyone could be listening."

"Fine. The witch's cottage, or the woodcutter's?" Hansel snapped. I noticed he pronounced his *ws* like *vs*. "Tell me quickly."

"The woodcutter's cottage. My people won't be going anywhere near your father."

"Very well," Hansel said. "When?"

"Tomorrow. *Fur die Freiheit.*"

"*Fur die Wildnis,*" said Hansel. "We will be."

And then there was nothing.

I pressed a hand to my temple. What on earth had I just overheard?

Witches and woodcutters and languages I didn't understand.

None of it made any sense to me.

And none of it concerns me, I reminded myself.

I knew only one thing: I needed to get out of Europe. There was too much danger here. Too many unknowns.

I needed to get home to Daddy, and to Potomac, where I'd be safe. Where Torden and I could *make* everyone safe.

I reached for the radio, tweaking the dial until I found her frequency again. But when I finally whittled my way back to 3.44, Godmother Althea was gone.

Anya never came back to her room. I lay on her bed alone, running my rosary through my fingers and turning over the strange conversation I'd heard, and went alone to meet her brothers by the stables.

I found them waiting beneath a moon like a pearl and flickering lamps like a constellation of stars. Skop and Anya were nowhere to be seen, but Fredrik and Bragi were laughing as though nothing was wrong at all. Though I was glad at Fredrik's return, their whooping and pushing and shoving sent a pang through me.

I wondered again if Torden could bear to leave them, to live with me in Potomac. Would he be whole without them?

I wanted to imagine the big brother he'd be to the little brother or sister Daddy and Alessandra had on the way. I wanted to imagine him by my side.

But watching him play with his brothers like so many overgrown little boys on the hillside, I couldn't even bring myself to ask.

"Why so glum, sunshine?" called Bragi.

I squinted at them, pounding the last few steps down the hill. "Pardon?"

Torden grinned. "I think it fits." He toyed with a bright streak in my hair before lifting me onto Gullfaxi. Aleksei smirked.

Fredrik winked. "It's because you're so bright and happy."

"And because Torden looks at you like the rising sun," Hermódr said, teasing.

Bragi shook his head. "He's useless till you come out in the morning."

Torden climbed into the saddle. I wrapped my arms around his waist and kissed the back of his shoulder. "And I'll scorch his eyes out if he looks at me too long?" His laugh rippled through the muscles of his stomach, and I grinned, absurdly delighted.

"Yes," Aleksei drawled. "And he gets hot around you and you'll eventually burn him."

"Aleksei!" Hermódr's face wrinkled in distaste.

Fredrik shook his head, frowning. Torden said nothing, but I felt him tense in my arms.

Aleksei's comment twisted in my ears as we rode to a clearing in the forest where *thegns* and *drengs* and *heerthmen* and noblewomen stood silhouetted by huge blossoms of flame. I spotted Huginn and Muninn immediately in their black cloaks, and a crowd surrounded the oldest Asgard boys, their shadows stretching out past the edge of the woods. A group of small boys trundled a wheel along the tree line to whoops from those watching. But as Torden helped me off Gullfaxi's back, the night and the crowd suddenly pressed in on me, and I wished I could shrink into myself and disappear.

"Don't be nervous." Torden's beard rasped against my cheeks as he kissed my temple. "Come on. Tonight is going to be fun."

I nodded, and as he led me after his brothers through the reeking smoke, J.J. bounded over, grinning from ear to ear. "Hey! Selah! Hey, guys!"

"You didn't want to trundle the wheel with the other boys?" Torden rumpled the toboggan on his head, his smile a little regretful. "Or are you too old for that?"

"I was too late. We almost didn't come." J.J. frowned at the protocol officer approaching us, with Lang close behind. "Sir Perrault doesn't like to go outside."

"I wasn't going to miss it." Perrault eyed me keenly. He nodded at the nearest bonfire, belching noxious smoke. "Still, can you blame me? They're burning garbage. And are those— bones?" His pretty lips curled in disgust.

"To keep the dragons away," Bragi called cheerfully. Hermódr rolled his eyes and laughed.

Aleksei leaned close, voice conspiratorial but loud enough for everyone to hear. "The old wives' tales say that dragons, ah, get excited in the summer." He laced his fingers together. "When they *come together* in the air—"

I clapped my hands over J.J.'s ears.

Torden cut Aleksei off with a look. "The stench is to keep dragons away so they don't poison the wells."

"I'm not a baby," J.J. protested, squirming in my grasp.

"I know, but you're my favorite." I hugged him impulsively, then let him escape.

Lang laughed, clapping a hand on the boy's shoulder. "Girls like her will look different in a year or two, J.J."

Fredrik took a drink and cocked his head sharply. "You think so, Captain?"

Lang coughed, rubbing at the back of his neck. "I only meant—"

"We also pick mistletoe on Midsummer's Eve," Hermódr broke in. His eyes darted around behind his glasses, his smile looking oddly pasted on. "All the old stories say that if it is cut without an iron tool and doesn't touch the ground, mistletoe picked on the full moon can heal and keep harm away."

Aleksei tipped his chin at Torden and me, eyes innocent. "It helps couples make babies, too—I'd be careful."

This time, it was Perrault who clapped his hands over J.J.'s ears.

"Enough," Hermódr bellowed, the only one of the boys to answer in English, and probably the only one not swearing up a storm.

Lang's jaw hung slack. We'd hardly spoken since the first ball. But as he took in Torden and me—his tensed arm around my waist, me curled against his side—an odd pang of guilt rang through me.

I jutted a thumb over my shoulder toward the woods and glanced up at Torden. "Should we—?"

"Yes." Torden nodded firmly. He threw another annoyed glance at Aleksei as we left the fires behind.

48

At first, our search turned up only bare branches and the sounds of laughter and bodies crashing through the brush. "The mistletoe near the bonfires will have been gathered up quickly," Torden said, gently thumbing my knuckles. "We'll have to search further in."

Fewer and fewer people crossed our path as we walked on. Soon the only noises were our boots in the undergrowth and the creak of the lamp in Torden's hand, its light sweeping the boughs of oaks and pear trees.

"There!" I suddenly whispered. From a clump of green overhead, white berries shone like moonstones in the dark.

Torden grinned. "Good eye. Here, take this." He passed me the lamp and fit his boot into a cleft in the tree trunk, gripping a pair of low branches.

"What are you doing?"

He twisted to look at me. "How did you expect we would get the mistletoe down?"

"I don't know. Not like that." I wrung my hands. "Just be careful."

Torden's back and shoulders worked beneath his sleeves, pulling him easily from branch to branch. "Selah, I begin to suspect you consider most of my hobbies dangerous." There was no mistaking the laugh in his voice.

I crossed my arms as well as I could while holding the lamp. "Like what?"

"Like climbing trees with knives in my belt." I caught a flash of bronze and the *snap* of stems as he cut the mistletoe where it clung to the old oak. "But you can't fuss over me. I insist on that rule if we get married."

I bit my lip, fighting a smile. "Can I suggest others?"

"Such as?"

"Such as . . . no dead animals in our personal spaces?" I asked. "Time set aside just for reading?"

"More books and no taxidermy in our bedroom? I'll consider it." Something in my chest flared at the phrase *our bedroom*.

Torden dropped the last five feet from the tree and hit the ground with a *thud*. I started forward before drawing myself up. "Oh—sorry, I forgot. No fretting." I leaned against a tree, setting the lamp down to examine my cuticles.

He stood slowly, a mischievous grin playing around his mouth. "I said no worrying when I go away. I didn't say you couldn't be happy to see me when I got back."

Torden sidled over, square jaw, square shoulders, scruffy red beard—so handsome it made me foolish. I scrambled for a reply. "You know, it's funny, mistletoe in the summer," I blurted out. "I only remember it at Christmastime."

Something flickered in his gaze. "We hang it all over Asgard. Do you use it in Potomac?"

"Yes." I twisted my fingers, my voice sounding very small. "If someone catches you underneath it, you're supposed to kiss them."

"We do the same."

I stilled as he approached, panting a little from his drop, lamplight glinting on his hair and in his eyes.

Torden tugged the mistletoe from his shirt pocket. As he dangled it overhead, his free arm snaked around my waist and he bent to kiss me. I was so dazed from his mouth against mine and his hand cupping my face that I hardly noticed the mistletoe slip from his grasp and fall to the ground.

"Any excuse to kiss you, or none," he said, voice husky against my lips. "Christmas or Midsummer, under the mistletoe or at a church altar or somewhere alone in the dark. As long as you are mine, *elskede*, because I am yours."

His mouth was a bonfire that set my skin aglow. As Torden kissed me, warm and relentless, I wondered if it were possible for two people to fall in real love as quickly as we had thrust our hearts at one another.

I wanted it to be. I wanted to keep his red-blooded heart, rough and strange and good as it was. And I wanted him to keep mine safe for me.

Torden held me, and we held the dark between us until we heard the crack of twigs nearby. He glanced up, arms taut around me.

"What is—"

"Shh." Torden's jaw grazed my temple, breath tense against my cheek. "I don't—oh." He suddenly relaxed. I followed his gaze to Aleksei, standing beneath a scraggly dead tree a few yards away.

"Aleksei!" Torden's embarrassed laugh shook me. "No mistletoe around here. Keep walking." I buried my face in his chest, smiling.

But his brother didn't answer his good-natured grin in kind. "Dronning Rihttá is asking for you."

Torden cleared his throat and cut his eyes at me. "Right now?"

"Look, she needs you, all right?"

I winced. Aleksei's tone was caustic.

I shivered at Torden's sigh in my ear. "This is a difficult night for my mother. I need to make sure she is all right. But I meant what I said." He bent his forehead to mine and kissed me again, lips certain, lingering. "I'll come to you later tonight. We have more to say."

I nodded, knowing full well my heart was in my eyes, not caring if I looked foolish.

I knew what I wanted. I wanted Torden to propose to me, to take him home to meet my father, to show him the place that I loved. To love him as long as I lived. If only he'd ask.

"Finished?" Aleksei's arms were crossed, one long, skinny leg jiggling impatiently.

"She's back at the fortress?" Torden asked. The other boy nodded wordlessly. "See that Selah gets back to the bonfires, would you?"

Aleksei bobbed, rolling his eyes. "Would you just get going?"

Torden gave my hand a squeeze before he took off through the woods. I watched him jog off, feeling forlorn.

Aleksei sized me up. "So." He barked a short, humorless laugh.

"So." I stuffed my hands in my pockets, ignoring the edge in his tone. "Why did Dronning Rihttá need Torden?"

Aleksei picked up the lamp. His hair was black as pitch, his skin ghostly white beneath its glow. "Selah, you've heard Baldr's and Hodr's names whispered here and there since you arrived."

Disquiet unfurled in my stomach, like blood twisting faintly in water. "Yes. They passed away last year, didn't they?"

"Yes and no," Aleksei said. "Baldr died last Midsummer's Eve in a horrible accident."

"He died a year ago—today?" I stared at him openmouthed, stumbling over a fallen log, my words faltering as my feet did. "And you pushed the king and queen to throw a party?"

Aleksei's voice was sharp. "People expected it. Tradition is important. Keeping up morale is important."

"Dronning Rihttá and her *son* are important," I said, my voice likewise carrying the hint of a barb. I shook my head. "H-how did it happen? Where's her other son?"

"Baldr and Hodr always wanted to look for mistletoe on

360

Midsummer's Eve. They said the wheel trundling was for kids," Aleksei said. "Hodr was a skinny, clinging little thing. Idolized Torden and Fredrik. Baldr would wake up screaming and sweating and thrashing around from nightmares. He worried Dronning Rihttá, so she tried to keep Baldr close, protect him," said Aleksei. "But what twelve-year-old can endure that?"

A bush off the path covered in thorns dug at my skin. I winced, swiping at the blood that rose on my forearm. "And?" I asked, feeling sick.

Aleksei wet his lips. His eyes were liquid in the dark. "They took off on their own last year when no one was watching," he finally said. "Baldr probably fell twenty feet out of that pear tree. Hodr didn't know what to do."

My lungs turned to stone. "They were out in the forest alone?"

Aleksei ignored me. "Hodr couldn't see very well during the day, but at night he was totally blind. He heard something hit the ground, and he knew something was wrong when Baldr didn't answer him."

My shoe caught on a rock, and I stifled a gasp. Aleksei seemed not to notice.

"Baldr was dead before we found him. Hodr had screamed himself into hysterics."

We were walking so quickly I'd begun to sweat, but ice skulked over my skin.

"It was tragic," Aleksei said. "Baldr was a beautiful child, with black hair like Dronning Rihttá's and a face like a cherub's. No one in Asgard would have ever done him any harm.

The tsarytsya herself came for his wake."

The tsarytsya. In Asgard. Anxiety jolted so sharply through me I felt it in my teeth. I closed my eyes and took a breath.

"And . . . what happened to Hodr?" I asked.

"He was sent away."

"What?" I blurted. "Where?"

"A monastery, somewhere in Iceland." Aleksei shrugged.

I shook my head, stomach churning. "But he was a child. It was an accident."

"Hodr wasn't a child. He was fourteen. He knew his vision was impaired in the dark." Aleksei's sidelong glance dragged a shiver up my spine, and his voice grew hard. "Alfödr cannot afford to suffer fools."

I stared, his hideous words scraping goose bumps over my skin. *Fourteen* made a child, whatever Asgard thought.

Perhaps it didn't matter to Aleksei. He hadn't been allowed to be a child for a very long time.

"Baldr had been the one to keep peace between us brothers, the reason Týr and Vidarr and Váli could accept their father's marriage to another woman," said Aleksei. "But the *kongen* could hardly look at Hodr after he died."

Horror trickled into my stomach like cold water. Dronning Rihttá hadn't been watching J.J. because he reminded her of her dead son. He reminded her of the living child who had been ripped from her arms.

It may have been Midsummer, but I was suddenly freezing.

I stopped short, limbs trembling, as Aleksei walked on. "I want to go find Torden."

"Torden's inside," he said, irritated, not turning. In the bobbing lamplight, the nose and teeth of his wolf tattoo snarled above his shirt neck. "I'm supposed to take you back to the bonfires."

My pitch and my pulse spiked. "No. I want to go find him now."

"Fine." Aleksei pointed in the direction Torden had jogged earlier. "The fortress is that way."

Panic gripped me by the throat. "I can't get there alone in the dark."

Aleksei held the lamp out to me without a word.

49

Our ride to the woods had been brief. It took much longer to reach Asgard's gates on foot.

As I stole through the night, jumping at the cries of owls and the croaks of ravens, at the *snap* of every twig beneath my own feet, Aleksei's story took form in my mind.

Baldr lying dead on the forest floor, his delicate bones broken.

Hodr, blind and alone and shrieking into the dark.

Dronning Rihttá gathering her limp child's body into her lap, anguish and loss clawing at her skin.

Dronning Rihttá, stripped of a son who had died and of a son who had not.

How had it happened? How had two boys who stuck so close to their older brothers sneaked into the dark where there was no one to keep them safe? How had they found themselves alone in this place where no one was ever alone?

Nausea hit me in waves. I ran panting inside the fortress, grateful for light and dying for company. But tonight, Valaskjálf's cheerful roar was replaced with one angry, echoing voice.

I skidded to a stop outside the great hall's doors and hid, watching.

They'd clustered into three camps inside, like three little armies in a standoff. The first centered around Skop, looking sick and pale beneath his light brown complexion. At his sides, Lang and Perrault were a shifting mass of restless glances and muttered words.

Anya stood inside the second camp, encircled protectively by her brothers. The Asgard boys' arms were clasped behind their backs, their cheeks pale, their eyes trained on the ground.

At the head of the third camp towered Konge Alfödr, eye blazing like the bonfires outside, flanked by Rihttá and his eldest sons. Huginn and Muninn circled the scene, cloaks flapping, eyes sharp.

"Koniag, you had no right," shouted Alfödr, stabbing a finger at Skop. "No right!"

"And you!" said Dronning Rihttá, arms outstretched to Anya. Her tone was considerably calmer than her husband's, but she was visibly upset. "Haven't we taught you better than this?"

"Nothing happened!" Anya choked. "I did not plan this— to fall in love."

Alfödr missed the pained pinch of Bragi's mouth, but not the joy that lit Skop's face. "Not planned?" he roared, striding toward her. "The fortress was empty but for the pair of you! I did not raise you a liar or a lovesick *girl*, to grow faint of heart over a boy. You are a shield-maiden and a *prinsessa* of Varsinais-Suomi, but tonight you have disgraced both your peoples."

A furious blue vein stood out on Anya's pale forehead. "I did not—we—" She broke off, eyes wide, nostrils flared.

I burst from my hiding place. "What is going on?"

A dozen pairs of eyes cut my way. "Seneschal-elect, this has nothing to do with you," Muninn croaked gravely, creaking forward on aged joints as if to block me from the hall.

I nearly backed down, but Anya's lips began to tremble. I steeled myself. "Skop is in Potomac's employ, so it certainly does."

"Very well." Alfödr glared, stomping toward the *Beholder* crew. "Your first mate and my daughter were alone in his room. Alone!"

It explained Anya's absence, and Skop's. I ground my teeth. *So reckless.*

Torden had warned Skop what his father would do. He'd known what he risked.

And yet Alfödr's hypocrisy gnawed at me. He had eight children by six different women, and no one had called him a disgrace to Asgard. At least Dronning Rihttá's moral qualms might be sincere. The king was only afraid his bargaining chip had been sullied.

"Is this true?" I whispered to Skop, hardly moving my lips as I took my place beside them. "Is it just hearsay? Please tell me there's some circumstance they're leaving out."

"It's quite simple." Huginn impaled me with his sharp blue stare. "We received information. They were found together."

I crossed my arms, steeling myself. "So you were informed," I fired back. "Have you been spying on my people? On your guests?"

Muninn shook his head. "We cannot disclose that."

"Konge Alfödr, First Mate Koniag is a good man," Lang offered earnestly. "His intentions were honorable. They were only talking."

The king's jaw tightened. "More is at stake than their feelings. Your first mate tried to seduce Asgard's *prinsessa*."

Skop burst forward. "*I'm* not the one using her, you selfish piece of—"

Alfödr cut him off with a punch to the jaw.

It was quicker than a drop from a gallows. One minute, Skop was upright, and the next, he was sprawling.

The sound of the blow was sickening, like a stone being dropped in the mud. But the empty silence that followed was worse, a world away from the Asgard boys' cheerful scrapping. Even the fireplaces were quiet, their embers cold and lifeless.

Torden looked stricken, but he and his brothers kept quiet.

I was going to cry. I was going to throw up right on the floor.

I stared at the *konge*'s clenched fist, at this man who commanded his servants and his armies and his children with equal ease and total confidence he'd be obeyed. Before his confidence and power, I felt weak, chubby, timid, foolish.

Anya's chest rose and fell in shallow breaths. Skop panted on his hands and knees, his face an angry red where the king had struck him. One hand rose to his cheekbone, and he flinched.

Nobody spoke up.

I was still in Norge, but somehow I was back home in Arbor Hall, aching and humiliated; I was at the Council meeting in the Roots, in a room full of silent men and entirely at Alessandra's mercy.

It was the pain in their eyes that did it—the pain in Skop's and Anya's eyes, and the total lack of awareness in Alfödr's.

Nobody had stood up for me at that meeting in the Roots. But I was not going to leave my friends twisting in the wind.

My feet grew roots into Valaskjálf's floor. "Lay a hand on one of my people again, Alfödr, and you will regret it."

The king's eyebrows arched. "Lay a hand on what is *mine*"— he nodded at Anya—"and a price must be paid."

"She is not *yours*." I stared at him as levelly as I could, squared my shoulders, and spoke as I wished I could have in my own defense so many weeks ago. "Her people had the good fortune to reach Asgard, to seek protection from the Shield of the North, and you were gifted your only daughter in the process."

Alfödr's eyes narrowed. "And this is her rightful duty and obligation."

I swallowed. "So say you."

"Yes." He stalked forward. "So say I, and in Norge, my word is law."

We stood closer than was decorous or diplomatic, the king towering a foot overhead. His voice was low when he spoke again. "The Imperiya never ceases to feast, Seneschal-elect. It only grows quieter in the hunt. Was it only last week"—he glanced at Huginn, who nodded in assent—"last week, we received word that the Imperiya is moving from Varsinais-Suomi into the Åland Islands. They will use it as a beachhead, to gain inroads into Svealand to the west, and from there into Norrland and Götaland, and thence to our very gates." His eyes were stern. "As long as the North is mine to guard, I can never forget, or grow complacent. Alliances must be maintained. Our strength must be gathered and waiting."

"Anya is not an alliance. She is a *person*," I said softly. "She loves you like a father, and she loves Skop. You can't force them apart. You can't force her to marry for this."

"And yet, Seneschal-elect," said Alfödr, "here you stand."

I pressed my lips together.

Perhaps he was right. Perhaps Peter had been pressured into turning me down, so I could be sent away.

That didn't change the fact that I was here, choosing his son, of my own accord. It didn't change the fact that Anya had the right to do the same thing.

"I am not infrastructure. I am not a tool," I said tightly. "I am a girl, and if my Council is backward enough to believe I cannot lead without a guide, at least I am neither a bridge nor a wall. And I will make my own choices, their mandates aside."

"I am sorry to have offended your delicate sensibilities," said the king, not looking sorry at all. "But in time, you will understand how things must be at Asgard."

"That's unlikely." My voice was crisp. The king crossed his arms. I glanced at Torden and the other boys behind him and found them watching me, as pale and wide-eyed as if they'd found a wounded animal in the woods and it had begun to spit and snarl with no warning. But I couldn't quit now.

"And I'll tell you something else." I pointed at Alfödr, my voice shaking slightly. "I didn't know this was happening, but if I had, I wouldn't have told you, and I'd have done my best to help them. Because they're people, not weapons or possessions. And they decide who they belong to."

"You've got a mouth on you." Alfödr's lips were a thin line.

"And a brain," I said unsteadily. "And a heart."

He turned away, scoffing, rubbing the back of his neck.

My voice rose, shaking. "So what do you intend to do?"

"Prinsessa Anya's past illicit liaisons have been exiled or imprisoned," Huginn answered dispassionately.

I'd done and said all I could. I turned desperate eyes on Lang. "Do something."

But it wasn't Lang who stepped forward.

Sir Perrault broke in, glowering at Skop. "Your Majesty, your daughter's honor has been sullied, and we are ashamed."

My mouth fell open, horrified. Frozen solid, utterly useless to my friend, I stared at Perrault as he continued. "Rest assured, my lord, that if you leave the first mate to our judgment, his punishment will be more than adequate." The protocol officer's expression was sober, his brows knitted slightly together, and I suddenly noticed his stance mirrored the one the Asgard boys took—back straight, chin level, hands clasped behind him. Perrault hadn't spoken in his usual charming tenor, either; he'd been direct, concise, even pitched his voice a note lower than usual.

Like a chameleon, Perrault had shifted colors before my eyes.

He looked and sounded faintly like one of the men of Asgard, like one of Alfödr's *thegns*—not imitating them so closely that the king would notice and think himself mocked, but near enough the *konge*'s own language that he might listen.

Perrault was acting. If it worked, I'd be indebted to him.

Perhaps his New York education was more useful than I'd given him credit for.

"Pappa," Váli began in protest, but Konge Alfödr held up a hand. He pressed his lips together and jabbed a thick finger at Skop. "Koniag, I leave you to the judgment of your captain and protocol officer. *Go.*" The word was weighty in his mouth. "Come back, though, and see if you find me so restrained."

Then the king turned his good eye on me. "Seneschal-elect, everyone here knows their place. If you're to marry my son, you'll have to learn yours."

I couldn't answer him. I couldn't do anything. I could only watch as Perrault hauled Skop away by his shirt collar, his eyes on Anya even as the protocol officer dragged him out the door.

50

Alfödr and his entourage left the hall, and I sank onto the nearest bench.

"What *happened?*"

Torden studied his hands, muscled and pale, like his father's. "Skop did not listen."

"Do not blame him. I chose this." Anya's voice was defiant, even as it broke. Her halo braid had half fallen down, and her eyes were red. "He was so sad, Torden. And I am so tired," she spat, "of being told I am not my own." She swiped angrily at the tears leaking down her cheeks.

The boys fidgeted, avoiding her gaze. None of them spoke.

Finally, Bragi held out a hand. "Let me take you upstairs," he offered quietly.

"No, I'll do it." Fredrik pushed past him and put an arm around Anya's shoulder. Bragi watched, frustrated, as Fredrik steered his sister out of the silent hall.

Suddenly, Lang was at my side. "Are you all right?"

Torden crouched before me, running his rough palms over my arms. "I thought Aleksei was taking you back to the bon-fires."

"I wanted you," I whispered. I glanced up, and Lang's eyes skipped away, searching the dead ashes in the fireplace. "Alek-sei told me an awful story."

Torden glanced at me sharply. "What did he tell you?"

"About your brothers," I said. "About how Baldr passed away. A year ago tonight."

Torden met Hermódr's eyes, and his mouth twisted, reluc-tant and miserable. "I see."

It seemed impossible that hands with so many split knuck-les and calluses could be tender, but Torden was gentle as he led me from Valaskjálf, bidding the others a quiet good night. "I was waiting for the right time to explain. I'm so sorry you heard it from Aleksei."

My stomach turned. "It's a horrible story. I understand why you weren't in a hurry to tell it."

"Hermódr was the one who found him," he said. "He went looking for help alone after he found the boys. He had to com-fort Rihttá alone when he finally reached her and my father. He's practically her own son now, but neither of them has been the same since."

Hermódr had looked ill at Aleksei's very first mention of Midsummer's Eve. Now I understood the disquiet in his face, the sadness in his mother's eyes.

Worry for Skop and Anya consumed me, but I wished I

knew Rihttá well enough to offer her some comfort on this miserable anniversary.

"Who do you think told on them?" I asked. "Skop and Anya, I mean."

Torden sighed. "Things were probably getting too quiet around here for Aleksei."

"Aleksei?" I stared at him. "Aleksei told on them? Didn't he know what would happen?"

"Selah, I told you, he loves to stir the pot. He is not malicious, but his childhood in Yotunkheym, it—" Torden broke off. "He strikes the matches because he wants to watch something burn. Because then, maybe, my father will pay attention. Maybe he can forget last Midsummer." He shook his head, pressing his fingers to his brow.

Another bid for attention, I imagine, Torden had said that one night, when Aleksei had shown up in the Imperiya uniform.

He's determined to shock, if that's what it takes to get Pappa to notice him.

What else would Aleksei do to make Alfödr see him? Who else would he betray for his approval? And what would Aleksei do if, despite all his best efforts, Alfödr never looked at him the way he looked at his blood sons? If he never belonged?

Would he seek to belong somewhere else?

Torden swallowed, looking troubled. "I wish you had stayed in the woods."

"I wish you had *said* something!" I put a hand to my forehead. "How could you just stand there while your father spoke to Anya that way?"

"What would I have said?" Torden asked, bewildered. "I did what I could. I warned them. But our *konge* is not to be questioned. He commands, and we obey." He cleared his throat, lowering his eyes. "Like Pappa said, you'll understand, someday."

I blinked at him, thinking of Daddy. He hardly ever raised his voice, and even at his angriest, I'd never seen him lay a hand on anyone. I'd envied these boys their powerful father.

Now, I just wanted to see mine.

"I don't think a lifetime here could convince me," I finally answered, "let alone a few more days."

Torden stilled. "A few more—" He seized my shoulders, and my pulse sparked. "Selah, I am falling in love with you."

Despite the night's disaster, his words were a firework in my heart. "I'm falling for you, too," I whispered. "I want you to come to Potomac with me."

"Of course." Torden gathered me into his arms, his heart hammering beneath my palms. "Of course we can go to Potomac for a little while before we—before anything happens. I have to meet your family."

I wanted to melt in his arms when he bent to kiss me, but I held up a hand, and he paused. "Go to Potomac—for a little while?"

He wet his lips. "If we get married, it could be there, even."

I met his anxious eyes and shook my head, hardly hearing his tacit proposal. "Torden, I have to live in Potomac. Permanently. You know that, right?"

Torden paled, freckles stark against his bloodless cheeks.

"What are you talking about?"

"My father's sick, and I'm worried about him. I don't trust my stepmother. Besides, I'm seneschal-elect. I'll be seneschal of Potomac someday." When he didn't reply, I kept babbling. "I got lucky. I thought it was lucky you took Týr's place, because you're only fifth in line, you're not— Torden, what is it?"

"Daughters are not heirs to the throne in Norge." Torden sounded strangled. He scrubbed a hand through his hair. "I had no idea."

"But my title—I thought it was clear." I shook my head, more a twitch than an actual gesture. "And I couldn't presume you'd marry me, regardless. I didn't know for certain how you felt."

Torden eased his arms back around me. "You don't know the half of it," he murmured into my neck.

"So come with me." I gave a shivering laugh.

He swallowed hard. "I can't."

My heart stopped. "Why not?"

"Because if Asgard's daughters are its bridges, Asgard's sons are its walls." He grit his teeth, closing his eyes. "And Asgard's sons do not leave."

51

I sat on Torden's bed and stared at him, dumbfounded.

He'd shucked off his flannel shirt and his boots when we reached his room, mopping his forehead with the shirt before adding it to a heap of laundry on the floor. The boots now sat neatly beside the large closet to one end of the room, and Torden sat backward on a chair across from me. Knees bouncing, head propped on his muscular forearms, he looked like an overgrown little boy.

We'd been silent a long time.

"I thought I explained everything," I finally said. "What Alessandra did. That Daddy is unwell. What I have to do."

Torden wet his lips. "Selah, your stepmother said when she opened negotiations that you would resign your title for the right suitor. You would never have been invited to visit if my father had known the truth."

"But I *told* you that morning by the Bilröst that she wanted me gone."

"Huginn and Muninn accepted her words as fact, and I never thought to question them. We don't lie like that here," he said, agitated. "Besides, you told me yourself that first day you hated the pressure, being in the public eye! Why didn't you say anything?" The spread of his hands was frustrated. Helpless.

"Ask you to give up your brothers for me? Your home?" I whispered. "I just—I couldn't. I didn't know if you would, but I couldn't even bring myself to ask."

I lowered my head into my hands. He drummed his fingers on the back of his chair.

"There is one more reason I have to stay," Torden finally said. "Dronning Rihttá. I have a promise to keep, to take care of her. To hold things together here."

Hodr. Baldr.

I thought I understood. I wanted to protect the little brother or sister I hadn't even met yet.

I only wished I'd had a chance to know the love he and his mother shared. Rihttá was family to Torden in a way Alessandra had never wanted to be to me.

I nodded. "No. I know. You're a good son. I—" I sprang off the bed and walked to the door, stifling a sob with my fist.

My heart was a mallet inside my rib cage. I was so *sick* of its abuse.

Torden caught up to me easily. "Shhh." He folded me against his chest, beard catching at my hair. I breathed him in, letting my mind grow quiet with the smell of his skin and the feel of his nearness.

When I finally calmed down, I wiped my eyes, glancing around at the four bunk beds lining one wall and the four desks opposite.

I needed to talk about something—anything—else. I didn't want to cry anymore.

Anya had mentioned the boys bunked together in the *brakker*. I cleared my throat. "Who do you share this room with?"

"Aleksei, Fredrik, and Bragi. Týr, Vidarr, Váli, and Hermódr have the one next door."

I nodded, thinking of Torden's gentle brother, pushing up his glasses as he worked uncomplainingly beside his father. How different he was from his roommates. "Poor Hermódr."

Torden blew out a long breath. "All the *drengs* bunk four to a room. Pappa can't make exceptions for us."

In time, you will understand how things must be at Asgard.

I swallowed and looked away. Opposite the beds—two of them tidy, two complete disasters—their four desks were stacked with books and papers. One, probably Fredrik's, was piled with notes in various brands of pretty female handwriting; another held a stack of letters signed *Anya*. I pretended not to notice them, a bit stunned Bragi would risk leaving them out—unless, of course, he wanted to establish among the *drengs* that she was off-limits. A third desk was nearly bare, with a map of Europe taped to the wall above.

"Aleksei's." Torden tipped his head at the almost-empty

desk. He cleared his throat, gesturing to the fourth desk and the bunk I'd been sitting on. "And these are mine, of course."

Torden had made his bed—not with hospital corners, but neatly enough. His sheets and blankets still hugged the spot where I'd been sitting. On his desk were a few books, an open notebook covered in neat handwriting, and several stacks of memos. I couldn't read the Norsk reports or the notes he'd scrawled in their margins, but he'd clearly labored over them; his writing, so square in the little notebook, grew uneven and heavily punctuated between the lines of the official documents.

"Plans to renovate the old forge, training strategy updates from the *valkyrja*." His scruffy chin grazed the hollow of my neck as he leaned over my shoulder, planting one palm on the desktop and spreading a few of the papers out for me.

"Who are the *valkyrja*?"

"My father's top twelve generals. All women, by tradition. Don't give away our secrets." He gave my waist a squeeze.

I bit my lip, blushing despite myself. "Luckily for you, I don't speak Norsk." I pointed at the notebook covered in his handwriting. "What's this?"

"My times and training progress."

I laughed out loud, tipping my head back against his shoulder. It felt good to laugh, after such a long night. "You're a man obsessed."

He gathered me more snugly against him, and my stomach began tying itself in knots; his skin was warm against my back. "I'm disciplined," he corrected me, grinning.

I cleared my throat. "I see that. You're tidy, too—Fredrik

and Bragi are pigs." I picked up the notebook to try and make sense of his scrawled records.

"Wait—" Torden blurted, too late. A thick sheet of paper sailed from between its pages.

There I was, miserable fuchsia dress, gray velvet chair, blank expression. My portrait.

"This is me," I said stupidly. Torden rolled one shoulder and scratched at his beard, his discomfort palpable.

"I, ah. I just—had that," he offered. I waited for him to meet my eyes, but they darted anxiously to the far corner of the room.

I set down the notebook, cocking my head at him. "Why?"

"Why what?" He shifted nervously.

The evening had gone to pieces so quickly, I couldn't help comparing it to the night I'd left England, hurt and humiliated. But the truth about Bear's lies had turned my bones to ice, and their coming to light in public had left me raw.

Now, glancing between my portrait and Torden's face, gone as red as his hair, I felt warmth unfurl in my chest.

And here, it was just the two of us.

Torden wasn't Bear, and he wouldn't hurt me.

I crossed my arms. "Don't you see enough of me all day?"

Torden rubbed at a muscle in his neck. "You must understand, I have lived in the *brakker* since I was seven. Four boys in twenty square meters is all I know. Even when I told my father I'd court you, perhaps marry you—I could not comprehend it."

I raised my eyebrows. "Being married?"

"Leaving my brothers, the dirty clothes, the bunk beds. The

noise and fights in the corridor. *Det er koselig.* In its way."

I cocked my head. "*Koselig?*"

"You might say *cozy* in English." Torden frowned, apparently dissatisfied with the translation. "But it means—home. Simplicity. Warmth." He glanced around, eyes affectionate, then uncertain. "I could not imagine sleeping in a quiet room, in a real bed, making a home with one person—a woman. But I've been trying."

"Trying to imagine living with me."

Torden nodded silently, winding his arms around my waist again. "I wondered what it would be like to live in a room that smelled like you instead of stinking soldiers. To wake up beside you in the morning." One warm hand rubbed my lower back. Even through my shirt, his fingers burned my skin.

Down by the Bilröst, Torden had told me he saw that I was trying to be brave, to be open, to stretch, even when it frightened me. I realized now that he was doing the same thing.

When Torden looked at this room, he didn't see sparse furnishings or gross boys; he saw his family. Marriage to me—a relationship apart from them—would be as strange for him as fitting in among the Asgard boys had been for me. In his own way, he'd been *trying*, too, the same as I had.

I wanted to kiss him well and thoroughly.

He cleared his throat. "You asked me once if I'd ever seen us side by side. The truth is, sometimes it is all I can think about."

Pictures flooded my mind.

Torden coming into Valaskjálf for dinner, worn out but smiling, engulfing me in a hug. He'd want to hear about my day, and I'd listen to him talk about his.

Torden kissing me first thing in the morning before he left for his run, wide awake when I was still hazy with sleep.

Horseback riding and reading, training and lying in the sun doing nothing.

Special days and regular days. Anniversaries and children. A thousand other moments that would be perfect because we spent them together.

"That's distracting." His voice was uneven as he stilled my fingers against the carved planes of his chest. I'd been absently tracing the ink over his heart.

"Oh. Sorry." But his ragged grin assured me he hadn't minded much. I tapped my knuckles against the tattoo, shaped like a letter *F* with its arms broken. "Torden, what does this mean?"

"*Ash,*" he said. "It is Asgard's rune. All our blood wear this over their hearts. And this"—he raised his left wrist, inked on the inside with a letter almost like an R—"is *Reid*. It means *ride*, the work and the journey of our lives."

The tattoos were everything he held dear, everything that made him a mystery to me, everything I admired about him.

But they were also everything that tied him to this place. Everything that meant where I had to go, he could not follow; that he could never be mine.

My chest tightened.

I slid my palms to his shoulders, past two sets of tan lines to his wrists, and swiped my thumb across the soft skin there. "You make me want one, except I bet they hurt." My voice was broken.

Torden took a pot of ink from his desk, face unreadable. "Can I?"

I nodded. His hands were gentle as he traced the skin over my hectic pulse with his little finger. I studied the shape, like a backward N. "What is it?"

"*Sol.* This rune means *sun.*" He lifted my wrist to blow on the ink, and goose bumps raced up my arm, my skin thrilling beneath his breath.

As long as you are mine, he had said, *because I am yours.*

Asgard was nothing like Potomac, could never be home to me.

But I was beginning to suspect Torden could be.

"Is it possible," I asked, "that it's only Friday?"

"What do you mean?"

"We've known each other for nine days." I thought of all the tick marks I'd added to the back page of my godmother's book the night before, correcting my error born of distraction. "Is this too much, too soon?"

"Everything feels *more* with so little time." Torden gestured, as though either English or words in general failed him. "More. Faster. Sooner."

I shook my head. "I wish we had more time."

More time to make such a huge decision. More time to reconcile an immovable object and an unstoppable force. If he had to stay, and I had to go, was there a middle where we could meet?

"We have a few days to work it out." Torden brushed a curl from my face. "Let's take our time."

He leaned forward and kissed me, slowly. I let my hands

wander back up his arms and into his hair, let my mind drift into thoughtless bliss.

Pounding footsteps and rumbling male voices filled the hall. Their door swung open, and Aleksei stopped short in the entryway, stumbling forward as Bragi and Fredrik plowed into him. "Aleksei, don't— Oh. *Hei,* Selah!" Bragi said. Hermódr loped in behind them.

We flew apart, faces flushed.

Fredrik grinned wanly. "Did we interrupt something?"

"*Idiot.*" Bragi punched Fredrik in the shoulder and pushed past Aleksei toward his desk. The word—the same in both our languages!—usually delighted me, but as Bragi swept Anya's notes into a drawer, his regretful eyes sank my heart. I'd assumed Bragi and Fredrik were two peas in a pod, but where Anya's brother simply chased women—*any* women—Bragi loved only Anya.

"What's on your—" Aleksei seized my wrist and snorted, rolling his eyes.

I snatched my arm away. "What was that for?"

Aleksei held up his palms and turned away. "Nothing."

I stalked after him. "What, Aleksei? What's your problem now?" A few blond and brunet heads appeared in the doorway, *drengs* I didn't know coming back from the bonfire.

Aleksei smirked. "There is no problem. I am only surprised at how quickly you got him housebroken."

"Selah . . ." Torden laid a hand on my shoulder.

"You just got my friend kicked out," I spat. "Skop is *gone.* Did you know that?"

Aleksei rolled his eyes. "I did you a favor. You thought Asgard was all happy days and handsome soldiers? I tried to tell you. But now you know the price of order here. Now you know who our father is and how far his sons will go to defend the ones they love. Exactly how far"—he glanced at Torden—"and no further."

"Let's not pretend any of this was about me." I stared at Aleksei, my teeth clenched. "Or about anyone but you."

You, and your father, and everything he refuses to give you.

This quest had humiliated me, crushed me, made me sob till I had no tears left. And I ached for Aleksei; I did. But I didn't feel like crying now.

I closed the distance between us in one, two, three strides, stopping just beneath Aleksei's pale, fine-boned chin. "Maybe you light fires for fun, or to get someone's attention," I hissed, "but consider this your warning to *start them someplace else.*"

As I stomped off toward the door, Aleksei mumbled something in Norsk. Bragi sucked a sharp breath through his teeth. The boys outside the room stiffened, expressions freezing.

I turned around in time to see Aleksei stumbling backward over a desk chair as Torden pounded toward him.

"Torden—" he stammered, pitch frantic over the crash of wooden furniture.

"Torden!" Fredrik threw himself forward, gripping his brother's forearm before he could take a swing at Aleksei, who was backed against the far wall. Bragi seized Torden's other wrist.

Glasses half sliding off his nose, Hermódr snatched their

cowering brother up by the collar. "Take a walk, Aleksei," he bellowed, shoving him toward the hallway.

"Why me?" Aleksei demanded. "Why am I always the one being thrown out?"

"Because you are the one who did this! Again!" Torden shouted. "Because Midsummer is for luck, and you turned it into ashes!"

The room was suddenly cold with silence, thick with stillness, crowded with boys who wouldn't look at one another. It was so different from the heat of the moment before.

Again?

I frowned a little, glancing between them. Bragi. Hermódr. Fredrik. Torden. Aleksei.

When I met Aleksei's eyes, he cocked his head, stalking near Torden again. "So you didn't tell her," he marveled. "You didn't tell her. We're still not talking about it."

Torden said nothing. His brothers stayed silent.

I was choking on the quiet. "Somebody please say something."

"Yes. Let's defy all our Asgardian instincts and say what we're really thinking." Aleksei turned to me, spreading his arms out like a ringmaster. "It's my fault," he pronounced grandly. "I am the reason that Baldr is dead."

I stared at him blankly, not comprehending. "But—but you said he fell."

"He did," Aleksei said. His mouth was a flat line, his tone almost philosophical. "He fell because he and Hodr were alone in the woods, and they tried to climb for mistletoe. Because they were alone, with no one to look after them. Because I told Baldr and Hodr that I had better things to do than watch them all night."

I was as cold as a stone, standing in the midst of them. I half expected my breath to fog on the air.

"Aleksei," I said cautiously. "It was an accident."

He laughed, and the sound tore at the quiet in the room. "Selah, I already *told* you," Aleksei said, bitter and earnest.

He *had* already told me—that night Alfödr had thrown him out of the ball.

Because you haven't made a mistake yet and been forced to taste the consequences.

"Alfödr cannot afford to suffer fools," Aleksei snarled softly. "And I'm the king of them all. And I'm still in his house, but I might as well be exiled with Hodr."

52

The *drengs* outside muttered to one another as Aleksei straightened his clothes and shunted past them, looking shaken and furious.

When I faced him again, Torden's hands were in fists, his expression fierce despite Fredrik's hand on his shoulder and Bragi's even, low tones. I suddenly felt childish, out of place in their barracks. "Should I go?"

Torden yanked his shirt off the laundry pile and pulled it back on. "No, wait. Please." When he crossed to my side and kissed my temple, I nearly burst into tears.

Torden had been respectful of me, so restrained at first and then so steadily affectionate that I'd struggled to imagine him fighting, arriving in his father's office with black eyes. I didn't know what to make of this version of him. I didn't know what to make of Torden's fury, Aleksei's bitterness and guilt.

Only his arm around my shoulder felt the same. Everything else felt wrong.

We left the *brakker* in silence and mounted the stairs. "What did he say?" I suddenly asked. "That made you so angry?"

"I would not repeat it in front of you if my life depended on it."

"That bad?"

Torden's eyes tightened. "Obscene."

"Can't you just—explain what he meant?" I asked uncertainly.

"No."

"Torden, I'm a girl, not a porcelain figurine. More important things have come up tonight. And I'll feel worse if you leave me in the dark about something your whole barracks heard."

He took a long breath, leaning back against Anya's door. "Aleksei asked if you'd traded your innocence for my manhood," he finally said, "because I'd lost all my nerve and you'd found some."

My skin crawled, and I looked away.

Torden put his palm against my cheek. "I have not implied that you've been in my bed," he said, voice low but intent. "I don't talk about women that way, least of all you, Selah."

"Of course not. You would never." I sagged.

He traced my cheekbones, brushing hair away from my face. "What's wrong, *elskede?*"

"*Everything* is wrong," I whispered. "You, fighting with Aleksei." My heart felt shipwrecked, sunk somewhere around my gut.

"I'm always fighting with Aleksei," Torden said, shaking his head.

"And this—impossibility—between us." My eyes shut, then flew open. "I need to talk to my godmother."

Torden frowned. "A letter would take weeks."

"No," I said quickly. "I have a radio." Curiosity sparked in his eyes. "But it's too small to act as a transmitter, unless there's a radio tower somewhere close by." I paused, swallowing hard. "I have to talk to her."

He nodded, eyes focused, somewhere far off. "We'll find a way."

I swallowed hard. "Promise?"

"I said I'd never lie to you."

His lips nudged my temple and my cheek before finding my mouth. We kissed each other like drowning swimmers dying for oxygen, his arms straining around me, my hands trapped in his hair.

But it wasn't until I'd climbed into bed that I understood why I'd felt less passion than desperation in Torden's kiss, that I understood why he'd held me so tightly in the hall outside my room. In the short time I'd known him, I'd never seen him this way.

He was afraid.

53

The others sensed that something was coming. I saw it more clearly with every frantic hour we spent together, riding and fishing and hiking and swimming, moving ceaselessly from dawn till dusk.

Aleksei skulked and avoided us, but J.J. and Cobie came along every day, J.J. basking in Anya's affection, Cobie intimidating even the boys with her lap times across the fjord and earning shy smiles from Hermódr. She was unusually kind to me, either because she saw how sad I was at Skop's absence or because, by now, the whole fortress knew what had happened after the bonfires.

But though no one could forget why Skop was gone, why Anya's eyes were red all the time, what Aleksei had said about Torden and me, the silent war he'd finally spoken of aloud—the boys never brought it up. They left those conversations unsaid, I guessed, for the same reasons that they never talked about

Hermódr struggling with their older brothers, about Bragi's painful feelings for Anya, about Fredrik's being twenty-three and refusing to take a single relationship seriously. About what had happened the summer before.

Aleksei had been right about the boys' Asgardian instincts.

They hated to be alone, but they kept everything hard or hurtful to themselves. I couldn't understand it.

They felt time slipping through our fingers, responded to it without acknowledging it out loud. Even as Torden and I recycled the same conversation when we were alone—*I can't stay; you can't go. I want to be together; I want to be with you*—he never said a word to Anya or his brothers.

Monday morning, Torden pulled me aside after breakfast, eyes bright. "No training today. Get your"—he glanced around and lowered his voice—"your radio. Meet me at the stables."

I seized his arm, hands trembling. "I'll be back in ten minutes."

I was going to talk to my godmother.

We rode on separate horses this time, Torden on Gullfaxi, me on Skeithbrimir, racing, racing over five miles of rocky cliffs, beneath five miles of blue sky, toward the mouth of the fjord.

A tower rose in the distance.

It was a massive thing, metallic, like a pen poised to scrawl messages across the sky itself. "You found one," I breathed.

"Turns out the old forge wasn't just a forge." Torden jumped down from Gullfaxi's back. "I found it reviewing the renovation plans. We're going to turn it into a second stronghold."

I climbed out of the saddle and crept to the edge of the cliff. Thousands of wooden planks descended in a curving staircase down to the Lysefjord, the drop as long as the tower was high.

"How close do you think we need to be?" I swallowed hard and turned, my neck bending back to take in the tower's height. "Do I—have to climb it?"

"No, no, I don't think so." Torden guided me underneath the massive structure. "If I'm right, the extension at the top of the tower does just what your antenna does, only it can transmit and receive a signal over much greater distances."

I unfolded the antenna. Radio in one hand, book in the other, I tilted my head back again, squinting against the sun. Bars and beams segmented the blue sky overhead in geometric patterns as intricate as the veins on a leaf.

I tuned the radio's frequency carefully to 3.44 and switched it on.

"Godmother?" My voice was hoarse. "Godmother Al—"
"Selah?"

For a moment, I couldn't breathe. I hadn't expected her to respond so quickly.

"Selah, sweet girl, is that you?" My godmother's voice was bright as the sky above, damp with tears.

I put a hand to my mouth to stifle a sob.

She was there. My godmother was really there, waiting for me, all the way across the world.

Torden wrapped an arm around me until I was in control again.

"Yes, ma'am," I choked.

"Oh, Selah. Oh, my baby girl. Where are you?"

"I'm in Norge. How are things?" I blurted. "How is he?"

"He—" She hesitated.

"Godmother?"

"He's fine." But her voice was tentative. Althea sighed. "No, he's not. He's not fine, honey." I put a hand to my mouth again, felt tears running over my fingers.

"Is he—is—" But I couldn't say it. I couldn't bring myself to use the word *dying*.

"No," Godmother Althea said. This time, she meant it. I lifted my eyes to Torden's, and he nodded, encouraging. "He can't do much without getting real tired. But Dr. Pugh and Dr. Gold say they're doing their best."

Torden passed me a handkerchief and I wiped my nose, nodding, though she couldn't see me. "Has Alessandra made any moves?"

"Nothing obvious." Godmother sighed. "She seems just to be . . . waiting." She paused. "Do what you have to do, sweet girl, but don't stay away any longer than you have to. I just don't know what's gonna happen."

I buried my face in my hands, racked by silent sobs.

Torden cleared his throat. "Miss—ah, Sister Althea?"

"Yes?" My godmother's voice turned curious. "Who's this?"

"I'm Prins Torden of Norge," he said evenly. "I'm Selah's— well, she's here visiting me."

"I see." My godmother's voice was wry. I swallowed, wiping my nose with Torden's handkerchief.

"Sister, I wanted to ask Selah a very particular question,"

he said slowly, brown eyes never leaving mine. "I know your government chose me, but it sounds like your opinion and her father's are what really matter to her."

My heart stilled in my chest at the desperate bob of his Adam's apple, the nervous blink of his perfect rose-gold eyelashes. Not all the spears in Asgard had such power to undo me.

"A question, hmm?" Godmother Althea asked.

"Yes."

I didn't understand. Torden and I had worn in the lines of our exchange so well I could have recited them in my sleep. *I can't stay. You can't go.* "What are you doing?" My voice shook.

"What if I went home with you, just for a little while?" Torden asked.

But you can't, I almost blurted. Not with things as they were.

"For a little while?" asked Godmother Althea before I could speak.

"Yes," I said quickly. "Godmother, the Council set me up with all suitors with hereditary obligations, who couldn't come back to Potomac. I—" But I didn't want to talk about other boys. Not with Torden standing here, eyes burning into mine.

"I see."

I could imagine my godmother's face, forehead furrowed, one eyebrow cocked.

"If I come back with you, you can see to your father and appease your Council," said Torden. "Then, Sister Althea, maybe you can help us figure something out."

"But what about . . ." I trailed off.

About Aleksei and your father. About your mother and Týr and Vidarr and Váli. About Hodr, exiled, and your house, falling apart around your ears.

"Just for a while," Torden insisted.

Slowly, I nodded.

It wasn't a permanent solution, but it didn't matter. We'd go to Potomac and make sure Daddy was all right. Alessandra and the Council would have to agree I'd done my duty.

And Torden would love it—the woods and the fields and the *freedom* he'd feel, away from his father and all the rules that went with life in Asgard.

Maybe he'd love it so much he'd agree to stay.

It was such a selfish idea. It filled me with guilt. It filled me with greedy hope.

My godmother gave an enormous sniffle. "Do you love her?"

Torden watched me steadily. "Yes."

"Will you take care of her, and let her take care of you?"

"Yes."

"And you'll always be true to her? Never manipulate her goodwill, or deceive her, always tell her the truth?"

Torden silently kissed my forehead. "On my brothers' lives," he finally said.

"Then, sweet boy, as long as she'll have you, you have my blessing."

I blinked back tears, but to no avail. They poured down my cheeks, ill-matched to the laughter that rang from my mouth and his. "I love you," I said to her, and to him.

"I love you, too, baby girl. Everything's going to be okay."

"Nice to meet you, Sister Althea." Torden's voice was as solid as his smile.

"See you in a few weeks, boy. You better be good to my girl."

I switched off the radio. Torden passed a hand over my hair and bent to kiss me, and I threw my arms around him. I let myself forget the past few days, all the fighting and the tears and the pain I'd felt and uncovered.

I was going home. And I was already there.

Torden's smile was triumphant, relentless. He ate his dinner with one arm wrapped around me, laughing with his brothers, unconcerned with his father's *drengs* and *thegns* watching. I fluttered, distracted; Anya'd had to do the buttons on my gown, a beautiful thing in rose-gold chiffon, because my hands shook too hard for me to do it myself. "You look like a sunrise," she'd said, squeezing my fingers, beaming at me.

It was only Monday, still two days from the end of our trip. But Torden had told me to wear my favorite dress to dinner.

He was planning something. I hoped it was what I hoped it was.

I'd wandered out of her room and through the crowded halls, unable to sit still while she'd stayed behind to finish getting ready. But Anya hadn't shown up to supper.

I hoped she wasn't crying again, alone in her room. I wanted her there for whatever Torden was planning.

When the meal was finished, Alfödr stood, and Valaskjálf quieted.

"The house of Asgard has long been the shield of the North, defender against the shadow to the south," said the *konge*, brows tense.

"I wish to see Asgard's walls secured. And for the honor and strength of Norge to be preserved, its sons need fierce, faithful mates at their sides."

Torden nodded, heart in his eyes. My own heart was thundering; it sounded loud in the noiseless hall.

Every person in the room watched Alfödr. No one had been expecting an announcement tonight.

Torden reached into his pocket. Something tiny glittered in his pale hand, catching the firelight—a ring. But his eyes were on me.

For once, despite the cost, I was glad to feel beautiful, in a beautiful gown.

But then his father spoke.

"Selah, Seneschal-elect of Potomac," said Alfödr. "You have brought spies and treason into our midst. Therefore, I decline to extend a proposal to you on behalf of my fifth son, Torden of Asgard."

Valaskjálf was cemetery-silent, lead-heavy with the stares of Alfödr's *heerthmen*. I stared at the king, paralyzed, cold all over.

Torden's hand was very still around mine.

For a long moment, I couldn't speak.

"Spies?" I finally blurted. "Treason? Konge Alfödr, what do you mean?"

"Perhaps you ought to ask your captain." The king stared at me. "Perhaps you ought to get to know your crew."

I glanced at the high table. Cobie and Lang were tense, as if ready to run for the door. Torden's brothers were pale with horror. Aleksei's mouth was wry and sharp and strained as a garrote wire. Anya was still nowhere to be seen.

"It pains me," Alfödr said, glancing down the table, "to cause my children pain. But my true-born children must serve Asgard first and truly, even if my adopted children do not." His eyes lit on Aleksei, then drifted away, searching for something, then narrowing.

And even as his father's eyes moved on, something hardened in Aleksei's face, some determination I didn't understand.

"Father," Torden began, shaking his head.

Suddenly, Valaskjálf erupted in whispers. Huginn and Muninn swept down the great hall's center aisle, like ravens descending on a wind.

The room held its breath as Alfödr conferred with them, then turned a fierce glare on me. "This is your doing, isn't it?" he demanded. He looked down the table again, on his left and on his right, his gaze fixing on the empty chair next to Fredrik.

"What?" I stammered. The *konge* stomped toward me, lowering his voice so the rest of the hall couldn't hear.

"Anya," he said furiously, "is missing."

54

"I have no idea what you're talking about." My voice was unsteady, even above the noise of the dancers and musicians the *konge* had ordered to begin.

The hall full of *drengs* and *thegns* and *heerthmen* and noblewomen pretended not to watch as Alfödr planted his hands on the table and leaned down so his single eye was on a level with mine. "I don't believe you." His gravelly voice was low, his gaze on fire.

I shook my head hard. "She helped me get dressed earlier. That's the last time I saw her."

"You told me yourself you would back her," he said. "That you approved of her insubordination."

"Pappa, Selah would never flout your authority that way," Torden cut in.

Alfödr dismissed him with a wave. "Of course she would."

Of course I would, I wanted to add. But one glance at Torden silenced me. His back was ramrod straight in his chair, his voice confident, but his eyes on Alfödr were almost pleading.

Torden sat before his *konge* a soldier of Asgard. But he wanted his father to see his son.

"Your Majesty," Huginn said, "it is unlikely that Prinsessa Anya will make an effective match if she is not found soon."

Alfödr turned his furious gaze on me. "Do you hear that?" he whispered. "You helped her run away. You have lost me an ally. With the Imperiya drawing nearer every season, we lose a marriage alliance for the sake of a *crush*."

I gripped Torden's hand. "But I didn't—"

Aleksei stepped to his father's side. "It's okay, Selah."

"You—" Torden's jaw tightened, but Aleksei held out a hand.

"Pappa," Aleksei said reasonably, sidling over to Torden and me. "Let me talk to her."

"Let you?" Alfödr stared at his Yotne son. "Why?"

"Because I know Selah, and I can make her see reason," Aleksei said, sounding as reasonable as I'd ever heard him. "She doesn't understand the way we do things here." His black eyes met Torden's, then mine. "But she knows how far we'll go for family."

"Majesty, if Anya is not found, and soon—" Huginn tried again.

"But if we send out search parties, the kingdom will know, and word will spread to our allies of the *prinsessa's* . . . dalliance,"

Muninn cut in. "If we exercise patience—judgment—this may yet be resolved quietly."

The king stared at me for a long moment. I could practically hear his teeth grinding over the scrape of the bow against the strings of the *hardingfele*.

"Three hours," he muttered, just loud enough that all his sons could hear. "You have three hours to bring her back. If my daughter is not home by the end of the ball, the world will know why." Alfödr stepped nearer to me. "You will not marry my son. You will not find a husband anywhere in the civilized world who will accept such a wayward wife."

"Three hours," I stammered back. "I'm sure she just lost track of time. I'll find her."

"Yes," said Alfödr. "You will."

I left Valaskjálf as if I were making for my room, then doubled back through darkened corridors and empty halls. I kept quiet as I could as I slipped through the front door and through Asgard's gates.

Evidently, it was easier to get out than it was to get in.

Anya had figured out as much.

The others were waiting among Yggdrasil's roots beside the Bilröst when we arrived—the Asgard boys, plus Cobie and Lang. The moon washed their faces pale and serious.

I wanted to talk to Torden. But I owed our captain some words.

"What did you do?" I demanded, stalking toward Lang. My

words echoed off the water. "'Treason and spies'?"

I had trusted him. I had accepted the terms of his ceasefire and let him keep his secrets. If only I'd known what a mistake that would be.

"Selah," Lang said. "This isn't the t—"

"It *is* the time," I fired back.

Aleksei put a hand on my arm. "Selah," he said flatly, "you have to run."

I flinched away from his ghostly face, his eyes like pits.

I was not inclined to trust him.

He'd betrayed Anya and Skop just days ago, and tried to humiliate me the same night. He'd delivered a horrible truth with the sole intent of horrifying me. But Aleksei was as sincere as I'd ever seen him.

And in the dark, with Asgard looming overhead, it was hard not to listen.

I pressed my lips together and shook my head. "But I didn't do it. I don't know where Anya is."

Torden stepped to my side, and I gripped his hand.

"Are you certain?" Lang asked. His face was composed, but anger swelled in me at the skepticism in his tone.

"What do you mean, *am I certain*?" I spat. "I either know or I don't, and I told you I didn't. You're the one who ruined absolutely everything!"

Cobie put a lean hand on my shoulder. "I just think everyone needs to calm down."

"Selah, I'm on your side," Lang began.

"Try acting like it," I snarled.

"We're dawdling," Hermódr said softly. "If Anya isn't found, you'll be punished, Selah."

"Leave tonight." Fredrik's voice was urgent. "Go. We'll cover for you. Get your people and get out of here."

"Tonight?" Cobie exclaimed.

Hermódr and I both jumped. But Cobie was watching Lang.

"Yes, tonight," Aleksei retorted. He ran a hand through his hair, standing its dark strands wildly on end. "What did you think he meant by 'three hours'? If you can't produce Anya, tonight is all you've got."

Could it have been just this afternoon that Torden had asked my godmother's permission to marry me?

I buried my face in my hands, near tears.

"Selah," Aleksei said. His voice broke, and I looked up at him. "You can't be here when she doesn't return. You don't want to watch what happens." He met Torden's eyes. "Trust me."

I was straw in a breath of wind. I was glass shattered on stone. I was the soft red flesh of a heart, vulnerable to every sharp thing in its path.

I couldn't go home now, without a fiancé. But what would Althea think when I didn't reappear in a month, if I couldn't tell her what had happened?

Hermódr turned to Cobie. "Can your navigator manage the Lysefjord after dark?"

"Ever practical," Cobie said, giving a wan smile. Hermódr

pushed his glasses up, looking forlorn.

"Homer's the best there is," Lang said, tentative. "But unfortunately, that's not our problem."

I lifted my head. "What *is* our problem, Lang?"

He wet his lips and looked away. Into his silence, Cobie spoke instead. Her hazel eyes were sharp as knives in the dark.

"Selah, the ship is gone."

55

I stared at her, as if she'd slapped me instead of speaking aloud. "Gone?" It came out confused, as if I didn't know what the word meant.

"Yes," Cobie said carefully. Beside her, Lang crossed his arms, silent.

Slowly, my gaze shifted to him. "Lang, where's my ship?"

He didn't answer, and I took two steps toward him. "Lang," I said slowly. "Where. Is. My. Ship?"

Lang stuffed his hands in his jacket pockets and finally met my eyes. "The *Beholder* made a run to Odense while we were in Norge. It should be back tonight."

I clenched my hands into fists at my sides. I was shaking with fury.

"Selah?" Cobie said quietly. "Do you trust me?"

I swung to face her. "Did you sign off on this decision?"

Her brows arched in surprise. "I'm a rigger, Seneschal-elect.

I don't sign off on decisions. I obey orders."

"Then sure," I said flatly.

"Good." Cobie turned to Fredrik. "Take everyone to your boat and wait for us there."

Fredrik blinked. *"My boat?"*

She nodded slowly, then with more certainty. "Make sure *Skídbladnir* is ready to sail." She turned to Hermódr. "You, come with me to the castle. We have to get her things out. Lang's going to get Perrault and J.J."

"I should stay with Selah." Lang's voice was low, and his eyes were urgent in the dark.

"No," I said tautly. "You should not stay with me. You should get the people you've put in danger out of it."

"I'll take care of Selah," Torden said evenly. His arm tightened around my waist, and I wondered if I was imagining the possessiveness in his voice.

"Fine." Cobie nodded at Aleksei. "You have to convince Alfödr that Anya's in her room, that she took a walk because she was upset, and now she's embarrassed to come downstairs."

Aleksei nodded, dark eyes bitter and confident. "Leave the tricks to me."

I hiked back up from the banks of the Bilröst in silence with the others, angry and afraid and already lonely for everything I was about to leave behind.

I hated Lang. I feared Alfödr. I loved these boys, with their broad shoulders and their stupid mouths and their loyal hearts.

We split apart, each to our stations. One by one, I hugged

the Asgard brothers, their jaws working silently, their eyes sad.

Bragi.

Hermódr.

Even Aleksei. Even after everything. He stiffened in my arms but returned my embrace, then set off away from the fjord.

Gone.

"Don't worry." Cobie squeezed my hand. "I'm going to handle everything." And then she was gone, too, hurrying after Hermódr into the dark.

"I'll get them out," Lang promised.

"You had better." My warning was sharp-edged and angry.

I watched them all disappear in the direction of the fortress, then followed Fredrik and Torden.

The three of us reached the harbor in due course. Fog rolled between the cliffs, and Alfödr's warships and Asgard's fishing boats bobbed at the dark edge of the water. I automatically sought out the *Beholder* and her open arms, but she was nowhere to be found.

Fredrik, Torden, and I made *Skídbladnir* ready to sail, and Lang, Cobie, J.J., and Perrault appeared on the horizon far too soon. J.J.'s skinny arms were wrapped around himself, his hollow eyes darting around the unfamiliar ship, and Perrault looked as confused as I felt. The Asgard boys were strangely quiet—the very quiet strange on them. I didn't know what to make of them, wordless and sad.

They made me ache for Anya. I hadn't even given her a proper goodbye.

"It's time to go," Lang said briefly. I shot him a furious look.

"And the *Beholder* will meet you?" Torden asked, urgent. "You're sure?"

Cobie nodded, certain. "Yes. We'll reach them. They were supposed to be here by midnight."

Only a few hours away. They'd truly believed I'd never know what they'd done.

And if Lang hadn't sent everything to hell two days early, I might not have.

What fortune was mine.

I pounded toward the gangplank after Cobie and Lang, but stopped short at a tug on my arm.

"Selah." Torden's voice was soft. He didn't move.

"You're not coming?" I blurted. "Not even to meet the ship?"

Torden shook his head.

I'd let anger drive me thus far, let my fury at Lang make me strong. But there was nowhere left to go. Nothing left to plan or do but climb aboard. I didn't need to be strong anymore.

I needed Torden.

The dam broke, and I burst into tears.

Silently, the *Beholder* crew began to move our things aboard.

Torden drew me into himself with a wretched groan. I held him, memorizing the feel of his fingers on my neck, breathing him in as he kissed my hair.

This was the end. I'd never see him again.

"Selah, won't you change your mind? Can't you stay?"

"Your father called me a spy. Will he change his mind?" I took Torden's hand in one of mine, wiping my eyes with the other. "And what about my father? Could *you* leave?"

"How can I, with the Imperiya hell-bent on our destruction?" The shape of his mouth was desperate. "Rihttá needs me. Asgard needs me."

"Exactly," I whispered. "Except my enemies are already inside the gates."

I imagined arriving home with an escaped Torden in tow—out of favor in Asgard, useless as an ally. Alessandra and the Council would rip me to shreds.

Torden nodded silently, his hangnails and calluses scratching gently at my palms. I kissed his pale knuckles, freckled and muscled and bruised and kind, so kind.

He pressed something into my left hand. A ring.

The rough rose-gold band was set with stones blue like the sky, like the Bilröst, like his brothers' eyes. Pain squeezed my heart.

"You'll want this back."

"No. This could never belong to anyone else." He slid the ring onto my finger. "I would still choose you."

"I—" I bit back another sob, tears spilling from my eyes. "I'm sorry, I'm not one of your *valkyrja*. This is killing me."

"You're more a shield-maiden than you think."

My crying blunted and broke my words. "I wish I didn't have to be."

We remained a bare half inch apart for a few breaths before Torden closed the distance between us, putting his lips to my ear. "You will always be the sun to me. Bright and beautiful and the warmest thing in my world." He paused. "Be free, *elskede*."

Free.

It meant riding like a wild thing over the cliff tops with Anya and the Asgard boys, jumping into the lake when I couldn't swim. *Free* meant being unafraid to tell him the truth about Bear, to kiss him by the Bilröst.

It meant wind in my hair. Water in my eyes. Sweat on my skin. Adrenaline in my blood.

I hadn't been afraid to jump, because he'd been a safe place to land.

I'd changed, because he'd helped me grow.

"I am free, because you *made* me free." I cupped his cheek, saw his heart in his eyes. The blue stones of the ring sparkled against the red of his beard. "No matter what happens, Torden Asgard, I will always love you for what you've given me." I bent my head to his chest, feeling the blood race beneath the rune tattooed there. *Ash. Asgard. Home.*

"I gave you nothing you did not already have." His voice was husky. "But Asgard will feel a little less like home without you here."

I could feel myself breaking apart there in his arms. Pieces of me scattered across the banks of the Bilröst, never to be recovered.

I wondered if I'd ever be whole again.

The dark was tense with our wanting and our sadness and our certainty as Torden's mouth found mine. I didn't understand the Norsk words he whispered in my ears, but I knew his voice. I knew what he meant.

And with his ring on my finger and his voice in my ears, I left him behind.

56

Skídbladnir cut through the Bilröst's dark water under Fredrik's deft steering. Our sails and the fjord glowed in the fog and the moonlight. My eyes tracked the great stone walls as we sailed, certain I'd see Alfödr's men descending upon us at any moment.

Once, I swore I saw Aleksei standing on top of a high rock, only his shock of black hair moving in the wind. When I blinked, he was gone, a shadow disappearing on the wind over the Lysefjord.

But when I closed my eyes again, it wasn't Aleksei I saw.

Torden's face filled my mind as we sailed over the midnight fjord, his half smile and forlorn mouth that broke my thudding heart as we sailed away from Norge. Red hair and red blood and freckles and muscles, honor and rashness and strength and fidelity, all of it enough to break me like a bottle of wine against the hull.

"There she is!" Fredrik's soft call was a shot across the bow.

And when I turned, the blank, starry eyes of the *Beholder* were watching me, her arms flung wide.

Welcome home, I heard her say.

Skídbladnir drew as near our ship as Fredrik was able. J.J. and Cobie and Lang brought the *Beholder*'s proffered rowboat close, moving our things into it one trunk at a time.

I nearly collapsed against the deck in relief.

Fredrik leaned against the rail beside me. "Any last words?" He looked nothing like Torden, but he was every inch his brother—the broad shoulders, the wry grin.

I bit my lip. "Tell him thank you. Tell him . . . I miss him already."

Fredrik nodded. "He misses you, too. I know it." He paused, scratching at the crown of his head. "I've never seen him happier, lucky bastard. So-serious Torden and the girl of his dreams."

"And now I have to go."

"For now," Fredrik said simply. "But this isn't over."

I watched Vishnu summon another boatload of luggage from the deck rail, watched Cobie and Basile and Jeanne adjust our sails, and swallowed hard. "It looks pretty over to me. Your father seemed to think so, anyway."

Fredrik's mouth hooked in a sharp grin. "I know a thing or two about relationships turning permanent, Selah, because those signs are my cue to run. But Torden—" His gaze narrowed. "This is not over tonight. Not for him."

"Selah!"

My heart leapt in my chest, and I turned back to face the

Beholder, eager to see Skop's face for myself, to put days of worry to rest. And there he was.

With Anya beside him. She waved at us happily, blond hair aglow in the moonlight. Fredrik's breath went out in a huff.

"Selah, take the helm." Without another moment's warning, Fredrik loosened a line and swung from *Skídbladnir* to the *Beholder*'s deck.

I pushed my hands into my hair, unable to believe the sight of her. Anya must have found Skop somewhere and struck out with him to meet the ship.

I was so glad to see her safe. But Anya's escape had precipitated mine. And I hadn't been ready to say goodbye.

Relief and frustration were a thunderstorm in my chest.

Fredrik covered the distance between himself and his sister in four long strides and wrapped her in an embrace. I couldn't hear what he said, but the crumpled shape of his mouth and the tight squeeze of his closed eyes told me things Fredrik had never said aloud.

"I have to," Anya said, her words clear even across the distance between us.

Fredrik nodded, exhaling a long breath. "I know." He swallowed hard and squeezed his sister again. The muscles in his back were trembling when he let go, and his jaw was tight as he extended one hand to Skop and clapped the other on his broad shoulder.

I looked away, back to my fingers white-knuckled on *Skídbladnir*'s rudder. I wished I could turn the boat around and sail back up the fjord, back to Asgard and back into Torden's arms.

Instead, when Fredrik returned, I hugged him goodbye and left the way he came, ignoring the rowboat Basile and Vishnu were already lowering into the water for me. When my feet hit the *Beholder*'s deck, I turned and saluted him, swallowing around the lump in my throat, blinking away the tears in my eyes. Fredrik barked a laugh that echoed against the rock walls of the fjord and dipped into a bow.

Then, shaking his head, he threw his weight against *Skíd-bladnir*'s steering oar and turned around. Back to Alfödr's hall. Back to pay the piper.

And there would be hell to pay.

Anya's hand slipped around my waist as we watched her brother leave us. When he was out of sight, I gave her a kiss on the cheek and stomped off after our captain.

Torden had told me to be free. And I was finally tall enough to jump Alessandra's fences.

Og er de ikke døde, så lever de ennå.

And if they're not dead,
they still live.
—Traditional ending, Norsk tale

57

The crew worked busily, feet pounding the deck, calling out to one another as we navigated the fjord by the shifting light of the moon. Nobody paid me any mind as I strode after Lang.

I stopped him as he reached for Homer's door.

"What have you done, Lang?"

He stilled but didn't turn.

"Selah, I can talk about this with you later, but right now—"

"No. Now." I seized Lang by the shoulder and turned him to face me. "Right now, you are going to let me in on whatever you've been keeping from me." My chest rose and fell quickly, heart beating fast. "You're going to tell me everything."

"Why would I do that?"

"Because this has been going on long enough!" I shouted. "Because when I needed to get out of Norge, my ship—*my ship*—was somewhere else."

Lang swallowed. "I've done all of this for a reason."

I pushed past him, pushed through Homer's open door. "Excellent," I said sharply. "I can't wait to hear all about it."

Homer, Yu, and Andersen stood over the map in the navigator's quarters, Andersen's face guilty, Yu's impassive, Homer's looking rather satisfied.

"I wondered when this day would come," said the navigator.

I refused to bask in his approval. I steeled myself, crossed my arms. "What was my ship doing in Odense, Homer?" I was going to ask the same question as many times as it took to get a direct answer. "And what kind of spying and treachery lost me my fiancé?"

Andersen turned to Lang, eyebrows arched. "Would you care to explain?"

The four of them stood silent over the map for a long moment, like the four winds at the corners of the world. Homer's chapped hands were planted heavily on the table; Yu's arms were crossed. Andersen looked strained, his gray-gold hair straggling around his sunburned face. Lang's eyes were closed, dark lashes fanning out in the exhausted hollows above his cheeks.

"Looking after her is our prime objective," said Andersen, his low drawl intent. "How are you going to defend her if your head is always somewhere else?"

"Andersen." Homer gave him a warning look. "Just tell them what you told me."

"No," I said. "No. Start at the beginning."

Yu raised his eyebrows. "Which beginning, Seneschal-elect? The night the *Beholder* left Norge? The night we met you? Or

420

the night we accepted a mission you're safer if you know nothing about?"

"I'm safer knowing who you are." I fired the words like shots. "I'm safer knowing what's happening around me than I am blind and blundering around, one stray spark from burning everything down."

Lang put a hand on my shoulder. His lean fingers and his thin lips were tense. "Selah, isn't it enough to know the rules and to trust us?"

I shrugged Lang off. "It might have been, once," I said sharply, "but not anymore. Trusting you and letting you keep me in the dark aren't the same thing."

"I agree," Andersen said.

"Fine," Lang snapped. He leaned over the map as if poised to spring. "Fine. You want to know the truth? You want to talk about sparks and burning things down? The truth, Selah, is that beneath your feet are enough guns to arm the resistance in old Deutschland and enough gunpowder to blow the *Beholder* to pieces."

I stared at him.

I'd always thought the captain's upturned nose and sweet-bowed upper lip looked refined—almost delicate. But his eyes were wild, and they lent an otherworldly look to the rest of his features.

The four sailors and I were silent, listening to the creak of Homer's lamps on their hinges and the lapping of the water against the hull.

"To arm the resistance?" I finally breathed. "Why?"

This was why Lang had stood with Perrault—why he had insisted on continuing into the Imperiya. He wasn't concerned with me. He hadn't been thinking of me at all.

"Because the president of Zhōng Guó gave them to us," said Yu simply.

"So the *zŏngtŏng* paid you off," I said slowly, "to arm the resistance to the Imperiya, and you decided that it was all right to use my ship to ferry weapons across the Atlantic without telling me?"

Homer frowned. "This isn't about cash, girl."

"Then what is it about?" I demanded. "Because right now, I'm thinking about the political ramifications of Potomac undermining one great power on behalf of another. And my father and the Council don't even know it's happening." I smacked the table.

"If you only understood—" Yu said.

"Then help me understand!" I shouted.

Andersen sighed. "The tsarytsya has done her best to break Deutschland. But her armies have met too much resistance. Yotunkheym is barely present in the Shvartsval'd now. The forest has grown wild, swallowed the Neukatzenelnbogen completely. The tsarytsya barely acknowledges Katz Castle."

The Neukatzenelnbogen, I knew, was the home of the *hertsoh* and my Shvartsval'd suitor. But—*Katz Castle*. Were they the same place? Why did that name sound familiar?

Yu scratched his head. "Our contacts have confirmed there's activity under the surface, just as the *zŏngtŏng* suspected. And arming the Waldleute is strategically the wisest way to help dismantle the Imperiya in Deutschland and the rest of Europe."

I frowned. "The Waldleute?"

"The rebels. Those who resist the Imperiya." Homer drew me nearer by my forearm, pointing down at the map. "They call themselves the Waldleute in old Deutschland, the Rusalka in Yotunkheym itself, by other names elsewhere. Lang met with a representative at Bertilak's court—the Sidhe, they call themselves in that neck of the woods." He rapped his knuckles on the map, against the word that curved around the southeastern edge of the island.

My heart threw itself against the walls of my chest, slammed to a stop.

I'd wondered idly at the start of our voyage how the word was pronounced, what it meant.

With a jolt, I remembered Lang and Yu conspiring in the corridor our first night in Winchester, whispering about *she*.

Not "she." *The Sidhe*. The woman with the cowslips.

I shut my eyes.

I couldn't get caught up in this. I had my father and Potomac to worry about.

"People are suffering, Seneschal-elect," Yu said quietly. His dark, angular eyes were so intent on my face I gritted my teeth.

"I know the tsarytsya is evil!" I burst out. "I've been telling you for weeks that I don't want to go into the Imperiya!"

"You don't know the half of it, girl." Homer thumped the gray center of the map and fixed me with his steely gaze. "You haven't seen it. But I've fought at the edge of her world. I've seen how she takes power first with spies, and then with armies. No one can trust anyone. She's swift. Cold. Merciless."

"She's closed mosques, temples, and churches," said Lang, dark eyes entreating me. "But she's also destroyed libraries from one end of the Imperiya to the other. Made bonfires of books and music."

"And children are raised apart from their families," Yu added grimly. "Citizens of the Imperiya have to live in registered villages—anyone caught living outside a town is immediately imprisoned."

Anya had told me as much. That the tsarytsya claimed Yotunkheym's children.

I thought of Anya and Fredrik, fleeing to Norge with the gray armies after them.

Of Aleksei, adopted for convenience's sake, left damaged from his childhood in the Imperiya in a way I didn't fully understand.

When Baba Yaga locks the door,

Children pass thereby no more.

"There's only enough space for one story in the Imperiya, Seneschal-elect," Andersen said softly. "Europe is being strangled. People only want room to breathe. To make their own decisions. To live free."

"That's their call sign," Yu added. "*Fur die Freiheit. Fur die Wildnis.* 'For freedom. For the wild.' If you go to Burg Katz, as planned, you can help fight for that."

A shiver ran up my spine as the Deutsch phrase brought back the conversation I'd stumbled across on the radio, the tryst I'd heard two strangers planning in a place I'd never heard of.

Burg Cats. *Burg Katz. Katz Castle.*

Fur die Freiheit.

Fur die Wildnis.

I stared at Lang.

He had been the first to see my radio smuggled inside God-mother Althea's book. This was second nature to these people. Hiding their purposes, hiding things where they didn't belong.

No—this was their real errand. *I* was the thing that didn't belong.

I put my hands on my hips, trying to breathe.

"Where are they?" I asked. "The Waldleute?"

"We don't know where yet," Andersen said. "I went to Odense, like our Sidhe contact told me to. I waited in the tavern night after night, for as long as we could risk staying—no sign of him."

Yu sighed, his practical face frowning. "I don't care how tight their networks are; England to Shvartsval'd is a long way. The intel could have been old; your man could have been way-laid." He nodded at Lang.

"We'll find them," said Homer bracingly.

I blew out a breath. "My godmother. My father. They're expecting me. They're expecting *Torden*." I turned to Yu. "I asked you weeks ago what you made of my father's condition. It's time to talk."

Yu paused. "It could be nerve damage," he said slowly. "Which can have many causes. Diabetes mellitus. Injury. Alcoholism."

I shook my head. None of those made sense for Daddy.

He cleared his throat. "But to me, it sounds like poison."

Poison.

I reeled, backing one, two steps away from the table until I hit the wall.

Poison. She was poisoning him.

I knew Alessandra was selfish. I'd suspected she wanted for her baby the future that should have been mine.

But I never believed she'd hurt Daddy—the father of her own child—to make that happen.

"How long does he have?" I asked. My heart beat jaggedly, slashing at my lungs.

"It's hard to say," Yu faltered. "It would depend on the specific poison. On the quantity he's ingesting. It could be months. It could be years."

"Or weeks. Or days!" I gave a hysterical laugh. My knees threatened to give way, and my head dropped into my hands.

"We can take you home," Andersen blurted. "Or we can take you back to England first."

To England. To Bear.

Somewhere between the outer gates of Winchester Castle and our location here in the Lysefjord, my anger at him had faded.

I knew why he'd lied to me. I saw now he hadn't meant to hurt me. As desperate as I'd felt in the last few weeks, for my home and my family, I thought I understood.

It would be so simple. Winchester was so much less complicated than Asgard. It felt so much safer than the Imperiya.

But my path didn't lie backward.

Lang's head jerked up. "I'm the captain here—"

"And it's *her* decision," Andersen shot back.

"We have a responsibility," Yu argued.

Andersen raised his voice. "Potomac's alliances are at risk. Her position. Her life. Her father's life." He pointed at me, determined. "It's well past time we started trusting her."

My hands made fists on the table. My engagement ring caught the gleam of Homer's lamp, flashing a warning. Or an invitation.

You can see more by some lights than others.

Be free, elskede.

I thought of the Saint George of Constantine's England, who did not wander abroad, searching for other people's dragons to slay. He had changed his ways, and of that, I was glad.

But this dragon had landed directly in my path. And I had the power to put a sword in the right hands to help those it threatened fight back.

They were still arguing when I strode out of the office and across the deck.

The ship pitched and swayed beneath me. But I was rock steady.

"Selah, wait!" Lang called.

Yu and Andersen and Homer scrambled close behind him.

The crew kept working around us—Yasumaro steering, Jeanne watching the fjords above, her amber eyes scanning the cliffs carefully for any sign of someone following. Vishnu's and Basile's muscles knotted with strain as they pulled at the lines. J.J. hurried into the galley, and through its swinging door, I saw

Will hurrying around, no doubt fixing us a late supper. Overhead, Cobie scrambled across the rigging, unfurling our sails like jasmine in moonlight. Anya and Skop watched each other.

Perrault stopped in front of me, utterly still, eyes boring into mine, black as secrets in the dark.

Funny, how I'd never noticed the fear there before.

"I don't know what you're planning, Seneschal-elect," he began unevenly. "But I will say one final time: we cannot avoid the court at Shvartsval'd. You are obliged to court Fürst Fritz."

"I'm surprised you came quietly, Perrault." I cut him a glance as I strode around him. "Weren't you afraid of slighting our Norsk hosts?"

"It's not as though things could've gotten much worse. Treason and spies, indeed." Perrault scrambled after me, pitch rising. "The *hertsoh* will be waiting! Seneschal-elect, you know what is at stake. You know what happens to the tsarytsya's enemies."

Don't I, though. I stomped on, undeterred.

"I don't know what my stepmother has on you, Perrault, but you don't need to worry."

Yasumaro was at the helm. I surveyed the horizon over his shoulder.

"Don't you know I always do what I'm supposed to do?" I asked Perrault.

Homer, Lang, and Yu stood around me.

Yasumaro glanced from their faces to mine, eyes serious in his round, gentle face. "What are my orders, Seneschal-elect?"

For once, Lang didn't bother to remind us that he was the captain and that this was mutiny. Yasumaro didn't seem to care.

I swallowed hard, thought of my father at home, wasting away.

I could turn the *Beholder* around. Fight Alessandra. Try to save him.

Poison, Yu had said.

My enemies are already inside the gates, I'd said to Torden.

But so were the enemies of Shvartsval'd. Of Finlyandiya. Of all the *terytoriy* that'd been stolen and stripped of their names and their stories by the Imperiya Yotne.

I was a long way from home. But we were nearly beneath the shadow at the center of the map. Nearly in the Shvartsval'd, where my third suitor waited for me. Where I could offer the crew the cover they needed to seek out the resistance.

I could help the Waldleute. And they could defend their homes—their stories—their people.

One detour. A few weeks of my life—and my father's. To help save a continent.

I was done looking for suitors. Whether or not I'd ever see Torden again, I'd already fallen in love.

It was time to stop playing Alessandra's games and join a fight that mattered.

Time to begin writing my own story. To begin doing something worth writing about at all.

I set my jaw, and set my face forward.

"Yasumaro, hold course for Deutschland."

Acknowledgments

To Stephanie Stein: it has been a privilege to have you as my editor. Thank you for the space you've given me to breathe as a writer and the guidance you've offered me as an author. This book would not be what it is without your care, your talent, and your friendship. I am so grateful.

To Elana Roth Parker: You were my dream agent. What a delight to find the reality of working with you to be even better. You are the advocate and the sharp eye and the understanding reader that every author hopes for, and I got you. Thank you.

To the rest of the indefatigable ladies of Laura Dail Literary Agency, especially Samantha Fabien, and to Tamar Rydzinski: thank you for your hard work, support, and guidance. I'm lucky to have such a team of all-stars at my back.

To The Beholder's incredible team at HarperCollins, including Jon Howard, Erica Ferguson, Monique Vescia, Kimberly Stella, Vanessa Nuttry, Michael D'Angelo, Bess Braswell,

Kris Kam, Jane Lee, and Tyler Breitfeller: you have made my story a book, and you have told people about it, and you have put it in their hands, and I'm in awe. I wish I could tell my teen self the kind of people I would get to work with someday. I am so grateful for your blood, sweat, and sheer talent. Thank you.

To Michelle Taormina and the team at Vault49: You gave me a fairy-tale dream of a cover. Your artistic ability is truly its own kind of magic. My sincerest gratitude to you.

My gratitude to Momma and to Amber Sisenstein, who advised me on all matters medical, and to Dr. Barry Rumack, who was my consultant on all things toxicology. To Nick, Kristin Istre, Tom Schrandt, and Sally Anderson, for answering my Russian, Ukrainian, Norwegian, German, and French language questions: Спасибо, спасибі, takk, danke, merci. Thank you so much. All errors are, obviously, my own, and not the fault of my generous guides.

To Kiera Cass, Evelyn Skye, and Jodi Meadows: I admire each of you so much as creators and as humans. It's special to have your words on my work. My gratitude to you all. To Angele McQuade, Poppy Parfomak, Brigid Kemmerer, Lisa Maxwell, Jodi Meadows again, Sarah Glenn Marsh, Miranda Kenneally, Lindsay Smith, Robin Talley, Jessica Spotswood, Martina Boone, Diana Peterfreund, Mary G. Thompson, Pintip Dunn, Christina June, Katy Upperman, and the rest of the DMV writer crew: it has been such fun befriending you guys. Thanks for the warm welcome. I adore you. And to my fellow Novel19s: it has been a pleasure to debut alongside you all. All my love.

So many musicians opened emotional doors for me as I wrote the scenes that make up this story. To Delta Rae, NEEDTOBREATHE, Handsome Ghost, Taylor Swift, Hozier, Howard Shore, Phillip Phillips, Brooke Fraser, Ed Sheeran, Lights, and so many other artists: thank you for your work. Art begets art. I will always be grateful for what you gave to mine.

To Mrs. Lois Gidcumb: thank you for putting *Ella Enchanted* into my hands when I was nine. It's still one of my favorites. You were a truly kind and wonderful librarian.

To the Georgetown small group at Grace Downtown church: I am braver for having you all in my life. I love you guys. See you Wednesday.

To the handful of friends who first read these pages so many years ago, including Julia Kiewit, Anna Sims, Sally Anderson, Katie Kump, and Rosiee Thor: Your elated texts and emails were what kept my fragile little snowflake heart beating for so many months. I owe you a great debt of comfort, friendship, and enthusiasm. And to Lei'La' Bryant, who read every iteration of everything: you are my soul sister. Thank you for always lending me a little of your bravery when I run out of my own. I love you so much, friend.

To #TeamElana—Shannon Price, Lily Meade, Leigh Mar, June Tan, Deeba Zargarpur, and Alexa Donne: I adore you guys. Rose-gold glitter hearts and cherry PopTarts to each of you.

To Eileen McGervey, the owner of One More Page Books in Arlington, Virginia: thank you for taking a chance on me when

I didn't know [insert poop emoji] about being a bookseller. You are the kindest boss I could have asked for and working for you changed the game for me. To Lelia Nebeker, Amanda Quain, Rebecca Speas, Lauren Wengrovitz, Rosie Dauval, Eileen O'Connor, Trish Brown, Sally McConnell, and everyone else, your support and enthusiasm have meant the world. It is a joy to see your faces every day at work. Thanks also to Rosie for your tireless efforts to get one (1) photo that I won't make a face at. Or in. You are a gem.

To the Pod—Hannah Whitten, Jen Fulmer, Joanna Meyer, Laura Weymouth, and Steph "Stephinephrine" Messa: publishing is scary, uncharted territory. Here be dragons. Being friends with you guys feels like having a map, and a sword, and a whole army at my back. All my love to you, always, my imaginary housemates. Tea in my attic room at four.

To Abbey Carter Jack and Erin Whatley Andrews: thank you for believing in me and for being my friends. I love you both so much.

To my family, the Gardners, Dormineys, Sernas, Andersons, Burkhalters, Shafers, Simkinses, Stiglishes, Hayeses, Bischoffs, and everyone else: I love you all. Thank you for your support while I waited for this day to come.

To Mamaw: thank you for your imagination. I love you so much. I like to think Holly and Molly and Genevieve live in a corner of one of the worlds I've created. To Grandmother and Granddaddy/Washing Machine: thank you for all the time you spent with me when I was a teen. I will always be your girl. I love you.

To Brother Bear: so much of me is also you. I hope you enjoy this story. I love you, Chelsie, Cohen, and Callan with all my heart.

To Momma: thank you for being the legs I stood on for so many years. You did everything it took to get me to where I am. I will never not be grateful. To Daddy: thank you for teaching me how to dig, and fight, and not be afraid. I love you both so much.

To Wade: oh, my love. For believing in me, for holding my hand when I was too afraid to step out alone, for giving me the courage to take this leap—I can never thank you enough. This book is for you.

And to my gracious Father: thank you for the stories. Thank you for the story about the cup, the sword, the tree, the green hill. Thank you for telling it to me always.

Keep reading for a sneak peek at
THE BOUNDLESS, the breathtaking
sequel to THE BEHOLDER

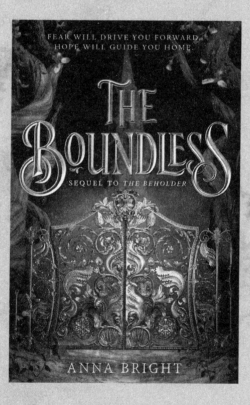

1

THE *BEHOLDER*

A storm was building. Dark birds circled the crow's nest. Cold salt water surged around us, crashing against the *Beholder*'s hull and the rocky Norsk coast at our back.

They were ill omens, all.

My stomach lurched as the ship rolled, the deck dozens of feet below me, little but mist and trembling ropes between us. Clouds hung low in the sky, gray as pewter, heavy as lead. They threatened to smother me.

Everything looked different from the crow's nest. Everything looked different in the aftermath of their deception.

When we'd left England, after everything that happened at court in Winchester, I'd been relieved to find myself aboard ship again. I'd felt safe out on the ocean, my path ahead clear, the *Beholder* my home away from home.

But I'd been wrong about everything. Lang was a liar, and the *Beholder* was no haven for lost girls.

I knew the truth now. With every gust of wind, every wash of water over the *Beholder*'s sides, our route would carry us farther away from my father and my home and the stepmother who had wanted me gone and toward Shvartsval'd and its tsarytsya. Toward the rebellion Lang and the rest had been seeking since before we left Potomac.

But now we traveled east on my orders. Alessandra would never have dreamed of such success when she expelled me from Potomac to search for a husband.

From this height, too, the crew looked different. It wasn't just that I'd never seen the top of Basile's head and broad shoulders before, or noticed quite how gracefully Jeanne loped across the deck; from the towering height of the crow's nest, I could keep eyes on all of them at once.

I hadn't felt I'd needed to in weeks, since I'd come to trust them.

I'd been unwise.

I leaned back against the mainmast and tried to let the salt wind soothe the betrayal that still burned in my gut. The fear that ran cold up my spine when I thought of how far I was from home. How far I had yet to go. How every moment, Asgard and Torden slipped farther behind me.

Lang stood outside Homer's quarters, hands in his pockets, chin lifted as he listened to Andersen. The older sailor was arguing with him about something, his hands waving dramatically as he tried to make his point, his gray-gold hair drifting around his thin face in the breeze. Lang settled his hands in his pockets, arching his brows at Andersen as he rattled on.

But his dark eyes darted up to me, as if they couldn't help seeking me out.

Talk to me, they seemed to plead. *Let me explain.*

Lang was my captain. My friend. The boy with the sensitive face and the wry laugh and lean, ink-covered hands, who I'd come to trust. But I wasn't interested in his explanations.

He'd talked on and on after we'd left Norge the night before, justified himself and his choice to smuggle the *zŏngtŏng*'s weapons to those resisting the Imperiya Yotne and waited for me to say that I understood.

On and on he'd talked. I'd said nothing.

I refused to set him at ease. I wasn't happy or comfortable; why should he be?

The crow's nest shifted beneath me. I sat up straight, tensing, then slumped again. "Cobie, you scared me."

"Well, you're scaring a lot of people. You really shouldn't be up here." Cobie glanced at me sidelong, pushing a lock of shiny, dark hair out of her eyes. "Not that I care."

"I don't care, either," I said, staring straight ahead. "What are you doing up here, anyway?" Cobie Grimm was our rigger; the maze above deck was her rightful place, and I was an interloper. But I didn't care about that now.

Cobie squinted at me. "You're aware there's a purpose to the crow's nest beyond your need for a spot to brood, right?"

"I'm not brooding," I mumbled.

"Well, you're not keeping an eye on the horizon for obstacles,

3

either," Cobie said wryly. She arched an eyebrow. "Are you all right?"

I stared down at my hands clasped in my lap, at the ring Torden had given me. It felt heavy on my finger, but that was nothing to the weight of my heart inside my chest.

I missed Torden. I felt every mile between us, stretching taut and painful.

I was brooding.

Fury bubbled in my veins when I thought of Lang and Homer and Yu and the way they'd treated me like a bit of porcelain. Breakable, easily set on the shelf and out of the way. Entirely ornamental to their true purposes.

Torden had never treated me that way. I'd felt strong and free when he looked at me, his eyes steady as the flow of the Bilröst.

Lang hadn't so much acknowledged my fury as tried to smooth it over, tried with explanations and excuses and repeated protests to convince me I wasn't really angry with him.

"You have to understand—" Lang had begun again as I'd walked away from the helm.

"Who knew?" I'd demanded, whirling on him.

Lang had swallowed hard but lacked the good grace to look guilty. He'd eyed me carefully, long lashes shadowing his dark eyes. "Some did, some didn't."

"That's not a straight answer," I'd spat. My gaze had darted between the faces of the crew, uncertain where to land. Uncertain which of them were safe.

They stared at me, expressions strained, nothing like the family who'd sat with me at dinners in the galley, telling stories by lamplight. Homer, who'd felt like my guardian. Vishnu and Basile and Will, who'd been so kind to me. Skop, whom I'd defended to Konge Alfödr of Norge, when he'd fallen for his ward Anya.

I'd thought he was my friend. I'd thought they all were.

And yet, there I'd stood on the deck again, feeling just as I had on the day I'd left Potomac, the water choppy enough to throw me off-balance: friendless and alone and an utter fool.

Except this time was worse. Because my place beside Torden and my place aboard the *Beholder* were homes I had chosen for myself.

They were all in ruins now.

"Say something," Lang had said, voice low and soft as moonlight. He'd drawn near to me, as if he had any right to lay a hand on my arm, to touch me like a friend.

I'd pulled away.

"I don't know what I can say to you right now that I won't regret," I'd answered tightly. I'd hardly recognized the tone of my own voice.

Out of the corner of my eye, I'd noticed a rope ladder swinging loose and uncertain from the mainmast, leading to the crow's nest. I'd stomped across the deck and taken the rope between my hands, gulping down my fear.

"Selah!" Lang had dashed after me and wrapped a hand around the rope, just higher than my shaking grip. "Selah, stop. What are you doing?"

"I need to clear my head." I'd suddenly been dying to get away from him, dying to find a quiet space above all the noise, though my palms were growing clammy at the prospect of the climb. The crow's nest was a dizzying height above deck.

"Selah, don't be silly." Lang's cheeks had been pale as the clouds overhead, his bowed mouth shadowed by his upturned nose, his eyes dark, dark, dark.

"Silly?" I'd demanded, my anger rising. "Is that what I am? A silly girl, too occupied with falling in love at court to notice you lying and lying—"

"No!" Lang had burst out. "No, it's just not safe for you to be up there."

"Not safe?" My words had been bitter as bile. "Not safe— like sailing a powder keg across the Atlantic? Like not knowing who my crew members are really working for?" Another step toward him had put us mere inches apart. "Like navigating the English court blind while you hunted for rebels, or passing Asgard's gates not knowing my crew are smugglers?" I'd studied him, desperate for some hint of remorse in his face, but I'd found none. "I'll do a better job looking after myself, if that's the best you can do."

With that, I'd turned away from him, grasping the ladder again in my hands, and begun to climb.

"Selah!" Cobie had called from the deck. "What are you doing?"

I hadn't been able to answer her *and* climb *and* keep breathing. So I'd chosen climbing, and breathing. I'd concentrated on the rough feel of the rope between my fingers and not on the way the ladder twisted and swung in the wind blowing straight through my clothes, sharp as my own anger.

My ears had told me that all movement on deck below me had stopped. I hadn't paused to look down.

The landing at the top of the mainmast was about six feet by six feet, a square with a small lip at its edge. I'd hoisted myself up onto it, out of sight of the crew, feeling it pitch beneath me like the mist swirling in the fjord.

But the roll of the sea and the fog had been nothing to the rage churning in my stomach. To the angry tears dripping sideways across the bridge of my nose and pooling beneath my cheek as I huddled on my side.

I lay that way now, curled up toward Cobie, studying the ring on my finger. Its cluster of stones was as blue as the Bil-röst and the Asgard boys' eyes, its rose-gold band the color of Torden's lashes.

I'd left him behind. Torden. The only thing I'd been sure of in months.

How I loved him. How I longed to feel his hands in mine, to feel him at my side, close as breathing.

But Asgard was at our stern, not our prow. And Torden had promises to keep. To Asgard. To his father, whose only concern was defending their home against the Imperiya Yotne. To his stepmother, who had lost one child to death and another to exile.

I had promises to keep, as well—to my crew, as they searched for the resistance, but also to Potomac and my father, whose sadness and sickness weighed constantly on my mind.

I'd marked the days as they passed in the back of the book my godmother had given me before I'd left; the marching army of tick marks never failed to make my chest grow tight with worry.

Time loomed vast and substantial behind and before me. So many days, so many miles, and my father's fate still unknown.

I thought of the bones that pressed at Daddy's skin, of the tremors that ran through his limbs. Of the heaviness that had seemed to weigh on his heart for so long.

I believed he would want me to help others defend themselves. I hoped I would get home in time for him to tell me so.

Always seems to be so much noise, he'd said to me the night of the Arbor Day ball.

Only the crow's nest seemed to be above all the clamor.

"No." I shook my head. "No, I'm not all right."

Cobie wet her lips. "It won't kill you," she said. She crossed her arms and leaned against the mast, black shirt flapping in the breeze.

My head knew she was right. The fear and the pain and the emptiness: they would not be the death of me.

But the depth and the breadth and the height of my loss felt as boundless as the ocean I'd crossed to reach this place. And my heart found it hard to believe her.

2

Fat drops of rain began to fall as I climbed down from the crow's nest. My movements were clumsy as I crept toward deck, my palms still sweating a little over the rope.

I couldn't stay up top forever. But I wasn't ready to talk to the crew. I made for the galley instead and found Will soaking dried beans and kneading bread.

"Can you take this over?" he asked with no preamble as the galley door swung shut behind me. "I need to go to the storeroom below." He laughed. "*Need. Knead.* Get it?"

Did Will know? I wondered.

My mind rejected the idea. Will was too comfortable, too kind. Too focused on working hard and feeding the crew, surely, to occupy himself with scheming.

But Yu was a doctor; he'd cared for me when I felt unwell. Andersen had made me paper ships and dragons, just to make me smile. They'd lied so easily. Could Will?

I huffed a laugh at him, but it sounded tense and unnatural. "You're silly. Go."

Will left me alone in the galley. Lanterns creaked from the low-beamed ceiling overhead, and dishes shifted gently in the copper sink. The smells of yeast and fat drifted on the air. I closed my eyes and tried to let them comfort me. But I couldn't help thinking of the guns and gunpowder stashed right near the flour and the salt and everything else we needed to survive.

I tied an apron around my waist, shook out my hands, and began to work the bread. As rain pattered on the galley roof, I pushed the heels of my hands into the dough, trying to stretch out the anxious knots in my neck and shoulders. I let my muscles lead, let my mind wander, drifting across the sea and across time. From my godmother to Bear to Torden to Daddy; from Fritz, my waiting suitor at Katz Castle, to the Waldleute rebels we were on our way to aid.

The galley door swung open again, feet crossing the floor in time with the thump of the dough as I worked. But it wasn't Will I saw standing over me when I looked up.

"Should I expect an end to the aerial performances anytime soon?" Lang asked.

I stiffened. Stilled.

Always more talking. He was so clever with words. I should've known he wasn't going to give me space to think.

I shook my head and resumed my work. "I'm not playing games with you, Lang."

"You're still angry at me," he said quietly. "And I don't like it."

He leaned against the counter, hands tucked in his pockets. Golden lamplight slanted across his cheeks and his upturned nose; his hair and his shoulders were spattered with rain.

I bent back toward my bread, pounding the last of the unincorporated flour and salt into the dough, wincing as the salt stung a shallow scrape on my wrist.

Lang passed me a damp cloth. I didn't look at him as I took it.

"You have to accept the consequences of your choices, Lang," I said, wiping my smarting skin. "I'm angry at you, and I don't trust you, and it's because of your own decisions."

He made a noise of frustration. "Come on, Selah."

"No, *you* come on," I snapped. I thought of Daddy, all patience, all gentle listening. Of Torden, of the night he'd told me he couldn't follow me back to Potomac. Of how he'd presented me the truth and then waited quietly while I decided what to do with it. "You think the answer to everything is words and words and more words. You can't wait even a day while I figure out how to cope with this, you're so obsessed with your own agenda."

"Everyone has their own agenda," Lang shot back. "Even you."

"Me?" I demanded, tossing down the cloth.

"Yes, you! As far as your suitors know, you're walking into your courtships with the aim of marriage. None of these poor saps know they don't have a chance. That you're just passing the time with them until you can turn tail and race home."

11

"I'm trying to protect my father and my country. You know what's at stake."

Lang held up his hands. "And I'm trying to protect millions of innocent people. You're lying for a good reason, just like I did. Are we really that different?"

I stepped close to him, jutting a finger at his chest. "My plan didn't put anyone's safety at risk."

"Selah, you were never in danger." Lang bent his head, casting both of us in shadow. A few droplets of rain trembled in his hair. "I had everything under control before y— Well, before." His face was close to mine, earnest enough to infuriate me.

My breath left me in a rush. Red burned my neck and cheeks.

"Do not treat me like a child," I said through gritted teeth. "I'm not a fool, and you are not all-knowing. Anything could've happened while I was stumbling around blind."

"I would've kept you safe." He swallowed, and his throat bobbed. "I *would* have."

I turned back to the bread, too angry to look at him anymore. Angry at his lies. Angry at my own weakness.

Lang came closer to me, two steps in the silent kitchen. I paused, wrist-deep in my work. When he put his hands on my shoulders, heat spread over my skin, furious and faltering.

"I don't mind if you're angry." Lang's thumbs stretched and tensed against my shoulder blades. He was close enough I could feel the words against the back of my neck. "I can take your anger. I just can't take you shutting me out."

"You were guilty of that long before I was, Lang." I closed

my eyes tightly. "I trusted you from the beginning. You were the one who wouldn't let me in." I looked over my shoulder and met his gaze. "And now you're going to have to wait while I come to terms with this."

My skin was colder when his hands fell away from it.

In *The Boundless*, Selah will chart her own course.

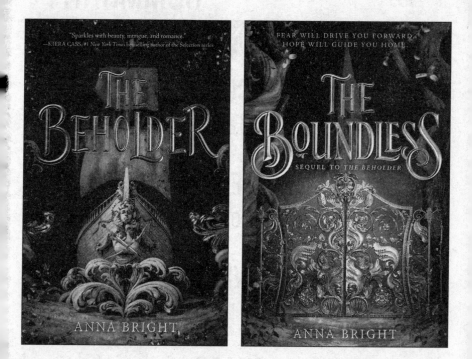

Don't miss the dazzling sequel!